FIC
Ram

Ramsay, Caro

Absolution

DUE DATE

12-11-07

Absolution

Absolution

CARO RAMSAY

PEGASUS BOOKS
NEW YORK

ABSOLUTION

Pegasus Books LLC
45 Wall Street, Suite 1021
New York, NY 10005

Copyright © 2007 by Caro Ramsay

First Pegasus Books edition 2007

Library of Congress Cataloging-in-Publication Data is available.

ISBN: 978-1-933648-41-5

10 9 8 7 8 6 5 4 3 2 1

Printed in the United States of America
Distributed by Consortium

To Jessie Ramsay
Born 1904

You can tell a Sheffield lass,
You just cannot tell her much.

Anna
Glasgow, 1984

White.

Nothing but white.

No sense. No awareness. Only white.

Nothing.

Then breathing.

Rhythmic breathing.

Nothing more than the ebb and flow of life.

She slept.

Pain picked at her as she emerged slowly from the depths. Her hands were strapped to her sides, and she could feel bindings cutting into her wrists. The pain in her face – cracking, burning – was unbearable.

Thirsty. She was thirsty.

She tried to lick her lips, but her tongue was swollen, and as immobile as leather. Something rigid filled her mouth; she could taste chloroform and rotten meat. She sensed her face was covered, her mouth and nose blocked. Panic rose until she could not breathe, and she tried to roll her shoulders to break free. Deep-seated agony skewered her stomach, and she lay still, thinking she might die if she moved again.

A voice, indistinct, insistent, was repeating words over and over.

There was a distant memory . . . somewhere . . . too far away to be recalled . . .

She felt a prick in her forearm and sank down deep into the dark once more.

PC Alan McAlpine climbed the concrete stairs to the DCI's office, past the rusty filing cabinet that had been stuck on the first-floor landing for two years. The yucca that crowned it, never a vital specimen at the best of times, had died in his absence.

'Alan?'

He hadn't noticed DI Forsythe pass him on the stairs, and turned at the sound of his voice.

'Good to see you, McAlpine. How are you? We weren't expecting you back for a while yet.'

'I'm fine,' he said bluntly.

'Sorry to hear about your brother – Bobby, was it?'

'Robbie,' answered McAlpine mechanically.

'No matter how heroic he was, it's still a terrible accident.'

McAlpine's only response was a casual shrug of thin shoulders.

'How is your dad coping?' Forsythe persisted.

McAlpine flicked his eyes up the stairs, wanting to get away. 'He's as you'd expect.'

'And your mother?'

McAlpine looked past him to a powdery, white patch of damp plaster. An image of his mother screaming burned into his consciousness, sobs racking her emaciated body so violently he heard her rib crack, as loud as rifle-fire. The doctor holding up the syringe, tapping it to draw clear fluid into the plastic chamber, putting his knee on her chest to hold her still as he exposed bare wasted flesh to the needle . . .

He glanced at his watch. 'My mother's fine,' he said flatly.

Forsythe tapped him on the arm, a touch, nothing more. 'If there's anything I can do, just let me know. We've missed you in the office.'

McAlpine nodded up towards the DCI's office. 'Do you know what he wants me for? Graham?'

'DCI Graham to you,' corrected Forsythe. 'There was an acid attack on Highburgh Road, about two weeks ago, the 26th.'

'I know. So?'

'Surveillance at the Western, a watching brief. The lassie got it right in the face, very nasty. She's been in a coma until now, but there are signs of recovery. The minute she talks, we want somebody there.'

'So I'm bloody babysitting.'

'Think of it as a gradual return to work. You start tomorrow, day shift for now. All those pretty nurses in black stockings, they'll be all over a handsome wee laddie like yourself,' Forsythe chuckled. 'Gives a new meaning to getting back into uniform.'

On the twelfth day she woke. She lay not moving, and knowing she could not move, her face dry and crusty, so tight she could feel it crack. Something had happened, something so painful, she couldn't remember. And something else had happened – something wonderful . . .

Her brain gently probed each of her senses.

Her eyes were covered; she had a feeling of daylight from somewhere, yet all she could sense from her eyes was cold emptiness, a void where something warm and comforting used to be.

Her ears were full of fog, but she could hear somebody trying to move around and not cause disturbance, the flick of newspaper pages, swing doors opening and closing, soft bleeps and pings, the constant low hum of fluorescent lights, whispers . . .

She couldn't breathe through her nose, but she could still smell burned flesh, and fresh air tinged with the tart smell of anaesthetic.

There was a tube in her mouth. Something was keeping her breathing, wafting air in and out of her lungs, pain on the breath in and pain on the breath out, a peaceful calm in between.

She sensed somebody, someone else breathing, their face close to hers,

*a touch on her arm. She couldn't tell them she was awake. She wasn't
sure she wanted them to know . . .*

PC Alan McAlpine was bored, more bored than he'd have
thought possible while still breathing, and he'd only been
on duty for ten minutes.

Glasgow, July, and midday on the hottest day of the year.
The sun streamed in through the high Victorian windows
of the Western Infirmary to highlight the dancing dust
motes. It was his own fault. He'd told DCI Graham he'd
rather be back at work than sitting at home watching dust
settle.

And here he was, back at work – and watching dust settle.
On a Saturday.

The cheap plastic seat was making his bum numb and
his brain wasn't far behind. Five minutes finished the *Daily
Record* quick crossword. He made a start on the *Herald*'s wee
stinker and got stuck at five down. He started doodling
ampersands in the margin, waiting for inspiration.

Nobody spoke to him. He was invisible – though he'd
been smiled at a few times by a slim red-headed nurse, her
light blue cotton skirt swinging as she passed. Her shoes
squeaked annoyingly on the lino, leaving a little trail of
marks.

She had fat ankles, ugly feet. His interest died.

His glance kept returning to the clock, the jerky long
black hand showing how slowly time moves for the living.

He thought he'd better phone home and find out how
his mum was doing. Not that he really wanted to be told.

*When she woke for the third time, they were close by, waiting for her
to come round. A voice spoke – a man's – low, monotone. She picked
up the words 'baby', 'daughter', 'doing fine' . . .*

She heard a scream, a strangled cry that rose to a howl; felt skin rip from the roof of her mouth, blood swamp her throat. The tide of air stopped. She choked.

The ventilator tube was abruptly removed, and something else was thrust into her mouth, something that gurgled and bubbled as it sucked the blood out.

A hand patted her as if comforting a frightened horse. Another voice – female – spoke kindly as the needle went in, and she felt herself floating again . . .

A baby. A daughter.

Their daughter.

They had almost made it . . .

PC McAlpine was staring into space. The smell of disinfectant reminded him of the morgue. The blue lino, great stretches of it as far as the eye could see, made him think of water, of somebody screaming and Robbie jumping into the darkness. Robbie having the breath crushed from him as the water enveloped him – screaming and more screaming. The blue hardened through his half-shut eyes, revealing itself as lino again.

He jerked fully awake when he realized the screaming was real, then felt a little foolish when he remembered where he was. The summary file of her admission had fallen on to the floor. Its contents, a single sheet of A4 paper, had floated out.

That piece of paper – the only key he had to her previous life. The file at the station was suspiciously thin. Ten badly typed pages, the sole result of days of police inquiries, had told him a grand total of nothing. A search of her bedsit had apparently thrown up nothing untoward. He decided to go and have a look for himself. The girl, early twenties, had been admitted, minus a handbag, a driving licence, a credit card. The only eyewitness statement said that a woman had walked out of a house; that a white car, maybe a taxi, had pulled up. The witness had not connected the car to the woman at all; the first thing she knew was when the car pulled into the traffic and she noticed the woman – 'young-ish, blonde, slim but very pregnant' – lying on the pavement. Six thirty on a bright summer Sunday evening in Partickhill. Nobody else saw anything.

McAlpine started to rub his temples, and something that had been curled in his subconscious began to flex and stretch. Why had she not screamed? Why had she not ducked or . . . ? And who was she? Where was her paper trail – National Insurance, mortgage, wages, tax? She had nothing. She had swept away every trace of her existence as she moved. So she had something to hide. And she was clever. Skilful.

He tensed in his chair, one ankle flexing rapidly up and down as his mind raced. He could feel a tingle of excitement: this was no longer a surveillance job; this was an intellectual pursuit. But who had she been hiding from? Who had tracked her down? And how? It suddenly dawned on him that DCI Graham had guessed there was more to this story and had rostered his star pupil, knowing he would rise to the bait. McAlpine smiled to himself.

Well, two could play at that game.

And DCI Graham would come second.

The redhead emerged from the room, dressed now in a white uniform, her shoes still squeaking. McAlpine looked past her through the door, catching a glimpse of a slim, tanned foot lying on a sheet, and was shocked. He hadn't expected the victim to be so young, so fragile. The foot framed itself perfectly in his mind, clear as a photograph, before the door closed.

*

8

The fourth time she woke, the squeaky shoes came close almost immediately. 'Just relax now, sweetheart.' Cold liquid dripped into the corner of her mouth, rolling sweetly over raw skin. She raised her head for more, feeling the skin round her lips crack, saw a shadow hover over her, then recede. 'Second time she's done that today.'

'It's been a fortnight but that's her oxygen stabilizing at last.' The tube in her mouth twitched, the voice receded. Then returned, louder. 'Your daughter's doing fine, the wee darlin'. She's along in the baby unit for now – we'll bring her in to you in a wee while –'

A harder voice, interrupting from the door. 'What do those police expect?'

'To question her, I suppose. She didn't do this to herself.'

'How's she going to tell them anything, the state she's in?'

The softer voice remained with her, droning on, confusing her. It was like a badly edited film: she was watching herself from a distance, closing the door, coming down the stairs carrying her bag, then clutching the handrail outside the door as a contraction hit her.

And?

On the street, falling . . .

Her skin on fire, her eyelids burned through, the pain in her eyes, the world going dark.

Then nothing.

The red-headed nurse squeaked along the corridor, a cup of tea in her outstretched hand. PC McAlpine took it, knocking her hand slightly, spilling a wave of tea down her white uniform.

'Sorry about that,' he said, getting to his feet. He smiled: he knew how to use his charm. 'Have there been any phone calls about her? Anybody asking after her? Any visitors? *Anything?*'

'No. No one. The hospital chaplain came immediately, and his assistant's been in a few times to see her and the baby. Just doing the usual. Apart from that, nothing.'

'So who is she? Any ideas?'

'Is that not what *you're* supposed to find out?' She raised a saucy eyebrow.

'You must have some idea.' He smiled again.

'She has no face,' replied the nurse, all sauciness gone, and McAlpine's smile faded.

'And when she was admitted? Was there nothing on her, no wee bit of paper with a phone number, a contact-in-the-event-of-an-emergency?' He gave her the full benefit of his charm.

'I was on when she was admitted, and she had an over-night bag, that's all. There was nothing that said anything about her.' She began to sense his frustration. 'Honestly.'

'But has she a name?'

'We gave her a number. She was in labour when they brought her in, so we did an emergency section, just past midnight. It was a wee girl. We've put her in with her just now.'

He sat back down, anger burning inside him, knocked the cup of tea down his throat and handed it back to the nurse.

Pregnant? Acid in her face? He shuddered at the cruelty of it.

With the warmth of morphine in her veins, she imagined the pain waving to her as it went, floating away on a sea of blood. It left her senses so sharp she could hear water gurgle in the pipes next door, could distinguish between the different phones at the end of the corridor. She could hear the policeman outside, stirring a cup of tea, the spoon tapping against the side of the cup. She could hear her daughter, breathing beside her . . .

In . . . out . . . in . . . out . . .

She could listen to that for ever.

They were talking about one of the policemen outside. 'He's lovely, isn't he, even though he's so short? Kind of bite-sized? Huge kind brown eyes, like pools of —'

'Sewage?' the older voice suggested. 'He's not a Labrador.'

'He doesn't have a girlfriend, you know.' There was a slight giggle. 'I bet I get a date with him before the end of the week.'

'Too good-looking for his own good, that one,' the other voice warned. 'It'll be tears before bedtime.'

She heard the creak of the door opening, a bump as it closed, then silence. She tried to imagine his face, a noble handsome face, eyes of burnt umber, hair the colour of sun on mahogany, and tried to give him a smile before he faded away to a cloud of morphine.

It was quiet in the hospital in the hour of the dead, that slow hour between 2 and 3 a.m. It reminded McAlpine of the night shift at the station. The clock clicked round, its tick ominously loud in the silence of the corridor, and music floated through from the IC station, where a nurse had a radio on quietly. He'd been sitting here, on and off, for the best part of four days. For something to do, he got up and went to the coffee machine down the landing.

The door of IC 2/3 opened; the red-headed nurse and the older one came out and returned to the station.

McAlpine also walked to the station, where he sat and sipped the vile coffee, deep in thought. He knew there was something nagging at the back of his mind, but he couldn't quite touch it. He crushed the cup in his hand and chucked it in the bin. He heard a noise, a faint squeak. The door of IC 2/3 had been left open, and it moved slightly to and fro in the draught.

He looked up and down the corridor. Nobody was paying the slightest attention to him. The older nurse was on the phone, and the redhead was looking at her knee, picking something from the skin.

He got up, placed his hand on the steel handle of the door.

The room was a tomb of dark silence. He looked round, giving his eyes time to adjust. He had a vague sense of freshness, the smell of sea salt, not the stale air of his mother's room. In the dull light he saw the incubator in the corner, empty, the white cellular blanket rumpled at the bottom. They must have taken the baby away for a wee while, to do whatever nurses do to babies.

She was lying in state. She could have been in a sarcophagus, the only movement the slight rise and fall of her stomach as the ventilator hissed and sighed life into her. He was unable to pull his eyes away, transfixed by the gauze that covered her face, her death mask, tantalizingly opaque, lines of blood beneath it like butterflies trapped in a web. He knew she was beautiful.

He stood back and took a deep breath.

He crossed himself.

Her feet looked cold in the blue light. He picked up each foot delicately by the heel and smoothed the white cotton underneath. Fine delicate feet with long elegant toes, a dancer's feet, fragile and cold under his hands. Chilled. His finger traced the length of a vein on her instep, then caressed a little flaw round the base of her toe, a perfect white smile of a scar.

She was being pulled from sleep, up to the light. She lay quietly, listening to the silence, listening to the breathing at the end of her bed. She knew she was being studied. All her life men had looked at her, and she knew this too was a man.

She heard a deep sigh, felt a hand touch her foot. She waited for the prick of the injection.

Nothing, only the soft stroke of flesh against flesh. Slow, soothing. A grip on her heel, firm yet delicate, almost a lover's caress . . .

'You're not supposed to be in here!' The redhead was standing behind him, the look of a dispossessed wife on her face. 'You could infect her.' Her voice dropped. 'Not that it's going to make any difference.'

'You don't think she's going to survive?' McAlpine asked. 'Why? Surely it's only her face?'

'Her face, her neck, her arms, her hands, her tummy.' The nurse's voice softened a little as she approached the bed, folding the yellow blanket over the bare feet. 'Poor lass. She was pregnant and lying in acid. It burned deep. It's sad. Come on.' She gestured to him to follow her to the sluice room, where they kept the spare kettle. He had to hurry to keep up. 'It's the depth of the burn that matters. You know your body is basically water? If your skin comes off, as hers has, you leak, leading to dehydration, leading to failure of all the major organs. There's nothing we can do for her, except wait.' She pulled two mugs from a cupboard. 'Sometimes they get an infection that glows in the dark. Gives them the heebie-jeebies in the morgue if they don't wash the body properly.'

'If she's as ill as all that, why keep her tied up? Hardly likely to do a runner is she?' asked McAlpine.

The nurse sighed, tilting her head to one side, as if forming an explanation for a slightly stupid child. 'Her instinct would be to claw the dressings off, and that would allow infection in, so she's tied for her own good.'

'So she lies there in frustration?'

'But safe from nasty bugs as long as daft cops don't keep going in and out, touching her.'

McAlpine ignored the jibe. 'She was pregnant. She would have attended a clinic. Where would she go, do you think, in the West End?'

'You not from round here?' she asked, fishing.

'No, Skelmorlie.'

'Now that's a one-horse town.'

'And the horse died of boredom. What prenatal clinics are near here, then?'

'Might be the Dumbarton Road Clinic, but women like that, you know, they don't exactly look after themselves, do they?'

'Women like what?' McAlpine bridled.

'Well, you know, that end of Highburgh Road, down on her arse. She's a hooker. Must have been.'

McAlpine shook his head. Vice would have had her on file. She had no phone numbers, no . . . He shook his head again.

'And you'd know?' The redhead licked her lips slowly. 'She was a hooker, I tell you.'

'You talk to her when you're in there? Do you think she can hear anything?'

The nurse blew on her coffee, pursing her lips and looking at him through the steam. 'It's never been proved that people in coma have any awareness of anything, but we put the baby in there just in case she can hear or sense something. She's probably brain-damaged, deaf, dumb and blind.'

'Should play a mean pinball,' McAlpine muttered.

Every day that passed her sense of smell got stronger. She knew he smoked. He wore aftershave, he smelled nice.

And she could smell the sweet milkiness, the soft breath of the little person, the little bit of herself who lay by her side, so close but too far away. More than anything she wanted to touch her baby, to cuddle

14

and caress her. She needed someone to lift her up and place her daughter in her arms.

She thought about the policeman, the young one with the kind brown eyes, sitting just beyond the door.

Kinstray, the landlord at 256A Highburgh Road, was blind and hunchbacked. He stood in the narrow crack of the door, wearing a beige cardigan that was more holes than wool, one red hand held up to protect rheumy eyes from the sun, the other feeling the card carefully between his thumb and the palm of his hand.

'Would that be more polis?' he asked.

Two minutes of monosyllabic conversation revealed that Kinstray had little to add to his statement. His speech was so Glaswegian McAlpine found himself subconsciously translating everything the man said. It was a sin what happened to the lassie, he said. She was quiet; he'd heard she was a looker, but he wouldn't know, would he? She paid her rent in advance.

'How far in advance?'

'Right up tae the end o' July. Paid it aw up front, the minute she arrived. Wisnae too bothered when ah said she wouldnae get it back if she left early.'

'And she'd been here for . . .'

The bony shoulders shrugged. 'Months.'

McAlpine sighed. 'How many months? Look, I'm not interested in how much she paid you, but I need to know when she came here.'

'April, it was. Four months.'

'You didn't know she was pregnant?'

'If I'd known that, she wouldnae've got her foot in the door. That's just trouble. I foond oot later, though.' He sniffed in disgust.

'And you didn't know her name?'

'Don't know she ever told me, son. Paid cash. No need for references, ah ask nae questions. It's no' against the law.'

McAlpine thought it probably was against some law somewhere, but continued, 'No visitors?'

'How would ah know, son? She wis in the top room, she'd her own bell. Came and went as she pleased.'

'But you did see – *meet* her, at some point?' McAlpine probed gently. 'You must have gained some sense of her, some impression? Tall? Thin? Fat? Clever? Thick?'

Kinstray's tongue probed at the side of his mouth, thinking. 'Slim, young, she moved light on her feet, even heavy with the child. She wore a nice scent, like spring flowers. She was polite . . .' He sighed slightly.

'Local?'

'Wouldnae've said so, son. She was polite but' – he considered – 'she wis carefully spoken, like, you know? Not stuck up but polite, like a lady. Well brought up now, that's what ah would say.' He nodded as if the answer was the best he could do and he was pleased with it.

'How long have you been here, Mr Kinstray? In this house?' McAlpine asked.

'Thirty-two years, thereabouts.'

'Could you place her accent?'

Kinstray smiled, a sudden rush of humour lightened his face. 'Wisnae English, she spoke it too well.'

'I know what you mean. You don't mind if I look around?' McAlpine chose his words carefully – this wasn't an official visit.

'Dae what ye want. You boys took a load o' stuff away. Told them, end o' the month, any'hing in her room is in the bin, unless ye can get somebody tae claim it. Shame.'

He tutted, arthritic fingers feeling for the door handle. 'Shame.'

The building was tall, narrow, stale and dark, and uneasily silent. As McAlpine reached the second-floor landing, someone came out of one of the rooms and locked the door behind them. McAlpine registered the prime example of Glaswegian manhood immediately: dirty-haired, undernourished, hardly out of his teens and scared of his own shadow.

'Just a minute,' McAlpine called, as the youngster made to scuttle past him to the stairs. 'Number 12A, up on the fourth floor – did you know her?'

McAlpine stood in his way, receiving a nervous flash of stained teeth.

'Did you?' he repeated.

'No. No ... I wouldn't be knowing about that. She never spoke to me, but she would pass a smile on the stairs. That's all.'

McAlpine noticed the Highland lilt. Not a Glaswegian, then. 'Pretty girl?'

The ratlike teeth flashed again, the thin fingers grasped the leather book he was holding even more tightly. McAlpine saw a glimpse of compassion, a slightly pained expression, before the young man dropped his eyes to the book he was holding, his thumb riffling the gold-edged pages. McAlpine recognized the Bible.

'I wouldn't be knowing about that,' he repeated, eyes still downcast.

McAlpine was about to ask him if he was blind as well, but the young man stood back, gave a slight bow and turned to go down the stairs. 'If you'll excuse me, I'll be late for a lecture.'

'But you know she was badly hurt? Sunday? 26th of June. Teatime? Do you remember –?'

'Sorry, I can't help you.' The blue eyes looked more troubled, guilty even.

'Look, pal, one question.' McAlpine's voice whiplashed down the stairs. 'Where would you say she was from?'

The other man stopped, shrugged. 'I couldn't tell you that. But I saw her with an *A to Z*, so she wasn't from round here.' He sighed and looked up to the ceiling. 'I'm sorry, I never spoke more than two words to her.' And he was gone, taking his guilt with him.

McAlpine lit up a Marlboro on the top landing after the four-flight climb, leaning outside the single toilet, flicking the cracked terracotta floor tiles with the toe of his boot. The smell of stale urine seeped out on to the stairwell. He tried to see those little feet padding their way through there, and couldn't. He pulled the nicotine deep into his lungs, kissing a plume of smoke from his lips to freshen the air.

The door of bedsit 12A opened with the touch of a fingertip to reveal a room frozen in time, circa 1974. The fluttering of the tiny drawings around the bed gave McAlpine the impression somebody had just walked out of sight. The air was heavy with mould and dampness; the chill in the air had been hanging there for years. McAlpine ground his cigarette underfoot and took a deep breath before going in. Going through dead men's stuff was one thing. This was something else.

A narrow single bed with a white plastic padded headboard under the cracked roof. The bedding had been dumped on the floor in a routine police search, the mattress left crooked on the base.

Everything was brown, beige or mouldy, and the room

stank of depression. He shivered. He couldn't imagine those beautiful feet treading across that filthy carpet, creeping down the cold stairs to the smelly toilet. He couldn't place *her* in this room at all; it was all wrong.

The smell was getting to him. He opened the door of the fridge and closed it again quickly. The meter had run out, the fridge had stopped chilling, and mould had launched biological warfare. He took a deep breath, opened it again and had a closer look. Nothing he could identify, but the botanical garden where the salad tray used to be suggested a healthy diet. Another thing that didn't add up.

Under the sink he found bleach, cloths, pan scourers, washing-up liquid and a rolled-up pair of rubber gloves. He sniffed around the drain, poked his finger down the plug-hole and withdrew it covered in black paper ash. In two minutes the ring holding the U-bend was off, and he watched as the plastic basin filled with thick inky water. Nearly a fortnight had passed, but he could still smell the evidence of burning. He swirled the basin as if panning for gold and fished out tiny flakes of unburned white paper. Thick paper, non-absorbent, glossy on one side, the remains of a photograph, maybe more than one. He stood up, staring at his blackened fingertips. Why – if she was thinking of coming back?

There was more here, more for him to learn. He took a closer look at the little drawings, each held by a single drawing pin: sketches of hands, feet, noses, arms, legs, ankles. Some were of faces, perfect tiny portraits, all of the same man.

He smiled to himself. 'Steve McQueen?'

A quick search of the small drawer by the bed revealed nothing; it had already been searched, he could tell by the casual disruption of the contents. She had folded over page 72 of *Jane Eyre*, a battered old copy bought from a charity shop for 10p, the only book in the room.

Behind the door was a coffin of a wardrobe showing signs of woodworm rampage. A quick look revealed a few clothes, carefully placed on individual padded hangers. He pushed them apart with his palms, knowing good silk and cashmere when he felt them, examining the names on the labels – MaxMara, Gianfranco Ferre. That was more like her.

A white dressing gown, thick heavy towelling, hung on a peg on the door. He read the label and smiled, sniffed the collar. It smelled of flowers, bluebells?

He glanced at the single pair of shoes lying in the bottom of the wardrobe, black, kitten-heeled, leather, with a perfect velvet bow. He flicked them over to glance at the size, knowing what he would see. Size 35. European.

Sitting among the detritus of evidence – the cardboard boxes of knives and assorted blunt instruments, bag upon bag of jumble – was a quiet little black handbag, its velvet bow clearly visible through the plastic.

'That one there, the black one,' McAlpine said, pointing. 'Middle shelf, third one from the end.'

The production officer bit a mouthful from his bacon roll before lifting the bag from the shelf and pushing it across the desk.

'What contents were listed?' asked McAlpine.

'See for yourself.' The production officer fixed the A4 sheet on to a graffitied clipboard and turned his attention back to his breakfast.

McAlpine read from the list. 'Perfume, Scent of Bluebells; three pencils, HB, 2B and 2H – somebody with an artistic touch ... a comb, blonde hair on it, a tube of mascara, a book of first-class stamps.' He flicked the page over, then back again. 'So – no bits of paper, no credit cards, no receipts. A normal woman's purse is full of crap.'

The production officer shrugged and wiped a smear of butter from the corner of his mouth.

McAlpine opened the plastic sleeve, lifting the bag clear. It was curiously heavy, lined in silk, hand-stitched, its clasp made of pleated goatskin. He tipped it, spilling the contents. And checked them against the list. Perfect match. He put the contents back in the bag, his sense of unease growing. Every answer he found led to another question. His fingers felt something hard trapped between the silk lining and the leather shell. He worked his fingers round the top, found it and passed it through a cut, not a tear. He pulled out a gold-faced man's watch and a fold of cardboard cut from a Kellogg's Cornflakes packet.

'You checked this?'

The officer backhanded some crumbs from his mouth. 'I wasn't on duty when it came in. No ID in it, so it's of no interest.'

McAlpine's fingers caressed the watch, the lizard-skin strap and the hinged fastening, which clipped down flat. She had petite wrists; this was a man's watch, far too big for her. Had she brought it with her because it was part of him? A way of bringing something of him with her? McAlpine turned his back slightly on the productions desk, making a point of looking closely at the bag, while prising the fold of cardboard open. Wrapped in a web of Sellotape was a ring, plain silver with a single diamond. A lover's ring. Another thing too precious to leave behind.

It was McAlpine's first Saturday night on duty, his third night shift in a row. He had come to prefer these nights to the day shift. Outside, Glasgow was sweating. The hospital was quieter, cooler, the nurses friendlier, and the sleeping beauty alone as often as not.

It had become a habit with him to slip into her room, to have one-sided chats about anything and everything. Sometimes he got the feeling she was listening, that there was an awareness behind that mask. Sometimes he wasn't so sure.

As far as the hospital was concerned, McAlpine was invisible. The nurses had dropped their guard around him completely, and he could harvest little snippets of information from their indiscreet conversations, or from the papers on the aluminium clipboard at the end of her bed. *Slight improvement, reflexes plus plus.* A list of drugs, mostly unpronounceable. He ran his finger down the column, some dosages the same, others getting less – even he could understand that. She was getting better.

He thought about the fine muslin that covered her face. He had got into the habit of screwing his eyes up when he looked at things, seeing the world her way. It was like looking up through thin ice, the ice getting thinner every day. When she broke through and took her first breath, he would be there. When she said, 'My name is . . .' he *would* be there. He could see her perfect features, hair wet and smoothed back like a marble sculpture, could see himself cradling her beautiful face in his hands, lifting her clear and carrying her away. *With this kiss I shall wake you.*

As he walked back, he heard a nurse on the phone, her little gurgling laugh like a teenager's. He'd bet she wasn't talking to her husband.

Their eyes met.

She looked away quickly and cut the call short.

He strolled back to his seat, thinking about women. How deceitful they could be. Or how wonderful.

He heard a cough, indistinct at first, then again. And again.

He looked up and down the corridor, opened the door and slipped inside. She was lying as usual, arms at her side, her body jerking with the spasm of each cough. The gauze was slipping from her face, revealing a line of fresh blood. He lifted her head a little, cradling the weight of it. She coughed again, louder, the force of it racking her body, but then the blockage cleared and her head lolled back slightly. He placed her head gently down on the pillow, and, as she slowly exhaled, he could feel her body deflate. Not like any corpse he had touched but not like a living person either; she was suspended in between.

He leaned over, looking at her closely, two faces separated by a wall of muslin and silence. He adjusted the gauze over the curve of her cheek; he twirled the wisp of blonde round his finger. She didn't pull away. He thought the veining of blood underneath was fainter, the scars beginning to heal. He stood back, regarding her, thinking how she would have been. She was young, slim and fit; her calves had been firm, her ankles still slender despite her pregnancy, her toenails perfectly cut. Even the scar round the base of her toe was smiling.

'Do you mind?' he said. 'I need to see.' He lifted up her left hand, rolling back the cotton wool padding on her palm, where the burning was deepest, where she had lifted her hands to her face. The nails were long and shaped, the back of her hand was covered in smooth tanned skin. He traced a thin band of white at the base of the third finger. He felt – imagined – that she pulled her finger away from his touch.

'I'm sorry, but I had to know. It's fine,' he said. 'It's fine.' He put the hand down carefully, reluctant to let her go and leave her. He held his hands over hers, warming them as he studied the monitor, a single fluorescent line firing across it, hiccuping every now and again, left to right, left to right.

There was a movement . . . a something . . .

He turned and looked at her. 'You OK?' he asked. *Bloody stupid question.*

Nothing, just the wheeze of the respirator.

He moved towards the door, opening it and closing it without leaving the room. She sighed, and he watched her relax, her head dropping slightly in heartfelt relief.

He smiled and took one last look. He walked back slowly to his seat in the corridor, deep in thought, and sat down, his arms folded, his eyes never leaving her door.

'I'm official this time. Official.' His voice was still deep, polite, conversational, sexy, but there was something else. This time it wasn't going to be a monologue. 'Look, sweetheart, I think – I know – you can hear me. And that leaves you with two options. Either I can sit here and talk to myself and feel like a right prick, or you could talk back.'

She so desperately wanted to talk to somebody; it had been months since she had said more than good morning to another human being. And she wanted to hold her baby in her arms; the pain of not having that was worse than anything. She considered her options, who she could trust, who she couldn't. She didn't have much choice.

'The fingers on your left hand aren't too bad. The right hand sustained a bit of damage, I'm afraid. Can you move your thumb?'

She knew she could not move her hands; her fingers were bound together, not tightly but restricted. She moved her thumb, felt her skin crack and a searing pain shoot through her palm.

'Good.' His hand rested on hers, his fingers warm.

She moved her thumb again, easier, less pain. She felt tearful, tense, yet she so wanted to say something. He kept talking, his voice steady and reassuring. He tapped the tip of her forefinger gently. 'What about this finger? Can you move that?'

It was difficult, a small movement, but he saw it. 'Good. So we'll make it a finger for yes, and the thumb for no. That OK with you, sweetheart?'

She thought for a moment, then twitched her finger.

'You fancy a wee chat? My name's Alan.'

Yes, I know. She twitched her finger.

'Look, love, we know what happened to you, and we can find out who did it.' Strong words, but the voice remained friendly. He sounded very young. 'But the first problem is, we don't know who you are . . .'

She listened hard to his voice, so young, so sympathetic. But so few words – could she judge? She kept still.

'Do you have any memory of what happened to you, anything at all?' Conversational? Concerned? She kept still.

'OK, OK.' He didn't speak for a while. She wondered if he was going to trip himself up, imagined him contemplating his next question. 'Look, I'm not stupid, and I don't think you are either.' The voice paused. 'You made a good attempt at covering your tracks, but a trained eye can always see things.' She felt fear prickle at the back of her neck. 'You were in labour, yet the last thing you did before you went out that door was to wash bits of burned photograph down the sink. Must have been important to you.'

She heard him move, shifting closer. 'Somebody got to you. They'll come after you again. You know they will. They might come after the baby.'

He wasn't threatening her; he was stating fact. She was sure he would hear the panic of her heart as it slapped against her chest. She kept her fingers still.

After a moment he said, 'If there's anybody we could contact for you, let them know how you are?'

She stayed still.

His voice softened. 'What about the guy who gave you the ring? Your husband? Fiancé? Was he involved in the attack?'

The thumb jerked. No.

'He's a good guy, then?'

Piet, smiling at her, on the yacht, the wind ruffling his hair, his Steve McQueen smile . . . she watching as the flames ate the photograph, the black flakes disappearing down the drain in a torrent of water . . .

Eventually her finger twitched.

'I see.' *She felt his fingers, warm and soft, caress her hand. He had the same gentle touch as Piet.*

This was a man used to talking to women.

I want to hold my daughter.

'But I'll have to call you something. What do you fancy?' *His hand was still stroking hers.* 'You have long blonde hair. Rapunzel?' *She had no idea what he was talking about, but she could tell he was teasing her.* 'Alice in Wonderland? Oh, I know – Anastasia. They can't work out who she is either. Anna for short.'

Anastasia and the rest of the Romanovs? They had had their precious stones, their diamonds, all the wealth they could take with them, sewn into their clothes. They didn't make it.

She could remember holding a pile of uncut pure diamonds, almost warm to the touch, in her hands. They were secure now, wrapped in black velvet in a safe-deposit box in Edinburgh. They were safe, safe for their child, but she herself wasn't. A tear of pain bit into her eyes to remind her. Her life was precarious.

'I've got a present for you . . . we took them from your room – your ring, the watch, it's all there.'

Her finger twitched.

'Here's the ring. I thought it was silver, but Mappin & Webb tell me it's an imperfect blue diamond set in platinum, a one-off. Why were you in a bedsit with a diamond worth a fortune?'

There was no response.

'Did the guy who owns the watch give you the ring?'

Again her thumb twitched, twice.

'OK.' *The voice was conciliatory.* 'Just make sure someone doesn't take them. Things go missing in hospitals, you know.'

Her finger twitched three – four – times.

Silence hung thick around them for a minute or two.

'Anna, are you saying you want me to keep them for you?'

A single twitch of her finger.

'All right, I'll keep them safe, I promise.'

She heard the chair scrape, sensed his shadow move, as he stood up.

'The wean looks fine.' Wean? A word she didn't know. 'They all look the same to me, but the nurses seem to think she's a pretty wee thing. Do you have a name for her?'

She heard him walk over to the cot. 'Can I pick her up?'

Her heart began to race. Maybe, if she concentrated really hard, he would know. She raised her finger.

'Well, look at you, eh? Oh, don't cry now.' Then his voice changed. 'Have you seen – sorry, held her?'

Please. *She twitched her thumb.* Oh, understand – please.

'She's got blue eyes, blonde hair, extremely pretty. Takes after her mum.'

She twitched her thumb at him, telling him he didn't know that, turned her head as far as the dressings would allow. The baby was quiet now.

Please.

'Here.' His voice was nearer now. She could smell mint – he had just cleaned his teeth. He guided her hand the inch or two the restraints would permit to something on the bed beside her, something warm, breathing, living. 'Anna, meet your daughter. Small person, this is your mother.'

Her daughter's head. Her fingers, stiffly at first and painfully, were exploring all the little pulses and bumps and fontanelles, seeing as blind people see, creating a picture in her mind of downy eyebrows, little wisps of eyelashes, the soft chubby flesh of a cheek. Her daughter.

'Here, feel this.' He moved her fingers down a little. A tiny hand. Her daughter's hand.

'You've no idea how small her hands are. So wee.' He was talking

like a daddy. 'My brother had hands like spades; always had to stick them in his pockets for photographs.'

She picked up the 'my brother had' – past tense – and the wistful tone. Had he lost his brother young? Yet he sounded so young himself, younger than her perhaps.

After a moment he spoke. 'So small, so full of life.' He fell silent again and then said, 'You wonder how they survive, that will to live. The older cops talk about cases – you know, abused kids, starved kids, battered kids – but somehow they keep going. As they say, the trick is to keep breathing, no matter what.' Minutes passed, and she could feel the silence congeal between them. Then he spoke again, his voice sounding desolate, bereaved.

'Do you think dying is a passive process? Because I think that's what my dad is doing. When you have had enough, you give up breathing. Maybe death isn't something that comes up and gets you. You just let it happen. But my mum . . .' He was holding back tears, she could hear it in his voice. For a while, all she heard was the rush of the ventilator; he didn't trust himself to speak. 'My mum – she's got cancer, you know. It's spread bloody everywhere. She'll die of a broken heart, of course. No bloody cure for that, for losing a favourite son. But she'll choose when she dies. And if Robbie hadn't died, then she'd have chosen to keep going' – she tried to crawl her fingers over the blanket towards his – 'because she'd have had something to live for. Her favourite son. I can't help thinking, when she heard, it must have flashed across her mind – why Robbie? Why not Al –' He stopped abruptly. She could hear a monitor bleeping somewhere outside, the banging of doors as somebody was rushed to Intensive Care, another human drama. 'Anyway, life goes on.'

She felt a caress on the top of her head, gone before it had registered. He had kissed her.

His mother was dead.

He was eating soggy chips from a newspaper, sitting on

a rock, nothing in front of him but Dunoon on a cold wet morning. The baking heat of the previous week had given way suddenly to overcast skies, and the brisk wind coming in off the Atlantic chopped up the water of the Clyde. The view gave him no comfort; it looked like eternity had been coloured grey.

Her passing had been simple in the end: no last-minute grasp at life, no desperation to hang on to the final breath.

McAlpine had popped his head through his mother's bedroom door at midnight, said good night, as he always did, and she was still. McAlpine's eyes had wandered to the empty morphine sulphate bottle. She had taken the lot. And that hurt him more than anything, her betrayal. Losing the son she loved had been the last straw, and it was too difficult for her to stay alive for the son she didn't love.

He threw the rest of his chips to the seagulls, then thrust his hands deep into his anorak pockets. He couldn't bear to go back to the house, couldn't bear to be alone with his dad, who had nothing to say at the best of times, couldn't bear even to think about what it meant to have lost his mother.

No, he wasn't going back.

A mother's grief. Those words had sunk deep into his conscience. A mother's grief. Sleeping Beauty and that tiny innocent little baby. He could feel a smile come to his face just thinking about her. Robbie had gone, his mum was gone. At that moment he didn't think he had anybody else, just his blonde angel, lying still in her cocoon, waiting. And that was enough.

Two seagulls squawked, fighting over a chip. It was time to go. He stood up, shook the sand from his shoes and started to walk back to the Victorian railway station at Wemyss Bay. He needed a place where death came with sirens blazing. He needed a place where it was quiet, and he was invisible. He needed to go back to the hospital. He needed Anna.

'Have a seat, Alan. I hear Robbie is to be nominated for a Queen's Commendation for Bravery. You must be very proud.' DCI Graham smiled gently.

A slight pause, a flash of insolence in the dark eyes before McAlpine sat down. 'Proud's not exactly top of the list just now. We don't even know yet when we'll get him back for burying.'

Graham coughed. 'I'm sorry,' he said, slightly abashed. 'What I meant is that it must be some consolation. And now the dreadful news about your mother.'

'They say good news travels fast,' said McAlpine sarcastically.

Graham closed the file, stood up and moved the picture of his wife to the side of his desk. He perched himself on the edge, closer to McAlpine. His voice was full of restraint. 'Putting all that aside, do you want me to list all the procedures you've broken during your association with this case?' he said.

'Do what you want.'

Graham folded his arms. 'I made a mistake. I thought this would be a good case for you, to get your brain back into gear. I knew there was a story about that girl, and I knew you'd get on to it. You were supposed to tell us her secrets, not vice versa; you were supposed to –'

'Supposed to what?' McAlpine was on his feet. 'Supposed to what? Just ignore her? Ignore the fact she's scared stiff? Just give her a bloody number, like the hospital?'

'Sit down and be quiet, Constable McAlpine.' Graham put his hand up. 'There are lines that you are not allowed to cross, and those lines are there for a reason. Put it this way: say we get on to who threw the acid, say we get to the bottom of it – you'll have ruined any chance we have of getting him to court, never mind securing a conviction. Interviewing a witness without corroboration of tape and without a colleague present, tampering with evidence, solo search, and without a warrant at that . . . the case would be thrown out before the ink was dry on the release sheet, and you know as well as I do, PC McAlpine, that kind of shit sticks. And it is not sticking to me, not in this station. You let her down. You let me down. Do I make myself clear?'

McAlpine folded his arms and looked out of the window with a teenager's petulance, reminding Graham just how young he was.

'Do I make myself clear?' Graham repeated.

'Indeed you do.'

'Those rules are there to protect you in cases like this. How are you going to survive the first time you see the body of a dead child? You can't react personally; you have to learn to walk away and move on. In the meantime Interpol have given us a promising lead on her, so I am *ordering you* to leave the girl alone. Just file your report and walk away.'

'And that's it? I'm supposed to just –'

'No, you are not *supposed* to, you have been ordered to. End of story. If you're not going to take time off, you've work to be getting on with. There's been a fatal traffic accident in Byres Road, woman driver killed, and daughter, a Helen – no, Helena – Farrell, she's at the Western Infirmary. Go and sort it out. And don't – just don't – start anything.'

McAlpine climbed the stairs at the Western two at a time and turned left, going quickly along the corridor, fuming, arguing with himself. How dare he? How dare he? It was just police talk; he was a human being and she needed him. She needed him.

Or did he need her?

He stopped at the sign for the Intensive Care Unit. The red-headed nurse went past, ignoring him. A uniform he didn't know was sitting in his seat, watching Anna's room. He was reading the *Sun*, his legs crossed, his foot bobbing up and down as he hummed to some secret melody. McAlpine paused as the uniform glanced up and down the empty corridor before going back to Page Three. A door clicked, and another uniform cop appeared with two cups of tea, settling into the seat opposite his mate. Two of them? There was no way McAlpine could get in there without being seen. He had somewhere else to go, somebody's daughter to sort out. He turned and kept walking.

'Helena Farrell?' At first he had thought it was a workman in the visitors' room, a tall figure in dungarees. Then she turned towards him, caught in the act of pulling a velvet scarf from her hair, leaving a smear of purple paint on her face as auburn curls cascaded down her shoulders. She flicked her head, freeing them, before restraining them once more in their velvet knot.

'When they said daughter, I imagined . . .' McAlpine held his hand out flat, indicating the height of a child.

'No,' she said. She pulled the handkerchief from her eyes, sniffing, and started to dab at the paint stains on her fingertips. He could smell turpentine from her. 'I was working when they called,' she said by way of explanation.

'I'm PC McAlpine, Partickhill Station. Have they told you what happened?'

'As much as I want to know,' she sighed. 'Seems Mum had a heart attack at the wheel and crashed the car on to the pavement.' She shrugged, and the auburn curls bounced slightly against their velvet restraint and resettled.

'Much to the distress of the pedestrians using it at the time. How are you feeling?'

The girl bit the corner of her mouth, almost managing to stop a lone tear in its tracks. 'We weren't close,' she said. Her eyes didn't leave his. She was looking down at him, being a few inches taller, and he wasn't sure he liked that. 'I'm surprised I feel so shocked. I just feel numb, really.'

'If that's the way you feel, that's the way you feel. There're no rules.' He paused. 'Is there anybody I can phone for you? Better that you're not on your own right now.'

Helena stood resolutely, then lifted her hands to her face, open palms covering her eyes. He took two steps forward, allowing her to drop her head on his shoulder before she started to sob. He had no option but to put his arm round her.

DCI Graham and DI Forsythe stood at the door of the DCI's office, listening as McAlpine's slow footfall came up the stairs towards them. Graham looked at his watch. 'Two weeks she was lying there, and we had no idea who she was. Now that we do know, I wish we hadn't bothered.'

'Best of luck with it.' Forsythe stood on the landing, looking down over the banister. 'He's a good copper, McAlpine. I worked with his dad for years. Had a passion for the job, he did.'

'Not always a good thing.'

McAlpine was climbing the stairs very reluctantly. On the landing, he stopped and remained silent, his eyes passing like a condemned man's from Graham to Forsythe.

Graham gently guided him into his office, saying nothing as he handed McAlpine a photograph and sat down.

She was sitting on a desolate beach, the dark mass of the sea to one side, dunes and reeds to the other, the sand spreading out behind her as far as the camera could see. The bleakness of the setting only emphasized the vitality of the subject. She sat half crouched, half sitting, her dark sweater pulled down over her knees, arms wrapped in front of her shins. She held her chin up, exposing her throat, and blonde hair caught by the wind framed her perfect face in brightness. Her grey eyes were full of humour, almost challenging, their stare intense, eyebrows elegantly arched. The lips twisted in a slight smile, the smile of a seductress. He didn't think he had ever seen such a beautiful face. And at the bottom of the photograph her little toes curled into the sand, the little scar bending into a crescent moon.

She was in love with whoever was behind the camera.

He was jealous.

Graham reached out to take the photograph. He pinned it to the board on the wall. Just a picture to him, McAlpine thought, just a cheap black-and-white photo of some blonde with nice legs. Yet there was a subtle change of expression in her sideways glance, catching him in the pit of his stomach. He couldn't quite read it.

The closest he could get was *Don't leave me*.

Graham's voice cut in, unpleasantly real.

'I'm glad you're sitting down, Alan. There's something we've found out, and you'll have to know. We think we know who she is. Interpol have been looking for a blonde female, twenty-four years old, grey eyes, Dutch, slim build, 1.76 metres tall. What's that – five foot six, seven?' He flicked the page over. 'Fingerprints have been lifted from the bedsit but none to compare . . . obviously. And they're sending dental records, but the medics won't let us X-ray her.'

'If she had an interest in art and an operation scar on the big toe of her right foot, I don't think you need look any further.'

Graham turned over another page on the file and sighed. 'Yip, degree in fine art and a ballet injury when she was twelve. Broke her big toe.'

The DCI took a deep breath and pressed on. 'This is going to be hard. Do you recognize any of these people?' He passed over another photograph. A young man who bore an uncanny resemblance to Steve McQueen had his arms round a dark-haired man and a beautiful blonde woman who was leaning lovingly towards him, obscuring the name of the yacht moored behind them. All three were laughing and smiling, the joke of the minute caught for eternity. McAlpine's eyes rested on her; there she was, her hand in the pocket of her shorts, long brown legs, barefoot on the wooden deck, her blonde hair catching in the sea breeze.

McAlpine pointed at Steve McQueen. 'Is that the baby's father? There were drawings of him at the bedsit. Drawn by her, I think . . .'

Graham took the photograph and put it face down on his desk. 'He's Pieter van der Kerkhof. A thief, an intelligent non-violent one, but still a thief. Two years ago he went to the theatre in Paris one night and met a blonde heiress who was studying at the Sorbonne.' Graham turned his gaze to the photograph of Anna on the beach; he knocked the sand with his knuckle. 'She was studying fine art, interested in jewellery design; her family are diamond merchants. Blonde, beautiful, with a brain – he was in love right from the off. Her name was Agnes Geertruijde de Zwaan.' Self-consciously, Graham pronounced the name correctly. 'Her friends called her Aggi.'

McAlpine smiled to himself. She would always be Anna to him.

'The other chap is interesting to us. Jan Michels. He was found dead at Schiphol Airport. He'd been tortured before being shot. There was a theft of uncut diamonds from a high-security warehouse in Brussels in March, and Interpol have been on the lookout for the happy threesome ever since.'

'According to Interpol, one Kommisaris Hauer to be exact, diamonds are fast becoming the purest form of currency these days. If you can get them uncut, unregistered, you have millions of pounds in untraceable assets. Diamonds are small and don't smell, handy if you're in organized crime.' Graham paused, flicking the photograph with his fingers. 'So, Alan, consider the chain of events as our friends at Interpol see it. Stealing stuff like that is a specialized job. They think somebody ordered Piet to steal them, probably threatened his life if he refused. Or threatened hers. Anyway, he does the job but doesn't get round to handing the merchandise over. He disappears, Jan disappears, Agnes disappears. Jan was trying to fly to Johannesburg, but fate caught up with him. Agnes took a circuitous route and entered Britain at Inverness Airport.'

'An airport with no customs, if you pick the right flight.'

'Really?' Graham paused. 'I didn't know that. Interpol think – and this is pure speculation – that Piet's paymasters persuaded Jan Michels the hard way to tell them where Agnes had fled to. No one knows where Piet went to ground. Possibly Jan didn't know. So either the Dutch gang came over to find Agnes, or they asked some Scottish associates to find her. It wouldn't take long: Glasgow's a small place, bedsit land is even smaller, and she was very beautiful. Not a face you would forget. A photograph would be all they'd need. We think she came here bringing the diamonds with her. Four months later Jan was caught trying to leave the country and was tortured. Then they tracked her down and, by making a very public statement that they had found her –'

'They flushed Piet out,' added McAlpine.

'And tried to flush the stones out. They didn't succeed.' This time Graham tapped Piet's photograph with his knuckles. 'He probably thought that by sending her away he was keeping her safe. The lovebirds had some way of communication, so that when he didn't hear from her he broke cover to go to find her. Which suggests she has the merchandise. And she would have put them somewhere safe, and we want to know where. Did she ever indicate to you where they might be?'

'No.'

'We're pulling that bedsit apart right now and interviewing everybody in the building.'

'What happened to the guy?'

'That's the difficult bit.' Graham coughed slightly. '"A" Division had received some intelligence in June that there might be a shipment of illegal diamonds coming in here, west coast. Not much interest to them; they're too busy chasing drugs. The boys at Customs and Excise, though, had a different take on it.' Graham paused a moment, holding another photograph in both hands, waiting for that to sink in.

'Robbie worked for the Excise, he was –'

Graham tapped his lips with the tip of the photograph. 'On HMS *Alba*.'

McAlpine nodded, but his expression had changed slightly; a look of apprehension clouded his brown eyes.

'And on 2 July, at 3.15 a.m. exactly, the *Alba* intercepted a yacht called the *Fluisteraar*, registered in Amsterdam.' He turned the photograph over – a small wooden yacht, a huge hole ripped in her hull, shards of raw wood sticking obscenely from her side – and put it side by side with the photograph of the same yacht moored in some resort in southern France. McAlpine looked away. 'The *Alba* sailed that night with a complement of seven –'

'And only six returned,' said McAlpine quietly.

McAlpine did what a hundred victims had done before him: he stated the obvious, trying to turn things to his own reality, where it all made sense. 'No, there's a mistake. He was just on manoeuvres. That boat collided with the *Alba*, it was just a routine thing . . . Robbie jumped in to effect a rescue; man overboard.' He looked up at Graham for reassurance.

'I'm sorry, Alan, but all Customs officers say they are on manoeuvres. Robbie died in the line of duty.' He handed the younger officer a glass of water, noticing the slight tremor in the hand as he passed it over.

McAlpine said nothing, so Graham continued. 'Small yachts like that aren't difficult to track; Kerkhof took a strange route, so he didn't have to register the boat anywhere. It took him only five days to sail from Amsterdam to the Clyde. God must have been with him going through the Caledonian Canal at this time of year, that's all I can say. You know the rest of the story: the *Fluisteraar* wasn't armed, she wasn't smuggling, there were no diamonds. On impact with the *Alba*, Piet went into the water. The witnesses say your brother didn't hesitate – just went straight in to get him. Robbie died a hero.'

McAlpine dropped his head and pinched the bridge of his nose, trying to take it all in, to shake off the appalling images that besieged his brain. He sighed deeply, and his eyes came to rest on Anna's picture, on her lovely face, her lips slightly shy, ready to break into a smile.

'He – Piet – was coming to join her,' McAlpine whispered, as though he hadn't heard. He looked up. 'So, there is some honour among thieves.'

'Maybe not honour, certainly love.'

The guy who gave you the ring – he's a good guy, then? And the finger twitching – slowly – yes.

'The story didn't end there, though. If she had brought the diamonds here, where are they now?' asked McAlpine.

'That was my question for you.'

'If they loved each other that much, they loved their daughter . . . So somewhere safe, untraceable . . .'

They sat for a minute or two in silence, thinking their own thoughts. A phone rang somewhere downstairs.

'But whoever did that to her is still out there. We're going to apply for specialized security for her and the baby; so rest assured, she will be safe.' Graham raised his head, his eyes uneasy. 'I'm so sorry, Alan. I would never have put you in this position, never let you anywhere near her, if I had known anything about the circumstances. I am genuinely very sorry.'

McAlpine stood up and bowed slightly in front of his superior officer. He seemed perfectly in control except that his brown eyes looked past Graham, staring at the photograph on the wall. 'The thing is, sir, it wasn't you who put me in this position, was it? It was her,' he said and left.

Graham picked up the phone and dialled the hospital, just in case.

She was relieved to be awake. Her dreams had been brutal and bloody: she was rolling in acid, watching through burned-out eyes as her own blood seeped into concrete. Yet, awake, her thoughts were a confused tumble running round her head.

Somebody knew exactly who and where she was. She was the only link in the chain left. If she stayed alive, the baby was in danger . . . but if the chain was broken . . .

Suddenly it was all so clear.

There was only one way she could protect her child.

Wide awake, more alert than she had felt for weeks, she began to plan.

Remembering everything she had learned, she mapped the room in her mind. The door to the corridor, the door to the toilet, the trolley laden with medical equipment, the waste bin with the clunking pedal, the sink with the mirror above it where the nurse with the squeaky shoes checked her mascara: all were plotted and fixed.

Just before afternoon visiting, the hospital was busy and noisy with people coming and going. The ward doors opened exactly on the hour, and, until visiting was over, no nurses would come unless her alarm sounded. She would be left alone for an hour or more.

Carefully she pulled herself up a little, her hands still tied to the frame of the bed. She felt the wound in her stomach twitch with the effort, then the dreadful sensation of her face falling. She collapsed again, waiting till the spinning in her head stopped. The gauze had slipped, nipping painfully where it had been tugging on underlying skin.

When the dizziness subsided, she tried again.

Take it carefully . . . a little bit at a time.

So far, so good.

Now the hands . . .

The wrist ties seemed to be of fabric, not a strap with a buckle but something stretchable. She pulled hard on one, feeling the bandages cut into the dressing on her arm. It lengthened a little. Why had she never tried to free herself before? It wasn't so hard. But until now she hadn't needed to. If she couldn't hold her daughter, she had no need to do anything. It was always easier to do nothing.

She lay there, moving her hand up and down, backwards and

forwards, sensing tightness and restriction, slack and give, working her wrist until she could slip her hand free.

Then she found that with her thumb and forefinger she could pull the soft bands on the other wrist to stretch, until she slipped her other hand out.

A quiet exhilaration overtook her. No more of this helplessness. She knew, at last, where peace lay.

The bitch! His vision was clouded with tears, but the burning in his eyes had nothing to do with the fumes from the traffic pulsating at the lights. He was running, down the hill at Highburgh Road on to Byres Road, past the Tennant's pub, to the traffic lights. He ran quickly, pacing himself along the pavement. Bitch. She had known! She had known! And all the time he had been pouring his heart out to her she had been hiding behind that mask. Laughing at his every word. He punctuated each step with the words as he went. *Bitch. Bitch. Bitch.* Along Church Street, he weaved through the traffic; a yellow Fiat blasted its horn, missing him by inches. He backstepped on to the pavement, wishing the traffic away. Once he reached Dumbarton Road, he stopped to gather his breath, feeling alone in the city's rush hour. The sandstone façade of the building opposite glowered down at him. She was in there, lying in her little cocoon, thinking she was safe, thinking she had fooled him. Impatiently shifting his weight from one foot to the other, he looked up at the hospital tower, stark white concrete against the old red of the college. The traffic jammed again, a juggernaut with W. H. Malcolm on the side stopped in front of him. He looked upward: John Anderson, the hospital's founder, was there, immortalized in stone, in the middle of a group, bending over benevolently, holding the hand of the sick. A scene of compassion. The lorry released its air brakes with a hiss and pulled away, the vibration juddering up through his boots.

The truck slowly moved from his view, revealing a woman standing on the other side of the road, looking up the street, wishing the lights would change. A wee girl, not more than four years old, looked back at him. She had a little pink dress on, pink ribbons, soft blonde hair that caught in the wind. McAlpine looked at her little chubby legs, her little pink shoes and little pink socks folded over at the ankle. Her fingers folded into the palm of her mother's hand, not at all sure. She looked at him, a thin man on the other side of the road, in a big hurry as if he was late for something. She ducked behind her mother's arm as he stared back at her, then she peeked out at him again with big blue eyes. A car passed between them and she was lost to him for a moment. Then she was back, and their eyes met. Another lorry thundered by. Her mother's hand tightened on hers, ready to cross. The girl smiled at him, a wide innocent summertime smile, and gave an absent-minded wave of her free hand. As they walked towards him, the mother tightened her grip further. She was keeping her child from danger, just as Anna had done with hers.

He couldn't blame her for that.

As soon as he entered the long corridor, McAlpine knew something was wrong. Two doctors in white coats stood at IC reception, on the point of arguing. There was a press of people outside her room. He saw the uniform, notebook out, writing something down, and felt his stomach tighten. He started to run, his eyes fixed on Anna's door.

An arm stretched out to stop him. 'Al, it's not –'

'Fuck off,' McAlpine told him quietly and punched him in the face.

*

The bed was empty.

So she had been moved, and he was in the wrong room. All this fuss was about someone or something else.

The red-headed nurse had the baby in her arms, the little head nestled into her neck. She avoided looking at him. Her eyes flicked warily to the bundle of bloodstained bed-clothes piled up on the floor near the sink, ready for the laundry.

Only . . .

It was not bedclothes.

It was her.

She was a marionette with cut strings, folded and crumpled, her face nothing but a pink and purple mulch blackened at the edges, a Halloween mask melted by a slow flame. In one eye, a tiny slip of white was visible. The other eye was closed flat, no eyeball in the socket to give it definition, and her nose was a bifurcated hole. Her out-stretched right hand, missing all but two fingers, seemed to point in benediction.

He saw the slits in her wrists, gaping, still moist, and so recent they glistened in the sunlight, the blood fanning out on the floor and soaking into her white gown. He registered the broken mirror and the slices of glass.

And a single wisp of blonde hair.

Graham's office was cold. Or maybe it was lack of sleep that was making him shiver. McAlpine, dressed in civvies, wrapped his fingers round his coffee.

'So, Interpol happy now? Got *all* the answers, have they?'

'Don't take that tone with me. This is a tragedy all round. I'm sorry she's dead.'

She's left me. 'What'll happen to the baby?'

'Kommisaris Hauer had hopes that Mummy and Daddy

43

might step up, but there's no forgiveness. They don't even want their daughter's body back, and that speaks volumes.'

'The baby?' McAlpine asked.

'Social services, who else? They're going to call her after her mother, now we know who she is.'

Graham turned back to his files. 'Land another punch like that one you stuck on PC Capstick, and I'll have you. This time, we'll say it was a mistake.' The DCI produced a ten-pound note out of his pocket. 'Look, have a whip round for the wee one, if it makes you feel any better. And take two weeks' compassionate leave. That's an order.'

The Western Necropolis sits high on a hill facing the soft verdant roll of the Campsies. It was a grey day and the double snub top of Dumgoyne blended into the dullness of the sky above and the higher peaks behind. He had no tears left, nothing. He had gone past sad, gone past grief, and was drifting in some no man's land devoid of the pain of purgatory. He was empty. He stood back from the road as a cortège passed, turning away at the last minute to look back out to the hills. He had wanted to be alone with her and her little wooden cross.

His mother had been buried at Skelmorlie. Robbie's body was still waiting for a release date, but his dad was insisting he be buried with his mother, putting them together for eternity.

And here was Anna, alone in foreign soil.

Some way from Anna's bare patch of fresh earth was another grave, carpeted with a sea of flowers. A crowd of people pressed round it, and the smell of the turned soil mingled with the scent of rosewater and Youth Dew. A tall man was officiously introducing people to each other, and a knot of women in hats seemed to be mobbing a young woman. Suddenly he caught a glimpse of flaming hair, and knew her.

Helena Farrell detached herself from the crowd and came over. 'I thought it was you. It's kind of you to come,' she said, and stopped on seeing that he was standing at a grave as recent as her mother's. She stepped back, shocked by her dreadful mistake. 'I'm so, so sorry . . . I didn't realize . . .'

'Your mother?' he asked.

She nodded. Her eyes strayed to the recent grave, marked only by a wooden cross, a laminated tag twitching in the wind.

'A friend,' he said, inviting no further comment.

'I'm really sorry if I've intruded.' She hesitated a moment. 'Somebody close?'

'No . . . maybe. Yes,' he smiled. 'Very.'

'Interesting flowers to put on a grave.'

He looked down at the white tulips in his hand, keeping one back in the curl of his fingers. 'She was Dutch. She'd have found these funny. She didn't have much to laugh about.'

'Where have all her other flowers gone?'

'She won't have any other flowers.'

'I'm sorry. That was tactless.'

'Your mother's got plenty.'

'Yes, but no one walked the length of Byres Road to find tulips in July.'

He looked at her in her black suit, purchased the day before. 'You know, I preferred you in your dungarees.'

'I had to buy this. I had nothing else to wear.' She turned to look out at the hills. 'It's a funny place to have a cemetery, up here, with all that . . . I think I'd need to be buried facing that way. To the hills.'

'To the hills, indeed.' He looked down at the tulips. 'Now,

if I was really organized, I'd have bought something to put these in.'

'Hang on a mo.' Helena walked over to her mother's grave, now bearing a resemblance to the Chelsea Flower Show, and returned a few moments later with a conical aluminium flask discreetly up her sleeve. 'They didn't notice,' she whispered. 'There's even water in it.' She bent down to screw the cone into the earth. 'Will that do?'

She stood back to let him put the flowers in himself, but his hands were shaking, and he handed them to her. She noticed how nicotine-stained his fingers were.

'There,' she said. 'What do you think of that?'

'Fine. Just fine.'

Rubbing the diamond ring in his pocket like a talisman, he turned back to the unmarked grave and laid a single red rose on it, just where he imagined her heart might be.

Alan

Glasgow, 2006

Saturday, 30 September

Elizabeth Jane Fulton had not been beautiful in life.

Death did her no favours either.

Detective Chief Inspector Alan McAlpine paused as he entered her sitting room, letting a thin stream of rainwater finish its meandering path down his back. He knew it was going to be bad, so he crossed himself and said a quick prayer.

Elizabeth Jane lay on her back, crucified against the soft scarlet wool of her living-room carpet, the deeper stain of her blood sinuously shadowing the curve of her body. She lay with her legs together, stockinged feet crossed at the ankle, arms outstretched, hands palm upward and fingers slightly curved in cadaveric spasm, the index finger of her left hand pointing, her head tilting, the roll of dead eyes looking at the door as if watching for Nemesis.

In the harsh light the skin of her face was waxy and blue, and McAlpine recognized the blistering of chloroform round the mouth and nose.

He wiped wet hair from his forehead, taking a closer look at her uniform: navy blue skirt, the matching neckerchief still round her neck. He couldn't quite place where he had seen it before. Bank? Hotel? The anonymous uniform of the professionally uninterested. The skirt had been pulled down to straighten the pleats, tan-coloured tights shrouding her legs, the toes stained blue with dye from her shoes. All the clothes over her stomach had been ripped apart as the knife ploughed its indecent path through skin and soft tissue.

The leather of the thin belt had held, dragged upward, framing the dark epicentre of the gaping wound. A fine dark line ran down from her sternum, opening out where the viscera nestled in the gentle arc of her hipbone. McAlpine couldn't help looking, trying not to breathe in the heavy mineral stench of blood.

The SOCO with the video camera stopped filming as Professor O'Hare stepped forward. He sideshifted his grey fringe with the back of his forearm, a dark smear of blood visible on his protective gloves, before he spoke. 'That's part of her intestine, DCI McAlpine. Little trick of Jack the Ripper, that one. Except he used to put them over the victim's right shoulder.'

'Thanks. I really needed to know that, Professor.' McAlpine glanced at the dead woman's left hand. The fingers were bare.

'In this case, I'm not sure it was intentional. I think he just cut the mesentery.' O'Hare tutted. 'I'll let you know ASAP. I heard last night you'd been put in charge; glad to have you on board.' O'Hare smiled slightly as he recoiled from the body, pulled the gloves from his hands, turned them inside out and placed them in a plastic bag. 'Don't drip on anything. Here.' He handed McAlpine a paper towel. 'How is DCI Duncan?'

'The bronchitis turned out to be chronic heart failure. He's stable, but that's all they're saying. At least he's not suffering the stress of this any more. I guess that's my job now.'

'He looked dreadful last time I saw him. When did you get the call to take over?' asked O'Hare.

'Thursday night. Duncan wasn't going to let go until they dragged him away in an ambulance . . . and in the end that's exactly what happened.'

'That's what the job does to you. Pass on my regards if you see him.'

'Will do.' McAlpine mopped the water from his hair, looking directly at Elizabeth Jane's open wound. 'Oh, the mess of her. Fucking bastard.'

They stood in silence, hands on hips, listening to the drumming of the rain on the window, and staring at Elizabeth Jane, who lay on the floor between them like some recalcitrant child exhausted at the end of a tantrum.

'Can we move her now?' the SOCO asked.

The pathologist and McAlpine stood back as the body was lifted, ready to be turned on to the white plastic sheet. A gloved hand steadied the loose intestine as the body moved. The camera clicked, catching everything, the blood-stained underskirt slipping over Elizabeth Jane's thigh to reveal fresh carpet underneath. The smell intensified as the body rolled, and McAlpine turned away, holding the paper towel to his nose, grimacing and cursing like a trooper.

The SOCOs held her, half turned, one leg balanced on the other, their plastic slippers crunching on plastic sheeting as they moved closer. Elizabeth Jane answered them with a slow exhalation, like a deflating tyre. Nobody spoke.

O'Hare bent to check her back, looking at the bruising. Then he nodded, the bodybag was zipped, and Elizabeth Jane disappeared.

'Same as Lynzi Traill?' McAlpine knew the answer before he asked.

'The pose, the cutting, the chloroform burns on the face? The wound's a bit deeper, but apart from that it's a carbon copy.'

McAlpine sighed. 'I'm only twelve hours into the Traill case, and this happens. What about chloroform – how easy is that to get hold of?'

'DCI Duncan asked the same question. It's a controlled substance. I know he had a check done, and none had been reported stolen recently; that was the last I heard. But I'll say to you exactly what I said to DCI Duncan about the Traill murder: efficient and confident use of a knife. This guy knows what he's doing.'

'Wish I did,' McAlpine sighed, looking at the exposed carpet outlined by the tidemark of drying blood. 'Nothing tasty about the knife?'

'Not yet.'

'But the same one?'

'Nothing tells me it's different,' O'Hare answered cautiously. 'Best of luck.' He touched the smaller man on the shoulder on his way past.

McAlpine wound the paper towel round his knuckles, tearing it as he flexed his fingers; it was damp but comforting. He scanned the walls around him. The TV, small and functional, a DVD player underneath, its clock reading 5.17, the figures flashing at him and reminding him how tired he was. He picked up a couple of family photographs from the wooden unit. One of the deceased at some grand function, grinning in glad rags and clutching champagne, her mother on one side, her dad on the other, their smiles broad for the camera. The other was of Elizabeth Jane with another girl, a sister or cousin from the look of her, with the same dark-rimmed eyes and serious expression. He put the photographs down, scanning the bookcase: DVDs of *David Copperfield*, *Upstairs Downstairs* and the BBC production of *Pride and Prejudice*. The books were all much of a muchness: Steel, Vincenzi, Taylor Bradford. A pile of magazines was stacked near by on the bottom shelf, topped by two sudoku booklets, one open with a pen attached.

One china coffee mug, half empty, sat on the pine mantelpiece; its partner was on the small table beside the sofa. He kneeled down. The second cup was still full, with a white and greasy film of floating milk.

McAlpine was thoughtful. Her number was ex-directory, and the name plate downstairs simply said FULTON, no Miss, no Mrs. The front door said E. J. FULTON. The car had a Stoplock and a gear lock on it. She was a careful woman . . . as the previous victim, Lynzi Traill, had been, from the accounts he had read. He walked to the window, pulling the curtain back slightly, looking through the net.

Elizabeth Jane Fulton had known her killer.

'Prof?' he called.

A reluctant shadow appeared at the door.

'What's the parking like out there?' McAlpine asked, flicking the net and wiping the condensation from the glass. A hive of activity in the dead of night, two police cars blocking Fortrose Street, another three up on the pavement. He watched as an officer, clipboard over his head to protect him from the rain, directed two others up the street, while another, half hidden behind the car, was bending over retching up the contents of his stomach, clearly finding the whole thing a trial by fire. Squad car 13 reversed to park between them, yellow light oscillating, highlighting the double curve of the digit 3 with every turn.

'It's busy. Permit parking only. A strange car might have been noticed, heard. Might be worth a shot,' O'Hare answered.

McAlpine looked up Fortrose Street, at the trees at the Wickets Hotel, the lights in the upper rooms making comets in the rain. Up the hill, turn right, ten minutes' walk, five if you hurried, and there was Victoria Gardens, where they had found Lynzi Traill. So close.

'Time of death?' he asked.

'At this stage, I'd plump for early last night. One of those mugs was half empty, so if it was hers, the coffee will still be in her stomach . . . if the stomach wall hasn't been punctured and leaked the –'

'Spare me, please.'

O'Hare smiled; he liked seeing hard-bitten detectives go green. 'I'll leave you to it. Helena sent me an invite to the exhibition, so I'll see you there if not before.'

It took McAlpine a little while to think what he was talking about. 'Yes, of course. It's sometime at the end of the week – Friday, isn't it?'

'Saturday,' corrected O'Hare.

The Professor departed, dipping his head by force of habit as he went out of the door. McAlpine stood in the perfectly square entrance hall, with its floor of cheap laminate, every door white-stained colonial. The only slash of colour was the mock-Persian rug, now littered with the machinery of investigation: lights, cameras, cases, everything covered in clear polythene. The two SOCOs, still in their plastic-coated paper suits, were packing up.

McAlpine opened the bathroom door. The ventilator purred into life with the light switch, wafting the scent of lavender through the air. All was pink. Wrapping his fingers in a piece of pink toilet roll, he opened the cabinet. One tube of toothpaste: Macleans' fluoride. One deodorant spray: Marks & Spencer's Peaches & Cream. One folded face cloth: pink. One shampoo: anti-dandruff. One conditioner: *for dry, fine, flyaway hair*. One Marks & Spencer body lotion, Peaches & Cream again. Not much else.

No contraceptives. No headache tablets. No hangover cure. He shut the cabinet door.

The bedroom was the same nauseating pink-with-a-hint-of-vomit. Even the teddy bear on the pillow was two-tone pink. McAlpine opened a few drawers, his fingers still curled in the tissue. The top drawer was full of very sensible underwear. Either Elizabeth Jane had no sex life or she went to hospital a lot. On a pink satin chair was a pile of clothes folded with army precision, blouses with sleeves tucked in, a jumper and cardigan to match her uniform. The few prints on the wall were from the same Marks & Spencer colour coordinated range as the wallpaper, the bed linen, the dressing gown and the teddy. More camouflage than coordination.

McAlpine turned back to the pristine white kitchen. Only Nescafé and the kettle on the worktop. The cupboard revealed a range of tins, all stacked label-side out, most of them WeightWatchers'. An open sachet of cat treats, carefully folded at the top, sat to one side. He looked for a water dish or litter tray, but couldn't see any. So – no resident cat. He opened the fridge: low-fat spread, skimmed milk, plenty of fruit and veg that all seemed fresh. He flipped open the bin. The only thing in it was the white bin liner.

The SOCOs said their goodbyes, wedging the door open as they left with their equipment. McAlpine saw a small black cat with a white kipper tie shivering with fear behind the cheese plant on the landing, its fur glittering with rainwater. McAlpine walked out into the hall and picked it up. 'Hello, little fella. I don't think you live here.' The cat regarded him with saucer eyes, then stared back at the white-suited men walking about his domain. 'Anybody know where this wee guy belongs?' asked McAlpine. Without waiting for a reply he put the cat into the hands of a SOCO who was coming up the stairs. 'Find out and give him back, will you?'

The SOCO took the cat in an outstretched arm as if it were a bomb. 'It lives in the next-door flat, I think. She's terrified it'll get out and run over by a police car. Wouldn't be the first time.'

'Make sure she keeps him locked up.'

'We've handed it in twice already; it escapes every time the nosy cow opens her door.'

'Well, tell her to lock him in the bathroom.' The DCI glanced at his watch. 'For the next twelve hours at least.'

McAlpine shivered himself in the draught that raced up the stairwell and bit at his legs. He entered the comparative warmth of the flat again, and went back into the kitchen for a look at the cork noticeboard and the plans for a future life that would never be: a wedding invitation with the ubiquitous Rennie Mackintosh rose motif and, clipped to it, a card with a date for a dress fitting. He opened the invitation with the tip of his pen. *Mr and Mrs Vincent Fulton request the pleasure* . . . That was a request for deaf ears now. Below it was a folded registration card for a Samsung 200 mobile purchased two days before; he made a note of the number. There were two more phone numbers written in the same neat disciplined hand, a list of three complaints about the flat and a note to phone the factors about a joiner.

McAlpine started opening and shutting cupboard doors again, searching.

He found no cigarettes, no alcohol, no chocolate.

He decided he would not have liked Elizabeth Jane Fulton.

McAlpine lingered for a long time over his last cigarette in the car park at the back of Partickhill Police Station, leaning against a battered old Corsa, letting the nicotine soothe his lungs. It had been six months since the Scottish Executive had banned smoking in all public buildings, and standing in the rain had become a popular pastime on the basis that pneumonia killed quicker than lung cancer. The police station was a long-lost friend he wasn't sure he wanted to know again. Working out of Stewart Street, he'd been able to pick and choose what station within the Glasgow Central and West Division he wanted to run an investigation from, and there were always a hundred and one perfectly valid reasons for it not to be Partickhill. Built in a gap in the tenements created by the Luftwaffe, it had come about by chance, not design. It fitted the space but was too small to do the job; the canteen was a joke, the car park was tiny, the lane too narrow for the meat wagon to get up. But the powers that be had decreed that what DCI Duncan had started, DCI McAlpine would continue. So here he was. How could he argue? He lived less than five minutes from the place.

He sighed and stubbed his cigarette out underfoot. Taking a deep breath, he closed his mind to the memories and walked up the hill to the entrance.

He nodded at the desk constable on his way past but kept moving, getting it over with. He went up the stairs of Partickhill Station for the first time in twenty-two years, wiping cold sweat from his upper lip, images best forgotten already flashing in his mind. The stairs were carpeted now. The window was new but still draughty; the filing cabinet had gone but a photocopier was parked in its place. A curled Post-it note was stuck to it, dated two years before.

He walked quickly through the doors of the main incident room, glancing up at the clock. That was new too but still told the wrong time. He checked his own watch, his gold-faced Cartier. It was ten to seven, ten minutes before he would know the first outcome of the silent conversation between O'Hare and Elizabeth Jane at the mortuary. He hoped it had been fruitful.

He strolled round the CID suite, watching the squad assemble. Some had been pulled from their beds; others had been here all night. Some wiped sleep from their eyes; others were chewing gum to stay awake. As he walked past a bank of computer screens, familiar faces looked up at him, arms stretched out to say hello and welcome, and there were a few pats on the back, a show of faith. McAlpine nodded back, saying hello here and there, *nice to work with you again; glad you're on the team.* He took his time to familiarize himself with twenty-odd years of change. The incident room still smelled the same: stale sweat and yesterday's coffee.

Memories were already stretching and yawning, uncoiling from sleep, memories of things he had never known, a voice he had never heard, a smile unfurling from lips he had never gazed at. Had never kissed.

A beauty he had never seen.

But it still felt like a reunion; even through the reek of staleness he could smell her in the air, in the scent of bluebells. The scent of *her.*

He closed his mind to the past and concentrated on the present.

The main room was a sea of desks and printers. He kicked a few cables with his toe on the way past; he would get them taped down. Dead coffee cups were piled up in pyramids; intrays and out-trays spilled over with printouts. DS Littlewood's tattered leather jacket was lying over his desk, and the early edition of the *News of the World* was open at Page Three. His tray was topped with the remnants of yesterday's bacon sandwich. McAlpine had met burglars who were tidier.

He stopped at the cork-board displaying the scene-of-crime pictures and pulled a piece of luminous orange card saying *wall of death*, crushing it with one fist and throwing it across the room. He didn't look round; he didn't want to know who had written it. He detested victims being treated with disrespect. He looked at Lynzi Traill, killed fourteen days before. Not a particularly attractive woman, with her round tanned face and eyebrows plucked to extinction, but there was nothing particularly unattractive about her either. She was neither fat nor thin, tall nor short; she worked part time in a charity shop; she had a lover. She had left her boring semidetached, left her boring hubby and left her child.

Left her child.

McAlpine looked closely at her wound, somebody's hand pulling the branches of a bush to the side, revealing hatred.

'Hello, DCI McAlpine,' a girl introduced herself. Her pulled-back tightly clipped hair was a sure sign she was just out of uniform. 'DC Irvine.'

'You have a first name, Irvine?'

'Gail.' She smiled, dark eyes twinkling. 'Professor O'Hare rang through just now. He says the preliminary examination has revealed no obvious forensics at the site. He's looking for trace evidence, but that will take some time.'

'Did he say anything about the scene-investigation report?'

'On its way, sir.'

'Good, good,' said McAlpine, looking over her left shoulder. DCI Graham's room, as such, was gone, and he was trying to figure out where the missing wall had been. The doorway had been moved from the hall to this room, a glass panel in place so the senior officer could survey the troops. The incident room was now twice the size, with a plastic concertinaed door folded to one side at the halfway point. He noticed that one door to the corridor was marked EXIT. So he had walked in through the out door.

So be it.

He continued his slow walk round the main room, breathing in the subdued tension, looking at the maps, the statistics, the duty roster. The fluorescent lights were humming exactly a semitone lower than the computers. There was the odd tap of a keyboard but mostly the squad were reading, a steady flick of paper, waiting. Two cops were debating why the coffee always tasted like chlorine.

McAlpine opened the door to Graham's old office. There it was again . . . that memory . . . *Graham's* old office. No, it was DCI Duncan's office. He shivered slightly; it was his own domain now. The room had two desks, two filing cabinets, one with a drawer missing, the compulsory computer monitor chasing a message from right to left, three dead plants and a memo from Assistant Chief Constable McCabe, asking him for a meeting to discuss the budget, details were on his email. His reputation for ignoring emails, and budgets, had clearly preceded him.

He reached into his pockets for a biro, finding his Marlboros. Something hard in his jacket pocket jabbed his fingertips. It was a small card, a hand-drawn caricature of himself in a deerstalker with a huge magnifying glass. He opened it.

Catch him!
See you when I see you,
Happy Anniversary,
All my love,
H.

She had slipped it into his pocket as he slept. He raised the card to his lips. It smelled of graphite, turpentine, pencil eraser and a touch of the Penhaligon's Bluebells he always bought for her. He smiled. The drawing of him was good;

she had even been kind enough to remove a few wrinkles. He hadn't remembered their anniversary. He never did. He thought there was supposed to be a dinner party but couldn't recall when. He made do with sticking the card up against the computer, obscuring the monitor.

He gazed out at the main office, then turned his back on his observers, the leather chair squeaking as it swivelled, and tore open the envelope of preliminary photographs. His breathing quickened as he flicked through grotesque images of Elizabeth Jane, the sheen of mesentery covering her exposed bowel, mucosa glistening in the flash of the camera. For a moment he looked closely at it, fascinated by its rich colour and gentle folds, then he remembered what he was looking at and shoved the prints back into their envelope.

He pulled out the small picture of Elizabeth Jane and held it up. From the corner of his eye he could see Lynzi's face looking at him through the glass, his eyes moving from short to long focus as he compared them, tapping a biro against his teeth and swinging on his seat, getting into a rhythm. To his untrained eye, it looked as though Elizabeth Jane's body had suffered the greater injury. Lynzi Traill, thirty-four, dark haired, dark eyed. Elizabeth Jane Fulton, twenty-six, a shy bank teller, slightly overweight, medium-brown hair. Both Ms Average. Both chloroformed, ripped open and left to bleed to death. No forensic evidence found at either site.

Lucky? Or clever? *Efficient and confident use of a knife.* O'Hare's phrase. Not many people could calmly push a blade into soft live flesh till blood ran like warm olive oil.

McAlpine looked at his watch. Three hours to the main briefing. He needed something to give them. And he needed nicotine and caffeine. Decent caffeine. He wondered where

61

Anderson was . . . he needed somebody to talk to. He looked at the photographs again. The direct comparison told him the attack on Elizabeth Jane had been more ferocious than that on Lynzi. Instinct told him that was not a good sign. Two post-mortem shots, a close-up of each wound with O'Hare's gloved hand in the frame, holding a rule, a scale to show how long, how deep, how brutal. Through the glass he could see Irvine bisecting the wall with a piece of orange gaffer tape, a half-legible case number on the second half. He could hear her chattering away about the previous night's *Coronation Street*. McAlpine scribbled on a piece of A4 paper and went out to hand it to Irvine.

'Type that out and put it up there. Her name was *Elizabeth Jane Fulton*, that's her date of birth and that's the date of her death. She is not a number.'

McAlpine walked on, not waiting for an answer. One step through the folded doors and he was back to 1984, memories crowding round him. He pulled the doors closed behind him. Alone, he stood, feeling the chill in the air, looking at the wall covered with a mosaic of pictures: Lynzi, her husband, her boyfriend, her son, the Glasgow Central train timetable, Victoria Gardens, a close-up of a single brass key. But all he could see was a black-and-white photograph of a blonde woman on a beach, her head flung back, smiling at the sun. It was quiet in here. He could almost hear the sea in the photograph, taste the salt on his lips. She was walking over his grave; he could feel that kiss, the soft brush of her lips against his. A smile that had never quite . . .

The door behind him bumped, and he closed his eyes, killing the memory.

'Roll, fried egg, potato scone, no butter, brown sauce,

one coffee, no milk. Did I get it right?' Detective Inspector Colin Anderson tried to elbow the door open holding two brown-paper bags and balancing a cardboard tray with two cups. 'How many sugars?'

'Three.'

'But I didn't stir it. I know you don't like it sweet.'

'The old jokes are the best. Good to have you back, Colin. *DI* Anderson now, I believe. Two years without me holding you back and you're promoted. Well, well. Congratulations.' McAlpine slapped him on the arm. 'How was life in the frozen east?'

Anderson grimaced. 'Thanks for the reference; it helped me get the job. But – well, it wasn't quite the job I expected.'

'Yeah, but you had to do it to find out, or you would have spent the rest of your career wondering otherwise. I debated whether to call you in on this, but I thought, what the hell – six months into a two-year secondment? You'll be pissed off with the driving already.'

'I was pissed off the first morning it took me forty minutes to get through the Newbridge Roundabout.' Anderson held out the roll, double-wrapped in a napkin. 'Eat it while it's hot, it's straight from the University Café.' He took a bite out of his own white roll – sausage, tomato sauce – and proceeded to talk with his mouth full with such relish McAlpine presumed he got a row for doing it at home. 'Edinburgh was shite; the office was too warm. After years of 23-hour shifts you think a nine-to-five will be fun.' He downed a mouthful of hot coffee. 'But it's boring. I couldn't settle. I'm glad to be back. Edinburgh's full of traffic lights and tourists. Bunch of chancers.' He pulled a face. 'The potato scones are iffy. There's a hill with a castle on it, a high street with no lamp-posts, and that's about it.'

'I can tell you were impressed. My mum always said you get more fun at a Glasgow stabbing than an Edinburgh wedding. Complaints and Investigations, wasn't it?'

'Yeah, but it's not real police work,' Anderson swirled his coffee. 'And I missed this, I really missed it. So how do we come to be here?'

'There were rumours DCI Duncan was struggling, then I was pulled into the office to be told he's in a high-dependency unit, and I'm being transferred to take over the Traill case. And they wanted it to be run from here.'

'You worked out of this place before?' Anderson looked round, staring at the ceiling. 'Small, isn't it?'

'Years ago, as a cadet,' McAlpine said bluntly. 'Anyway, next thing I know, I'm being dragged out of bed at five in the morning for victim number two.'

'Any ideas about what's behind all this?'

McAlpine looked round to see who was listening. 'None that go anywhere,' he said quietly. 'Colin, I'm a bit uneasy about this, and I'm not sure why.'

Anderson stuck the last bit of roll in his mouth. 'You've a hundred per cent record. Why shouldn't you get the case? Surely it was down to you or DCI Quinn. I tell you, if *she*'d been on the case, I'd have stayed in Edinburgh.' He sensed further disquiet. 'What's up?'

As McAlpine took his cigarette packet from his pocket, Anderson noticed the tremor in his hand. Sharp resolution came back to his voice. 'It's a difficult situation for us all. It's a big squad; they know each other much better than they know me. Or you.'

'But Costello's been on the team right from the start, hasn't she? Has she any ideas?'

'I phoned her from the scene this morning. I wanted her here before the others. But the lock's jammed on her car, she says, and she can't get into it. She'll be here soon.' McAlpine was walking up and down, looking at the photographs, like a sergeant major inspecting his troops. He stopped in front of Lynzi's face.

Anderson followed discreetly and took another mouthful of his coffee. 'How's Costello doing?'

'Sounded her usual self.' McAlpine inhaled deeply. 'Breathing fire and brimstone, champing at the bit. Relieved it wasn't Quinn taking over. You know a chap called Viktor Mulholland?' he asked sharply. 'That's Viktor with a *k*? He's being wished upon us from on high.'

Anderson shook his head. 'He a fast-track?'

'Talented, seemingly. But I'm out of touch, I don't know about him. A case like this, he'll sink or swim.'

'Pair him with Costello. She'll keep an eye on him,' suggested Anderson.

'Of course. I should have thought of that.' McAlpine sighed.

Anderson retreated round the partitioned wall and sat on the edge of the desk, rolling his empty coffee cup in the palms of his hands, his eyes passing over Lynzi and resting on Elizabeth Jane, looking at the arrangement of their feet, left over right. 'Sinister over dexter,' he mused. 'Do you think there's a religious thing behind all this? It's a bit precise, isn't it, the arrangement of the limbs?'

'Which means we have a psycho, and . . .' McAlpine turned, catching something said just out of earshot. 'Sorry, Col, I'm wanted on the phone. I'll take it on the moby and go out for a fag. See you in the office in a minute? Oh, and as I've been up since five, I'm going to nip home and have a shower before the briefing.' He looked at his watch. 'You can run me back in.'

The fried-egg-and-potato-scone roll with brown sauce

still lay on the desk, one bite taken out and the rest untouched. Some habits did not change.

DS Costello caught her toe on the step of Partickhill Police Station, as she had done every working day for the last six years.

'Enjoy your trip?' PC Wyngate asked, as he did every time he witnessed it.

Costello rolled her eyes and forced herself to remember that she was actually fond of young Wyngate, whose endless willingness and sheer bloody niceness made up for his not being the brightest. 'It's Baltic out there.' She pulled down the hood of her cream duffel coat, running her fingers through unruly blonde hair, and shivered in the warmth of the station, wishing her shoes didn't let water in. 'Briefing at ten?' she read off the board.

'Yes. I think that new guy wants you to do something first; you've to go up straight away.' He leaned over the desk. 'Guess what?'

'What?'

'I was there, at the scene. I was on the tape, then I started the door-to-door,' he said smugly, stirring his tea with deliberation, clinking the spoon repeatedly against the side of his Partick Thistle mug.

'I thought you were taken off the tape because you were spewing your guts on the pavement? Using the tape to keep yourself upright, in fact.'

'Oh, who told you?'

'It's on the noticeboard, Wingnut. You should be flattered, shows some kind of popularity.'

Wyngate could never quite tell when Costello was joking, so he shrugged. 'You going upstairs?'

'Yeah. Main incident room, is it?'

'You take these up with you, some more stuff about last night. That's the prelim report from the scene through already. Traill all over again,' Wyngate stated baldly.

'The same?' asked Costello, as she took the envelope of photographs.

'Exactly.'

'Oh . . . right,' said Costello cautiously. She turned round, tapping the envelopes on the counter, feeling them surreptitiously. The report was only one page; the other envelope had the stiff cardboard backing of photographs, the number code telling her these were the second batch to come through. God, how quick had they been with the first? She allowed herself a smile – DCI McAlpine was in charge, things were moving.

'So who else is up there?'

The stirring resumed. 'Vik Mulholland's not in yet.' Wyngate sniffed the air. 'You can always tell. No aftershave, therefore no Mulholland. Is he gay, d'you think?'

'No, but he helps them out if they're busy. Who else is up there?'

'A tall fair-haired bloke in a Barbour, polite, looks stressed.' Wyngate was looking down a list of names. 'Would that be DI Anderson?'

'Yeah, Colin Anderson. He's been dragged back from Edinburgh. Nice guy,' Costello said, smiling to herself.

Wyngate consulted a piece of paper. 'Was he not seconded from the L and B?'

'No, they seconded him from us, and we are having him back. Is McAlpine already here?'

'DCI McAlpine? Small, dark-haired bloke?'

'Yip, that'll be him,' said Costello, giving him a sweet smile, her sharp features blending into prettiness for the briefest of moments. She looked at the clock: it was going on seven.

'He wasn't fast-tracked, was he?' asked Wyngate.

'He made DCI at thirty-five. That's talent, not fast-track,' Costello whispered, letting him into a secret. 'He's good; you should watch and learn.'

'Yeah, right.' He dropped another two reports on the top of her pile, spinning round to talk to an old couple and a tartan-coated greyhound that had just walked in. 'Can I help you?' he said, tapping a keyboard, happy with his computer.

Seconds later Costello was taking the stairs two at a time up to the incident room. Every murder inquiry McAlpine had been on, he had called for her. Every time she met him again, she hoped she would feel different, that he would somehow *be* different. The door to the DCI's office was closed, but she could see them through the window, sitting close together, Anderson talking, McAlpine with his back to her. She took a deep breath, hoping again that time had caught up with Alan McAlpine: that the almond eyes had faded, the burnt umber had dulled to sepia, the beautiful profile had wrinkled with age. That maybe his seductive smile had been softened by the passing years. She felt her stomach twist.

She opened the door, her feet squelching. McAlpine and Anderson were deep in discussion. It was a while before McAlpine turned, flicking his hair from his face before his eyes met hers.

His face was just as it had ever been.

Perfect.

Winifred Prudence Costello had suffered many misfortunes in her life, not least of which was being named after both grandmothers. Another was the ability of her cars, like her men, to let her down just when they were needed. Like at six that morning when she'd been in a hurry, but the Toyota was more impregnable than Alcatraz, leaving her standing in a puddle and making her late for the meeting. The DCI, being his usual self, had got straight to the point.

'Glad to see you, Costello. Get your skates on and check this out.' He had handed her a piece of paper with Elizabeth Jane's neighbour's statement. There were a few too many vague comments in the initial interview, and he wanted it cleared up before the briefing at ten. The good news was that he trusted her to get the job done properly.

The bad news was she had to take Vik Mulholland with her.

McAlpine had spared her the embarrassment of explaining about her car by ordering Mulholland to take her in his. She was the senior officer, so she should be the one driven. That had gone down like a lead balloon.

She checked her watch. Mulholland had said he would be out in two ticks, and that was ten minutes ago. She began to stamp her feet, the water in her shoes warming nicely to skin temperature. Plunging her hands deep into the pockets of her duffel, she pulled her neck tight into the collar, humming 'A Policeman's Lot is Not a Happy One' to herself. All the time her fingers caressed the soft leather of her warrant card, the evidence of her promotion, to Detective Sergeant Winifred Prudence Costello.

She gestured through the doors of the station, tapping her fingertip on the face of her watch. Wyngate shrugged his shoulders at her; Mulholland was nowhere to be seen. Costello sniffled and looked up Hyndland Road. Brenda Muir was having an autumn sale, 50 per cent off. There was a dark green cocktail dress in the window, the colour of avocado skin. Who was she kidding? She never went anywhere, except work. If she wore good clothes, she looked as though she'd stolen them. She stamped her feet a little quicker, watching a piebald collie investigate a wheelie bin. She looked at its feathered tail rippling in the wind, letting her mind run. First Lynzi, now the Fulton girl. She shivered, nothing to do with the chill of the morning. The collie teased a chip paper from the bin and began to worry it, pinning it to the pavement and taking great delight in ripping the newspaper to shreds, which the wind promptly dumped in the gutter.

The rush hour had started, and cars were snaking up to the junction with the Great Western Road, amber and red lights smudging in the rain. Up there too stood the elegant four-storey terraces of Kirklee, one of the most prestigious addresses in Glasgow, a five-minute walk from the police station but socially a million miles distant. The McAlpines had lived there all their married life, in Helena's family home.

Still no sign of Mulholland, and Costello was getting impatient. Vik Mulholland was the new kid on the block, still had to prove his worth. The old musketeers were back together again. For the last ten years their careers had criss-crossed each other's like the weave of a hunting plaid. Costello herself had always been at this station or at Div-isional HQ less than a mile away since she graduated from Tulliallan Police College. McAlpine lived at the top of the hill. Anderson had done the rounds of the division like a good detective should as he climbed the career ladder. They all knew this area like they knew their own faces, but Mul-holland was a south-sider, and a posh one at that. He might just find himself a fish out of water. The thought pleased her.

The collie trotted off, a pie crust in its teeth as a prize. Costello began to pace back and forth, counting to ten before each turn. She knew this city and the people in it better than she had known her own mother, and it gave her an edge over the others. Mulholland was welcome to his designer suits and blind ambition. McAlpine had his handsome face, his aggressive genius, his electric charm and his beautiful wife; Anderson had a troubled marriage and two adorable kids ... Costello stopped pacing, halted by a thought. Over the years she'd been aware that Anderson had a great fondness for the Boss's wife. Not that there was anything in it – of course there wasn't – but Costello had always wondered. Then a sudden gust of rain stung her in the face, putting an end to her romantic notions.

She gestured impatiently through the door of the station again and breathed deeply as she looked up the street, the centre of the West End, the creative heart of the city, *her* city. She had an instinct for the place and its people, had always felt safe in its streets. The only move she had made in her life was from the south side of the Clyde to the north. Glasgow had warmth, and the humour of hard-working people. It was an *in-your-face* kind of city but one with a soft centre. But now her home town was keeping a secret from her, and she didn't like it.

Her foot came down in a puddle, and ice-cold water invaded her sock again. She had hoped she wouldn't still feel the same about McAlpine, but she did. She reminded herself that the way she felt about McAlpine was probably the way Anderson felt about Helena. The McAlpines were a difficult couple to dislike; she was rich and successful with an easy grace that put everybody at ease; he was ... well, he was himself, and that was enough.

The rain didn't look like giving up, so she pulled her hood right up over her head, tucking her hair underneath in an attempt to keep it dry. The sky in the east was slipping from dark to light grey, but it wasn't going to clear. A van pulling in to overtake on the inside went right through a puddle, and dark murky water splashed with uncanny accuracy on her cream chinos.

A black shining Beamer pulled out of Clarence Lane, stopping the traffic. Vik Mulholland leaned over to open the door for her. 'Don't get the upholstery wet, will you?'

'I'll hover in mid-air, will I?' she said. Mulholland looked very smug in his cashmere Crombie. He always looked immaculate, one of the many things about him that annoyed Costello. She fastened her seatbelt and nodded at his expensive overcoat. 'Sorry, did I interrupt you working as a body double for Johnny Depp? Or was it a photo shoot for Versace today?'

'Nice, isn't it?' he said, smiling imperturbably. 'So we have another one to add to our workload.' Mulholland indicated right. The traffic always stopped for the cop cars. 'He has a bit of a reputation, this McAlpine, but I didn't think much of him. Seems a bit soft.'

'You reckon? Underestimate him at your peril,' Costello muttered, pulling her coat beneath her. 'It should mean something to you that he's allowed you to stay on the team. What he says goes . . . or who he says goes.' She smiled at her own little witticism.

'Really? So why are we doing this routine stuff? Inappropriate use of resources. This is uniform.'

'It means he has a hunch about something.'

'About what?'

Costello sighed. 'The Boss isn't happy about the body being found by somebody looking through a letterbox at three this morning. Wants to know more.'

'Why would anybody be looking through a letterbox at three in the morning?' asked Mulholland, smoothing his eyebrow in the mirror.

'Exactly.' She leaned forward, sticking a Post-it note with the address on the dashboard and turning off some operatic warbling from his CD player. 'Take a left when you can.' She started scribbling in her notebook. 'I've phoned ahead; they're not going out till we speak to them.'

'But why are we doing it?'

'Because,' Costello said, with consummate patience, 'it's our job.'

'Can I give you a hand with that?'

Helena McAlpine was trying to manoeuvre a flat wooden crate out through the front door of the house in Kirklee Terrace. 'My God, that's a rarity – a policeman when you need one. How are you, Colin?' She smiled at Anderson. Her arms outstretched, leaning on *My Brother in Palestine*, she gave him a hug and a light kiss. Then she sideshifted a swathe of red hair from her face and smiled mischievously. 'How was Edinburgh?'

'Best forgotten. Do you need a hand with that?'

'It got delivered here last night, rather than to the gallery, and I have to be there to open up.'

Anderson twisted his wrist and looked at his watch. 'You're supposed to open at nine?'

'Yes.'

'You'd better get a move on, then.'

'My lord and master has been getting in my way since he came back. Can you lift that end?'

'This has a dent in it,' Anderson observed, lifting the crate and carrying it easily down the steps, reassured to feel needed in these days of equality.

'Yeah, your boss gave it a kicking when he eventually came home from the office last night. He said it was because

73

it was blocking the hall, but I think it was more of a comment on the state of modern art. It's only worth about twelve grand.'

Anderson automatically tightened his grip. 'I'll just drop it here,' he told her and lowered the painting delicately to the pavement. 'We need the keys . . . to open the boot . . .'

Helena looked at him, hands on hips. 'Keys . . . yes, they would help, wouldn't they? Can you give me a clue where that cantankerous old bastard I married might have put them?'

'He had on his leather jacket earlier this morning, the black one, over a dark blue suit, if that's any help.'

Anderson watched as Helena dashed up the stairs, her lion-red hair cascading down the back of a huge black jumper he was sure was one of Alan's.

She reappeared, keys in hand. 'Got them: leather jacket, just as you said. I told him you were here. He's on the phone, swearing at some poor minion. Does "effing profilers" mean anything to you?' She rolled her eyes and sighed as she opened the boot of the Five Series BMW.

Anderson smiled and hoisted the crate on to the bumper, watching Helena's fingers as they wrapped white cloth round the corners. Long strong fingers, a single wedding band and the light catching the single blue diamond above it.

'How are the kids?' she asked.

He winced as a splinter jammed in the skin of his thumb. 'Bloody skelf!' He lifted it to his mouth and sucked the blood. 'Expensive, cheeky. But not at the devious lying stage – yet.'

'Wait till Clare's out at night with unsuitable men. Sleepless nights for you then.'

'I'll be working. At the moment I'm psyching myself up

to sit and watch two hours of six-year-olds doing ballet without falling asleep.'

'Tough,' agreed Helena. 'You'll come to the exhibition, you and Brenda? I know it's not your thing but . . . Alan . . .'

'Free champers and raw fish. Wouldn't miss it for the world. I'm going to sell you some of wee Peter's paintings, people with big heads and no keeping within the lines.'

'You've been peeking at *My Brother in Palestine*,' she teased, tapping the crate. 'It's by a Canadian artist, very experimental.' She eased the boot shut and flicked her hair back, making the sun spark on the copper. That flirtatious smile again, looking at him as if he was the only person that mattered. 'God! It's cold!'

Alan McAlpine appeared at the door, and Helena's expression softened a little, as if she had warmed as she looked towards the house. Then McAlpine disappeared again, having forgotten something.

Helena turned back to Anderson. 'He's had about two hours' sleep, so you're working with Mr Grumpy today.'

'No change there, then. It'll get worse before it gets better.'

'Look after him, will you? Somebody has to.' Helena's head tilted to one side, her love for her husband silent on the upturn of her lips.

'Do you want us to follow you to the gallery and take this out for you? We'll have time before the briefing.'

'No, we won't,' said a voice behind them. 'Goodbye, dear.' McAlpine kissed his wife on the cheek. Anderson watched her incline her head towards him, eyes closed. More a promise than a kiss.

'You don't have time, apparently,' said Helena sweetly.

'Well, if you need a hand, let me know.'

'Ta! It's good to use other people's husbands. Mine's useless. Remind him he has a date with his wife tonight.'

'Got you.' Anderson tapped the side of his head as McAlpine got into the car and slammed the door.

'See you, Helena.'

'Bye, Colin. Thanks.'

Anderson pulled into the street, and in the driving mirror watched the wind blow fire into her hair as she waved.

Anderson walked into the chaos of the murder room, keeping four paces behind the Boss. By the time the clock had wound itself round to ten, thirty-three officers were busy chatting, reliving old glories and mistakes. They sat, they stood, they leaned against monitor screens and filing cabinets, they drummed fingers along the sides of polystyrene cups, they tapped pens off the top of clipboards, they paced the floor like condemned men.

Coffee cup in hand, Anderson picked his way through them to the back, aware that he was regarded as McAlpine's golden boy, conscious of not wanting to step on any toes, physically or metaphorically. He caught their whispers as he passed . . . *maybe we'll get something moving now – should have been on the case from the start.* It was natural; they wanted a second chance and new lines of investigation, something a fresh eye, a younger eye, could bring to the case.

McAlpine walked to the front. Everyone turned to look, conversations halted in mid sentence. The DCI was the smallest man in the room, but one flash of his almond-shaped eyes across the squad and the ruffle of noise was silenced. People shifted in their seats to get a better view. There was an air of expectation.

Vik Mulholland handed McAlpine a piece of paper and went to the back, looking around for a spare seat. Finding none, he wiped a desktop beside Anderson with the palm of his hand, tugged at the knees of his Versace trousers, then sat down.

McAlpine read the note, twice, his eyes narrowing before he looked up and settled on Mulholland. 'What the fuck does that mean – *System's gone down?*'

'If it's too busy, it collapses. It's done it four times so far.'

McAlpine dropped his forehead into his hands. The squad waited for a vitriolic eruption. It never came.

'Sir?' Costello spoke quietly, raising a tentative hand.

He opened his eyes and looked at her, tired already. 'Yes?'

'Wyngate, sir, he has a degree in IT. If it's true that upstairs aren't going to shell out for an expert, maybe we should use what we have. He's not much use at anything else, sir,' she added, with an affectionate grin at Wyngate.

McAlpine had to nip a smile, searching for the name. 'Wyngate? Gordon, isn't it?'

'Yes, sir.' PC Wyngate pulled on his over-large ears, more nervous than he looked.

'You recovered from last night?'

'Yes, sir.'

'Fancy the job?'

'Yes, sir.'

'Get to it. I'm not having that heap of shite jeopardizing the investigation.' McAlpine turned at a sudden draught and asked for the window to be closed. Ostentatiously, from the back of the room, Mulholland started fanning with an empty file. 'What do you need?' McAlpine asked Wyngate.

'More phone lines. The system's slowing down.' Wyngate spoke directly to McAlpine, keeping his voice low and respectful. 'We'll be in trouble if it crashes completely.'

McAlpine turned to look at the volume of paper, his face impassive. 'We have no budget for it. Do the best you can.'

'Well, maybe you could ask them not to pour coffee over the keyboards,' DC Irvine interjected.

'It's all our coffee's good for,' muttered Anderson, passing the paper cup under his nose, trying to identify the contents.

Wyngate turned to walk away, twisting around DS Littlewood, who was blocking his path between two desks. As he went past, Littlewood pulled on his own ears, like a schoolboy impersonating Dumbo. The smatter of laughter died at the DCI's expression.

'For those that don't know, I get called many things but my actual name is Detective Chief Inspector Alan McAlpine, and I'm in charge. DCI Duncan is doing well; he thanks you for your kind thoughts and the presents. He can't think of a use for the blow-up woman yet, but give him time.' A ripple of applause went round the room.

Anderson watched his boss carefully, hardly listening to what he said. He saw tension in the corner of McAlpine's lip, a nervousness in the fingers as they rippled his hair, the same edginess he had noticed that morning. Not quite the same old confident guv he knew.

McAlpine said, 'Stepping into another's shoes is never easy, but we just get on with it. Reviewing a case always implies criticism. But let's think of it as a chance to explore areas previously unexplored.'

'You think DCI Duncan was wrong?' asked Littlewood, chin up, arms folded, the challenge in his posture unmistakable.

Costello and Anderson exchanged glances: if he carried on like that, DS John Littlewood would be issuing parking tickets in Blythswood Square before nightfall.

'I'm the Senior Investigating Officer now,' McAlpine emphasized calmly. 'And I don't think Duncan was wrong. End of story. As you know, our friend struck again last night. The press had already christened him the Crucifixion Killer after Traill. Nice. We could do without it, but it happened.' He got up, perching on the side of his desk. 'We'll give you the latest on Fulton, and by the end of today I want the name of the guy who found his way into her flat. She was an ultra-careful woman, but she wasn't surprised when her doorbell went. So who was he?' He tapped the desk with his fingertip. 'Somebody offered Lynzi Traill a run home, and she took it. Two sensible women. Two dead women. Forensics are drawing a blank, so we need to review the circumstantial.' McAlpine rubbed his chin. 'By five this evening I want both their lives, inside out, upside down. Something will – *must* – connect one with the other.' He turned to Costello. 'So what was the script at three this morning? Why was somebody looking through Elizabeth Jane Fulton's letterbox?'

'To see if her cat was there.' Costello tucked her hair behind her ears.

'*Cat?*' asked Littlewood.

'Little black guy with a white chest?' McAlpine nodded to himself. 'Go on.'

'Kirsty Dougall looked through the letterbox of Elizabeth Jane's flat at three o'clock this morning to see if Mowgli the cat was there,' said Costello slowly, as if speaking to a simple child. 'The cat had been causing aggro. Well, Mowgli was fine. Kirsty told the officers at the scene that it was Elizabeth Jane who was causing the aggro, trapping the cat in her flat and then complaining.'

'She had catnip treats in her cupboard,' said McAlpine. 'Was she causing trouble deliberately?'

'It would seem so. The neighbours said a similar thing. And I expect we'll hear more of the same when we interview them properly. I've already rung her employers at the bank, and it seems she could be awkward at work too. She was the type who'd clype on her colleague for using the office printer to print a personal letter, for being five minutes late back from lunch –'

'For farting without permission. I know the type,' said Littlewood. He shot a look at Costello, who fired it back again.

'She was described as a narrow-minded perfectionist by someone who said they liked her and as a petty-minded bitch by someone I'd say didn't. Not a popular girl. So,' Costello went on, 'when Kirsty looked through the letterbox, she saw Elizabeth Jane's hand on the floor, and she dialled 999. Lights out, please!'

On cue, darkness fell, and the glare from a single spotlight dropped from the ceiling, casting harsh shadows on the wall. Costello pinned up pictures as she spoke. The photographs showed a young woman, her face running to fat already, her smile framed for eternity in brown curls and pearls. She had made an effort to look nice.

Costello spoke. 'Elizabeth Jane – she didn't like being called Liz – aged twenty-six, single, bank teller for the Bank of Scotland, living up in Fortrose Street, no boyfriends we have discovered, kept herself to herself, non-smoker, non-drinker, went to church a lot, sang in the choir. Elizabeth Jane's cousin Paula is getting married soon, and apparently she asked the girl next to her in the choir to go to the wedding meal with her, so maybe she had no really close female friends either. Her idea of a great night out was an evening class in accounting, which raises the question: who was it at the door?' Costello's hand, ghostly in the projected light, smoothed down another photograph. There was a ripple of movement as the team shifted to view the obscene image: Elizabeth Jane lying, arms out, legs crossed, dressed in her work uniform, her abdomen ripped open like a ripe fruit. 'Her mobile was a new one, and the phone records are being checked. We're waiting for a call back.'

'But all this . . . all *that*' – Anderson pointed at the photograph of the room – 'suggests preparation, a method, organization. He turned up at that flat knowing exactly what he was going to do. He let her make him a cup of coffee, but he didn't touch it. He didn't touch anything.'

'There's no doubt he knows what he's doing,' said Costello, as she checked her notes. 'O'Hare has done the prelim, puts death at around eight last night. We know she was alive at quarter to six, because she was helping with cashing up at the bank. But there was no answer when her mother phoned her at her flat just before nine. Same MO as Lynzi Traill: chloroformed, from behind, no struggle.'

'I've heard that chloroform doesn't knock you out instantly,' said Anderson. 'So why no struggle? No disruption?'

'He's bigger? He can hold them until it takes effect?' suggested Costello. 'They were both – what? – under ten stone? Probably lighter than he is . . . but they were short, which means he gains a totally controllable victim.' She folded her arms, her point made. 'Who was checking up on the chloroform?'

'Me,' said Mulholland. 'I've rechecked all the sources listed locally; no reported loss or theft. I've alerted HOLMES for a nation-wide check, but all registered sources have come up with a big zero.'

'Exactly what DCI Duncan found,' muttered McAlpine. 'Damn!'

The soft Hebridean accent of DC Donald Burns came through the darkness. 'That one single cut, right up the front, no messing around – there's strength in that.' The quiet lilting voice was authoritative. 'The leather belt has been nicked by the blade, and that takes a strong knife, moving with control and strength. And a bloody sharp blade.'

'And he knows how to use it, *where* to use it,' said Anderson. 'Do we have a field for that in the system?'

'I don't know. I'll see what I can do,' Wyngate said, scribbling it down.

'Get it in: people who are good with knives. Butchers?' said McAlpine.

'Surgeons?'

'Farmers? Slaughtermen? Chefs, I suppose,' offered Costello.

McAlpine's voice cut through the dark. 'I want that flat vacuumed and the dust gone through. We need some physical evidence of whoever she let in. If there's so much as a speck of dandruff, I want it. And try to think like Elizabeth Jane. Think precise, think pernickety, and then think who you would open your door to. Knives, small-minded women, sensible knickers . . . you get my drift.' McAlpine went to stand up, then paused. 'Tell us about Traill now.'

Costello looked round. 'Me?'

McAlpine nodded. 'Just to make sure Anderson, Mulholland and I are up to speed.'

'Lynzi Traill, as I understand her . . .' Costello idled, then closed her eyes as she clarified her thoughts. 'Aged thirty-four, housewife, body found in Victoria Gardens.' She indicated the location on the map with the point of a pencil. 'The gardens are kept locked. Ian Livingstone's house – he's the boyfriend – is here, in Victoria Crescent, overlooking the gardens. The fence is too high to punt the body over without leaving traces, and she was hidden in the bushes, so her killer must have had a key. And all known keys were accounted for?' Her voice faded on the query.

'Yes,' said Littlewood wearily. 'You know we spent days on that.'

'Yes, I do know.' Costello paused, recalling. 'Anyway, the distance between the two sites isn't much. Wyngate timed it as seven minutes' walk. Lynzi was last seen at eleven o'clock on Saturday, the 16th. Here she is, caught on a CCTV camera at Glasgow Central after a visit to the theatre with her friends.' The spotlight moved to a grainy coloured image of a crowd of people, Lynzi Traill just visible among them, her head turned animatedly to one side. Whoever she was talking to was obscured by a much taller man. 'They told us they were all going to travel back to Paisley Gilmour Street together. They said somebody – they assumed it was a man, but the station was busy, and they didn't see who it was – called to Lynzi, and Lynzi disappeared off to talk to him, while they waited. A minute or two later she waved across to her friends to indicate that they should go on without her; they assumed she was getting a lift.' Costello pointed at the peppered image. 'This friend –'

'Annette Rafferty?' asked Mulholland, flicking through a sheaf of papers.

'That's right. Annette says she knew that Lynzi was having an affair – the only other person who did know, by all accounts – so she thought Lynzi had bumped into the boyfriend and decided to stay, and persuaded the others it was OK. But it wasn't OK. A local resident walking her dog found Lynzi's body in the early hours of Sunday, the 17th, chloroformed, ripped from pubis to sternum.' Costello asked to have the spotlight moved to a picture of Traill's wound. In black and white, the carnage was highlighted by the brightness of the flash. 'Same injuries, same pattern as Elizabeth Jane Fulton, but not so severe. Lynzi was posed, as Elizabeth Jane was. Exactly. O'Hare says she was alive when her killer left her. He . . . just left her to die in the rhodies.'

Someone muttered, 'Where she gave the old dear and her Westie the fright of their wee lives.'

Costello continued, 'Lynzi would probably have had you believe she was happily married. Her parents and her sister, all her friends except for Annette, believed – or wanted to believe – that she and hubby were still together, but that she'd just moved out for a rest, because she was finding it so difficult to cope. She was living in a flat in Paisley.' Costello tucked her hair behind her ears, a sure sign she was anxious about something. 'Stuart Traill apparently went along with this, thinking she was having an early mid-life crisis. Their little boy, Barry, was told his mum was looking after a sick friend. Lynzi was there when the wee lad went to school in the morning; she was there when he came home. But in between times, despite telling people she was working at the charity shop and looking after a sick friend, she was having an affair. And she was totally oblivious to the fact that the neighbours were amusing themselves with her comings and goings at all hours of the day and night.'

A question was fired at her from the darkness: 'So what were the mechanics of that?'

'She kept her mobile phone switched off; she did a voluntary job with no pay and no regular hours; Annette may have fibbed for her . . . It's not that difficult. Lynzi's parents, sister, brother, the hubby's family, they all swear they had no idea what was going on. But I can't believe that . . .' Costello ran out of steam.

'So where is the boyfriend in all this?' asked McAlpine, pointing at the map.

'As I said, Ian Livingstone lives here, in Victoria Crescent.

But both he and Mr Traill have been turned inside out. Clean.'

'Are we satisfied with that?' asked McAlpine.

'We've checked them again and again,' Costello insisted. 'Triple-checked. Neither was alone for a minute between the time Lynzi was recorded at Glasgow Central Station and the time her body was found.'

'And Livingstone was really upset, absolutely devastated,' said Burns.

'Guilty,' muttered Littlewood.

'Nobody could have faked that. He asked for the minister to come from next door.' Burns shook his head. 'They even said a prayer together.'

'Definitely guilty, then.'

'He's been nothing but cooperative,' Irvine volunteered. 'And he seems a nice guy. Well, that's my opinion . . . for what it's worth.'

'So what about the husband?' asked Littlewood.

'At work. He worked nights, and his shift covered both ends of the time scale.'

'Bloody convenient. Check it again,' McAlpine persisted. Costello sighed inwardly.

'The son? Wee Barry?' Littlewood again.

'Home alone. And not for the first time.' Costello's tone of voice indicated exactly what she thought of that.

'There's that element of trust again, though, isn't there?' said Anderson. 'Elizabeth Jane let someone into her flat, someone she knew and trusted. And Lynzi left Glasgow Central, at night, again with somebody she knew and trusted, but not the husband, not the boyfriend.'

McAlpine stood up, his hand on Costello's shoulder. 'So we keep digging. This second killing means the location is important.' He paused and looked round the room again.

'Lynzi lived in Paisley, but she spent a lot of time here in the West End. The boyfriend lived here. She worked in a charity shop in Byres Road, she shopped here. But the charity shop and the boyfriend are her only real connections with this area. So there must be some connection between them and Elizabeth Jane. There has to be. So we get working on Lynzi Traill's connections in the West End. Who's in the shop, for instance? Try to crack those alibis. And get working on Elizabeth Jane's new-found freedom. Her flat was a recent refurb; she'd been in it for only a few months, first time she'd been away from her parents. What was she getting up to? The MO's being circulated nationwide, and so far we have nothing that comes close. So this is on our doorstep and nowhere else. Costello, you're coming with me for the tea-and-sympathy bit. The rest of you, get on with it.'

There was a murmur of assent, as the migration for the coffee machine started. It was going to be a long day.

It took a good two or three minutes' discussion before Sean McTiernan got what he wanted, and by then the mid-morning queue of Saturday shoppers behind him was stretching out to the street. The menu said 'Coffee Latte Light with Wings.' He didn't know what that meant.

It turned out to be bog-standard white coffee with a prong stuck in it that pulled the dark brown of the coffee through the white of the milk to form a pattern. It was, he presumed, supposed to be the Ashton Café logo. Or was there a 'right way up' to drink it?

He proffered a pound coin. The bored waitress with the plaits didn't look up. Her outstretched hand hovered in mid-air as the other pulled the receipt from the chattering till. A foreigner in his own city for a moment, he looked again at the price list and gave her another pound coin. The waitress flicked it over before depositing it in the till and scooping out some change with long red nails. She dumped the coins on his tray and walked away.

The only empty tables were at the back of the café. Sean chose a seat in the corner, his back against the wall and his eye on the door by force of habit. He moved the coffee cup back and forth under his nose, enjoying the aroma, trying to see the Betty Boop watch of the peroxide blonde sitting in the booth opposite. He couldn't make out the time. It must be nearly half eleven, and Nan believed there was an eleventh commandment . . . thou shalt not be tardy. He was about to lean over and ask Peroxide the time when a man slid into the other seat at her table. Sean glanced at the man's watch, its larger face easier to read backwards and upside down. Five to. He caught sight of white cuffs and a dog collar as a piece of paper passed from him to her. Peroxide looked at it, puzzled. The dog collar seemed to explain something, and she nodded. Then there was an abrupt goodbye, and he was away. The blonde crumpled up the paper and threw it dismissively across the table. For a minute she was lost in her own world, then she caught Sean looking and smiled alluringly, curving her wide red lips over a cup of espresso. He caught the scent of her musky perfume, cheap, too strong.

He didn't smile back.

A week to go. Seven days of being out more often than being in, a phased return to the community.

A week to go . . . and he would be with her again. Seven days of waiting. But he had waited four years. Seven days made no difference. He dipped his spoon into the coffee, drawing the black liquid at the bottom through the white foam, making patterns of his own. The last time he had seen her, she had been stomping down the road in a bomber jacket and baggy jeans, her blonde hair dyed black, cut short and spiky, looking like any Scottish teenage boy. He would never have recognized her, so what chance would anybody else have had? He remembered standing at the window of the dark green bedroom in the flat in Petrie Street, with the ceiling he never got round to painting, the bed still warm from their bodies, watching her go to the bus stop, carrying a bin bag full of her life, kicking it as she went. He had felt tears prickle at his eyes then.

He felt them again now.

He sipped at his coffee. It smelled better than it tasted. It tasted like cow piss.

Two weeks ago he had been released into the care of Martin the social worker, an anaemic-looking Geordie who walked down Sauchiehall Street dressed for the north face of the Eiger. Martin had never cautioned Sean to assess the psychological parameters of his crime, never asked him why he had kicked Malkie Steele to death with such prejudice he had burst his liver. Martin had simply asked if he preferred McEwan's or Tennent's, and had given him his own set of keys. All he had to do was take time to adjust.

In prison Sean had evolved an acute sense of when he was being observed; he knew Miss Peroxide with the red lips was looking at him, waiting for him to meet her eyes again. It was the same game he played. He knew he was good-looking, and inside or out it was something to trade.

He looked round the café, letting his eyes pass over the blonde without stopping. She was looking at him through the peroxide wire that covered her eyes. Her features were too heavy to be beautiful, but she was carefully made up, with an oriental tilt to her eyes, a wide nose, her lips beautifully painted pillarbox red.

Sean let a smile soften his lips. Soon he would be home;

he would go running every morning, running every night, along the beach from the white cottage under the shadow of the castle, along a beach that went on and on and on . . . to a beautiful blonde witch, waiting with her familiar.

Miss Peroxide smiled across at him. He smiled back, then looked away, noting the miniskirt, the chunky legs in green ankle boots.

She was far from perfection.

But after three and a half years she didn't have to bother to look decent. The fact that she was a female with a pulse was enough for him. She would have a comfy bed, clean sheets, a duvet, nice toilet paper.

He looked at her face again, giving her his James Dean smoulder, then let his eyes linger a little longer on her thighs.

'Aye!' A thin old woman dumped a plastic shopping bag on the table in front of him, sending a tidal wave of expensive coffee over the rim of his cup, obliterating the Ashton Café logo.

'Hello, Nan, how are you doing?' He stood up, planting a kiss on her cold bristled cheek, embarrassed to feel a tear in his eye.

Here was his Nan, miserable as usual, with her thrawn smile. The turquoise butterfly glasses had been changed for small gold rims, but the mole was hairier than ever, standing to attention on her top lip. She pulled her grey crocheted hat further down over her lank straight hair, then, just in case anybody thought she was enjoying herself, she began cursing under her breath about his choice of meeting place, the mole hairs twitching as she muttered.

Miss Peroxide, still watching, still interested, shot him a look of amused sympathy. The pigtailed waitress came over with a cup of tea.

'I told them you'd get it,' Nan said.

89

Sean paid, pushing the waitress's hand away, telling her to keep the change.

Miss Peroxide twisted her head slightly, the three gold chains round her neck narrowing down her cleavage, and crossed one chunky leg over the other. There was a lot of flesh between the top of her ankle boots and the bottom of her skirt. She raised her cup to her lips, smiled at him again and turned away.

Nan blew her nose on a napkin, giving her nostrils a good clear out. That brought back memories to him, memories of the kids' home, of paper hankies like steel wool and a hard slap every time he used his sleeve.

'You've lost weight,' she said. 'I've made you soup.'

'Oh, ta, what is it?' Images of home-made Scotch broth boiling away on his Baby Belling.

'Good for you, that's what it is. Better than that.' She pointed at Miss Peroxide. Nan never missed a trick.

'She's nothing,' he said quietly. 'How are you?'

'Who listens to me if I complain? Twenty minutes to wait for a train, I'm telling you, ma boy –'

'What else's in the bag?' He peered in the top.

'Soup, tablet, chocolate crispies. Where are you staying?'

'Just up the road.' He kept it vague.

'Good, good,' she said. She wasn't daft. 'Is it near Cleopatra's Disco?' She said it as though she had been rehearsing it.

'Everywhere in Partickhill is near Clatty Pat's.'

'You should go there.'

'Should I?'

'Oh, yes. Sunday night's good in there. Older folk like you.' She gave him a hard look, telling him something.

His heart began to thump against his chest. He had been prepared to wait; she wasn't.

'You look awfy peaky, you should get out more.' Only Nan could say that to someone who had been out of jail for a matter of hours.

'How are things?' he said, keeping his voice low and steady. It had been four long years since he had hatched the plan, and a faint flicker of doubt passed through his mind for the first time.

Nan nodded. 'All is fine.' Uneducated she might have been, but she was shrewd, very shrewd. 'And business is very well, very smooth,' she said, opening her palm on to the tabletop and looking down. 'Paintings are selling well. The staircase is just as you left it. Do you want to see the house?'

He cast his eyes left and right before nodding.

'I've photographs.'

'Not a painting, then?'

'Not too old for a slap, son.' She handed over a Kodak envelope.

He opened it, fanning out the fresh prints. A photograph of a dog, a huge silver husky, its intelligent blue eyes black-rimmed in a white mask.

'Gelert,' he said.

'By name and nature.'

'The brave and faithful hound. That was always my favourite story, you know. You used to tell it to us –'

'In the cleaning cupboard, aye.' Nan gave him a rare smile. 'He's a big dog now.' She tucked a roll of used twenty-pound notes into his fist with covert skill. 'Next one shows how far we've got with the veranda.'

A whitewashed cottage on a beach, the seaweed scar of the high-tide line black against the sand, big windows, a half-built wooden veranda bleached blond by strong west winds and weak Scottish sun.

The house looked exactly the same; so did the beach and the castle. Only the husky lying on the front step had grown.

He stared at the picture for a long time, aware that Nan was waving her fingers at him, wanting the photographs back. Two minutes and a quick trip to the toilet later, the money had been folded into his shoe.

'I'll see you around.'

'I'm sure you will.' Suddenly he wanted her to stay. 'Pass on my . . . regards.'

'Get that soup in you.' She ruffled his hair with her hand; she had been doing that since he was four years old, and she used to check him for lice. And then she was away, the photographs leaving with her.

He lifted his cup, looking at the milk separate on the top of the coffee. He leaned back, relaxing. It was all so close. He was happy. Miss Peroxide said something. Maybe if he closed his eyes . . .

'Excuse me,' Miss Peroxide repeated, 'do you have the time?'

Prettier with her mouth shut. He looked across to her table. Her Betty Boop watch was gone.

Fair enough. He thought about his nice new bedsit, with its hot running water and crisp white sheets. He'd done enough time at Her Majesty's pleasure. He wanted some of his own now.

McAlpine hated doing this. *I'm sorry, it's about your daughter.* 'Ready?' he asked.

Costello had been checking out the street. Affluent, middle class. She had no problem placing Elizabeth Jane here. 'Ready,' she agreed.

The door was opened by a squat gargoyle of a woman, blazing with anger, gold chains on her wrists rattling as she waved them away. 'Enough, I've told you. Enough already!' The closing door halted as she caught sight of two warrant cards. 'Oh, I *am* sorry,' she said, her eyes darting from one to the other. 'We've had reporters, knocking at the door, standing in the drive. No respect, some people.'

'It's a very difficult time,' Costello agreed, smiling her charming smile.

The gargoyle nodded, smiling too now. Not the mother, then. 'Oh, it's been a terrible day,' she said with thinly disguised relish. 'A terrible day. I mean – you never think, do you? Not someone you know, not in their own home. Do come in.'

They followed her into a large hall, terracotta-tiled floor, a winding staircase overhead. Elizabeth Jane's parents were not short of a bob or two.

'Betty and Jim are in there. The minister is with them.' She looked at her watch, a copper-brown fingernail tapping the face as if she was timing the visit. 'He hasn't been in very long.' She seemed reluctant to interrupt them.

'And you are?' asked Costello, sensing McAlpine's impatience.

'Isabel Cohen. I live next door. Twenty years I've known that girl, twenty years ... since she was knee-high to a grasshopper.'

'It must be very difficult for you, Isabel. Do you mind if we ...' Costello opened the door without waiting for an answer and then stood to one side, letting Mrs Cohen go through first. A smile passed between the two women. Clearly there was plenty Mrs Cohen could say, but she was too well brought up to say it.

'Betty?' she inquired quietly round the door. 'Some more police, detectives. They want a word.'

McAlpine and Costello walked into a room that was as

sterile as an operating theatre, three brilliant white walls, the fireplace wall a deep cobalt blue. Only one picture broke the colour, a professional portrait of Elizabeth Jane above the fireplace. On the mantelpiece below it an array of photographs of her throughout her life was lined up with regimental precision, a shrine to an only child. In the middle sat a gold anniversary clock, its weights spinning this way and that. Incongruously, behind it, McAlpine noticed, someone had propped up an invitation to a wedding. He was sure it was the same one that Elizabeth Jane had had; it bore the same stylized Mackintosh rose. He inclined his head to read covertly inside: *Mr and Mrs Vincent Fulton . . .*

Costello eased past him, further into the room. Three people were sitting at the dining table in the conservatory. The older man, white as a sheet, was stroking the tablecloth with the palm of his hand, comforting himself. The woman looked as though she had no tears left. The younger man – small, slender, early thirties – was the minister, she presumed. His fawn hair was neatly cut, a few stray strands curling on the collar of his Guernsey. As if aware of her scrutiny, he turned, his eyes meeting hers; there was a brief flicker of acknowledgement. The table showed evidence of recent cups of tea. Somebody had nibbled the crust from a slice of toast and left the rest.

Mrs Cohen stopped behind Betty Fulton's chair, placing her hands on the thin shoulders, bending to whisper in her ear. Betty placed her hands over Isabel's and gave them a gentle squeeze. Words of comfort that Costello could not hear passed between them. The minister got up, dusting crumbs from his jumper with slight feminine hands, and walked into the living room, into Costello's line of vision. She could see the dog collar now, a fine line piping the neck

94

of his Guernsey. A good-looking man, thin-faced, older than she had first thought, closer to forty than thirty, his skin finely lined, faint shadows under the eyes. Those eyes did not belong to one who had had an easy life. He raised his head, aware of her scrutiny, and looked at her with eyes as blue as the wallpaper behind him.

'If we hadn't let her move out . . .' Jim Fulton came towards the fire, shaking his head.

'All ifs and buts. She wanted her freedom.' Costello caught the lilt of a Highland accent as the minister turned to Elizabeth Jane's father. 'I'll leave you now. Let me know when you're ready to make arrangements, any time . . . I'll be in touch with Reverend Shand, to pass on the sad news. I know he would want to know as soon as possible.'

'And you will tell Tom?' Jim Fulton asked. 'It's difficult for me – my generation – that kind of thing.'

'No problem at all. I'll see to it. Don't you go concerning yourself with that. You've got enough on your plate now.' A double handshake, four hands clasped together.

Costello gave them both her concerned professional smile and committed 'Tom' to memory.

The minister drew his eyes briefly over her and looked away. 'They are in need of comfort,' he said, speaking directly to McAlpine. Costello saw the DCI narrow his eyes slightly, as if trying to place some vague recognition. 'I'm George Leask.'

'DCI McAlpine. And my colleague is DS Costello.'

The minister shook McAlpine's hand, then shook hers, but when he spoke it was directly to McAlpine. 'You'll be here for Elizabeth Jane. I shall leave you to continue with your sad business.' He turned and again clasped Mr Fulton's rheumatic hand with both of his. 'I'm so sorry, Jim; there are so many victims in this. I'll be back home this afternoon if you need me. You have my number, so if you need anything, any time, please don't hesitate to call me.'

The older man nodded numbly.

'I've written it down,' said Mrs Cohen self-importantly. 'Don't worry.'

'Good bye, God bless.'

'And where can *we* find you, if necessary?' Costello chipped in sweetly, stopping the minister as he made to leave.

He smiled directly at her, blue eyes heavy with pain. His red lips moved as if to say something, but he checked himself and sighed. 'Beaumont Street Church. Or at the Phoenix Refuge. A terrible business, yet again.'

'Again?' she asked.

Leask started talking, the rhythm of his Highland brogue making it sound like sweet poetry. 'You'll be familiar with Ian Livingstone? He is my next-door neighbour, a good friend. If you'll excuse me, I think I need to speak to him, tell him it looks as if Lynzi's killer has struck again, before he hears of it from . . .' He paused, the hint of something pejorative about the police on his lips. 'Before he hears of it from some other source.'

'Of course,' Costello said, her smile still in place as she stepped aside to allow him to pass.

'Wait a second,' McAlpine cut in. 'Did you know her – Lynzi Traill?'

'No, I never met her. It's Ian I know.'

'Have you spoken to the police about him?'

The minister frowned. 'No. I doubt there'd be anything I could tell them.'

'There might be –'

Costello interrupted McAlpine with a discreet cough and

an imperceptible shake of her head in the direction of the stunned and grieving Fultons.

Leask bowed slightly at Costello, then hesitantly shook McAlpine's hand again and left.

Costello backed up to the fire and stood warming her legs, watching the minister go down the chipped driveway and get into a red Fiat Punto. He had the same arrogant walk as the DCI. Both were handsome men, intelligent men. She stopped thinking about McAlpine just in time to get the plate number and commit it to memory as the car turned out of the driveway and vanished from sight.

McAlpine turned to the Fultons. 'So,' he said. 'I know this is a difficult time, but I need to ask a few questions for now, and then we'll leave you alone.'

The Fultons nodded in unison, and Betty lifted her cup and saucer to Mrs Cohen's proffered hand. Costello opened the kitchen door for Mrs Cohen and followed her in, and the door closed on McAlpine's voice.

'How are they coping?' Costello asked conversationally.

'It hasn't hit them yet.' Mrs Cohen busied herself, rinsing the teacups and dusting crumbs from the plates into the flip-top bin. She obviously felt at home in this kitchen. 'Like I said, you never expect this, on your own doorstep, do you? Not somebody you know.'

'And did you know Elizabeth?' asked Costello, pulling a plate from the rack and drying it very slowly. 'Know her well, I mean?'

'I certainly knew her well enough not to call her Elizabeth. She was always Elizabeth Jane.' Mrs Cohen added in a whisper, 'She was a bit funny that way. She was that type. Even from a wee girl, she was that type.'

'What type, Mrs Cohen?' Costello softened the intrusive question. 'You've known her a long time, then?'

'Oh, yes, she and my Sophie are much of an age; they used to play together. Elizabeth Jane was a lovely girl, of course, but . . . stubborn. Very stubborn.' She dried her hands on a towel, twiddling the cloth round her wedding ring. 'She was to be a bridesmaid, you know. I wonder what will happen now.'

'The wedding – ?'

'Yes, Paula. She'll want to go ahead with it, I don't doubt. She's as stubborn as Elizabeth Jane – cousins, you see. Like peas out a pod. And that'll upset Jim and Betty, I can see it coming.' Isabel Cohen nodded as though she was rather looking forward to the prospect.

'When's the wedding? I saw the invite on the mantel-piece –'

'Three weeks. Oh, they've all been up to high doh about it. There was a fair bit of friction between the girls . . .' Then she added in a whisper, 'But that's families for you. You're better putting a ladder at the window and letting them elope.'

'You seem very close to the family, Mrs Cohen?'

She sniffed, folding the towel back on itself. 'The same dressmaker who did Sophie's dress is doing Paula's. No problem with the bride's dress, but Elizabeth Jane's dress was causing trouble. Oh, it was going to be such a happy occasion . . .'

Costello didn't think it sounded as if it was going to be happy at all. 'And where will I find Paula?' she asked, her hand on the door as if to open it, but letting it linger until Mrs Cohen answered.

Brown's Gym was busy. The deep thud of an aerobics class somewhere in the building echoed over the pool, and the noise of Lycra-clad bodies in constant motion was everywhere, with bottles of water clutched in sweaty little hands.

It reminded Costello of Fritz Lang's *Metropolis*. It was her idea of hell.

'Judging from what DCI McAlpine got from the parents, Elizabeth Jane was a cross between Maria von Trapp and Mother Teresa. The next-door neighbour had a slightly different take on her, though.'

'She didn't sound like a walk in the park at the briefing,' Irvine agreed.

'The neighbour said the cousins were like peas in a pod, so she should be easy to spot,' Costello said, her eyes scanning the line of bobbing heads on the running machines.

It was easy to find Paula Fulton. She did indeed bear a close resemblance to her cousin, with the same plain face, the same brown curls, the incipient double chin. But, judging from the sweat on her face and neck, she worked much harder at keeping the weight off. She didn't look surprised when Costello and Irvine showed her their cards.

'Hang on a mo,' she said, getting off the running machine. She bent down and pulled a sweatshirt over her head.

'Can we talk somewhere, quietly?' Costello asked.

Paula didn't have to ask the gym attendant. News had got round. The attendant pointed them in the direction of the first-aid room. Costello gestured that the other two should have a seat.

Irvine seemed lost for words, and Costello was about to prompt her when Paula suddenly started chattering. 'I bet you think I'm terrible, being here.'

'Not at all,' said Costello.

'Couldn't stand it at home. Had to get out. They've already started talking about cancelling the wedding, and I'm not having it.' She shook her head. 'I'll not.'

'I quite agree with you,' said Costello. 'Don't you, Gail?'

'Oh, yes,' said Irvine, finding her tongue. 'Elizabeth Jane was going to be your bridesmaid?'

'Yeah.' Paula grimaced. 'I didn't want her, but we're cousins, and Dad insisted. Families – you know how it is.'

The conversation stalled, and Irvine lost her train of thought.

'Paula,' said Costello, taking over. 'We need to know a bit about the victim, about Elizabeth Jane. It can be really difficult for the police when all you get is sweetness and light about the deceased. What was she like, really?'

'Impossible,' said Paula with no hesitation whatever. 'Oh, I don't mean to speak ill of the dead, but she always had to be the centre of attention. Only she did it in a quiet kind of way. She was always allergic to stuff, and couldn't do this and couldn't do that. I mean, I'd invite her round and I'd take the trouble to cook something nice, and she'd say, "I don't want to make a fuss, but I couldn't possibly eat that." You know the type.'

'I do indeed,' said Costello. *So Elizabeth Jane was the passive-aggressive type, was she?*

'I had my colour scheme for the wedding all planned,' Paula went on, clearly getting rid of a certain amount of aggression of her own. That suited Costello just fine. 'I wanted scarlet for her dress, because I was going to have all red flowers, and it would suit our colouring. Then, at the final fitting, she says she doesn't think the red suits her and she wants turquoise instead. I said no, and she burst into tears, and, before I know it, it's "Oh, poor Elizabeth Jane!"' She spanned her hands in frustration. 'Like, the wedding's three weeks away, and I need to reorder the flowers. I mean – *turquoise*! The dressmaker threw a hissy fit and charged us double to do another dress so quickly. Then, as if she hasn't caused us enough upset, Elizabeth Jane goes and has her hair cut so the headdress won't fit. And puts blonde highlights in! Oh, she made a real freak of herself! Even her parents, who thought the sun shone out of her arse, were angry with her. I was ready for strangling her.' Paula put her hands to her mouth. 'Oh, I didn't mean that! Anyway, she changed the colour of her hair back again. But she stuck to her guns about the dress.'

Costello kept her face expressionless as Paula unscrewed the top off a plastic water bottle and took a few swigs.

She wiped her mouth with the back of her hand. 'I'll tell you something,' she said. 'You'll probably think badly of me for saying it, but I'm glad she's not going to be my bridesmaid. And I'm not cancelling my wedding for anyone.'

Costello smiled. 'I don't think you should. The best advice I can give you is that it's your day, and those who love you will want it to be your day. Those who complain can go and organize their own weddings and leave you to yours. Life is too short . . . as your cousin found out, unfortunately.'

Paula smiled. 'Thanks.' She rubbed her face with her sleeve.

'Had she ever had a boyfriend? Elizabeth Jane?' asked Irvine.

Paula paused, the rubbing stopped.

'Come on, Paula,' Costello prompted. 'Anything might be a help.'

'Well, my fiancé is not a stupid man, he doesn't imagine things or make things up, but he said Elizabeth Jane was trying to cause trouble between us.'

'What kind of trouble?'

'Oh, she'd say things to him about me. Not really putting me down, but –'

'A put-down all the same?' Irvine said.

Paula nodded. 'And she seemed to be trying to flirt with

him all the time. Trouble was, she'd no idea how to do it. He said it was just embarrassing.'

'Did she ever mention somebody called Tom?'

'Not that I remember. And if she did have somebody, I would have been the first to hear about it. I would have had to rearrange the seating plan to make him guest of honour.'

'Thanks. That's all for now. You'd better go and have a shower before you get chilled.'

Paula thanked them and walked back into the gym, looking happier with her lot.

'Well, I'd say we had a potential murderer right there,' Irvine said.

'From the sound of what Paula says, potential murderers would have to form an orderly queue.'

'Three–nil is a bit of an insult,' said McAlpine, closing the sports page of the *Evening Times* and flinging the paper into the rear seat of Anderson's Astra, where it joined a litter of empty Ribena cartons and a green Tweenie. It was late on Saturday night, and his head was thumping. He had spent all day chasing the ghost of Elizabeth Jane Fulton – a woman with few enemies and even fewer friends – and had got absolutely nowhere. He put his hand on the car-door handle but made no move to get out. 'We'd better get a break tomorrow,' he said to nobody in particular.

'It's early days yet.' Anderson pulled on the handbrake and pointed at the Volvo in front. 'Helena got friends in? LLB 11, nice plate, worth more than the car.'

McAlpine looked at the number plate and the National Trust badge on the back bumper, vaguely recognizing the vehicle; he couldn't recall who drove it, but he knew he didn't like them. He just couldn't remember who it was.

He checked his watch. Then he began slowly and deliberately to slap his forehead with the palm of his hand. Saturday night, eleven thirty. 'She's having a dinner party. They'll be well into the liqueurs by now.'

'Shit,' said Anderson with feeling. 'Were you supposed to be there?'

'Our anniversary. I am – was – indeed supposed to be there. I was at the wedding, after all.'

'Shit,' said Anderson again. 'Was I supposed to remind you?'

'Yeah, it's your fault.'

'At least I remembered to phone my mother-in-law, least I got the kids covered . . .'

'I didn't phone.' Suddenly McAlpine sounded very tired. 'Didn't even remember to forget. She's been planning this for ages.'

'Helena'll understand. Brenda would go apeshit.'

'Yeah,' said McAlpine, more cheery. 'It could be worse. I could be married to your wife.'

'Cheers for that, Boss,' Anderson muttered sourly as the DCI walked away through the dark drizzle.

The dining-room door was open, and McAlpine was immediately assaulted by the smells of coffee and garlic, the voices of adult, clever debate. He could hear Terry Gilfillan making some tedious speech about the Scottish Parliament and the Arts Council, could hear Denise Gilfillan answering wittily in her advocate's voice. He felt like a kid spying on grown-up fun as he sneaked past the door, hoping to get in unseen, steal ten minutes in a hot shower and then slip under a duvet for some wonderful, uninterrupted sleep. Small talk had never been one of his fortes and certainly not after a day like this. He needed to de-stress, stop the chattering in his head and think. He needed to forget Elizabeth Jane and her immaculately sterile flat, forget Lynzi and her double life. One woman with no life, the other with two.

But the dead were not always silenced by sleep.

A burst of laughter filled the hall, a response to some witticism, as McAlpine slipped into the sitting room and closed the door. He kicked off his shoes, slipped his jacket off and dropped it on the floor. He lay full length on the sofa, half pulling the throw over him, listening to the easy hum of conversation drifting from the dining room, punctuated with laughter, against a background of Diana Krall crying a river over somebody. The music lulled him as images of Elizabeth Jane and Lynzi chased each other across his mind, his subconscious juggling random thoughts, searching for coincidence and serendipity. Suddenly he thought of the minister, George Leask. He knew that face from somewhere. But where?

McAlpine slipped into a dreamful sleep – *the dead woman lying with arms outstretched, her thin elegant wrists, the leather strap of her watch* . . . not Elizabeth Jane's, not Lynzi Traill's, but Anna's. As she accepted his kiss with her wide sunshine smile, enveloping him with the rapturous scent of bluebells, she woke, and he heard somebody say, 'Hello, honey.'

'Hello? Hello, sleepyhead,' Helena said. She kissed her husband on the forehead; he smelled of whisky, cigarettes and apple shampoo. More often than not she would find him unconscious on the sofa when he was on a big case; he ate nothing, drank more and slept less, living on adrenalin and fresh air.

'You ruin every suit by doing this,' she murmured, turning

up the thermostat on the radiator and turning down the dimmer switch. As the light faded, she paused, studying his face, almost childlike in sleep, the handsome profile she had painted a hundred times in her mind. She kissed her fingertips and pressed them to his lips. Just as she was pulling the throw over his feet, a triangle of light ghosted across the carpet.

She turned to find Denise Gilfillan standing at the door. 'Everything OK?'

'Yeah, fine.'

'Why doesn't he go to bed?'

'It's a genius thing. He thinks better on the sofa.' She pulled the door closed behind her, forcing Denise back into the hall.

'Do you want me to get the coffee? The Robertsons don't look like shifting,' she asked. She was holding three empty wine glasses in her hand, ready for the dishwasher.

She took them from her. 'No, Denise, it's fine. I have it all ready.'

Denise followed her into the brightness of the kitchen. 'How are you keeping?'

'I'm fine. How was the cheese? It seemed very strong. I wasn't aware there was a difference between vegetarian cheese and carnivorous cheese.' She poured boiling water into the cafetière and, conscious of her best friend watching her back, wiped its bronze lid.

'Depends on the rennet. Are you sure you don't need a hand?' Denise stood with her hands outstretched.

Helena looked at her reflection, pale, a smudge of mascara under her left eye. She licked the pad of her thumb and rubbed at it. 'You can get the cream out of the fridge if you want.' She knew where this conversation was going.

'The cheese was excellent, my favourite.' She would say that. 'You know what I mean – how *are* you? You can't avoid the question.'

Helena bit back her annoyance. 'You told Terry, didn't you? I spotted all those *poor Helena* looks over the goat's cheese tartlets.'

'They were lovely goat's cheese tartlets.' Denise patted her on the shoulder. 'But, Helena, we think of you as part of the family. We worry about you.'

'Well, don't. There's nothing to worry about.'

'But I saw a letter from the Beatson on the hall table. Unopened. Is that the results of the mammogram?'

'If you're that observant, you should be in the force along with him on the sofa.'

'Helena, with these things you have to move quickly, you have to be –'

'Never mind what I have to be.'

'But the letter is unopened, and –'

'And it will stay unopened until I'm ready. It's just the appointment to get the results, and I have deliberately set up the appointment for after the exhibition, so it makes no difference, does it?' Helena said sweetly, her friend's insistence making her dig her heels in.

Denise stopped at the door. 'Well, I think you are wrong but give me a shout if you want anything.'

'I will.'

'Make sure you do.'

Helena thrust the plunger of the cafetière deep with the palm of her hand, quicker than was necessary, causing the grains to billow up the side in anger.

Sunday, 1 October

Helena woke from a restless sleep, caffeine fuelling her thoughts, thinking about all the things she still had to do, worrying about her little lump, worrying about the future. She had agreed with herself to put it all to the back of her mind until after the exhibition. She could cope with only so much at a time, and right at this moment she didn't have time to be ill. Two weeks wouldn't make any difference.

Denise, being helpful in her confrontational way, had just robbed her of a good night's sleep, and the one thing she needed right now was sleep. But it wasn't Denise who had the problem. She hit her head angrily into the pillow.

But then she reached out across an expanse of cool lemon cotton sheeting and smiled to herself. She was used to hearing the front door open and close at all hours of the day and night, a pause as a jacket was slung on the stairs, feet going straight into the sitting room, the clink of glass. Alan had the ability to move around the house with ghostly silence, but she always knew he was there. Even in her deepest sleep, she always knew. He would come into the bedroom eventually, sit on his side of the bed, thinking, staring into his whisky, waiting for the day's thoughts to disappear. She would roll over, curving her body round his back, and his hand would rest on the side of her face, his thumb caressing the tendril of hair above her ear, and she would sleep easy once he was there.

This time she waited, her hand automatically stroking the blank sheet beside her. The clock said 3.59. She smiled again, glad he was at home, resting on the sofa in the room below, cuddling the velvet throw. Then the vague thoughts in her mind crystallized. She had *already* heard him come up the stairs, she had waited for him, gazing into the darkness with half-open eyes. But the footsteps had continued up the stairs to her studio. She thought she had misheard, remembered opening her eyes wide, looking at the ceiling, listening as his footfalls betrayed him. She'd heard the clunk of the ladder up to the attic being pulled down. And then nothing. She remembered lying, in silence, staring at the fronds of lace on the lampshade as they danced in the draught, wondering what he was doing in the attic. If he wasn't in bed, he must still be up there. She slipped out of bed and out on to the landing. The downstairs light was on, casting faint shadows on the stairs. She could hear nothing apart from the occasional tick of the central heating and the odd creak of an old house waking to a new day.

'Alan?' she called, looking both up and down the stairs. 'Alan? Are you there? Alan? Hello?'

'Yeah,' came a quiet voice from somewhere below her. She could see him, bathed in the dull light from the stairwell, sitting on the stairs like a child beneath the oriel window, looking very small and alone.

'You OK?'

'Yeah.' Something about his voice was unwelcoming. 'I'm fine,' he said. He didn't get up, but sniffed and slipped something into its tissue-paper wrapper, then pushed it under his leg on the stair.

'What have you got there?' she asked softly, sliding on to the step above him.

'Can I answer *nothing much*?' He rested his head on her knees. She felt the damp on his cheek; he had been crying.

'If I was a detective, I wouldn't accept it. But as I am a

mere wife, I shall.' She kissed him on the back of his head, letting the weight of her lips rest in his hair, waiting for him to respond.

'I was looking at photographs of Mum.'

'Yes, I know.'

'So why did you ask?'

'I wanted to know why you were looking,' she asked softly.

McAlpine didn't answer. Helena felt his shoulders stiffen, holding back something he did not want to say. 'Just thinking about Mum,' he said eventually.

'Your mum died, Alan, when you were young and vulnerable.' She sighed. 'I have far too much nagging to do ever to leave you. Come on, let's get some sleep.' She got up and made her way back to the bedroom, leaving her husband sitting on the stairs. She heard him sigh, and she knew she was right to leave him alone with his thoughts.

Later that morning it was her usual post-dinner party routine: two glasses of mineral water, strong coffee, Dinah Washington on the CD and the dishwasher humming away doing all the hard work. She looked at her watch. There was plenty of time to get the kitchen squared up, and she could leave at half eleven and be at the gallery by one. She pulled on her rubber gloves ready to tackle the delicate glassware in the sink, her mind miles away. Peter Kolster was being demanding, wanting his *My Brother in Palestine* to have top billing in the exhibition, but he was an unknown . . . so far. And she had five Old Dutch paintings at Customs at Glasgow Airport, waiting to be signed for.

The doorbell sounded, and she cursed under her breath. Terry Gilfillan back to fetch the car he had been too drunk to drive the night before, no doubt. She had enough on her plate today, and she could do without his dripping sympathy. Immediately, her hand went to her breast, feeling for the little lump that was trying not to be found. And there it was, her body betraying itself. She rolled the gloves from her hands, picked up the car keys from the hall table and opened the door.

Colin Anderson looked at the keys in her hands and raised an eyebrow. 'That kind of night, was it?'

'It sort of turned out that way.' She smiled, glad it was him. 'Come in, Colin. Alan's upstairs messing about. He'll be down in a minute.' Helena swung the gloves from her hands, dangling them inside out. 'Coffee? I have some on.'

'Great.' Anderson noticed how tired she looked, paler than usual, her skin transparent under her eyes.

'Is that more work for our lord and master?' She nodded at the file he was carrying.

'Yeah.' He slumped in a chair at the breakfast bar, spanning his fingers at the heat radiating from the Aga behind him. He wished he could take his shoes off and warm his feet as well. 'I've just picked up Michael Batten, Ph.D., B.Sc., BBC, GTi, etc. The *effing profiler,*' he expanded. He nodded upstairs. 'What kind of mood is *he* in?'

'The same.'

'Christ.' He looked longingly at the remnants of the crème brûlée.

'Have you had any breakfast?' Helena could see flecks of grey in the blond and an insidious puffiness under the eyes. Colin needed a shave and a sleep; he was looking worse than her husband.

'Those going a-begging?' He pointed at some cold duchesse potatoes and an abandoned goat's cheese tartlet.

'Yes, help yourself. Do you want them warmed up?'

'No, I'm used to eating leftovers, believe me.'

She leaned against the worktop, watching him as he stabbed at the potato whorls with a fork. 'Do you want to investigate some cheese and bickies while you're at it? Or I could put on some toast for you? Or both?' she added.

He hesitated, then scooped a mouthful of crème brûlée with the same fork. 'Toast would be great. Our toaster's on the blink after hitting the wall, narrowly missing my head.' He licked cream from the fork, his other hand reaching for the Ritz crackers. 'This is lovely.'

'You know, over the years, the amount of Alan's food I've tipped into the bin would probably feed a small African nation.'

'He doesn't eat at the best of times,' said Anderson, slicing a big piece of Caboc and sticking it awkwardly between two crackers.

'How do *you* think he is?' she asked, keeping her voice steady.

'Who knows?' said Colin, his voice non-committal.

She tried a different tack, her fingers swiping imaginary crumbs from the worktop in front of the toaster. 'Does he seem the same at work?'

Anderson took his time to answer. 'Maybe a bit nervy, that's all, but it was his first day on the case. Why do you ask?'

'No reason.' Helena folded her arms, deep in thought.

Anderson munched away at a cracker, then felt the need to break the silence. 'Why, is he not OK?'

'Oh, he's fine.'

Anderson noticed the slight emphasis on the *he*.

'You know how the mind races at four in the morning.' She started rubbing the worktop with her forefinger, erasing a mark that didn't exist. 'You know he was at Partickhill Station when he was a cadet? He interviewed me when my mother died . . . and we got married three months later. It was our anniversary yesterday.'

Anderson paused in mid crunch. He said, 'Congratulations. You deserve a medal, being married to him that long.'

'Divorce has never crossed my mind. Murdering him is a daily thought, though.' She smiled, then was serious again. 'His mother had died just before mine. That means he was at Partickhill when he lost his mum, and he hasn't been back to that station since. Christ, he even drives down Byres Road rather than going up Hyndland to get to the station.'

'There's always been a bit of a rumour that he avoids the place like the plague.'

'It's true; he said it was too small a station to be effective.'

'We're all allowed to avoid our demons,' said Anderson. 'I should know: I married mine.'

'But that's all there is to it as far as you know?' She folded her arms automatically, protective of the perfidious little lump.

'Helena, he'd just lost his brother and his mum. Like you say, he was a cadet then,' Anderson reminded her gently, scooping up congealed cream with another cracker. 'Cadets answer the phone, they make the tea. He wouldn't be allowed to get involved in anything that would affect him. So don't worry. He'll have his reasons; he always does.'

Helena looked at her watch, easing the strap from her skin, running her forefinger round under the leather. She had lost weight. 'It wasn't like him not to come in and annoy Terry. He never misses an opportunity to wind him up.'

'He was very tired, Helena. He nearly fell asleep when I was driving, and that speaks volumes.'

But Helena was miles away, curling her hair round her finger. She was thinking back to the summer of '84, the day of her mother's funeral, and how kind Alan had been. He had been looking at that unmarked grave, a young, shattered, broken man, gaunt and bloodless. She had always suspected that whoever was in that grave was buried as deep in his heart as they were in the earth. But twenty-two years of marriage had taught her it was not a subject for discussion. Well, not with her. She watched as Anderson nibbled at another pyramid of potato, wondering how much he knew. She circled her toes a few times, making the tendons on her ankle snap, still thinking about the white tulips lying in their aluminium cone, about the single rose that he had added later. She knew she had intruded on his grief then; she sometimes thought she still did.

'I'll let him know his carriage awaits.' She walked out of the kitchen, leaving Anderson munching hot granary toast and melted butter, his feet stretched out to the Aga. He could have sat there for ever, but the peace was shattered by McAlpine coming down the stairs, stuffing the day's mail into his breast pocket while shouting down his mobile at Costello.

Anderson got to his feet. 'Another day, another dollar,' he sighed.

The word 'tenement' is often misused and misunderstood; the term 'vertical village' coined by some social anthropologists is much more apposite. At that moment, standing on the marbled floor, feeling the curve of the tiles at her back and marvelling at the Rennie Mackintosh stained glass, Costello wondered if she would ever be able to afford a place like this. The ground-floor flats with their own front steps and the use of the Victoria Gardens were going for more than a quarter of a million. So much for housing for the masses. It was all architects and surgeons up here now.

How on earth, she wondered, did a minister and a man who'd presumably had to pay off his three wives manage to afford it?

Costello leaned against the wall, waiting for her superior officers. Again. McAlpine had said noon. She sighed, wondering what the hell she was doing here. At least she was out of the drizzle. She gazed at the stained-glass window, Mackintosh's fallen roses, the light spiralling down towards her in a kaleidoscope of colour. She climbed the stairs up to the half-landing, the stone worn down with a hundred years of feet. At the window she checked her phone; no messages. Anderson and McAlpine had been held up somewhere. She leaned against the windowsill, looking through a panel of clear glass to the back of the tenement beyond, across the midden, as she would have called it. Fine for Castlemilk but not for Partickhill; they probably called it the courtyard or . . . the patio? She smiled to herself. It was still a midden; no matter how many little wooden gazebos they had, how pretty they made them, they still housed the bins. Here the paving stones were laid out in neat geometric patterns, a yellow-brick road to follow while hanging out the weekly wash. The weather was clearing at last, the sun coming out from behind a cloud highlighting the rain as it fell and pooled, a slight wind eddying in the back court making the border of pyracantha tremble. It caught her eye, the way the yellow berries danced; she had seen that before. On the loci photographs. The block of flats on the right-hand side was cut off by the shrubs; on the other side was Victoria Lane, the leafy grass way from Victoria Crescent to Victoria Gardens, the last walk Lynzi Traill ever made. Costello felt an eerie shiver creep up her spine. Why would Lynzi walk from Central Station and pass so close to her boyfriend's house without going in? Why go up the lane, across a road to the garden and . . . well, maybe she hadn't been conscious. The lane wasn't often used; it was more a narrow garden running between the blocks, and most people walked round on the pavement. The grass was thick and full, no mud for footprints. Costello sighed. She was the same age as Lynzi, give or take a year, and she couldn't think whether she would trust anyone enough to follow them up a lane on a dark Saturday night.

So who had Lynzi trusted? The boyfriend, the elusive Ian Livingstone, who'd had three wives already and him not yet forty? Yet his life had been turned upside down far more effectively than he could have managed himself. He was a womanizer, yes, she thought, but not a murderer. She knew he had been in the Rock Pub all Saturday night, in the company of some respectably solid citizens. To judge from their signed witness statements, Ian Livingstone hadn't even gone to the toilet on his own. Costello looked at the stairs, imagined Livingstone and Leask going up and down them. Strange bedfellows, those two, the minister and the womanizer. She wondered about the relationship between them.

She heard a car pull to a halt. She went to the door, to see McAlpine and Anderson get out of the battered Astra, not bothering to park. She could tell McAlpine was in a mood, scowling at the sky, daring it to rain on him. He banged the door hard, and Anderson glared. Costello presumed there had been words in the car.

There were no pleasantries. 'We want to interview Livingstone.'

'Good morning, sir,' she said politely. 'His alibi has checked out.'

'Twice,' said Anderson, dusting crumbs from his jacket.

'Three times, to be exact,' stressed Costello. 'It's watertight. He was with eighteen scouts and five parents, two of whom ran him home and then went into the Rock with him to watch the footie. He even went to the loo with his disabled friend to help him with the door,' Costello added drily.

'And what idiot looked into that? Was it thorough? Was it precise?'

Costello stood her ground. 'I did, sir.'

'And I checked it,' Anderson confirmed. 'Independently.'

'Right.' McAlpine sighed.

Costello and Anderson looked vaguely up the stairs, waiting for orders.

It was Costello who spoke first. 'I think we need to get a feel for him first, sir. I've just realized how close we are here to Victoria Gardens; the lane runs down this side of the flats. I'm going to go out and have a look.'

'And?' McAlpine was interested but not quite following.

'Maybe she was lured here. She wouldn't come out this way for nothing.'

'Livingstone must be involved somehow,' agreed McAlpine. 'Bait? *I'll run you to Ian's* type of thing?'

'Don't forget the minister lives here too,' said Costello, twisting the doorknob again, holding the door open with her foot. She pointed at the aluminium entry box, with six neatly typed names behind glass. Two were covered by greying white stickers; one said LEASK, G. 'He lives right across from Lynzi's boyfriend. And he knows Elizabeth Jane's parents. So he has a connection with them both.'

'But he wasn't Elizabeth Jane's minister; somebody called Shand was, if you remember,' McAlpine said irritably. 'And Shand is the minister who'll be officiating at the wedding where Elizabeth Jane was going to be a bridesmaid.'

'I know I said there was a religious slant to this,' Anderson said. 'But a minister, cutting up women and arranging them as if they were on a cross?'

Costello reached for her notebook, thinking about what McAlpine had just said. 'But Shand is away on holiday. OK, Reverend Leask knows the parents. But do we know for certain that he knew Elizabeth Jane?'

McAlpine cut her short impatiently. 'He was quick enough to the parents the minute she died. Where's Livingstone's flat?'

'Third floor, right.'

'And the minister's?'

'Third floor, left.'

'OK. You go out, have a poke around.' McAlpine went to move up the stairs. 'Come on, Colin.'

The grey storm doors over the third right were locked. Anderson pulled a letter from the brass opening. 'No post on a Sunday, so this is yesterday's. He's not here now, but he was until recently.'

'And when did you get your degree in stating the bloody obvious? Where is he? Now, I mean.' McAlpine looked round, as though expecting Ian Livingstone to jump out behind him.

'Don't know. Leask is in, though.' Anderson gestured at the stained glass of the left-hand flat. 'The hall light is on. Strange for a minister, to be in on a Sunday morning. But they're friends, sir. You said so. We could ask him maybe?'

'I'll do it. You phone the station, find out if Livingstone said he was going anywhere. He should have told us.' McAlpine lifted his own phone from his pocket. 'I've got no signal in here.'

Anderson scanned his own mobile round the landing. Nothing. 'Me neither. I'm waiting for a call to bring Batten in from the hotel.'

'He can walk. It's only round the bloody corner.'

'Beautiful glass, that, isn't it?' Anderson observed, trying to change the conversation.

McAlpine ignored him. Their house up on the terrace was full of stuff like that. It meant the insurance premium went up with every door-slamming argument. 'What's the background on Leask? Do we have any?' he asked quietly.

'West Highland Presbyterian Kirk.'

'Never heard of them. Who are they in the great scheme of things?'

'A little less tolerant than the Gestapo, from all accounts,' said Anderson, adjusting the collar of his jacket. 'This phone is hopeless. Hello?' he said to nobody in particular.

'Worse than the Wee Frees?'

'Much. But Leask checks out OK,' said Anderson, slapping his phone with the palm of his hand. 'I'll try again in a minute. He's from Stornoway, a bright pleasant man from all accounts. Burns has been doing some digging. One half-brother, a sensitive soul, apparently. Mother married twice. First hubby – Leask's dad, Alasdair George Leask – killed in a farm accident, no great loss from the sound of the local gossip. Mother was a long-suffering soul. Apart from reading theology at Glasgow Uni, George worked locally, looking after things at home when his mother was widowed a second time. He was the dutiful elder son, leaving his brother free to move down here. But the brother passed away . . .' Anderson paused to listen to the phone, then shook his head. 'Still nothing. Anyway, once the mother died, there was nothing to keep Leask in Stornoway, so he took the chance to get back to the big city. He's helping out at Beaumont Street Church, but he works mostly in that place for the homeless, the Phoenix Refuge, Father O'Keefe's place, looking at how we cope with drugs down here. Seems a nice guy, quiet. He's never married. Spends any free time with his uncle in Ballachulish.'

'How did you get all that?' asked McAlpine, impressed. 'Burns got some super-duper search engine?'

'Burns may look like a woolly mammoth, but he's a terrier when it comes to finding things out. However, in this case his search engine is his Auntie Dolina, who lives at Back, near Stornoway. Leask used to be the local eligible bachelor. Do you think it's worth asking the local nick for a background search?'

McAlpine smiled. 'What for? Convictions for sheep-shagging?'

'That's not an offence up there; it's compulsory. I'm going outside to get a signal.' Anderson dropped his voice, in case the door opened. 'Might be worth digging a bit deeper. He could be stoating about at all times of day and night. They would trust him.'

'They would have to *know* him, DI Anderson.'

'Well, he has a connection with Elizabeth's family, and a connection with Lynzi's boyfriend, DCI McAlpine,' said Anderson cheerily.

The door opened before McAlpine could reply.

If the Reverend Leask was surprised at finding the police on his doorstep, he didn't show it. His face took on a slightly quizzical look as he glanced at Anderson's warrant card.

'Hello,' he said. 'What can I do for you?' He stood to one side to let them in, but Anderson hung around on the landing.

'We're looking for Ian.'

'Mr Livingstone, I presume?' Leask smiled a little. 'Sorry, old joke. Ian isn't here. He's gone down south to stay with his mother. Come in.'

Anderson stayed put.

'When did he leave?' asked McAlpine.

'Come in. I've just put the kettle on.' Leask walked into a long hall with a beautifully polished wood floor; it struck McAlpine that Leask must have a cleaner.

Anderson tapped his phone again. 'I'll go down and make that call now, sir.'

McAlpine nodded and followed Leask inside. 'When did he go?'

'He left sometime Friday. I was busy, but he put a note through the door saying that he was going away and asking if I would feed the cat. I didn't see it until I got home yesterday.'

'That usual?' McAlpine asked.

'Yes. He would have let you know. He's' – Leask stopped at the living-room door – 'keen to get all this sorted. What do you want to talk to him for? Could I help?'

'One of those scenarios where he probably knows more than he realizes he knows. We'll show him some pictures, Elizabeth Jane's friends, see if the two women have anybody in common.'

'He told me you'd already phoned him about Elizabeth.'

'And we will speak to him again. And again.'

'I see. Do go through.' Leask walked over to the bay window and closed the sash as McAlpine looked around the room, thinking that Helena would approve of the polished floors, the oriental rug woven from fine silk, the dried grasses in the pitchpine fireplace. He placed his hand on the radiator. Warm. Such easy comfort wasn't where he would have pictured Leask.

'Have we met before, Mr Leask?' asked McAlpine. 'I mean, before this inquiry? You look familiar.'

'Yes, we have.' The minister smiled, a wry regretful smile.

'I'm not one for forgetting faces. The minute I saw you, it came to my mind. The girl from the bedsit? She had an accident.'

McAlpine thought he had heard wrong. Somebody suddenly speaking of her, sparking her to reality. 'I'm sorry?'

'When I was a student, years ago, I lived in a bedsit on the Highburgh Road. A girl upstairs had a terrible accident. You were there. We met on the stairs.'

'On the stairs . . . yes.' McAlpine's fingers curled round the radiator, as he remembered why he was on those stairs that day more than twenty years ago. 'You've changed a bit since then.'

Leask rubbed at his chin. 'A car dashboard and I had an argument once, and my face came second. The NHS provided me with new teeth, did a really good job. Not that I'd go through it again: too painful. I must be one of the few men whose looks have improved as the years have passed.'

'You knew her, though? The blonde girl upstairs?'

Leask nodded. 'I should never have walked away from you like that. I confess it's one of the few times in my life I have lied. I still feel terrible about it.'

McAlpine raised an eyebrow but stayed silent.

'The thing was, I was very young, studying to be a minister, and well . . . she was nice. Very nice indeed. Always pleasant, with such a friendly smile, and I thought rather lonely for one so young. My faith has obvious problems with unmarried mothers – how pompous that sounds now – so I tried not to speak to her because she was pregnant. But when I did I found her enchanting.' Leask had the grace to look embarrassed. 'A beautiful woman. She had the most amazing grey eyes. A face that wasn't easy to forget.'

'Not a face I ever saw, not in the flesh.'

'She taught me a lesson in tolerance,' Leask went on.

'And, unwittingly, she taught me a lot about myself. I knew her better than I told you. I wanted nothing to do with the investigation. If people had found out . . . I felt really bad about it. Every 26th of June I think about her wee girl . . .'

'How did you know she had a wee girl?'

'I went to the hospital a few times, just to see how she was. They knew me slightly, as I was assistant to the chaplain, so they were happy to tell me she'd had a daughter. It had to be by Caesarean, she was in such a bad way. Just two days after my own birthday, so I always remember it. Then later all sorts of things came to light, and the police turned up mob-handed at Highburgh Road and really tore the place apart. I've no idea what they were after.'

McAlpine remained silent, thinking of the little drawings of Steve McQueen, fluttering in the draught.

'Well, it's in the past now. She gave me a taste for good coffee, I remember.' Leask smiled at the memory. 'I was skint. I went to ask her for a tea bag. In that little hovel, she gave me the best coffee I've ever tasted. Dutch stuff it was, her one pleasure, she said. Would you like a cup of coffee? Mine's only instant.' Leask smiled. 'She wouldn't have approved.'

'That's fine,' McAlpine replied, a thousand thoughts racing through his head.

Leask left the door open, leaving McAlpine to walk slowly round, looking at the pictures on the wall, trying to keep his mind on the job when all he wanted to do was to sit down and say *So tell me about her, how did she sound, what did she say?* He hoped she had laughed, and laughed often.

'What do you want to know?' said the detached voice from the kitchen.

How did she sound when she laughed? 'When did you last speak to Ian?'

'I rang him this morning. He said he had already phoned the police about it. I had tried to call him last night, but he wasn't in. And it's not the sort of message you'd leave with somebody's mother, is it?'

McAlpine coughed slightly, clearing his mind more than his throat. 'We just want to talk to him. DS Costello was going to take him down to the station to look through photographs – places, people, Elizabeth Jane's family album, people he knew, people Lynzi knew . . .' He realized he was rambling, but he wanted to stay, wanted to talk. About *her*.

'DS Costello? The blonde girl?' Leask sounded surprised.

'Yes.' McAlpine looked to the kitchen, alerted by Leask's tone.

'It's not a job for a woman.'

'Not a popular opinion these days. So you think they should still be nurses and typists, and leave work when –'

'There'd be less trouble in the world if women remembered their responsibility to their children.' Leask held out a Millennium china mug full of Nescafé. 'You have no children, have you?' He stated it as fact, but he was smiling as he spoke. 'It would make your job quieter.'

'Indeed.' McAlpine leaned against the radiator, placing the cup down. 'Do you mind if I . . . ?' he asked, rolling a Marlboro between finger and thumb. 'How do you know that?'

'Smoke if you want. There was a piece about your wife in the *Herald* supplement. She sounds like a fine artist, a talented woman. Too busy for children, I suppose.'

McAlpine noticed an implied criticism. 'I didn't read that article.' He moved along the wall, looking at a photograph of an owl. 'What's that?'

'Scops Owl, photographed in Beith in 1995, very rare, not found on British soil much.' Leask was rubbing the bridge of his nose with each forefinger, as if he could easily have slipped his hands down to prayer. He changed the subject. 'You have me thinking that maybe I should remember something, and I can't.'

McAlpine let his eyes flit around the room, trying to concentrate. He eyed up the bookcases: some books in Gaelic, a selection on the flora and fauna of the British Isles, a fair smattering of science fiction and Stephen Hawking's *A Brief History of Time*. The man of God reading the man of science. 'You said, yesterday, that you didn't know Lynzi. Could you clarify that? Are you sure you didn't ever meet her? Here, perhaps? You know Ian well enough to feed his cat,' he said casually.

'I don't *think* I met her.'

'You would know, though. You have a good memory for faces.'

'I knew *of* her, obviously, but I can't recall ever setting eyes on her. But Ian has a photograph of her in his flat.'

'Were she and Ian happy?'

Leask answered carefully, enunciating every syllable, letting his tongue roll on the *r*'s. 'What there was of the relationship was happy. But –'

'But you couldn't have agreed to it. It was adultery after all.'

Leask winced at the word. 'I counselled him that maybe a woman who could leave her child wasn't everything a woman should be. There are things a woman should not walk away from . . . marriage, a family, a child.'

'But did Ian Livingstone not leave his wife – and two other wives before her?' Costello put in quietly. She had come in uninvited, her boots leaving marks on the polished floor. 'He sounds like a marriage wrecker to me.'

Leask's face remained impassive. He watched as Costello

folded her arms and leaned against the doorjamb. There was silence for a moment, the only sound the gentle gurgle of the central heating. Leask turned back to McAlpine. 'That was one of the things I tried to . . . to counsel him about,' he said eventually. 'But none of his relationships was what you would call *satisfactory*. Not honest women.'

And Ian Livingstone was in no way to blame, I suppose? Costello thought. But this time she kept her silence.

McAlpine's eyes clouded over, wondering which woman Leask was actually talking about. 'Are you here for a reason, DS Costello?'

'I've just two questions. Mr Leask, is that your car in the second garage in the lane? Across Victoria Crescent?' she added for emphasis.

Leask nodded. 'It's not my car, technically, but the red Punto is the car I use.'

'You walk down the lane to get to this flat from the garage?'

Leask nodded again.

'And you mentioned a "Tom" in relation to Elizabeth, at her parents' house.' She paused. 'You were to tell him about Elizabeth, pass on the bad news? A boyfriend?'

'Hardly. Tom O'Keefe is a priest. A colleague of mine,' Leask said coldly. 'The Fultons' own minister is away, so they contacted me and asked if I would pass it on. At a time like this, the last thing you want is everybody phoning the house.'

'I'm sure they're grateful for that, Mr Leask. That's all I wanted to know. I'll leave you two to it, then.' And she was gone.

McAlpine inwardly cursed Costello. 'Sorry about that,' he said.

'Doing her job, I suppose.'

McAlpine changed the subject. 'That your mother?' He pointed at a collection of snapshots, one of Leask and an elderly woman sitting on a wall in a harsh bleak landscape. 'Is that home?'

'Stornoway, yes. My mother died recently.' Leask's voice was brusque. He turned away and sat down.

'You must miss it, the island?'

'I do. Glasgow's noisy. And dirty. I still have family in Ballachulish, so I get up there as often as I can. I was there on Friday, but I came straight back when I heard about Elizabeth Jane.'

McAlpine looked at another photograph, faded with the passing years, of a family group posed outside a croft. He couldn't help noticing there was no father in the picture. And a more recent one: a young Leask with an even younger boy. A broad italic hand had scribbled something on the mount, but it was too ornate to read. The two boys were fishing, standing with a small and extremely woolly sheep. McAlpine supposed every family had photographs like that. The McAlpine family version was him and Robbie in front of a snowman. They'd put their dad's helmet on the snowman and warped the band . . . that got them kicked arses all round. The picture had stayed on the mantelpiece for years after the snowman had melted, and was still there when the priest came and told them that the water had taken Robbie. McAlpine brought it home the day his mother died. It had been waiting for him.

'Who's the other boy?'

'My half-brother,' said Leask, clipping his speech. 'Brother.'

Recognizing a raw nerve, McAlpine turned to look at Leask. 'He's . . . passed away, then?'

'Recently, yes.'

'I'm sorry to hear that. Had he been ill?'

'A kind of illness, you could say. That's Alasdair, there.' Leask pointed to a silver-framed photograph on the side table, a young handsome man, his tight smile not quite managing to cover squint front teeth. A bare arm bordered one side of the picture: it looked as if somebody had been cut out. 'As I'm sure you know, these things are not always the hand of God.'

'In my experience, it's more often the hand of man,' said McAlpine.

'Indeed. It doesn't matter, not in my job. The Lord will repay, that's all I need to know.'

McAlpine smiled. 'It matters in mine.'

McAlpine was leaning over the sink, staring at himself in the mirror, realizing he had grown old without noticing it. Anderson inclined his head to check for feet under the remaining cubicle doors. They were empty.

'How did it go with Leask?' he asked.

McAlpine looked up. 'Fine.'

'You feeling OK? You were grumpy as hell earlier. Did you get a good night's sleep?'

'No, why do you ask? Spit it out.'

'Helena thought you were unsettled. She thought you'd been . . .'

McAlpine was evasive. 'She had too much to drink. I should have known. She was nice to me when I got home, a sure sign she's had a dram too many.' He changed the subject back. 'Interesting guy, Leask. He sounded out OK about Ian Livingstone. I don't think that's an avenue worth pursuing. The alibi is watertight.'

'Do you mean Leask or Livingstone's not worth pursuing?'

McAlpine ignored him totally. 'So, what's he like, this profiler tosser?'

'Thought you'd forgotten all about him.' Anderson pursed his lips. 'Not what I expected. Younger, no ponytail, no polo neck, seems OK. First question he asked me was where was a good place to get bevied.'

'An alcoholic psychologist? Interesting.' McAlpine plugged the sink and ran in some cold water, and an indistinct thumping echoed along the pipe. Anderson noticed the tremor in his boss's hands was getting worse.

'He says he can read people like he can read a book.'

'Slowly? With his lips moving?' McAlpine shook his head at the innocence of fools. 'Where did you say you left him?'

'I dropped him off on the way to pick you up, so he's been in your office for – what?' Anderson flicked his eyes at his watch. 'An hour? An hour and a bit? I told Wyngate to look after him. He's requested the newspapers, to see how they're carrying the story.'

'All he has to do is shout out the window and ask them.'

'Better get a move on. Leave him any longer in your office and he'll have done a thesis on "The Effect of Macallan Malt on the Investigative Mind".'

Dr Mick Batten got to his feet as McAlpine entered the office. The DCI was determined not to apologize for the mess of the place and was equally determined not to let it show that he was deliberately not apologizing. Batten looked like a football hooligan, hair all one length, cut blunt into his collar, unshaven beyond the point of designer stubble, and wearing ripped jeans and a rugby shirt from a country that McAlpine, a football man, couldn't identify.

Batten, leaning on the filing cabinet, seemed comfortable in the silence. McAlpine gestured to him to sit down.

'I'll get somebody to get us a coffee.' McAlpine looked round.

'I already have one, I've been well looked after.' Batten pulled a packet of Silk Cut from his jeans. 'Am I right in thinking I'm not allowed to smoke in here?'

'Only on the street, mate. The car park is quite sheltered.'

'I'm on the patches, but I still need these to kick them in.' He nodded at the picture stuck to the monitor. 'Your wife do that?'

'Yes,' said McAlpine guardedly.

'I thought so. Helena Farrell. She's talented. There was an exhibition at the Academy in Liverpool a while back. My brother bought one of her paintings. He reckons it'll be worth a bit one day.'

'Indeed,' said McAlpine shortly. 'PC Wyngate was told to show you around. Is there anything else you want to see?'

Batten nodded. 'ACC McCabe had everything sent on to me through Pitt Street. Gordon took me through the local papers. Always interesting to see how they're carrying the story.' His accent was pure Merseyside, and McAlpine found it difficult to take him seriously. The casual use of Wyngate's first name didn't escape him. 'Do you allow feet up on your desk? I think better with my feet up on the desk.'

'Please, go ahead.' McAlpine said, his voice flat, aware he was sounding like his own father.

'Thinking's what I get paid for, so I try to do it well,' Batten said, closing his eyes. He rubbed the threadbare denim that covered his knees absent-mindedly. When he spoke, his eyes screwed up. 'I reckon you're close to catching him, though, definitely close. Converging paths, I feel, you and him.' He spanned his fingers. 'Converging paths.'

'Who?'

'This Christopher Robin. I always call them by a name.

129

Helps me to focus on them as people. I don't like the media calling him the Crucifixion Killer – makes him sound superhuman somehow. He's human all right; he was a baby once, then a child, then an adult. If you lose sight of that, you'll never find out why he is what he is, why he does what he does.'

McAlpine let all that pass. 'My definition of "close" in this case would be a guilty verdict or a signed confession – either would do.'

'Neither would guarantee you'd got the right man or that the killings would stop. You've a good team. Anderson is honest and loyal, a good man. Gordon Wyngate is a non-academic technophile who's found his own niche. You've played him well, to your advantage.'

McAlpine ignored that, aware that it had been Costello's idea.

'Is this a young team? You're – what – early forties? Anderson, late thirties? Wyngate's just a boy.'

'We don't lack experience, if that's what you're getting at,' said McAlpine coldly.

'Not at all. I've read all your records – exemplary. This Costello – a female from the look of the loopy handwriting – how old?'

'Does it matter?'

'Yes.'

'Mid thirties? Maybe a bit less.'

'Good. Nice to have a team whose average age is the same as that of the man we're chasing.' Batten was suddenly businesslike again. 'You've not established any connection between these women yet?'

'Maybe,' said McAlpine quietly. 'But it's tenuous. Costello is typing up a report for you. I think we've established a connection, but I can't see the significance of it yet.'

'I look forward to reading it.' Batten examined his fingernails closely. 'How are you coping?'

'Why does everybody keep asking that?'

'Because you can get drawn in. *When you look into the abyss, the abyss also looks into you.* Robert Kessler, the man who coined the phrase "serial killer".'

'I think Friedrich Nietzsche said it first,' said McAlpine blandly. 'Unless I'm mistaken.'

'Correct,' Batten said, impressed. He moved the topic back a step. 'I've been through most of your files, nothing in depth as yet but enough to hypothesize. I'd say the connection between the victims will be something non-tangible, something perceived. So when we learn to think like him, we'll catch him.'

'You make it sound so easy.'

'In theory it is. The trouble is, the link doesn't have to actually be there, it only has to be *perceived* to be there. Who did this report? Costello? Same handwriting.' He flicked the page of a report to read the signature.

'Yeah, she's doing the report, like I said.'

'It's an interesting read with regard to Elizabeth Jane. An intuitive copper, Costello?'

'Intuitive is one word for her.'

'Meaning?' said Batten.

'Meaning nothing. She's good, doesn't always take the party line. What about her?' McAlpine was defensive.

'I'd like a word with her, that's all.'

'You have an idea?'

'I'll speak to her first. Firm up a few things.' Batten put the report back on the desk. 'I'd like a car and a driver. Just for a few hours, to take me round the loci.'

'Ten minutes would do it, mate. By foot.'

'That close together?'

'As close as a gnat's testicles, as the saying goes.' He looked through the glass, indicating the map. 'That covers two square miles at most.'

There was a gentle knock on the door, and Costello popped her head round. 'There's a taxi outside to take you to the Hilton, Dr Batten.'

'And you are?' asked Batten.

'If you're such a good profiler, you should have worked that out for yourself,' said McAlpine, smiling.

'DS Costello, I presume,' said Batten, putting his arm out. He then walked out with Costello like a keen suitor at a prom.

McAlpine reclaimed his seat while shaking his head. Batten had spent twelve years at university only to go with female intuition. No wonder nobody took profilers seriously. Bloody waste of taxpayers' money. He looked at his computer, then at his watch. It was time to open his email. He decided to open his mail instead.

There was a knock on the glass door of the gallery. Helena didn't look round, continuing to direct the joiner, who was up a ladder. 'Left a bit, left a bit.' She waved her hand at the door irritably, but the knocking was insistent. She turned round to give the interrupter a mouthful, then realized it was her husband.

'Oh, shit. Look, guys, could you leave it there? I'll come back to it.' She pulled the keys from her belt as *My Brother in Palestine* was carefully lowered to the ground, her assistant Fiona easing the painting on to the floor and then propping it against the wall. 'Hello,' Helena said, opening the double locks. 'And to what do I owe this pleasure?'

'Hello, dear wife.' He kissed her on his way past, walking quickly towards her private office, stepping over wooden crates and toolboxes. 'It's looking good. She keeping you busy?' he asked Fiona, not stopping for an answer.

Fiona looked at Helena, who shrugged helplessly.

Alan McAlpine walked into his wife's office, smiling, and held the door open for her. He slammed it behind her with a violence that rattled the glass.

She watched as he placed a letter on the desk, skimming it across to her. She recognized the health authority logo. 'That is personal!' she hissed. 'Why did you open it?'

'When were you going to tell me?' he asked, keeping his temper in check, his voice steady and quiet. He moved towards her. She stepped back. '*Were* you going to tell me? Why did you keep this from me?'

'I haven't kept anything from you,' she said, her voice challenging. 'It's just a letter telling me about an appointment I already have. See for yourself.'

'About what?'

'Nothing much, just a small lump, happens to women all the time and –'

'So why didn't you say? What is it?' His face paled.

'Alan, I knew you would panic, and it *is* nothing.' She reached out to him, but he pulled away, leaving her arm in mid-air stretched across her desk.

'But why are you leaving it? Why not go now? If there's a bloody waiting list, we'll go private.'

'Alan, stop it,' she said very quietly. 'I need a bit of breathing space.' She opened the door and called out, 'It's half two – do you two want to go for lunch now? Back at three? We'll finish it then.' She shut the door. 'I really don't have time for this.' She closed her eyes. 'I don't have the emotion for it just now. I'm busy.'

'Busy?' he hissed at her. 'Hanging polka-dot nonsense on the wall for people to gawp at?'

'A major event in a lifetime of promoting new artists is how I would put it. It's my problem, and I will solve it my way.' She leaned forward, putting her forefinger on the letter and pushing it back to him. 'I have an exhibition to organize. *Now*. And it's a bit difficult keeping this to the back of my mind when you fling it in my face. So please back off. I am trying to be calm about it, and I know you are worried, but people are constantly reminding me of things I would rather forget and . . .'

He sidestepped, keeping her against the door. 'Who? Who else knows?'

'There's nothing to know yet.'

'Who?'

'Denise.'

'So how does she know?' He leaned against the desk.

'Girl chat,' Helena sighed. 'And then she told Terry. You should have seen them on Saturday night, looking at me as if I might break.'

'At least they got the chance.'

'It was your decision not to turn up, remember? If you had known, you would have been just as bad as them. You're doing it now. The "Poor Helena" look. In fact I could exhibit myself here. And you can all look at the same time.' She reached out again to touch his face. 'Sorry, you OK?'

'Not really.'

'Well, I am not *going* to worry.' She refolded the letter, lifting her bag, ready to go. 'And I am not going to worry *you*.'

'Until it's too late?' He caught her elbow, standing very close to her now, his voice almost whispering in her ear.

'If they thought it was dangerous, they would have said at the time.'

'You being honest with me?'

'As honest as I am being with myself. And it doesn't help when you sit on the stairs all night like a muppet. Your head is right up your arse at the moment, even more than usual. We're both busy – and I need to have time to deal with it. End of story.'

'Fine!' he said, heading out the door. He slammed it so hard a miniature jumped from its hanging and crashed to the floor.

Helena swore loudly as her husband went on to slam the outer door behind him, killing the sudden noise of traffic on Bath Street.

Silence.

'Bastard!' she whispered. No point in talking aloud: there was nobody there to hear. She sat down. She should have sat down right at the start and told him calmly, drip-feeding it a bit at a time, but hindsight was a marvellous thing. Back then she'd thought it was all about nothing. Now it looked as though it was about a wee bit more than nothing. *My Brother in Palestine* was lying against the wall, looking at her; she decided to go to the shop for a sandwich and to get some fresh air.

Monday, 2 October

Shortly after midnight, the disco was heaving like a huge animal that pulsed and grooved to the insistent rhythm. The noise was deafening. Dark, dirty walls glistened with dripping sweat, the air heavy and thick with dry-ice smoke, cloying at his lungs. The constant rhythmic thumping of the bass pounded his stomach. Sean McTiernan had often felt caged in prison, but this was worse.

He started to shake. Nerves, he muttered to himself to keep calm. This was it.

After three years, six months, two days.

He seemed just another punter in a nightclub, looking for a woman, any woman. But Sean was looking for one woman in particular. A redhead leered at him as she went past, paused and came back for another look. He squinted into the middle distance, looking past her, avoiding her eyes, losing her in the smoke. The music assaulted his ears and the redhead joined in the attack, squawking something at him and laughing. Her hair moved like a brick, he noticed. Anybody running their hands through that risked losing a finger. He smiled back at her and again fixed his eyes on the point over her shoulder: an old Chevy bumper was stuck on the wall, decorated by two pairs of knickers. He wanted a woman, but not this travesty.

The redhead's friend bumped into her and the redhead dominoed into him, spilling her Bloody Mary down his shirt. Sean pulled away from them, steadying the redhead as she stumbled before releasing her and letting her fall to the floor. And then he knew. He knew she was close. If he closed his eyes, he could see her, coming through the haze, smiling at him . . .

She might not be safe, but she was here.

His throat began to hurt. He needed a drink. He stepped over the redhead, making his way doggedly towards the bar, ploughing a course where there were only men. It was more difficult to elbow women aside; their flesh was softer, barer. He didn't like to touch. They weren't wearing much: skirts up to their arse and see-through tops with no bras. At the bar, trying to understand what you had to do to get a drink, the queue still bopping up and down to the music, he found it easier to move than to stand still. In the end, the transaction was done by sign language, the can being pointed at and paid for with Sean having no idea what he had bought or how much he had paid. It was Miller, and the lager was warm to his tongue. He felt himself being sucked back towards the crowd on the dance floor.

A skinhead in a Saltire T-shirt elbowed him and spilled the Miller down his shirt, spreading further the stain of the Bloody Mary. 'Sorry, mate.' Then he added, 'Some result, big man, eh?'

Sean nodded. In Glasgow it was always *some result*. And always better to agree. The smell of skinhead aftershave could have disinfected a dog kennel, but somewhere in his senses Sean caught the smell of the sea and salt and the scent of a woman. Blonde.

His eyes scanned the dance floor, the crowd at the periphery, the dancers on the stairs, the people at the bar. He knew he was being watched.

Three years and six months and two days.

He made his way towards the dancing. The wooden floor was separated from the rest of the nightclub by a single brass rail. He leaned against it, trying to appear non-chalant, his eyes scanning the dance floor, from left to right and then back again, through the mist of dry ice to the ghostlike figures gyrating and thrusting like demented marionettes.

A girl noticed him and started dancing, sideways on, her chin on her shoulder, moving her body with comic mistiming. She was a piece of Glaswegian glamour, red leather miniskirt and a black bra nearly covered by a black plastic waistcoat, peroxide blonde hair the colour of straw piled on top of her head. A wide mouth was painted scarlet to match the talon nails.

And green ankle boots.

Those ankle boots. It was only when she moved closer, smiling at him, stubby fingers opening and closing in greeting, that he realized it was bloody Arlene from the café.

Sean looked away, but the eye contact had lasted a little too long, and she misread the sign.

'You said you'd be here.'

'Did I?'

'Nae, I wiz earwigging.' She leaned over the rail and started to grind her legs against his, jutting her pelvis backwards and forwards like a cheap lap dancer revving up. Sean's eyes shot past her to the dance floor, catching a glimpse of something that was gone. His heart stopped for a moment.

He stayed still, looking. Arlene caught the line of his vision.

'Yer up for it? Again?' Her tongue ran across her upper teeth, then she raised her glass to her lips and swayed drunkenly, spilling most of it down the Grand Canyon of her cleavage. 'Again,' she repeated, pulling his ear close to her mouth, her grasp firm on his shirt. She blew a bubble with her gum, the sickly sweet smell of it exploding in his face.

'Fuck off, and fuck off now.' He ducked under the rail.

He stood still for a moment, raising his eyes through the mist of dry ice, and she was there, slowly revealed to him. Short black hair, a dark dress that skimmed the top of slender bare white thighs. Dark mirrored glasses covered her eyes, her pouting lips curved to smile. Seductively she raised a forefinger to touch the bridge of the glasses and pulled them down the length of her nose, revealing large grey eyes. She winked and pushed the glasses back up, her eyes hidden, her face lost in the smoke.

When it passed, she had gone.

This one was his.

Outside in the street, the wind caught the breath from Sean's lungs and the rain stung his eyes, but Glasgow had never smelled or looked so good. She stopped at the corner of Torness Street, looking back to make sure he was following, pulling her cloak up over her head before slipping, ethereal and ghostly, into the stormy night.

Byres Road was busy, singletons hurrying past to get out of the weather, smokers sheltering under the canopies, couples hand in hand, absorbed in each other, on their way home from the Chip and the Cul de Sac. Most of the pubs had closed their doors, though a few people were still hanging around the alleyways, too drunk to notice how wet they were getting. A football supporter in Celtic hoops was standing in the middle of the pavement, arms out, the wind filling his jacket, laughing, letting the gusts spin him among the traffic. Sean McTiernan walked past slowly, watching the small figure swathed in black standing at the corner, one foot in the road, one foot on the pavement. She swayed slightly in the wind, moving to one side as a taxi passed, then out into the road again, so she could be seen. Then she was gone.

Sean went after her, resisting the urge to break into a run, keeping his head down, protecting his eyes from the rain. He careered into somebody, saying sorry and continuing on, his stride never breaking. He sidestepped round a couple, too busy sheltering their faces from the rain to watch where they were going. He jogged a few yards to make up the lost distance, his eyes on her all the time. He was high on emotion. Three years, six months and two days. Now that she was there for the taking, he could hardly stand it. There was only one constant thing in his life. Her love.

He lost her for a moment, then caught sight of her again. Hide and seek. In sight, then gone.

He stopped at the supermarket window, looked up and down the street. A blonde came by, staggering slightly, and as she walked past an illuminated window he recognized the green ankle boots.

Oh, no, not now. She was trash. How could she even walk on the same pavement, stand under the same rain, as perfection? He turned to face the glass, letting her pass behind him. But she didn't notice him; she just kept going, raising her hand in greeting to some other poor sucker she had lined up. He kept his head down, not seeing her, not seeing anything but the little figure costumed in black that danced ahead of him. Where was she going?

His bedsit was near here, but she was too clever for that; she wouldn't go there. He walked to the edge of the pavement, looking: nothing to the left, nothing to the right. She hadn't crossed the road. His eyes darted up the side road opposite. Nothing. He felt a familiar tickle in the hairs on the back of his neck, that familiar sense of *her*. He turned slowly round.

Three years, six months, two days.

Behind him was an alley, a dead end, the goods entrance to the supermarket, finishing in a yard with a high mesh fence, a skip abandoned at the far end. He squinted his eyes against the rain.

Whistler's Lane. He had killed Malkie Steele there.

Of all the places, why this one?

To say thank you.

Whistler's Lane was empty. Then a glimpse of flesh in the darkness, here, then gone, seen, then unseen. She had dipped into a door recess. Sean could not help but feel like John Wayne as he walked down the lane. He had the measure of her game now; she wanted him, and she was not going to wait until it was safe.

She had come to get him.

Just as she said she would.

The lane was cobbled at the end, the walls covered with graffiti. King Billy and the Pope were due for a rematch. Good for them, thought Sean, so are Sean and Truli.

She was leaning dramatically against the door at the back of the recess, not smiling but looking at him almost warily, her black cloak furled round her slender arms, one leg up, bare foot against the wall, silk slippers kicked on to the concrete. Her face was turned into the wind, her skin wet, the light glistening off perfect cheekbones.

She could have been twelve years old, waiting for him outside school again.

He reached out with both hands, cupping her face, holding it up to the light and the rain so that he could see her clearly. Nothing had changed. He frowned slightly and pulled the wig from her head.

Blonde hair tumbled to her shoulders.

His angel was back. She smiled as he pulled her face to his, kissing her deeply and passionately, biting into her face. Her thin arms moved round his waist, the cloak falling from her shoulders to the ground. He could feel the erotic slenderness of her pelvis, her ribs through her dress, the tenderness of bone moving beneath his fingers. She smelled of the sea and of salt and of home. He needed that more than he needed oxygen, more than life itself. His cheek felt wet, her tears mixing with the rain as the light grey eyes filled and overflowed. She looked frightened. Only then did he understand that maybe the last four years had been hard for her too. He kissed the tears from her cheek, tasting salt on his tongue.

Then, pulling at her lips with his, his hands moved down, feeling the thinness of her spine, the curve of her hips, fingers walking their way down, then up . . .

She did not stop him.

He realized that she was wearing no underwear; in fact, she was wearing hardly any clothes at all. His breathing quickened. She paused, pulling away from him, and then tugged at the belt round his waist, trying to undo the buckle with fingers made clumsy by passion. His heart was light; she wanted him as much as he wanted her. He leaned against her, hard, pinning her to the wall as he undid the belt himself, his hands moving hurriedly, not wanting to lose any contact with her body. Then he took her hands in his, opening them out to her sides. He stood, looking at her spread against the wall as if crucified, strands of blonde hair falling over her face, grey eyes staring directly back at his, wide and vulnerable. An erotic Madonna. She pulled him back into her, and he slipped his hands under her bottom, lifting her from the ground. She gasped, whether with pain or pleasure he couldn't tell and didn't care. He felt her small teeth bite into his neck, her nails grip on to his arm. Four years, a long time to be away from this. He breathed her in, the smell of her, gasping, tasting her, biting her. Then it was over, too quickly. Gently he lowered her back to the ground, catching his breath, and simply held her as though he would never be able to let her go. He felt her body stiffen against his. Her hand tapped on his shoulder, a warning.

He nuzzled closer to her neck, but she slid out from underneath him and leaned out to look down the alleyway. In one movement she had picked up the wig and coiled her hair underneath it, pulled the cloak back around her and stepped into her shoes. Then she was gone down the lane, careering straight into two policemen.

She turned on them, her face dark and angry, chin up and petulant before storming off, soaking her shoes in the puddles.

Sean looked after her, her slight figure receding, walking away. The two beat constables looked at Sean, who had just about got his belt buckled, and smiled at each other.

The digital clock flicked over to three fifteen. McAlpine sat up, and heaved his feet out from under the duvet and on to the floor. His head was pounding. He picked up the bill for the room service, a bottle of Pinot Grigio, smoked-salmon salad, a bottle of Taittinger. All at Turnberry prices. Natalie had insisted on it, saying she was used to five-star hotels now. Now.

Now what?

Now she thought she had him in her little claws.

Beside the clock was his mobile, the display blank. He

picked it up and stared at it, as if the act of looking would bring it to life. She had turned it off. The stupid cow had turned his mobile off! He began to hit it slowly off his forehead.

He had to distance himself from this, from her.

He stilled as she moved, turning over under the duvet, exposing a bare brown satin shoulder. She was lovely but empty, and he had had enough of her. She was asleep and quiet, though she wouldn't stay that way. Like the rest, she was young and blonde and beautiful. The artistry of the surgeon had to be admired. Pity he had neglected to sew up her mouth.

He looked at the folded curves of the sheet shaping into her body, the contour of her thighs, her stomach rising and falling. He put his hand on the fine cotton that covered her feet, feeling their warmth, a gentle pulse. Anna, deathly quiet for weeks on end. A yes. A no. But a thousand times more interesting. He sat down on the side of the bed, wishing it was another year, another time, and that he was sitting on another bed with another blonde. One so quiet and so perfect. This one so manufactured and so cheap. He put the mobile down, and started to pull notes from the roll of twenties in his wallet. As he closed it, the light of the digital clock caught the picture of Helena tucked into the billfold.

'It's all shite,' he said loudly, his tongue revelling in the noise. 'All shite.' His mind drifted back to the Crucifixion Killer. What had Batten called him – Christopher Robin? McAlpine wondered if this was what went through his mind. Women. Anger. Hatred.

Power?

He held his hand out over the sleeping woman. He could crush her throat with the palm of one hand, right now.

Tempting.

Drunkenly he rose to his feet, got more or less dressed in the dark and swung his jacket over his shoulders, not trusting himself to get his arms down the correct sleeves. He looked away.

Anna? What would she have looked like now, if she had survived? *Anna.*

He had to distance himself from this.

He was going to get a drink.

Helena had had another restless night. Her body was tired, she was emotional, and she ached for sleep. She had tried a glass of wine and a warm bath with lavender oil, before resorting to Zimovane. Just as the sleeping tablet was taking effect, the storm hit Glasgow and she was wide awake again. She had no idea where Alan was; his mobile was turned off, and the station didn't know his whereabouts. She had even phoned Colin, who had been polite but vague. She rolled over, pulling the pillow beneath her head. Then over her head as the wind gusted again. She gave up on sleep and got up. Pulling on a pair of jeans and an old black jumper of Alan's, she padded down to the kitchen, switched on the kettle and walked away, forgetting all about it. She poured a glass of red wine and picked up a box of Carswells' truffles somebody had brought for the dinner party. She didn't like them, but she took one out anyway, sitting on the edge of the sofa and nibbling at the chocolate. She wondered where all the rain was coming from. She wondered about the exhibition. She wondered about the small treacherous lump that had no right to be there.

She picked up the bottle of wine and, tucking the box of chocolates under her arm, walked towards the window. The traffic was quiet on the Great Western Road, the occasional orange tail light glittering in the rain. No cars pulled into the terrace, and she leaned against the wooden shutters, annoyed at herself for looking and hoping. There was no point; he wasn't coming home. Suddenly lightning silhouetted the street, pointing out to her that her car was missing.

The commissionaire of the Turnberry Hotel held the door open for him, offering the cover of an umbrella for the short walk to the car park. McAlpine refused politely.

'If you're heading up the coast road, sir, just take care. It's a bad road, and there's a fair blow on.'

McAlpine thanked him.

In the car park, away from the shelter of the building, the wind had whipped itself up to gale force, the rain slashing across the golf links and up on to the car park in horizontal sheets. Alan McAlpine held his jacket over his head as he ran to the BMW.

'Sober, sober, sober,' he said to himself, thanking God it was Helena's car and had remote locking; it could almost drive itself. He concentrated hard to press the key fob and then to aim it at the car, his thumb missing the black button. It took ages to bleep.

McAlpine tumbled in, pulling his wet hair back from his face. He felt a little better, refreshed after a cold power shower of Scottish rain. He adjusted and readjusted the mirror to look behind him, taking care to fire the engine and select reverse, and drove out of the space in what he hoped was a sedate manner, not the over-cautious of the mildly drunk or the slapdash of the too-pissed-to-care. He turned north and drove into the darkness, heading towards the coast road, towards the city, as the clock clicked round to 3.30 a.m.

'No, we can't!'

'Yes, we can. Come on, it'll be great.'

'No way!' But the girl was laughing and letting him pull her along, her head back, face up to the sky, letting the rain drizzle down her face, dragging her make-up with it.

The lightning flashed again, and momentarily the world turned black and white, showing up her white skin and panda eyes.

'You look like Alice Cooper.' He laughed, one hand dragging her, the other round her shoulders, guiding her along. She held her skirt down against the wind, her knees knocking together as her high heels clipped unsteadily along the cobbles of Whistler's Lane.

'Here! In here.' They ran up the lane, the girl stumbling as her stiletto caught on a cobble, and turned into the yard of the supermarket, where they were sheltered from the worst of the wind. The rancid smell of decay, rotting veg and sour milk, hung heavy in the air, making their stomachs churn. But beyond that lay a stack of pallets under a tent of tarpaulin.

'We can have this place to ourselves,' he said, pulling out a pile of flattened cardboard boxes waiting to be bound.

She was holding her nose. 'I can't believe we're doing this; that smell is disgusting.' She wound her hair over her face, then round her neck in mock strangulation, her coat hanging open, the way she pulled her arms pushing her breasts together. She couldn't stop laughing.

The boy advanced, his hands wriggling. 'And where are the *r-r-rats*, my dear?' he questioned her in his best Vincent Price accent.

She shrieked, playing her part. 'My dear sir! What would you want with a maiden like me?' She held the back of her hand to her forehead, her chest heaving in the best Hammer House of Horror tradition.

The wriggling fingers came closer. 'Rats, my dear! Rats,

and more rats! Don't worry, I'm here to protect you,' said Peter Cushing, putting his arm round her. She nestled into his neck, eyes wide, as with his other hand he pulled the tarpaulin free. 'Look out for the rats! They could come creeping up your leg and under your –'

She started screaming. A moment later, so did he.

Rain, rain and more rain, it was bloody everywhere. He could hardly see the convolutions of the road in front of him. The rear end of Helena's Five Series seemed to have problems gripping the road, and McAlpine sobered up more quickly than he would have thought physiologically possible. Then he realized it was the strength of the wind catching the car side-on as the isolated road was exposed on the contour line of the hill. He drove on past the dunes, past the links at Turnberry. The Golf Club and the hotel had disappeared behind him into the whirl of wind and rain. Pushing his foot down, he turned up the road to Culzean, Croy, the Electric Brae and then to the Heads of Ayr. He concentrated, fighting sleep, fighting drink, fighting nausea, as the car jerked sideways with every gust of the gale. The windscreen wipers danced madly, barely clearing the water from the glass. He drove, fingers gripped on the leather wheel, eyes straining as the road, the clouds and the sea merged, water coming at the car like some breathless animal desperate to get in.

It was as dark as he had ever seen. He leaned forward, wiping the inside of the windscreen with the back of his hand. The car's back end shuddered violently, and he pulled on the steering wheel, the road suddenly twisting and rising. The battering of water on the windscreen came and went as the car turned headlong into the wind, rain coming at the glass by the bucketful.

He was fully awake now, and he could not ignore the bile

rising in his throat. Bright diamonds of water danced in front of him: now you see them, now you don't. Desperate for fresh air, he reached for the button to open his window, but his fingers couldn't find it. He glanced at the dashboard display; the speedo was reading seventy. He flicked the switch for the passenger window, and it hummed open two inches, then jammed. The CD player burst into life; he'd pressed the wrong button, and Orff filled the car. *Carmina Burana*, Helena's favourite. Soundtrack from *The Omen* to him. He smiled to himself, wiped the inside of the wind-screen again, making the shape of a smile with the back of his hand, and started to laugh. He pushed the car up to the next corner, braking at the last minute, the sliding rear end gaining momentum as it rounded the bend. He dotted a couple of eyes over the smile in the condensation. The car over-straightened, and the engine shrieked as it aquaplaned, fighting the weight as the back of the car started to slide. He over-corrected, the front whiplashed round quicker than his reflex response, and the car began to spin like a waltzer into the darkness.

Helena pulled a pristine sheet of Ingres 47 from its pad and pinned it on to her board, smoothing her fingers over it, comforted by its familiar grain. She watched the chiaro-scuro shadows of her hand as the lightning flashed through the Velux. Two bright flashes – she blinked – then it passed. Only the stair light remained, highlighting the shadows in the room. If she hadn't lived here all her life and known the house to be a kind one, she would have shivered at her ghostly thoughts. The power of the storm invigorated her, just as it had invigorated Mary Shelley, whose Dr Frankenstein had created his monster on such a night as this. She must create too, from the heart, something ethereal, instinctual, primal. Something to suit the moment. She lifted the bottle again, took a good mouthful, swilling the Merlot round her mouth. She watched for the lightning, counting *a hundred and one, a hundred and two*, until the thunder, and then she swallowed. It was getting closer. She toyed with the idea of opening the windows and letting the rain in, but she wasn't as drunk as that.

She put the bottle down and picked up her small box of pastels, all her favourites; some were beyond use, no pigment left under the paper, but she could never bring herself to dump them. She began to draw nothing in particular, just instinct, chalk against paper, and felt the tension flow from her. She was drawing a man, broad shouldered, slim hipped, walking in fine rain along a path. The path wound its way among trees. She added a jacket and put his hood up, clouding his face in darkness. She took the side of her thumb and narrowed his shoulders. She knew this man. And these were not small trees. She crossed their trunks, not trees at all. She knew this scene . . . she was painting from memory . . . there was a flash of lightning, the room brightened, and for a moment she thought the house was screaming, then realized it was the phone. She swore, wiping her mouth with the back of her hand. Her watch said four o'clock. No matter *what* Alan had to say, she wasn't having any of it.

'Yip,' she said curtly.

'Hello? Helena?' The voice was uncertain.

She shook her head clear of Merlot. 'Is that you, Colin?' 'Yes.'

'You sound as though you're out on the high seas?'

'Is the Boss there?' Anderson was quietly insistent.

'No,' she answered curtly. 'He isn't.' She put the phone down. 'Bastard!'

She looked at the picture: a lonely man, not much more

than a boy, walking up a path surrounded by graves, a stick in his hand. No, she could see it clearly now, not a stick, a single rose. A single red rose, for . . .

She leaned against the wall, staring at the picture, tormenting herself, thinking how small he seemed, how vulnerable.

That was one memory too much for her. 'You've never really been mine, have you, Alan?' she said to herself, and sleepily slid down the wall, still looking at the pastel, her own creation – her own monster – mocking her. 'Never been mine.'

McAlpine felt a knife being slowly inserted into his eyeball and twisted to the left. Then to the right. It settled into a rhythm, pain skewering this way and that. Pain was the only thing he was aware of.

He breathed out, recognizing the smell of vomit. He tried to open his eyes, but they were locked tight with a crust that he didn't have the energy to break. He tried to move his head, but the pain suddenly intensified. He thought better of it and kept still.

As consciousness slipped away, he realized his head was resting on the steering wheel, his face being rearranged by the pressure of leather on broken bone. He could taste the blood in his mouth. There was a tooth lying on his tongue.

He tried to spit it out.

He passed out instead.

McAlpine woke again. This time he was aware of urgency; this time he could smell vomit and blood, and whisky, and something heady. Perfume? Petrol. He heard a gentle *drip* – then another – getting steadily louder. He felt himself slide back into unconsciousness, trying to ignore that little voice urging him to stay awake.

The smell of petrol feasted on the lining of his nostrils. The stench was getting stronger, the drips steadily bigger and louder. The petrol was meandering around the engine of the car, gathering, forming a puddle, which formed a stream that ran along the outer metalwork of the car body. It snaked towards the live wire of the alarm that sparked and twitched against its metal casing.

The effort of thinking hurt. He was dreaming. Of Anna. Of petrol. Anna and then . . . petrol.

The switch in his brain flicked to survival. His eyes opened.

He was awake, in a strange half-life of non-sleep, but his body was refusing to cooperate. He was thinking through mist. It was every nightmare he had ever had: he was falling and could not stop, he could not run, he could not escape to where Anna was calling, and he could not answer. He couldn't get out. And all the time, he knew, the smell of petrol was getting stronger. His eyes failed to focus on a dark shadow that passed over the front windscreen. He thought he heard somebody trying to open the door, thought he heard somebody climb on to the bonnet. He felt the car shudder. Was that the wind? Or salvation?

The smell of petrol was burning his throat. He tried to reach the central locking switch, but his arm would not move. He felt bone grind on bloody bone, and was sick.

He didn't hear the knuckles knocking hard on the window, nor the stick hitting against the door. He woke with a start as something hooded and dark landed monkey-like on the bonnet of the car, lifted winged arms and brought a stick down hard on the windscreen, and he closed his eyes as glass and water rained down on him, again and again. As the creature stretched and turned, as it raised the stick yet again, the hood fell from her head and her face was lit by a sliver of lightning.

It nearly stopped his heart.

Salvation.

Arlene lay, as both the others had, flat on her back, her green boots crossed at the ankles, arms outstretched, palms up, as if crucified. Her head was turned to one side, her face looking out of the gap in the wall of the tent as if she was checking the progress of the storm. The police had erected a polythene cover over her to protect the scene till the SOCOs had finished. Her face lay in the path of the rain that entered the gap, peppering her skin and darkening her peroxide hair.

Outside the tent, Anderson's jacket was getting wet; rain trickled under his collar and down his back, but his head was dry, stuck as it was through the gap, viewing the scene but ignoring the lump of intestine that glimmered on the cardboard beside the body.

Mulholland had been the first to arrive, summoned by text from the nearby casino. He was kneeling beside her, scribbling in his notebook. He was wearing polythene slips over his immaculate shoes, his knees protected by another piece of plastic. Every time he moved, he squeaked.

He reached over to turn her head towards him and said queasily, 'There's nothing of her face left round this side. Looks like someone kicked her. Hard.'

'That's a change from the norm,' said Anderson, too tired to think about its significance.

'Any luck finding the Boss?' Mulholland asked without looking up.

'No, not yet.'

'Probably lying pissed as a fart somewhere.'

Anderson didn't dignify that with an answer.

'She was a prostitute. Known as Arlene, among other names. Well known in the area,' said Mulholland, still on his knees, peering at her neck. 'Do you think her neck's broken? Her head wobbles about a lot.' He gently pushed her chin with his gloved fingertip. Arlene looked upward momentarily, then turned back to the gap in the tent.

'Don't do that, Vik. Was she a big-time pro?'

'More hooking than a Loch Fyne fisherman, according to Littlewood. She used to be a stripper in her young days, before she had her kid. She did things with a banana that would make your mouth water. Or your eyes, depending on your point of view.'

'If Littlewood knows her from vice, she'll be on file. Cavalry's arrived.' Anderson stood to one side to let O'Hare in.

'Either this is too early in the morning or I'm getting old.' O'Hare shook the rain from his hair, careful not to let it spatter the body at his feet. 'Right, so what's pulled me from my bed at this ungodly hour ... again?' he asked, unnecessarily.

Anderson answered. 'Female, late twenties. Mulholland thinks she might have a broken neck.'

O'Hare looked at the bloodied viscera, congealing slowly. 'I would guess at a more obvious cause of death.'

'He meant broken neck ... as well as a change from ... I feel sick,' said Anderson.

'I know what you mean, DI Anderson. Go out and take a breath of fresh air.'

'That skip stinks, the air's better in here.'

Costello stuck her head into the tent. 'Yeah, it's Vik Mulholland's aftershave. Kills 99 per cent of all known germs and confuses the rest. Hello, Doc. Col? The two that found the body, they're just a couple of kids. He's as white as a sheet; she's in the back of the panda crying her eyes out. They came up here for a quick shag.'

'Beside the rubbish skip?' said O'Hare. 'And they say romance is dead.'

'Can't snog in Ashton Lane now with the smoking ban, it's too busy. So they came up here to Whistler's Lane instead. Two policemen walked past. That's four people in the locus, so what do you want me to do?'

'What time was this?' asked Anderson, holding his stomach.

'Must have been only minutes before the body was discovered. Once all this is over, I'll organize a run-through for better timing,' said Costello. 'Do you have a time of death?'

Four sets of eyes looked at O'Hare. He shrugged. 'I'll take her temp now.'

'Check out the policemen. They must be on the current night shift.'

'I've been in touch with the station. Just waiting for them to phone back.' Typical Costello, she had already done it. 'Is the Boss here?' she asked.

'Not yet,' replied Anderson. 'What about the boy? Did he see anything?'

'The Goth? No, he was thinking with his dick. OK for Wyngate to take them back to the station? And can they have Mulholland to help do the taxi queue before it dwindles away? I really want to see him get that suit wet.'

Anderson nodded. She would have done it anyway. He heard Costello's ringtone shrill from her pocket. She withdrew from the tent to answer it.

The pattering of rain on the tight plastic roof was quieter now as the storm passed, and they could hear Costello's voice and others talking outside. The tent started pulsing with yellow light, heralding the arrival of another panda.

O'Hare went through the motions of looking for a pulse, making a cursory examination of the body. He touched the forehead with the fingertips of his gloved hands, flicked a strand of blonde hair from lifeless eyes.

Costello's head came back through the gap. 'A witness on the street saw her talking to someone. "A man in an anorak with a hat on" was as good as we got description-wise. Didn't hear the conversation, but thought the guy was Irish.'

'Good,' said Anderson, surprised at the relief he felt. Something at last. 'Take Mulholland, and keep everybody at the station until they sober up; make sure there've plenty of hot coffee and towels. Before you go, Costello, get that skip picked up, lock, stock and barrel, get it taken to Stewart Street or Pitt Street, or let the Keystone Kops have a look. All you want is a garage out of the rain. Let the uniforms loose on it, they'll enjoy it.'

'I'll pull that tarp over it for now; stop any more rain getting in. Vik can climb in and give me a hand.' Costello left, and Mulholland followed her reluctantly, cursing her behind her back.

The pathologist took a dictating machine from his pocket. For a long time he said nothing, reading Arlene before speaking.

'Note the position of the limbs, the burn marks around the mouth.' He pointed to what was left of her face with his finger. 'All the actual wounds are made with a weapon similar, if not identical, to that used on Fulton and Traill, but inflicted with greater ferocity.' He prodded the bloodied mass of her lower abdomen with a rubberized finger. 'Jesus!' he swore quietly, as the intestine slipped with a syrupy sound on to the gravel with her stomach, leaving a smear of mucus and blood. 'He's gone right through the mesentery. Whether he meant to is another thing.'

Anderson felt the acid rise in his throat and just made it out of the tent before the contents of his own stomach contaminated the scene.

'Look,' O'Hare went on, 'she was killed an hour or so before she was found. Somebody has been walking about covered in blood; there's no way he walked away from this one with his hands clean. And get that profiler down here, show him what he's missing. Are you OK, Colin?'

'Not really.' Anderson put the back of his hand to his mouth, feeling his eyes water.

O'Hare pointed at the injuries on the face again, taking a paper rule from the photographer and holding it against the marks as the camera flashed and buzzed.

'Mulholland thought he'd kicked her in the face,' Anderson contributed.

'I don't think so,' said O'Hare. 'I'd say he jumped on it.'

Alan McAlpine had been sick again. Twice. The first time he barely made it to the toilet before throwing up a mixture of blood and bile into the pristine white bowl. He sat on the side of the bath, resting his arms on the sink, building up his strength before he looked in the mirror. It was a woman's bathroom; he could tell that from the lotions and potions on the window ledge. The plastic basin for the false teeth made him retch again. He looked in the small round mirror. He had a bad cut down the side of his face, and a bruise was forming on the left side of his lower jaw. His tongue delicately probed the gaping hole as his brain suddenly registered that a tooth was missing, and the side of his face began to throb. He soaked a small white towel with cold water and pressed it to his cheekbone. It seemed to help.

He made his way back to the bedroom, carefully stepping across a Bri-Nylon rug, and lay down on the single divan, the green candlewick rumpled under him. He tried to ignore the pain in his face, the pain in his shoulder, the sensation that his mouth was filling slowly with blood. The taste of fresh blood was everywhere. He lowered his head gently on to a single pillow, turning on his side to relieve the pressure on his shoulder. The small gold face of his Cartier watch smiled back at him – ten to nine.

He could smell bluebells, could smell the sea, again felt hands reaching to him, slender fingers holding him back as they freed his arm, loving fingers picking the glass from his face . . .

She had been there, slight and blonde and winged like an angel. She had come to save him. Of course.

When he woke again, somebody had been in to see him. His makeshift compress had been folded and put on a radiator, and the curtains and window had been opened, dissipating the smell. He got up, moving carefully as his shoulder crunched and grated. If he moved it too far from his side, it hurt – it hurt like hell even when he took a deep breath.

He painfully straightened the bedspread, put on his shoes and pulled his jacket from the peg on the back of the door. He reached into the inner pocket for his mobile, but it was empty. His brain clouded over again. Had he dropped it at the hotel? No, he had put it in his pocket. The stupid cow had turned it off, but he had put it in his jacket. Hadn't he? He couldn't remember. But he remembered the flames in the car, the *whoosh* as it ignited, the sudden flash of flame as he walked away, supported by two . . . two arms, one either side. Two people? He tried to slip his arm into the sleeve – *Christ!* – and waited for the gritty agony to pass.

He folded the jacket, swinging it over his shoulder, trying to appear casual as he went down the stairs. Careful not to make any creaking noises, he moved slowly when placing his weight on the next step of the narrow winding staircase.

She was in the kitchen, a spry old woman, thin, her grey short-cropped hair held back with an uncompromising kirby grip. She stood at the sink, tartan slippers on grey lino, cutting vegetables with deft, deadly movements, her hands guiding the knife as it cut with force and precision. McAlpine found he could not take his eyes off the blade as it rose and fell. *Efficient and confident use of a knife.*

'Hello,' he said, trying to sound as casual as he could.

'Do you want the phone?' she asked, gathering the vegetables together with thin blue fingers and putting them in a colander. She seemed to have chopped a lot of vegetables for a single person, but then she looked like the sort of person who would eat a lot of vegetables and keep a diary of associated bowel movements.

'Yes,' he said, looking around the clinically white kitchen, so like Elizabeth Jane's. 'That would be great.' He looked at the draining board – two cups, one teaspoon.

'In the front room.' She gestured to the hall, the front of the house. She turned, wiping her hands on her pinny. She looked old but up close her skin was smooth except for a huge mole on her top lip. Behind steel-rimmed glasses, the eyes were clear and intelligent.

He walked through to the front room, her slippers scuffing the carpet behind him. All the windows were open at the front of the cottage, the glass running the full length of the room for a magnificent view of the sea. On a clear day like this you could see Ireland lying low on the horizon,

Arran snaking down from Goat Fell. Cotton wool clouds in the sky. The brightness of the sun shimmering in through the window made his headache a hundred times worse.

The woman pointed a bony finger at an old cream dial phone on a wooden sideboard. She pursed her lips in disapproval as she passed him on her way out of the door.

He asked, 'My car?'

'Well, it went up in flames. Nobody noticed, they never do. It'll be exactly where you left it. You'll find it up there in the top field. It's a bad bend. He'll be wanting you to shift it.'

McAlpine didn't bother to inquire who 'he' was.

She left the room, and he dialled the station, requesting to be connected to the murder room, asking for Costello, Anderson, the only two he could trust to keep their mouths shut.

Somebody picked up the phone but was too busy continuing another conversation. He could hear papers being shuffled about, distant voices, then one close by saying, 'Hello. Can I help you?'

He asked again for Anderson. The voice at the other end shouted, 'Has anybody seen Anderson?' Then, 'No, sorry, he's out.'

'Can you give me his mobile?'

'We don't give out . . .'

'For fuck's sake, it's DCI McAlpine! Give me his bloody number!'

The voice at the other end hesitated. 'Can you identify yourself, sir?'

'Yes, now give me his fucking phone number!'

'Aye, OK.'

Was that all it took?

He dialled the number, moving the phone to his left hand,

the shoulder feeling better for being up and about. He ran his fingers through his hair as he waited, wincing at the reek of vomit, petrol and unwashed scalp.

As the number clicked to be connected, he moved to one side to get out of the glare of the sun and looked round the room. On the floor beside an old sideboard, the sort that usually housed an old record player, was a pile of LPs: Frank Sinatra, Dean Martin, Hits for the Swinging Sixties. She looked sixty at least, but he bet it was a long time since she'd swung. He smiled, and his mouth cracked.

A package was leaning against the wall next to the tiled fireplace. Something about it struck him as odd. It had been torn at the top to reveal bare strips of carved wood obviously forming part of a frame. There were a few of them. She must be an artist, this old biddy. He recognized them easily enough; Christ knew, Helena's studio was littered with them. But they were incongruous here. It took a while for the reason why to penetrate. No smell of turps, no paintings drying, no paper stretching, no canvases being sized, no mess. No pictures on the wall. He could read the plain white label on the front, if he angled his head enough and held on to his neck. *Nan McDougall, Shiprids Cottage, Shiprids Lane, Heads of Ayr Road, Croy, Ayrshire.* He scratched at the cut above his eye, committing the name and address to memory.

'Get a bloody move on,' he muttered down the phone.

The phone was answered; there was a clattering of cups. 'Hello?'

'Hello, Colin, McAlpine here. Do me a favour?'

'*Where the fuck have you been?*'

McAlpine went back into the kitchen, then remembered his manners. He searched through his pockets for a pound coin. She was passing the colander under the running tap.

'Did you get a lift?' she asked without turning round.

'Yeah, fine, thanks.'

'Your wallet is on the table in the hall.'

'Oh . . . right.' He hadn't even registered it was missing. She wiped the spots of water off the sink with a folded J-cloth. The two cups had been put away. She still had not looked up.

'Thank you for all . . . well, everything.'

'No problem. You were not the first, you won't be the last. I've told the council.' She said this as though she had spoken to God.

'How did you get me from the car?'

'You could walk. If you can walk and you call an ambulance, they expect you to pay a fortune. A good sleep, and you'd be fine. Like I said, you weren't the first.'

'Well, thanks anyway. There was someone else there, though? Helping you? I would like to thank them.' He scratched his head, searching for a vision of the monkey-like creature on the bonnet, breaking the glass. He had a sense of someone younger, smaller, agile, angelic.

For the first time, she looked at him, her eyes reptilian behind the glass. He sensed the lie before it left her lips. 'No. There was only me.'

Arlene lay on the stainless-steel table, her head on a pillow carved from marble, waiting for her meeting with Chief Forensic Pathologist John O'Hare and his assistant Dr Jessica Gibson. She looked cold. There was a constant draught from the air filter, but the air stayed cold, chilled to the point of biting. A sudden rush of water from the sluice interrupted the silence.

The dead do not always look at peace. Arlene's blonde hair framed her face unflatteringly, dark roots showing through in a thin scar along the parting. The cheekbone and jaw sat an inch lower on the left side than the right. Her lips had been cut, forcing her mouth to a charmless grimace that looked like a remnant of life. Death did not suit her; like a flower that needs the sun to show its colour, she was ugly now.

Costello looked exhausted, her eyes shadowed in grey. Dressed in scrubs, she was walking up and down the far side of the table, every so often inclining her head, bobbing as if inspecting a dodgy second-hand car, concentrating hard on the wounds. Arlene did not seem to care, her sightless eyes staring at the ceiling from her wrecked face.

She was still wearing the black plastic waistcoat and red leather miniskirt she had worn at the disco. The obscene stain covering her abdomen and the top of her thighs had darkened to the colour of junkyard rust. The jelly mess of her intestines had also dried out, wrapped now like prime butcher's tripe. Chunky white legs stuck out from the skirt, one foot covered by a green plastic ankle boot with a four-inch stiletto, the other bare and bloodstained, red varnish scraped from her toes, one nail missing. Both feet, both hands, were wrapped in polythene bags that Costello pulled slightly, flattening out the surface for a better view. She was peering at the label, then at the nail-less toe.

'Formal ID yet?' Mulholland asked, resting on a stool at the wall, crossing one tailored trouser leg over the other.

Costello nodded. 'Her friend Tracey. We'll have to press harder, get another word with her. She's a right −' She stopped abruptly as Davidson, the younger assistant, came in. He nodded, his gloved hand moving quickly over the paper on the clipboard. 'Arlene Haggerty?' He flicked the tag on the toe.

'DI Mulholland, DS Costello,' Costello said formally,

feeling that the presence of the dead merited some small show of manners.

'Cheers! Nice when they make the first incision for us.'

'Spare us,' she muttered.

Costello walked slowly towards Mulholland on the pretext of moving around to keep her feet warm.

Davidson misinterpreted it. 'Squeamish?'

'No, not at all. It's never the dead that hurt you; those with a pulse are always that tad trickier.' She looked directly at Davidson, who pulled a face and left, the door closing behind him, with a hiss of something that Costello presumed was negative air pressure.

Mulholland shuddered. They could all be being microscopically murdered while standing here, some bullet-shaped virus making its way into their lungs to infect them with a deadly, as yet unknown disease. He coughed, holding his handkerchief to his nose, using the linen as a filter against whatever might be flying around, and looked longingly at the door.

On cue, it swung open and O'Hare came in. 'Just have to wait for Dr Gibson. Any nearer to a result?' He leaned on the slab, scrupulously looking Arlene up and down.

'We're waiting to see what Dr Batten says.'

'So, no nearer.'

Costello shook her head.

'I would rather not have yet another victim on my slab,' said O'Hare.

'I would rather like to get something nice, something solid, forensic,' countered Mulholland, keeping his distance.

The door hissed open. 'Good morning, Dr O'Hare.'

'Good morning, Dr Gibson. Do you mind if we get started?'

'No, please, carry on.' Jessica Gibson leaned against the

wall. Her hair was sticking out at odd angles, waiting to be introduced to a brush. 'The law only states I have to be here.'

'Here and involved,' corrected O'Hare.

'Here,' muttered Gibson. 'I don't have to get involved. I only have to agree to everything you say. Hello, DS Costello, how's tricks?'

Costello shrugged at the body on the slab. 'Just another day at the office.'

O'Hare walked round the table, pulling on a pair of gloves. He pushed the overhead microphone to one side, leaning over the body on outstretched arms, his head low over the table. 'Well, the same MO as before, but as you can see this one is much more violent.' He pointed to her face. 'The tell-tale burning of the chloroform round her upper lip. This piece of flesh here used to be the lower part of her nose. We may be able to get a shoe print from the face. There are some slight marks here, on the upper arms, which would have developed to contusions if she had lived long enough.'

'Bruises, then,' translated Costello, who was leaning in, her blonde hair now covered by a blue cap.

Gibson looked at the upper part of the arm as O'Hare said, 'Suggestive of being held around the upper arm, squeezed bodily. I think that she was gripped forcibly by the arms, which would suggest the assailant came up behind her and bear-hugged her to give her the chloroform. That gives us some indication of his height. She's a wee bit overweight round the hips and thighs, but she's slim across the rib cage, so the knife might have hit bone.'

'Could you ID the weapon from that?' asked Costello.

'Maybe.' O'Hare was on a roll. 'It's the first indication of the depth of cut this knife is capable of making, which reduces the search a bit. We'll excise the tissue at the edge of the wound; it might tell us if the blade was serrated. There are also signs of her being dragged, so it's probable she was knocked out, stabbed, then died where you found her. Her heart was pumping long enough for the cuts and grazes on her toes to bleed. But examination of the site shows most blood at the start of the drag, not where it stopped.'

'Meaning?'

'I'll demonstrate. What height are you, Costello?' O'Hare crooked his finger at her.

'Five five.'

'Stand here.' O'Hare stood behind her, encircled her in his arms, lifting his left hand to her mouth. 'Collapse forward now.'

As she did, she slumped on to his right fist, which pressed into her stomach.

'And if I had a knife in my right hand – the knife going up, your body weight going down' – he pointed at Arlene, as Costello straightened – 'that's what you'd get.' He stepped back to the table. 'What would be really helpful is something that would tell us a bit more about the knife. Jess, could you shine that in here?'

Gibson angled the overhead light, and a bright fluorescent glow illuminated the intestine, every fold and convolution of the mesentery. 'Fingers crossed,' Mulholland said, looking away. 'Sooner or later our luck must turn.'

'Well, going through a haystack is easier when you know you're looking for a needle. I'll be ready as soon as I can.'

The two detectives walked towards the door, Costello subconsciously rubbing her stomach, as O'Hare started his dictation. 'The body is that of a young white female . . .'

*

Helena peered into the back of the larder fridge, looking for a quick bite of lunch before she headed off to work. She rummaged among the remnants in the salad tray, bits of lettuce tinged brown, celery that had given up its fight for life.

She stood up, fingers drumming along the door of the fridge. There was nothing here worth eating; Alan had scoffed the lot in one of his midnight feasts. A half-bottle of whisky, two fried eggs, square sausage and potato scones. No wonder he found it difficult to sleep. She pulled down the notepad, making another list. She would soon need an index for her lists.

She heard the front door open and shut, very quietly. She braced herself. It took a while for her husband to get from the front door to the kitchen. Helena was staring at the carpet, her arms folded, ready. She could imagine him checking the study, the sitting room, pausing at the bottom of the stairs to listen. His next stop would be the kitchen.

His face was bloodied and bruised, but his expression was impassive as he appeared at the door, looking at her as if she had no right to be there. He bit the side of his lip, holding his hand to the side of his face. She knew he was trying to draw attention to the pain he was in, non-verbally changing the subject before she had started.

It wasn't going to work.

'You look as though you've been in a fight.' She refolded her arms. 'You're about to walk into another.'

He tried for levity. 'At your worst, when you had PMT and had stopped smoking, you weren't as dangerous as a BMW with a mind of its own.'

'Drove itself, did it?' she snorted. 'Don't blame the monkey, blame the organ grinder.' Helena looked him up and down, then the smell hit her. He had got drunk and had been lying all night in a gutter somewhere, throwing up on himself. She saw his bloodshot eye and the deep angry cut on the side of his face, a bloodied gap in his lower jaw. She resisted the thought that he might be badly hurt.

'Do you mind having a shower? You smell,' she said calmly, keeping her eyes from his face.

'I'm fine, thank you for asking.'

'I didn't.'

'I don't think I have any broken bones, but your car is lying in a field somewhere. I managed to get out before it exploded into a million pieces.' He went to lean on the worktop, but the pain ricocheted through him and he shot back upright. 'I've dislocated my shoulder, though,' he said.

'Does it hurt?'

'Yes, I'm in agony.'

'Good. We all have our crosses to bear. You chose yours; some of us aren't so lucky.' She raised her chin, a sign that she was going on the attack. 'You were the one out shagging some brainless bimbo. In the throes of passion, you forgot your mobile. She phoned. She phoned *here!*' Helena walked past him. 'You owe me an explanation as well as a new car, but it can wait. I'm busy right now. And you stink.'

He heard the front door shut. He couldn't disagree with her.

Upstairs, he spent a good hour in the en suite bathroom, using all of Helena's bottles that smelled nice but not too girlie. He punished himself by dabbing Dettol into the cuts on his face, managing to get copious amounts of blood on the towel. He wanted Helena to see it, to know how much he was hurting. He wanted her to apologize. First.

In another suit and a fresh shirt, he began to feel a little more human. He dumped his soiled clothes in the laundry basket, took them out, carried them into the bedroom and dumped them in the middle of the floor, arranging them so the blood looked as bad as he could make it. Mick Batten would have a field day with them. *Why not go the whole hog?* He went downstairs and scribbled a note saying he was going to the Western to get his shoulder X-rayed. He folded up the piece of paper and walked into the sitting room, placing it on the coffee table.

He needed to get to the hospital, but from the look of the traffic the taxi would take ages. He turned to go, then noticed the photographs lying on the sideboard, still wrapped in their envelope of fragile tissue paper, still covered in dust from the loft. On top of them, folded and dog-eared, was Robbie's Queen's Commendation. He picked them up and held them to his nose, inhaling dust and old memories. He sensed that somebody else had gone through them. Frowning, he slipped them into the inside pocket of his jacket. He wouldn't let them out of his sight again.

Hurriedly, he left the house, walking out to Great Western Road to get a taxi to the hospital. He had an hour to get to A&E, jump the queue and get his shoulder sorted and the cut on his face cleaned properly. Then it would be back to the station, to face another atrocity with a head full of sepia-tinted memories, memories of two little boys and a snowman.

Helena got round the corner and was in the back of a taxi before she burst into tears, her hands to her mouth as she wept uncontrollably. What if he was really hurt? Why should she care? The stupid selfish bastard. So why was she crying? She didn't know. She blew her nose, wiped the tears from her eyes and stabbed out the station number on her mobile, trying to remember the last two digits. She didn't get the number right until the taxi was outside the gallery. She asked for DI Anderson to be paged and left a number for him to call. She then went into her office and slammed the door. Fiona looked up but said nothing and returned to cataloguing the Dutch imports.

Helena was mindlessly opening a pile of envelopes, ripping up the junk mail, placing the bills on a neat pile, when the phone went. 'Hello,' she said.

'Helena?'

'That you, Colin?' She found she couldn't speak any more, her throat closed with tears.

'Are you OK?'

'I'm sorry. I've just seen the state of him. It was a bit of a shock.'

'Yes, but are *you* OK? That couldn't have been easy for you.'

There was an unmistakable tenderness in his voice. *He knows.* His kindness provoked a tear that ran slowly down her cheek.

'Helena?'

'Sorry, Colin. I'm a bit shattered by all this, that's all.'

'Well, he's doing a good impression of the walking wounded. A uniform went and got him. Judging by the state of the Beamer, he was lucky to walk out of it.' A pause. 'I'm not making this any better, am I?' He sounded somewhere busy; she could imagine him talking, one hand to his ear.

'Had he been to hospital before he came home?'

'Don't think so. He was probably saving the whole horror of it for you. Do you know where he is now?'

'Probably still at home, licking his wounds,' said Helena.

'I have a profiler champing at the bit; no matter what

state Alan's in, we need him here. If the press get on to this . . .'

'Bloody-minded arsehole,' said Helena stabbing the next envelope with a pencil, shattering its point. 'My car's a write-off, I take it?'

'I guess so.'

Helena thought before asking the next question, never exactly sure how far Anderson's twenty-year loyalty to her husband could be stretched, or how far she wanted to stretch it. 'Where did it happen?'

Silence.

'I want to know where it happened.'

'On the coast road, near Culzean Castle.'

'The Heads of Ayr Road?'

'Yes. I presume he was avoiding the police. No sober normal person would choose to go home that way. It's an accident black spot at the best of times. And, before you ask, I don't know who he was with.' There was silence on the line.

'Don't worry, Colin. I don't want to know the gory details. He'll have his reasons.'

By six o'clock on Monday night the incident room was busier than Glasgow Central in the rush hour. Colin Anderson was holding his head in his hands, staring at the screen in front of him, about to read something for the third time and no nearer making any sense of it. He needed sleep.

Wyngate tapped him on the shoulder. 'It's the wife on the phone.'

'Whose wife?'

'Yours.'

Anderson shook his head, 'Tell her I'm not here.'

'Told her that at lunchtime.'

'Well, you haven't found me yet.'

Wyngate walked away, muttering platitudes down the phone. Anderson checked his mobile was off and began rattling his thumbs on the keyboard. There was no point in reading any of this; he needed action, and he could feel the adrenalin building up in his blood.

'I'm ready, DI Anderson,' said Batten into his ear. 'How's the Boss? He looks a little delicate.'

'Aquaplaning BMW. Best not to ask.' Anderson had to hand it to McAlpine. When the Boss had returned from Accident and Emergency with a strapped-up shoulder and a bumful of analgesic, he had strutted into the office looking fresh and calm. His face looked as though he had gone two rounds with Mike Tyson, but he was smiling, tentatively trying to hide the gap in his teeth.

Anderson knocked gently on the open door, wary of the Boss's mood. 'Alan?'

'Yip.'

'We're ready to roll.'

'I'll be out in a minute.'

Anderson looked at the piles of painkillers, coffee cups, reams of statements and papers covering the DCI's desk, and realized that in that small amount of time he had been absorbing every detail of Arlene, had tasted and digested every morsel of information. The distinct smell of alcohol, wound-cleaning or recreational, didn't escape him.

McAlpine gestured at the photographs in front of him. 'And all this was in Whistler's Lane?'

'Yeah, in behind Savaways to be precise; it was one of their skips.'

McAlpine sucked air in through pursed lips. It caught the bloodied well where the tooth had been, and he grimaced.

'Whistler's Lane, eh?' He looked out of the window. 'Well, we'd better get on with it.'

Forty-two officers were waiting for them to get started, ending phone calls, sending off emails, doing a final scroll-through of screens of information. McAlpine walked to the back of the room, speaking to nobody, holding the side of his bruised face with bruised fingers.

Anderson rapped the bottom of a coffee cup against the tabletop. 'Look, guys, it's a big meeting, it's a small room. The longer we're here, the more unpleasant it is going to get.' He rubbed his forehead with his open palm. 'You all know Mick here, he's been floating around this station like Casper the friendly profiler.' Batten raised a hand in greeting but remained seated, feet up on a computer terminal, letting the string of leather he had been playing with swing like a metronome. 'You all know what he does. Well, he has a few interesting things to say, so settle down and pay attention.'

Costello lifted her eyes to look at McAlpine, but his face remained impassive as though he wasn't listening as Anderson continued to talk. 'The two policemen who emerged from Whistler's Lane saw' – Anderson ticked them off on his fingers – 'two loved-up Goths – the young kids who found the body – and another couple. The girl was described as wearing a Victorian-type cloak, very pretty, with matt-black hair, very dense, probably dyed.' He pointed at the identikit faces. 'The male, early twenties, blond, thin, not tall, slight build.' The group murmured; there had been a few sightings. 'They looked as though they'd been having sex up the lane and had been disturbed. We need to track them down, and we need to talk to them. The blond guy had a mark on his T-shirt that might have been blood, and he was seen earlier by Michaels, one of the cops, appearing, quote, "as if he was looking for somebody". He was first seen on his own, then with her, and again after she left him. He was on his own, twice, and might have been sexually charged up. So we concentrate on him. What we don't know is how to tie that precisely with the time of Arlene's death, but it was within thirty minutes.

'They're doing an e-fit as we speak,' said Anderson, 'and Michaels has a good idea in his head as to what they both look like. The two kids who found the body are in the clear. So we're more interested in these two, the shaggers with no names,' said Anderson. 'From two points of view. Was the dark-haired one in the cloak a potential vic who got away? Or was she the bait? Women tend to trust other women . . . so pay attention to what Mick Batten has to say.'

'The guy that the witness said was Irish, the guy who was seen speaking to the victim minutes before she died . . .' Littlewood said. 'The witness can't describe a face, but he got the impression he was about forty, dressed soberly in an anorak, and with a hat on, so we don't think he'd been out clubbing. Something about the exchange made the witness think Arlene knew him. We haven't traced him yet either.' The temperature dropped in the room. 'Note that this kind of echoes what they said when Lynzi left the train station, the same vague pick-up. So we might have found his method, or, as I said, it might be an innocent witness we haven't traced yet. And, for the record, Arlene was not working. She was out, celebrating the fact that she had got the keys for her new flat. Council flat down in Norval Street. We'll get there when we have time. Costello is going to interview Arlene's friend Tracey, once she's sobered up.' Littlewood smirked at his own joke. 'Once *Tracey*'s sobered up, not Costello.' .

'If she wasn't turning tricks, then what was she doing up Whistler's Lane?' asked Mulholland.

'That's what we have to find out.'

'The same reason Elizabeth Jane let him into her flat, maybe?' Costello challenged, glaring at Littlewood. 'The same reason Lynzi went up Victoria Lane?'

'What was her religion? If she was a hooker?' Batten asked out of the blue. Everybody looked blank. Batten was unruffled. 'Any connection? With the others, I mean?'

'Not that we can find.'

'Good,' said Batten firmly.

The door opened, and Irvine came in with a sheaf of white paper. 'E-fits, as close as we can get them.' Hands were raised, the pictures passed round.

McAlpine had been sipping a cup of cold coffee with the good side of his mouth. He then straightened, staring at the pixellated image as it was pinned on the wall, catching teasing glimpses as other people's copies were passed around the room. There was the semblance there of someone he knew. He took a copy and looked at it closely.

It took him a while to recall it. 'I think I can ID him,' said McAlpine quietly. 'Sean James McTiernan.'

Silence dropped on the room like darkness.

'He's on my list,' Costello almost shouted with delight. 'He came out of Penningham ten days ago.' She flicked through her papers.

'Penningham?' asked Batten.

'Open prison, down the coast. He would be there because his last address was Ayr,' explained Costello.

'What did he go down for?'

'Culpable homicide. He killed a Glasgow hard man, Malkie Steele, four – five – years ago. Should have got a medal, not a life licence.'

'Stabbing?'

'Kicked him to death. He did damage his face, though, if I remember right.'

'Faith?'

'Catholic? A name like Sean James McTiernan, must be.'

'Can we set up an interview?' asked Batten.

'No, we can't. Scots law. Once we nab him, we have only six hours, so that's the last thing we do.' McAlpine's voice was quiet but authoritative. 'Especially as the death of Malkie Steele happened in Whistler's Lane. I don't want anybody going near him without my precise say so. And I mean it. Costello? A word, please. My office, after Mick is through?' McAlpine's voice was sharp. Costello coloured at being singled out. She had been on her feet for fourteen hours, and had her mind set on a fish supper and a hot bath. No chance. 'Over to you, Doc.'

Michael Batten, B.Sc. (Hons.) Psych., Ph.D., perched himself on the table, his eyes on McAlpine, weighing something up in his mind. He stubbed out his cigarette into his Diet Coke before turning to face them. As he moved, his leather jacket opened, revealing a T-shirt that stated: 'Hug me, I'm sober.'

The room was as silent as a church full of mourners.

He stood there for a minute, both hands thrust into the back pockets of his jeans. 'Can I take it we've all seen *The Silence of the Lambs?*'

A wave of irony rippled its way round the incident room, a gentle laugh that said, *so fucking easy in the movies.*

'*Ten Rillington Place? The Boston Strangler?* So now we can forget the shite and forget the hype, we've eaten the pie and thrown up on the T-shirt. We are all experts in our own way; the only problem is' – he paused – 'we haven't caught the bastard yet, and he won't stop until we do.'

He pointed at the line of photographs behind him, pictures of women with life taken from them as easily as pinching the flame of a candle. They were lined up, their names written by Costello in her loopy feminine handwriting: *Lynzi, Elizabeth Jane, Arlene.*

'We haven't caught him yet because he's difficult to catch. Normal rules do not apply. This guy is in a class of his own. I've written this.' He held up a single piece of paper. 'A rough guide to Christopher Robin. Why Christopher Robin?'

'Christopher the Crucifier?' Mulholland guessed.

'Good but no coconut.' Batten held up a copy of the *Daily Record*, then the *Sun* and the *Evening Times*. '"The Crucifixion Killer",' he said. 'I won't have the newspapers demonizing him, giving him superhuman powers he simply doesn't possess. This guy eats and shits and sleeps.' He paused to let that point sink in. 'So let's call him after Winnie-the-Pooh's wee pal. I am going to give you a psychological idea of what this man is, an image to build on. Irvine has been photocopying it. It's a tick-box system, like you used to do in school. Every man you come across in the investigation gets put in here. *Everybody.* We will then slant the investigation towards somebody who ticks more boxes than most. Mr McTiernan, for instance. These three women were pre-selected victims. Christopher Robin will have his next victim already lined up. Time is a luxury we don't have.'

Littlewood looked at the ceiling as if he had better things to do than to listen to this crap.

'It's important that we understand this. He is an ordinary man but with an extraordinary past.'

'So it is a man?' Vik Mulholland asked. 'We have no evidence of that.'

'It is a man. And I think he works alone to kill, though

he may have a female accomplice to lure. The trust these women place in him is remarkable.' Batten nodded at Anderson, who nodded back, giving way to the expert. 'I know there is a lack of sexual interference, but this killer is a man. He may be getting his sexual kicks from the compliant female accomplice. If she does exist, he will have bonded with her, though he'll still have trouble with other women. If she doesn't exist, and he works alone, then I'd say he was a man brought up under the influence of a domineering mother. The dominance might have been benign, but it was there, and was maybe extreme. In simple terms, ask any suspect what they did on Mother's Day and watch the response you get.' Batten's eyes were twinkling, and Costello noticed that the whole team was listening with rapt attention.

'Sorry, I don't follow,' said Mulholland. 'How can it work both ways?'

Batten nodded his head. 'Young Christopher Robin might habitually take her side in a fight, try to protect her, but be too small to do it. So he'd feel guilty, and grow up fixated and inadequate. If he idolized her, other women who don't match up are in trouble. Or maybe she punished him by ignoring him, abandoning him or locking him in a cellar, and he's been punishing her and other women like her ever since. Whichever way you look at it, he has a huge emotional mother fixation.' Batten grinned. 'But what guy hasn't?'

The squad laughed. The mood had lifted; confidence was being restored.

'Is he escalating, though, as serial killers do?' asked Mulholland.

'He is not escalating,' said Batten, pulling his hair back into a ponytail. 'The violence to Arlene was greater, but he is still very controlled.' They looked at each other, eyes locked. 'Name me one mistake?' asked Batten. He easily endured the silence that followed, still folding his ponytail into an elastic band. 'In fact, he did make a mistake. He let the knife get close to bone. This is a job for instinct. This man feels he can neither love, nor be loved by, the object of his desire. So – any ideas? Any ideas at all? I'll be in the DCI's office if you need me.'

Costello took the sheet of paper that was handed to her, with points listed in double-spaced Times New Roman. On the back was a grid system, with boxes for letters, so it could be scanned by computer. She was impressed. Most of the squad had taken their papers, moving downstairs to the café like a herd to a waterhole. Only she, Batten, McAlpine and Anderson stayed in the room. Mulholland had got up to leave but changed his mind, got some water from the cooler and sat back down again. Batten stayed sitting on top of the desk at the front, swinging his legs back and forth, looking like an expectant father.

Costello pulled another chair over and put her feet up on it, reading the first line: *This profile was compiled in no particular order of priority.*

– *He knows the victims.*
– *He's sympathetic to them; he anaesthetizes them. He kills them quickly and efficiently. No torture.*
– *He is lucid. He sees perfect sense in what he is doing.*
– *He murders in the same frame of mind as he shops in Tesco's.*
– *He is executing these women. He will have grown up fixated on execution, the elimination of evildoers.*
– *These killings are not the result of a spontaneous urge; he has been working up to this all his life.*
– *The geographical profile is small. He lives here. He travels on foot between incidents. He knows the area well.*
– *We have spoken to him; he is already in the system.*

– His job takes him out and about at odd hours.

– He is inconspicuous.

– Women can't relate to him, yet cautious women trust him (or his accomplice). Is he disabled, or disfigured in some way, so that they feel safe with him?

– As a witness, he will have been helpful and cooperative.

– His upbringing was dominated by a woman.

– There was loss in childhood.

– His age is between twenty-five and forty.

– He doesn't see us as a threat to his liberty.

– He is well educated but not necessarily formally so.

– He is very intelligent.

– He has a religious belief of a kind. It might be an organized religion; it might not.

– He won't drink to excess. He won't swear to excess. But he might amend his behaviour to blend with that of his peers.

– He regards women as Madonna-mothers or whores, nothing in between. Note the deliberate pose, in particular the crossing of the legs; he hates women but wants to respect them.

– There is no interaction between Christopher Robin and the victims, no sexual assault. There is no emotional involvement with them; they are almost non-people. They represent what he wants to destroy, and he is the instrument of their destruction.

– He has been sparked by a recent incident. Recently divorced? Has his girlfriend aborted his child?

– He is selecting these girls. From people he knows.

– He is in the shadows, but he is there.

– We will find him.

Costello reread the list. *He is already in the system.* She sighed. 'So, Dr Batten, we tick the boxes and arrest the one with the most ticks, is that it?'

'Some hope,' said the psychologist. 'I'm nipping out for chips. Anybody want any?'

'I'd love some,' Costello sighed. 'I need fortifying for a date with the Boss.'

McAlpine lifted a pile of papers from his chair and flicked through them. 'Irvine?' he shouted through the open door. 'We need to wake up Costello. Coffee, please.'

'I wonder why I look tired. It's only been a sixteen-hour day. Do I have any chance of getting home before it's Tuesday?' Costello licked the salt from her fingertips and wished she had asked for a bigger portion of chips.

'Not a hope in hell,' McAlpine answered.

'Well, tea, for me, if it's going.'

'Right, sit down. My face is lowpin.'

'I have some paracetamol, if you want,' offered Costello.

'Not allowed anything till eight. Fucking doctors, what do they know?' McAlpine touched his jaw cautiously, as if expecting the bone to crumble under his fingertips.

Costello sat down on the edge of the seat, notebook in hand, like a secretary in her first week, hoping this meeting would not take long. Her hunger was sated, but she still longed for a bath.

'Kick the door shut, will you?'

Biting her tongue, she got up, closed the door and sat back down again.

'I want you to track down Davy Nicholson, ex-DI, would have retired about four years ago, from Stewart Street.'

'I remember *him*.' Costello tutted. 'Not the most inspirational boss I've ever had.' She pushed her hair back with her pencil, realizing she had the one with the Winnie-the-Pooh rubber on the end. She stuck it behind her ear.

'Is that a compliment?' said McAlpine, ruffling through some papers.

'No,' Costello said airily. 'Are you looking for something, sir?'

He didn't answer, but instead asked, 'Would you walk up a dark lane with Christopher Robin?'

'I might, if I knew him as somebody else. Last night – this morning, I should say – I walked up Whistler's Lane four times, with four different men. That was Batten's point. Trust.'

'But you have half a brain cell. On a good day.' McAlpine scribbled something down. 'I want you to track down Sean McTiernan, get the details from the record office. Davy Nicholson did the donkey work; he'll fill you in. You'll need to go back three, four years. There was something about that case . . . might be something, might be nothing. But I don't want this public until we have something concrete to move on.'

Costello shifted uneasily in her seat. 'Is that wise?'

'Bear with me. McTiernan is very clever. I want you to dance round him discreetly; I don't want the likes of Irvine and Mulholland marching in with their size tens. It was Nicholson's collar, and I'm not going to question that publicly.'

'Until we have a reason to.'

McAlpine nodded, slowly pressing his hand to his face, confining the pain. 'Sean McTiernan might have ended up serving three for a culp. hom. when it was actually a premeditated murder.'

'I didn't work the case, but I don't remember any great argument about it.'

'I don't think any officer on that case was going to argue. Malkie Steele had walked about Glasgow thirty years, putting knitting needles up people's noses and fucking non-consenting little boys, and always protected by Laing. We couldn't get near him.'

'Oh,' said Costello.

'Exactly. So imagine our delight when an unknown squirt appears from nowhere and takes him out of the game.' McAlpine stopped rubbing his face, suddenly deep in thought. 'Maybe it was mental sleight of hand – *I'm showing you this to stop you looking at that.* Review his case in light of what Batten was gibbering on about,' said McAlpine. 'There was something about that case that didn't add up, something about that lad that didn't add up. Sniff around him, have a good root around. And always remember that Sean McTiernan is one bright cookie.'

Costello heard the door behind her open. Irvine came in with two coffees, dumping them down on the desk and leaving. Costello, a tea drinker, left hers untouched.

'Find McTiernan, but don't go near him. You are the most senior female on the team. He won't fool you. I hope.'

'What was your version of events?' Costello prompted with a glance at her watch, still hopeful of a bath.

'Well, McTiernan phoned himself in, saying he'd had a fight and he thought the guy was dead. He had called the ambulance first of course.' McAlpine sipped his coffee delicately and cursed at the pain it provoked in his jaw.

'Hardly the act of a guilty man.'

'Or exactly the act of a guilty man. It was in Whistler's Lane; I don't know if that has any significance at all.' McAlpine's eyes scanned past Costello to the map on the wall. 'Might be significant to Arlene's murder.'

'Might just be he was up there with a girl. There aren't many private places left round here with the smoking ban and everything.'

McAlpine nodded. 'Keep it to yourself for the moment. If he is Christopher Robin, we'll have to tread carefully or he'll run for his lawyer and then we'll get bugger all.'

Costello realized what McAlpine had given her: the main lead in the biggest murder inquiry of the decade.

McAlpine was talking. '. . . and then McTiernan said a scout from Partick Thistle asked to meet him for a drink because he had seen him play and wanted to offer a trial. He went along, but the Whistler's Pub gets very noisy, so they went outside and casually walked up the lane. McTiernan went thinking the lane led somewhere. He said Steele made a pass at him, there was a scuffle, McTiernan got away. He walked towards Byres Road and heard Steele coming up behind him. He lashed out like some kind of Ninja and kicked Steele twice – once backward and once on a spinning turn. Forensic examination of the shoe print proved it: McTiernan was indeed walking away. Steele was hit with some accuracy, once in the stomach, once in the face. Malkie was a hard drinker, his liver sustained too much damage from the assault. Without the pre-existing condition, he might have pulled through, but who knows.'

'Dead with two kicks?' Costello was incredulous.

'Martial arts, don't know which one. It'll be in the trial transcript; an expert turned up and explained how an eleven-stone man can take on an eighteen-stone guy and win.'

'So far I'm convinced,' said Costello. 'You said Steele was a known homosexual, with a passion for clean-living thin little boys . . . legal, but only just?'

'Yes, but it would be obvious within two minutes of conversation that Malkie was no more a scout for Partick Thistle than I am for the Royal Ballet. McTiernan was young but too old to be a bright young talent. McTiernan cut his hand and cancelled the first meeting at a game in Ayr. He grew up at the Good Shepherd Orphanage, so he would have known damn well the lane went nowhere, but that wasn't mentioned at the trial. He had been training hard . . . practising . . . getting fit. Glasgow hard man taken out of the game. He serves three years. What way round do you want it?'

'Entrapment comes to mind,' said Costello slowly.

McAlpine nodded. 'Maybe. Steele was an evil bastard. So if McTiernan had a private score to settle, fair enough, we weren't going to dig too deep. But if he's evolved in prison to *this*, we need to be on him. McTiernan is nice, pleasant, articulate and intelligent. Charming, even. However, capable of great violence when sparked.' McAlpine stopped swinging in the chair. 'He grew up in the area. He's been away. Now he's back. And he's a carpenter, handy with a chisel. A knife? Who knows?'

'But wasn't he in jail when Lynzi was killed?'

'Penningham is an open jail. He would have been out at weekends. Lynzi was killed on a Saturday night. Find out what you can and report back to me. And Costello, never forget, he's clever. Don't go near him.'

'Not likely to, sir. I saw Arlene's face on the slab.'

'I thought you would be here,' Anderson said, dipping under the canopy of the Three Judges. 'Are you coming in for a pint or are you going to stay out here and get drowned?'

'I thought you were going home,' replied McAlpine.

'I went home for fifteen minutes, and Brenda didn't stop nagging to draw breath. It's ten o'clock at night, and the kids took no notice of me saying it was bedtime. So Clare will still be practising her ballet in the front room and Peter will still be having too-tired-to-sleep tantrums upstairs.

I knew the lads would be in here. You'll have to come in; I can't afford to get a round in.'

McAlpine popped his cigarette into the bin on the wall and followed Anderson through the lounge. 'I went home, but there was nobody in. No idea where Helena is.'

'At the gallery, I presume. She does have her big exhibition soon.'

'I hate the house being empty. So I walked round here. Byres Road is like Sauchiehall Street. Where do all those students get the money to drink like that?' There was a burst of laughter from Littlewood, who slapped the puny Wyngate on the back, nearly knocking him over. 'Where do *they* get the money to drink like that? Wyngate should be saving up to get married.'

'They seem to be having a good chinwag about something. Batten's over there too, bonding with the troops. Did you find his stuff helpful?'

'I grudgingly admit I did. It focused their thoughts.'

They found a table against the far wall. 'What do you want?' Anderson stuck his hands in his pocket, fishing out a fluffy blue hippo and a Mysteron hat before finding his last fiver.

'Here. I'll get it. Helena makes a fortune.' McAlpine pushed an empty pint glass away and held out a note to Anderson. 'Get me a Macallan.'

From the bar, Anderson looked back at his boss. There were winos on the street outside who looked better than the DCI did at the moment. He seemed thinner, the bruising emphasizing the gauntness of his face. Batten, however, looked relaxed and confident. He didn't fool Anderson for a minute. He caught the psychologist looking at McAlpine, apparently a casual observation, but an observation it was. As Batten turned back to the bar, emptying some Tennent's

90 Shilling down his throat, he caught Anderson looking and raised an inquiring eyebrow.

McAlpine didn't look up when Anderson put the glass in front of him. Anderson sipped his tomato juice and pulled a face. They'd put Lea & Perrins in it, even though he'd asked them not to.

McAlpine downed the Macallan in one.

'You'd better be careful,' Anderson warned, nodding in Batten's direction. 'I think *somebody* is noticing how much you're drinking. I know it's your way of working, but –'

'But what?' The almond eyes narrowed dangerously.

'But nothing,' Anderson said, not wanting a scene.

'What are they talking about anyway?' McAlpine growled, noticing that Wyngate and Littlewood had now been joined by Burns. 'Have they got nothing better to do with their time?'

'Women. Wyngate's getting married, or might not be, if he signs up for any more overtime. His fiancée has the hump.'

'Bloody women. Look at us – the three of them over there, miserable as sin, and the two of us over here. Not a decent woman between us. They do one thing, say another. Brenda wants you to earn more, then bites your balls at the first hint of overtime. Helena says she loves me, then keeps secrets from me and gets mad just 'cause I smash her car.'

'How much did you have to drink before I got here?' asked Anderson. 'Look, mate, I've known you a long time and it's none of my business, but it's usually Helena who has her head screwed on, and if she is keeping something to herself she'll have her own good reasons. Women do.'

'You're right; it is none of your business. And stop being right, Col, it's fucking annoying.'

'Helena is a good woman. You should be more careful where you lay your head.'

'And when did you become the Yoda of love? You're sitting here on your arse as well as me, you know.'

Anderson conceded his boss had a point and let the silence lie.

'Helena knows I would never leave her, never. And that's enough for her.'

'Is it?'

'That's the way our marriage works. She's not like other women; she's strong, she's independent, she knows the job I do, what I am, and lets me get on with it. She never interferes with my work or complains about the hours I put in.'

'Sounds bliss,' muttered Anderson.

'But this is –'

'But this is what?'

'A matter of life and death.' McAlpine spoke very quietly. 'I'm supposed to be the most important person in her life, but she doesn't confide in me. How do you think that makes me feel?'

Anderson remembered Helena's red-rimmed eyes, the pallor on her skin he'd thought was tiredness.

'My mum died of cancer,' said McAlpine suddenly, the Macallan in his voice making it sound as though he was proud of it. 'Well, that's not true. She killed herself once Robbie had died, but I had to watch her being eaten away. Her pain was unbearable. Helena knows that.'

Anderson read between the lines and trod carefully. 'Maybe it was because of your mum that she didn't tell you. Poor Helena, I didn't know ... So she's struggling with that –'

'Why's it always *poor Helena*? It's worse for those watching it than it is for those going through it.'

Anderson doubted that, but said, 'I wouldn't know, I've no experience of either.'

McAlpine stared deeply into his glass. 'I couldn't carry on if it wasn't for her,' he said quietly. 'And she knows that too. I was a mess when we met. And I'll be a mess if she . . . goes.'

'I know what you mean. She's the kind of woman that holds mere men together.'

'I couldn't face life without her, and she just . . .' McAlpine sighed and shook his head slowly, then asked for another Macallan. Suddenly his mood shifted. 'You know, Colin – you know that ability some women have, to appear to be one thing but be another? I think Christopher Robin's right – why not just slice the bitches up?'

'Christ, Al!'

'No, listen . . . women are the root of all evil.'

'Isn't that supposed to be the love of money? That's the popular theory anyway,' Anderson answered carefully.

'No, seriously. How would you feel if Brenda left you? Left wee Paul and Clare too? Left you for another man after years of accusing you of being unfaithful?'

'His name's Peter,' Anderson corrected. 'I'd feel a thousand times worse if she took the wee man with her.'

'So, we have Lynzi, a two-faced cow, leaving her kid and shagging everybody in sight. The girls in the disco with Arlene told us she was coming off the game, to get a flat, to get her kid back, to get respectable. From O'Hare's report, it seems she was making a good go at being clean.'

'I don't know how much credence we can give to those girls. We need to talk to one of them sober. Tracey nearly blurted out something about the stupid cow being caught. So we're leaving her to stew for now, and then we'll nail her. Leopards don't change their spots.'

189

'So, say Arlene's still a streetwalking pro. Lynzi fucks off with another man but doesn't tell anybody. Elizabeth Jane's all sweetness and light but has no friends to speak of. There'll be a pattern to all that if we can find it.' McAlpine steamrollered on. 'But I'm not seeing it. It's like a bad smell – the smell of *morality* – and I don't know where it's coming from.' McAlpine began to push his fingertip on the top of the table, drawing a convoluted pattern. 'I can nearly see it.'

Anderson had witnessed this before, the two minutes of genius McAlpine displayed between sobriety and being pissed. 'But Elizabeth Jane was respectable. Very respectable.'

'Wrong.' McAlpine's finger waved close to Anderson's face. 'The higher they are, the further they fall, morally. Get Costello talking about her; she knows how a woman's mind works.'

'She does have the advantage of being one,' said Anderson with ultimate logic.

'Just ask her.' McAlpine fell quiet again. 'Just ask her what goes on in the mind of a woman like that.' The pub fell silent as well. 'I had my first fatality here, you know, at Partickhill. That was the worst, the very worst. She was so beautiful . . .' He looked deep into the middle distance.

Anderson felt one of McAlpine's drunken soliloquies coming on and did his best to divert it. He wanted to go home. 'Have a mouthful of coffee, it'll make you feel better, and I'll drive you home. You have a long chat with Helena and remind her what an absolute arse you are.'

McAlpine ignored him. 'Young and beautiful – that's not right, is it?'

'No, it's not right. Neither's leaving your wife alone when she's faced with a long night of worry about –'

'How many dead kids have you dealt with?' asked Mc-Alpine, his finger waving in Anderson's face.

'Too many,' answered Anderson, with honesty.

'How many?'

'One. Only one. One is too many.'

'Colin, I'm serious.'

'So am I. How many times have I heard you say it: it's worse if it's female, worse if she's young. Once you add pretty and blonde, you're in severe trouble. And the guy you think's done for some blonde doe-eyed orphan gets lynched before we even get him to the nick. You know that. But at the end of the day you always have to remember they're all –'

'Someone's daughter.' McAlpine smiled drunkenly. 'I'm glad I taught you something.' He was palpating his face again, pushing his fingertips in hard. 'She was lovely.'

'So when was all this, then?' asked Anderson. He had an eerie feeling, heard Helena's words coming back to him. *He lost somebody close.* 'You haven't been at Partickhill for twenty years or so – is that why?'

McAlpine nodded slowly, his eyes fixed on something in the distance of his memory. 'She had acid flung in her face.' He held the palms of his hands before his own face, looking at them as if he had developed stigmata.

'Who did?'

McAlpine's eyes half focused themselves back on Anderson. 'It was a case I was involved in once.'

'That's a very personal thing to do to someone, especially someone who's pretty. It's so –'

'She wasn't pretty. She was *beautiful.*'

'Yeah, but what does acid-throwing do? Rips your face off, changes your identity, in some ways it removes you from being a person.'

'Oh, piss off with your psychobabble. They were using her as bait to lure out the boyfriend. It worked; the minute she got that in her face, he tried to get over here. They must have had some way of keeping in touch, and when he didn't hear from her, he was over. Must be terrible, to be so alone.'

'Sounds a bit heavy,' said Anderson, vaguely wondering why, in all the years he and McAlpine had known each other, this was the first he'd heard of this particular case.

Suddenly McAlpine leaned forward in his seat. 'She was eight months pregnant.'

'That's nasty,' said Anderson gently, the thought hitting him in the stomach. No wonder the Boss hadn't forgotten. 'That's really nasty.'

'I got a bollocking for getting too involved.'

'And then got fast-tracked?'

'I got traded off. Should have hung around and made it difficult for them.'

Anderson drained his already-empty glass, hoping the Boss would see it as a precursor to leaving, going home and getting some kip.

But McAlpine didn't move. 'It took her weeks to die.' He drew a forefinger across each wrist. 'Her decision. All those weeks, I'd been talking to a face, a personality, covered in blood and bandages and stuff. She had such, such . . .' He stared at the carpet for a long time. '. . . *life* about her. You see, Colin, after she was gone, I saw a photograph of her. Sitting on a beach, she was, without a care in the world. You have a picture in your mind of somebody and then – *pow!* – there she was. Beautiful.'

'Yes, you mentioned it,' said Anderson, wondering how the passing years had edited the memories. 'What about the baby?'

'Yeah, I still think of her. She'd be what, twenty-two? A couple of years older than I was when it all happened.' McAlpine suddenly stopped talking, started rubbing the top of his glass with the palm of his hand. 'The same age? I must be old now.' He squinted, remembering something. 'You see . . . you see, Colin.' He sounded very drunk now. 'She wasn't a Lynzi or an Arlene or a Brenda. Anna wasn't two-faced; what you saw was what you got. What was in front of you, that was it. You ever known a woman like that?'

Deep in Anderson's brain, something clicked. 'That must have been about the time you lost your mother.'

'And Robbie.' McAlpine stared into his empty glass. Anderson was about to ask him if he was OK when he said, 'You don't forget it. You never forget any of it.' He shook his head. 'What a fucking year that was. Never so glad to hear the bells as I was that Hogmanay.'

Burns came over, moving to the side to let the man in the next booth slide out, and stood waiting to be allowed to interrupt. 'Is your mobile off, sir? The station is trying to get you.'

'It's this new bloody thing.'

As soon as he pressed the switch, the screen flashed green, telling him to call back. For a while he listened to the voice at the other end, mouthing Mulholland to Anderson. 'Yeah, yeah, yeah . . . OK, right – Phoenix Refuge . . . yeah, I know it. What are they . . . Elizabeth Jane's mobile? And the number is the Phoenix? Anybody in particular? Father O'Keefe? And any connection to Arlene? You beauty!' He snapped the phone shut. 'Both Elizabeth Jane and Arlene had the Phoenix Refuge number in their mobiles. Do you know where the place is?'

'Up on the Circus. And you, sir, are pissed. Leave it till morning, eh?'

'Why?'

'Sobriety is the best policy when interviewing men of the cloth.'

Tuesday, 3 October

Costello sat down at the back of the canteen with the files on Sean James McTiernan. It was only nine o'clock in the morning but she had been in the station since six. There was no point in staying at home; her mind was too active for sleep. But so far her morning had been productive. She had sweet-talked the central records office, getting the files before breakfast, and was looking forward to a good read and a fried-egg sandwich while the canteen was quiet.

It was a still point in the investigation for her. Yesterday's feeling of euphoria had gone. The real goodies were going elsewhere this morning. Other officers were being detailed to go here, there and everywhere.

Davy Nicholson had been easy to track down but seemed reluctant to phone back. His voice, with its slightly effeminate tone, on the answering machine had reminded her of an old Kelvinside queen. It brought back a few unpleasant memories, and she had put down the phone feeling dirty.

If Nicholson wasn't as old as the hills, Costello thought, he would be a fit for Christopher Robin. Maybe McAlpine wasn't a million miles away either. Or Anderson with his narky wife. Or, if she thought about it long enough, almost any man she knew. Bloody profilers.

Right, Mr McTiernan, she said to herself, pulling a face, let's see what you have to say. She lifted a mugshot from the file: a handsome young man, with a hollow face, blond hair and flat, perfectly square teeth. There was a touch of the James Deans about him. He *appeared* to be approachable, friendly. Just like Christopher Robin.

She flicked through to the court papers, found a request for a social inquiry report from the Social Work Department. 'Oh, yeah?' She searched through the papers, forward and back again, eventually finding it: a photocopy on fine yellowed paper. McTiernan had been brought up in the Good Shepherd Orphanage. She smiled to herself; she drove past it every day on her way to work, but in ten years of working the area she had never met anyone who had been there. And here he was, Mr McTiernan. Abandoned as a baby, aged four months. Mindful of Batten's words about mothers and unhappy relationships, she scanned the typing, looking for details about Sean's mother. She herself didn't put too much credence in that theory, since her own mother had been drunk most of her childhood; she had never been abusive, she had just never been sober. Costello couldn't remember ever blaming her dad for leaving; she couldn't remember her dad at all. Life was what you made it. We all have choices. And Costello smiled to herself; was that why McAlpine had singled her out for this? Looking for the choices McTiernan had made.

It was all there: the official past of Sean James McTiernan. An unsuccessful reunion at the age of four, another at eight. All attempts to adopt Sean had been unsuccessful. He was an institutionalized child but mixed well within the school. She translated the educational psychologist's report: a bright child but not academic. She turned to the back. He had left school, worked for a local firm of joiners, done his apprenticeship; he was good, popular . . . So why did they say he was institutionalized? Why had he not been fostered and adopted? She flicked back but could see no further references. She began to feel a little uncomfortable, like a voyeur on his life, not a feeling she was used to. There was no history of criminal activity. His boss, Hugh White of White's the Joiners, had even offered to stand bail for him when he was charged, and had taken him on again after his early parole. He was a popular young man. It said it again. Popular. Sociable. There was no further mention of his mother. Costello made a note to track down the staff at the home; they would remember him, their killer pupil. But the picture forming in her imagination didn't fit.

She opened the flap at the back where the photographs were held in a protective plastic envelope. Still uncreased, they had not been looked at often. There were numerous views of the locus of Malkie Steele's murder, his body a bulky amorphous lump in a dark alleyway. He was lying, curled like a child, trying to protect himself from McTiernan's feet. She ran her hand along the inside of the envelope. There were a few scraps of paper, a petrol receipt and a scribbled phone number. She pulled out a small white card, turning it over carefully, revealing a much older picture, black and white, four children on a beach, three standing, arms round each other, a sand castle to the left, a single flag flying. She recognized the middle one as Sean, aged nine, maybe ten, fair hair flopping over his face, stick legs hanging from shorts that were too big for him. Her eye was drawn to the girl sitting to one side, younger by two or three years. She was one of the most beautiful children Costello had ever seen. Long blonde hair danced in the wind, her eyes were wide and innocent, yet there was something about the curve of her cheek and the acutely bowed but unsmiling lips that was slightly dangerous, enchanting even. And Sean's gaze was focused on her with utter devotion.

'Nice reading material,' said Mulholland, pulling up a chair and glancing at Steele's photograph. 'Nearly as nice as that.' A copy of Tuesday's *Daily Record* flew across the table. Arlene's battered face stared back at her.

'Oh, no!'

'The Boss will go nuts. Where is he anyway? Can he come out of his coffin in daylight hours?'

Costello didn't answer, but she watched as Mulholland broke a Wagon Wheel in half over a napkin, wiping his fingers before starting to eat. She pointedly folded the newspaper and shoved it back to him. 'Did O'Hare say something about a footprint from the shoe that did this?'

'Somebody said yesterday: nothing unless we can get hold of the shoe to get blood from and match it. Her face was too badly mangled.'

'You enjoying that?' Costello pointed at the Wagon Wheel.

'Yes.' He wiped his fingers again before picking up the photograph. 'What's that?'

'Malkie Steele's face.'

'The guy McTiernan walloped? He made a good job of it.'

'Apart from all that blood, look at the left side of the face: it's lower than the right. He stood on it and jumped. Oh, no, he didn't . . . it says here in this report, both Mc-Tiernan and Steele were upright at the time, which fits in with McTiernan's story that he was walking away and lashed out. I suppose that might be second nature to somebody who studied martial arts.' She picked up another photograph, narrowing her eyes for a better look. 'Look, the eyeball is missing. Is that it over there in the corner?'

Mulholland looked away. 'You are one sick woman, Costello.'

'What rage, though, for one human being to do that to another.' Costello passed him another napkin.

'Steele looks really fat in this one, nine months gone.'

'Bleeding from the liver. The Boss said McTiernan kicked him and it exploded.'

'Never heard of that happening before.' Mulholland was turning the picture in his hands, looking at it this way and that. 'Anderson has just phoned. We're going out to that Phoenix place.' He looked at his watch. 'Now.'

'The Phoenix? The refuge?'

'Indeed.'

'What are you going there for?'

'Major breakthrough. Haven't you heard?'

'I heard a bit.'

'Well, that's the price you pay for being McAlpine's blue-eyed girl.'

Green-eyed, she thought. 'Oh, piss off,' she snorted. 'What's happening?'

Mulholland took a long slow drink of his mineral water, his eyes twinkling at Costello, who was getting more irritated by the minute. 'Shall I piss off? Or shall I tell you?'

'Just tell me,' she spat through gritted teeth.

'Elizabeth Jane's minister . . . the Reverend Shand . . .'

'Is on the committee of the Phoenix?'

'And the Phoenix number is the only place she dialled on that mobile phone. The Phoenix office, to be exact, which would take you through to O'Keefe. Father Thomas O'Keefe.'

'The Tom her dad mentioned? And Leask said he was a colleague . . .'

'He's in charge of the day-to-day running of the place. Arlene was on a literacy programme, organized –'

'By the Phoenix.'

'Even started reading the Bible, apparently. Good girl, you should become a detective.' He screwed the top back on his mineral water, as if he had done a hard day's work.

'Not really, it was spadework by me and Wingnut that got us there, DC Mulholland. And Lynzi? Anything except Leask living across from her man?'

'No, nothing yet. But a load of religious do-gooders is just what this case needs, which is why we're doing background reports on them all, one by one. So let the boys get on with the big stuff. How are you doing with Seanie-boy? If the DCI has McTiernan in his sights, he should bring him in,' said Mulholland.

'It's all circumstantial and convenient timing. We'll bring him in when we're sure.'

'I think the pressure is getting to the DCI. He's disintegrating quicker than a chocolate chip pan.' He got up and pushed his chair in, the feet screeching against the tiled floor. 'You connect Sean to the Phoenix, then pick him up; that's what I would do.'

'If I was you, DC Mulholland, I would phone the charity shop Lynzi worked in. I would ask them what they do with their unsellable clothes. The local refuge for the homeless seems like a good bet, the Phoenix probably.' She could have earned the Brownie points herself, but it was more satisfying to smack Mulholland in the mouth with it.

He walked away, probably mentally kicking himself for not coming up with that first. Costello smiled and picked up her mobile, thinking of the geography of the area. A charity like the Phoenix got a lot of publicity; they would be sponsored by a local company. White's was the biggest local joinery company. Directory inquiries gave her the number. Their secretary was most helpful. Yes, the company did all the refurb at the Phoenix when it opened three years ago, but it wasn't sponsorship, it had been lottery-funded. And yes, they still had the maintenance contract. She seemed quite happy to talk away.

'Could you tell me if Sean McTiernan has been up at the Phoenix recently?' Costello held her breath. The voice at the other end paused, and Costello thought she was going to refuse to answer.

'Aye, he's getting his hand back in, after – well, after being away . . . He's spent quite a lot of time there – dry rot in the toilets.'

'Good, good,' said Costello encouragingly. 'There must be a lot to do. It's quite an old building, isn't it?'

The voice on the phone softened. 'Like the Forth Road Bridge.'

'Do you do the new flats at Fortrose Street?'

'We do all the work for their factors,' responded the voice, a little guarded now. 'Is there a problem? Can I ask the nature of your inquiry?'

'I'm DS Costello, Partickhill CID,' said Costello in her most girlie voice, hoping the receptionist would not connect the address with the murder. 'Just some background . . .'

'Oh, about the skylight at that house? Where the girl was murdered? It had been giving trouble for ages.'

Manna from heaven. 'And who did you send on that one?'

'It was . . . oh, let me see . . .' Costello heard the clicking of efficient fingers over a keyboard. 'Billy Evans went.'

Damn.

'But he couldn't get access. So someone else went back two days later.' Another tap-tap-tap. 'Sean McTiernan.'

The voice that answered the phone sounded young and strong.

'Hello,' Costello began. 'Can I speak to Alice Drummond please?'

The voice hesitated. 'Who's calling?'

Costello put a smile into her voice. 'I'm DS Costello from Partickhill Station.'

Another hesitation, 'Yes?'

'I'm looking for a Mrs Alice Drummond. She used to be in charge of the Good Shepherd Orphanage?'

'Yes.'

Costello laboured on. 'And this was the last-known contact number . . .' She let her voice trail off, inviting a reply.

'I'm afraid my mother's not keeping too well these days.'

'Oh, I'm sorry to hear that. And you are?'

'Patricia, her daughter. We're just emptying her house. I'm afraid Mum had to move into a home last week.' The guarded voice softened. 'She doesn't seem to know much about it, but what she does know, I don't think she's very happy about.' Costello's mind jumped back to Sean's file, a scribbled note in a margin. A right wee Miss Marple, this one, not much got past her. 'It was her third stroke, you see.'

'Is she able to talk?'

'No, not at all. Terrible thing to see, age taking its toll.' A little quietness rested on the phone. 'What do you want to know?'

'Just some background stuff on a child who passed through the Good Shepherd.'

'I really wouldn't want the police talking to my mother just now. I'm sure you understand. But this number might be of some help.' She rattled off a phone number. 'Lorna Shaw. I'm not sure what she did at the Good Shepherd.'

Costello glanced at the statements in front of her. 'It says here she was the senior housekeeper.'

'Yes, that's her. Nice woman. She's kept in touch with Mum all these years. And if she can't help you, she'll be able to put you on to someone who can.'

'That's great; you've been very helpful.' Costello looked again at the photograph of the future murderer, gazing with such devotion at the beautiful little girl. In deep thought she rattled her pencil between her teeth, aware of DS Littlewood's eyes resting on her.

Then she reached for the telephone to make an appointment to visit Lorna Shaw.

The Phoenix Refuge was housed in an old sandstone church sitting high above the city in one of the better parts of Partickhill Road, a jewel in the centre of the elegant curved terrace that separates the majestic villas to the north from the student-digs Victorian tenements to the south. The grass in front, though strewn with cigarette ends and empty Carlsberg cans, was as wide and even-cambered as a moat, and the original church still maintained its dignity.

Mulholland reversed the Beamer neatly into a space outside the Phoenix on the lower road, Anderson beside him, drumming his fingers against the dashboard. Anderson had trawled the system for details on Father O'Keefe, founder of the Phoenix, and had spent the short journey flicking through the printouts.

Mulholland sat for a moment. 'Well, sir?'

'Yes,' Anderson said, still not moving.

'The DCI said he would meet us here.'

'Yes, just give him a minute,' said Anderson, hoping the DCI would look clean and sober when he turned up. Anderson himself had eventually fallen asleep at McAlpine's house, to be woken by Helena coming in at half one in the morning. The image of her smile had stayed with him long into the night, as he tried to sleep on his own sofa, barred yet again from the marital bed.

'How long are we giving him?' asked Mulholland, thinking more along the lines of getting in there and getting on with it. He showed his irritation by looking at his watch.

Anderson ignored him.

Mulholland started fiddling with his impeccable cuffs. 'Do you know Thomas O'Keefe?' he asked.

'No,' replied Anderson. 'But, in view of Batten's initial profile, we should find him an interesting character. Richard Branson in a Roman collar.' He held up a photocopied newspaper interview. '*Father Thomas O'Keefe, aged thirty-four, says –*'

'The age is ticked in Batten's box.'

'Calm down. *We are not creating the drug problem in this area. If anything, we are moving the problem away from the general public. At least we give the homeless a bed, the hungry a meal.*'

'Druggies a warm place to shoot up.' Watching Mulholland constantly fiddling with his cuffs, Anderson realized why he irritated Costello so much.

'According to this, O'Keefe's next step is to start up a medically supervised programme at Partickhill Community Centre, handing out clean needles for use under supervision and providing heroin substitute as part of a detox programme. It seems to be some sort of stipulation they make; if you're not in a programme, they don't touch you. And so it goes on.'

'What does that sign say?' asked Mulholland, craning his neck to see.

'Can hardly read it from here.' Anderson leaned forward to peer through the windscreen. '*The Phoenix Centre. Open for Breakfast 9 to 10 a.m. Overnight accommodation by booking only. Abuse of our staff or neighbours will not be tolerated.*'

'Who the hell would book to stay here?'

'It'd feel like the Hilton once you'd had your arse felt on the floor of Central Station a few times. *Doctor here every day 11 to 12*. Hmm.'

'That the drug programme? When they move it here full time, I give it a week. The first hypodermic found on the street, and the middle-class majority of Partickhill will find their charity has run out. Maybe not as long as a week. How long has this place been here?'

'Two years in this location, but there's been a Phoenix for six years, in one place or another. It's O'Keefe's baby, apparently. He came over from Ireland as a very young newly ordained priest and set it up under a multi-denominational committee.'

'Clever bloke – imagine how many lottery grants he'd get.'

'You're so cynical, Vik. He has two GPs on board, and a rep from Pitt Street. Community Constable Elliot.'

'Never heard of him.'

'Well, I had a quiet word. He says the place gives very little trouble, apart from the neighbours complaining initially about undesirables hanging about when the place wasn't open. And admittance is refused if you smell of drink at all.'

'Strong-minded man, then, this O'Keefe? Does he tick Batten's boxes?'

'I'm not excluding anybody. From what it says here, the place appears to be well run. As far as I know, the policy on the homeless has been welcomed, the policy on the alcoholic problem is being tolerated, and I've a sneaking suspicion that even if the drug abusers do push the good citizens on the posh side of the hill too far, the good ship Phoenix will simply sail on, doing exactly what is required, regardless of public opinion. Elliot said O'Keefe is the kind of Irishman who keeps going regardless. The only stipulation the Phoenix seems to make is that no one under the influence of drink or drugs gets in, so you'd have to make some commitment to getting clean before you could queue up for your bowl of soup.' Anderson unclipped his safety belt. 'Let's go. McAlpine can catch up if he's interested.'

'Bit of a shitter if O'Keefe and Christopher Robin are one and the same,' said Mulholland, getting out of the car.

'It would tarnish his public image somewhat,' muttered Anderson.

The foyer of Lorna Shaw's block of flats was that mix of dark blue and white that Costello associated with the old fish shop in Paisley Road West her mother used to drag her into, with its smell of kippers and damp sawdust. The carpet in the hall was blue, the plaster on the walls was blue, and in the corner stood a blue wrought-iron stand housing plants that had dehydrated a long time ago. All it needed was a few plastic fishing nets and lobster pots hanging from the wall to complete the theme. The block had the look of an institution, not inappropriate for a woman who'd spent most of her working life as housekeeper in the Good Shepherd Orphanage.

When Lorna Shaw opened her front door, although introductions had been made over the intercom, Costello made a point of showing her ID.

Lorna looked at it closely, comparing it to the blonde woman in front of her, dressed in an ill-fitting suit, before waving her through as if welcoming royalty. She was a tall elegant woman, her plaid dress belted in the middle, a Peter Pan collar snug round a thin wrinkled neck. Her hair was the same blue as the ceiling.

'Last door on the right,' Lorna Shaw said, still waving.

The theme for the living room was brown, every shade of brown, except the carpet, which Costello classed as a very light beige, easily marked. She paused for a moment at the door; she did not like to think what was on the soles of her Dr Martens. The only colours in the room came from the inhabitants of the fish tank gurgling away in the corner.

'Tea?'

Costello shook her head. Tea would have been a welcome distraction, but she knew it would come in tiny white cups with handles too small for her fingers to get through. And shortbread.

On a doily.

Costello pulled her notebook from her bag, aware of Lorna's observation of her trouser suit, the trousers washed too often to still match the jacket, the knees slightly bagged.

Lorna pulled a face that said something about young people today, her narrow red lips pursing. 'So what can I do for you?'

'I was going through some old notes, a review for a current case. It's purely routine to check offenders who have recently been released . . .' Even as she spoke, she realized she was sounding defensive.

'Sean McTiernan comes to mind.'

'Sean, yes.'

'Our most notorious charge.' Lorna Shaw's face cracked into a smile, and she sat back on the sofa and relaxed, sticking her legs out and regarding her feet. 'I quite liked him, actually. A wee rascal but never a nasty boy, and we had enough of *them*, believe me. His nose was always running, his knees were always skinned, and he was always getting things wrong, but a nice kid.'

'It seems, from his notes, he was never fostered? The

background reports are a bit vague.' She guessed Lorna Shaw was the type to counter 'vague' wherever she heard it.

'Oh, my dear, the social services tried to home him many a time, but he always bounced back like a bad penny.'

'Why?'

'Destructive behaviour, usually. That's the reason he was sent back, but he was never like that with us. Quite the opposite. I could see we were being manipulated, but you can't tell a child psychologist just out of university anything, can you?' She sniffed with disapproval.

'We have to suffer them in our job as well,' Costello confided.

Lorna Shaw turned round suddenly. 'Are you sure I can't tempt you with a cuppa?'

To Costello's surprise the tea was served in bright Dunoon ceramic mugs. She had guessed the shortbread right, though. And the doily. As she stirred her tea, Lorna Shaw came back into the room with a photograph album.

'Sean was very friendly with one girl, very friendly. I mean, inseparable. Mrs Drummond referred them to the hospital. Psychological twinning, twinning between two people who aren't related, that's how the child psychologist explained it. They become two halves of the one; they can only function together, not apart. Like Morecambe and Wise. Tom and Jerry. And I think that had a lot to do with what happened later . . . the murder.'

Brady and Hindley, Bonnie and Clyde, West and West, thought Costello. 'And what happened when they were separated?'

'He went violent; she stopped eating. She was a very quiet child, not easy to get close to. In those days we were allowed to cuddle them. But not that one.' Lorna wrinkled her nose. 'She never seemed to invite it.'

'Was he a bright boy, Sean?' Costello asked, returning to her subject.

'Not in the academic sense. Bright enough if he was interested. If not, you might as well talk to the wall.' Lorna flicked the album open, scanning the pages.

Costello took a mouthful of strong tea; it reminded her of her granny. 'Were you surprised, the way he turned out?'

Lorna shrugged thin bony shoulders. 'He got into a fight, and the other man died as a result, is that right?'

'More or less.'

'Wrong place at the wrong time. He was fifteen or sixteen when I retired, and I didn't see him after that – no, that's not true; I met him once when he was doing his apprenticeship. I wasn't surprised when White's took him on; he was always good with his hands. As a little boy, he used to like taking things apart and putting them back together again. He was doing fine, still plenty of chat. Quite charming, really. He was always . . .' She paused, searching for the right word. 'Passionate about things.'

'No problem with substance abuse?'

'Drugs, you mean?'

Costello nodded.

Lorna shook her head. 'No, I remember the police asking us at the time. I worked in that place for over thirty years, ever since I finished my training, so I had a fair idea how most of them would turn out. I wasn't often wrong, Miss Costello.'

'And how did you think Sean would turn out?' Costello asked.

'He was committed to sport, running, and he was good. He's the sort of young man who would watch football simply because he liked football, regardless of who was playing. He was keen on Kung Fu or whatever it was called.'

'Do you know anything about his parents?'

'Well, I don't think Sean's mother ever had any real feeling for him. That's why we were always taking him back, poor wee mite.'

'What about the dad?'

'Your guess is as good as mine.' Lorna turned over a few more pages. 'The only request we ever received from his mother was that he be brought up Catholic. Sean had plenty of friends, he developed relationships within the place. I got on well with him, the kitchen staff always had time for him. The cleaners had a cupboard, you know, for keeping the buckets and brushes. He and Trude were in there more often than they were in the playground. In the cupboard, playing cops and robbers.' She shook her head in memory, holding out the album for Costello to see.

'This Trude – not a relative?'

'Oh, no, but I can tell you they were closer than some of the siblings we had. Everyone had a soft spot for those two, used to let them get away with things just so long as they were a pair. It made them – well, special.'

Lorna Shaw held out the album for Costello to see. The cleaner in her uniform, laughing, one foot holding her bucket steady. A gap-toothed Sean balancing on the other side of the rim. The little blonde girl, her hands to her face, shoulders hunched, covering her laughter. Costello looked at the cleaner, the big glasses, a mole or cold sore on her top lip. Add on twenty years? She would be in her late sixties by now.

'And can you tell me this woman's name?'

'Do you know, I can't. And here's me priding myself on my memory,' Lorna Shaw said, reaching for another triangle of shortbread. 'I heard she retired a while back, and I think she moved away.'

'Can I take this and make a copy? You'll get it back, I promise.'

'Yes, of course.' Lorna nibbled at her shortbread, edging the crumbs into her mouth with her finger, dusting them away before reaching for the album again. 'There might be some more here of interest to you.'

Costello looked at the picture in her hand. Sean, a thin, attractive little boy.

'Do you know his sexual orientation?'

'He preferred girls to boys.' Lorna started to flick the pages back and forward. 'There she is.' She showed Costello a picture, three boys eating ice creams, pulling faces. And, off to one side, that beautiful pale face with tumbling blonde hair. 'That was taken on the beach at Largs.' Lorna's voice drifted. 'Trude Swann. Two *n*'s.'

'Really?' Costello asked, intuition rising.

'Yes.' Lorna shook her head. 'Trude looks like an angel, but she was incredibly bright, IQ off the scale. Used to draw pictures all the time, not much use in the real world. Beautiful too – just look at her. Always using bits of this and that, just rags and stuff, to dress up, pretend to be a fairy or a princess, someone with a personality she didn't have.' Lorna Shaw sighed. 'Pretty, but distant, lived in her own head. Nowadays she'd be tested for autism or something like that. Sean was the only one who talked to her, really. He always called her Truli, after Truly Scrumptious.'

Costello smiled. '*Chitty Chitty Bang Bang*.' She had lost her train of thought completely.

Lorna looked at the picture again. 'Sean was a good-looking boy, she was a very beautiful girl. You don't have to read Mills and Boon to know what would happen as soon as they were older. Sean stayed in the area, working with

White's, and visited her until she was old enough to leave. I don't know what happened to them after that . . . well, I know what happened to Sean.'

'What did you think of that?'

Lorna shrugged. 'He was never a bad boy, never cruel. But who knows?' she said enigmatically, as she pulled the photograph from its protective film, looking at the perfect face of the little girl. 'Who knows what became of her? Without him? The only person – absolutely the only person – she trusted was Sean.'

'And she had no family, anything that would help me trace her?'

'No, no family. If my memory serves me right, her mother committed suicide.'

'Oh, that's awful.'

Lorna shrugged. 'One of those things. All we had was a letter left with a lawyer, and the lawyer insisted on being told if she was moved.'

'Why? That's not usual, is it?'

'No idea. It wasn't money; it was some kind of inheritance, but worth nothing. The orphanage made a point of checking that. It always stuck in my mind. It never happened with any other kid we had, this lawyer who tracked her every move. There was a rumour that all the lawyer had was a letter to contact another lawyer in Edinburgh.'

'Can you remember the lawyer's name, by any chance?'

Lorna shook her head. 'Somebody in town, no doubt. Not the sort of thing I dealt with. Sean's not in trouble again, is he? He was such a charismatic wee boy.' She passed the photograph over to Costello. 'It's a shame they went their separate ways.'

'If they did,' Costello muttered to herself.

*

'Do you think priests spend their lives celibate?' asked Mulholland.

'They're supposed to.'

They both took out their warrant cards as Anderson leaned on the warm brass button next to the great door. A plastic laminated sign stated: *Please ring bell between 9.30 a.m. and noon for attention. Kitchen opens at 12.15 daily. No queuing, please, it annoys the neighbours. Please use bins for cigarettes.*

Mulholland wrinkled his nose at the insistent smell of urine. 'Lovely!' he said.

The door was opened by a fresh-faced man with dark blond hair. He wore jeans and a faded denim shirt, and his hands were wet as if he had been interrupted doing housework. Despite the Roman collar, he bore more than a passing resemblance to David Cassidy.

'Police,' said Anderson, showing his warrant card. 'I'm DI Anderson; this is DC Mulholland. Could we have a word with Father Thomas O'Keefe, please?'

The priest nodded, retreating behind the door, wiping his hands down the front of his jeans. 'I'm Tom O'Keefe,' he said. 'Please come in. I've about finished the dishes.'

Mulholland's eyes flickered at his boss on hearing the soft Irish brogue.

O'Keefe disappeared into the darkness of the vestibule, picking up a chipped mug of black tea and a half-eaten custard cream from the ledge that held the phone. Anderson noticed the chains securing the phone to the wall and the bars on the window. O'Keefe strode down the hall with a purposeful vitality at variance with the smell of vegetable soup and Mansion Polish. It was easy to see why he was a success. The priest was about to turn to say something when the main door, which had not yet swung closed, banged open again. McAlpine walked in, glaring at Mulholland, his dark eyes rimmed with red, his face gaunt and wasted. For a moment, as he stood leaning against the doorframe, the faint sunlight casting his thin face in shadow, it ran through Anderson's mind that O'Keefe must have thought he was having a visitation from the devil himself.

'And this is DCI McAlpine,' Anderson said. 'Father O'Keefe.'

O'Keefe smiled. 'From a DC to a DCI in three minutes; I must be dangerous.' He started fishing in his pocket for a key, hip against the door, mug in hand, the remains of the custard cream between his teeth.

The office was small and dark, and smelled of stale dust. The wooden panelling had been scratched and engraved by a thousand penknives. A sloping ceiling, painted the same sickly yellow as the walls, was stained with dried blood where the unwary had stood up too quickly. An old wooden mantelpiece in the corner was piled high with books and papers. The chaos of the room seemed to be built around the central desk, on which the computer sat in isolation. A flash of light came from the corner, and McAlpine leaned forward to see a dumpy woman in jogging trousers and T-shirt, hair dyed bright red, using a photocopier that sat precariously on an old green-baize card table. She was standing with her hand out, impatient for the machine to finish, the bright light flashing, highlighting the slight thickening of hair on her chin.

'This is Leeza,' said O'Keefe, by way of formal introduction. 'I've forgotten your second name, Leeza.'

'McFadyean. M small C, F-A-D-Y-E-A-N,' she said. 'Just give me two minutes.'

O'Keefe had moved a pile of blankets from the seat behind the computer and was now standing with them, arms out, waiting for divine intervention to clear a space. Leeza finished her work, the paper still warm and curling, and plucked the blankets from the priest as she went past.

'I'll put them in the laundry.'

O'Keefe sat down, experience reminding him to bend his head. Anderson realized that the priest was a smaller, slighter man than he had first thought. Nobody spoke until Leeza had left the room, and McAlpine slowly closed the door with his foot, making sure nothing could be heard from the other side.

'You are, no doubt, aware that there's been a series of murders in the area. As part of our usual routine, we are flinging our net slightly wider, trying . . .' Anderson was placatory.

The priest held up his hand. 'I appreciate what you're saying, DI Anderson. I'm not daft. I know why you're here, and I don't have a problem with it. In some ways, I was wondering why it took you so long. You'll be wanting to talk about Arlene, I suppose.'

'And what can you tell us about her?'

'Not much, really.' O'Keefe shrugged lightly. 'We'd put her on a rehab programme, and an adult literacy course. Well, we were *trying* to get her on one. She had problems with reading.'

'Did you know her well yourself, Father?' Anderson asked mildly.

'I'd met her, but I would never say I knew her well,' the priest answered. 'This place may look deserted at the moment, but once the doors open dozens – hundreds – of people are in and out. For sure, I knew her name, so when I heard the poor girl had been murdered, I checked on our involvement with her. Your first thought when such a thing happens is whether there might have been anything you could have done . . .'

'So, a literacy programme – who would have been her initial contact here?'

'It depends what you mean by contact. I suppose her social worker or her GP would have referred her. It might even have been one of the outreach workers. But, if my memory serves me correctly, she came here of her own accord. Was there not a kid involved in all this?'

'Yes, she has a son, in care.'

O'Keefe nodded thoughtfully. 'And I suppose he will stay in care. Our clients come here because they have decided to change, to make a positive change. I say *they*, because nobody can do it on their behalf. So we welcome people like Arlene, and do what we can to help them to help themselves.'

The three policemen remained silent.

'So whoever it was first answered the phone,' said O'Keefe, 'could have been her point of contact. And I don't know who that was. I'm sorry.'

'What about the deliveries you get from the Save the Children shop?' Mulholland asked, abruptly changing the subject, provoking glances from his two companions.

'Sorry?'

'Did Lynzi Traill ever deliver stuff from the shop in Byres Road? You do take the stuff from there?'

'We're always glad to take whatever they are unable to sell, certainly.' O'Keefe looked totally nonplussed. 'I'm sorry,' he said again. 'I saw her photograph in the paper, but I don't think I ever set eyes on her, never knew her name. It meant nothing to me.' He shrugged, sounding truly sorry. If he was a liar, he was a good one.

Anderson looked past him to the wall behind, letting time pass. Silence was good for putting a witness slightly out of their comfort zone. Anderson studied the photographs hanging haphazardly along a length of the mahogany panelling, all framed differently, some in colour, some black-and-white, and some just photocopies of articles in the local paper. Most were of people doing strange things, obviously for charity. Anderson moved closer for a good look, and shuddered. Somebody looked as though they had raised money by sitting in a bath of worms.

He quickly asked O'Keefe, 'Elizabeth Jane Fulton. You knew her, though?'

O'Keefe looked uncomfortable. 'I'm not sure I do – did.'

'Maybe this will jog your memory.' Mulholland pulled out a photograph of Elizabeth Jane and handed it over.

O'Keefe took his time looking before handing the picture back. 'I still don't recall this girl. I'm sorry. She was another victim, wasn't she?'

'Yes.'

McAlpine sighed as if bored. 'So it would come as a surprise that her family thought you knew her?'

O'Keefe's blue eyes flitted from McAlpine to Anderson. Anderson's eyes stayed steady.

'Can you explain that?' asked McAlpine.

'No, I can't. It is as I say.' He bit his lip. 'I don't know why anybody would think that.'

Anderson cleared his throat. 'How well did she know the Reverend Shand? He was her minister. He's on your committee, isn't he?'

'Andrew? Yes, he is. He's on holiday at the moment. Majorca. Or Minorca, would it be? He's a great birdwatcher.'

'Maybe you would like to tell us where you were on Sunday night, Monday morning,' McAlpine asked, looking at Mulholland, instructing him to take notes.

'I would have to think. Sunday night, now . . . after Mass I went to the Western, visiting a friend. Then home, via Porters for a drink, Diet Coke because I was taking communion for a colleague up in Rose Street. That was at eight, so I would be home by half nine.' O'Keefe shrugged but less confidently now.

'And you were home alone in the small hours of the morning?'

'Priests usually are.'

'Some priests, Father O'Keefe,' retorted McAlpine.

'Not funny, DCI McAlpine,' said O'Keefe, offended.

McAlpine carried on without apology. 'What's the set-up here?' McAlpine was prowling round what space there was in the room. 'How is it going?'

O'Keefe had switched to friendly mode again. 'We're a registered charity, and we've been pretty well funded, so far.' He touched wood. 'We got lottery money to convert the church building to its current use. And routine maintenance is done at little more than cost, almost pro bono, by a local firm. It's their way of supporting us, and it makes a big difference. As far as running the place goes, the basic organization works by a rota system. I don't have a parish of my own, so I'm here full time, and local clergy of all denominations come in and help out.'

O'Keefe turned and viewed the gallery of pictures behind; the pride in his achievement was unmistakable. 'That's me, and there's Rabbi Shaffer. That's Reverend Shand . . .' He pointed to a photograph of a tall thin-faced man in a dog collar – definitely too old to be Christopher Robin. 'And Father Flynn, Reverend William Macdonald.' Two rotund, elderly men were clowning around, one on a space hopper, the other on a skateboard. Below them was a page from a local paper, a cheery line-up photo of a few old crocks playing football.

'Have you all been here since the Phoenix opened?'

'Apart from George. He's been around for ages, but he

became official two, three months ago?' O'Keefe sighed into a smile. 'His brother died recently, so he found time on his hands. Otherwise I don't know much about his personal circumstances.'

McAlpine leaned forward, speaking softly. 'Father O'Keefe, could you tell us what you do know about his personal circumstances? Gossip and speculation are all we've been getting.'

O'Keefe bit his lip, as if reluctant to say much. 'As far as I know, George came down here after his brother died. Alasdair had been struggling with things for a while and finally took his own life – George has never told me the details, and I have never asked. Those circumstances drove him to stay here and "live in the real world", as he put it.'

'And how does he fit in? He comes from such a strict faith.'

'I was worried about that when he applied to join us. You do tend to think that anybody in the West Highland Presbyterian Kirk will be totally intolerant of all we are trying to do. But then' – O'Keefe smiled charmingly – 'that's just us being intolerant of them. But George is fine. He knew he needed to get out into the big wide world. It couldn't have been easy for him to come down here after his home – the land his family had farmed for years – was sold. But I don't suppose there was anything to keep him there, with everything gone.' The priest nodded. 'He's a good man, George.'

McAlpine said. 'There's nothing else. We'll leave you to get on.'

Anderson looked at his notebook. 'There is one more thing,' he said as O'Keefe got to his feet. 'Cooking goes on here, on the premises. You use knives. None have gone missing?'

O'Keefe straightened up and bumped his head on the ceiling. 'No. They're kept locked up in an old glass display cabinet. All the knives are numbered with Dymo tape for security. Two of the guys who make the soup were in the Catering Corps, so they keep the knives very sharp. But there have never been any missing.'

'Where are the keys kept?'

'On a hook, beside the cabinet.' O'Keefe seemed not to notice any lack of logic.

By the time Costello left Lorna Shaw's flat it was nearly one o'clock. She decided not to go back through the Clyde Tunnel and instead turned left to Pollok Park and the Burrell in search of some peace and quiet and a green field. She had been born a south-sider, in Mosspark, less than half a mile from here physically, but socially it could have been the other side of the moon.

She allowed her head to roll like a puppet's as her Corolla bounced over the sleeping policemen on the boundary road. She went past Dumbreck Riding School and the fat hairy little ponies grazing in the drizzle. Then past the mounted police stables, where the horses were bigger, much more shiny. By the time she reached the car park the drizzle had stopped and the sun was thinking about coming out. Two tourist coaches were disgorging their load at that precise moment. One quick glance at Degas's *Jockeys in the Rain* and then they'd start to queue at the café. She got out of the car and went to sit on the fence instead, listening to the steady grind and grunt of two Highland cattle grazing near by.

She took the envelope from her duffel-coat pocket and opened it, thinking she was beginning to understand Sean, except that she couldn't get the Trude thing to fit. Had they been together, and had she left him while he was in prison?

Or were they together and seeking revenge on society? Either would fit Batten's profile. She could match Lorna's Sean with the Sean from the file. But she could not reconcile that with the evidence of Malkie Steele's body and the pulpy mess Sean had made of it. She watched as one of the cows lifted her head to regard her through plum-brown eyes. Costello looked back, realizing how much she and Sean had in common, except that Sean had been surrounded by friends and staff who held him in genuine affection. Somebody had always looked out for his welfare, which was more than she could say for herself.

She was going to ask Wyngate to track Trude. And she wasn't even going to ask permission, in case McAlpine said no. She flicked open her mobile.

'Wingnut, can you do your computer magic for me? See what you can come up with on Trude Swann – that's with two *n*'s. And get back to me, before anyone else.' She snapped her phone shut. In today's world, Trude's footprints would be visible in the electronic snow. Somewhere.

The cow snorted warm air from her nostrils; Costello was boring her. So she said goodbye and slid from the fence. She had an appointment with Nicholson in an hour's time, and she was looking forward to it like toothache.

The flat was crammed full of furniture, most of it far too big for such a small room, remnants of a life in a larger, grander home. Former DI David Nicholson walked back into the living room, pushing a leather chair to one side. Costello had the feeling she was not exactly welcome. The big, well-worn chair had been right in front of the widescreen television; a half-drunk cup of tea was on the floor, with two ginger nuts on a side plate beside it. She had interrupted him watching the cricket highlights from Australia on Sky.

Folded over on the seat was that morning's *Herald*. Costello could see Lynzi and Elizabeth Jane looking out at her in black-and-white. Arlene was in colour.

'You're looking well. Retirement suits you,' she said in a voice she hoped sounded genuine.

He didn't answer but walked into the tiny kitchen, holding on to the doorframe, shuffling his feet as he went, his slippers not quite clearing the carpet. He had aged badly; life in the retirement apartment did not suit him. She saw a few small plastic brown pill bottles on a side table. Maybe he wasn't keeping too grand.

'I'll just stick the kettle on.'

'Lovely,' said Costello through the door. She pulled a chair out from the dining table, turning it so it faced the leather one, wishing he would come back and open the window or turn the fire off or something.

Nicholson appeared with a china cup and more ginger nuts. 'So what can I do for you, DS Costello? What's your first name again, petal?'

'Costello. I just get called Costello. I'm here about Sean McTiernan.' She had already explained all this on the phone. He handed her the cup, his clammy hand clasped over hers, and she shivered despite the heat, relieved that Batten was sure Christopher Robin was a young man.

'So!' she said enthusiastically. 'You were quite famous for the work you did on this case. Anything you can tell me?'

'Can I ask why?'

'Well, it's all background stuff, anybody who's recently come out of jail, anybody with a criminal history involving violence . . . of any kind.' Her voice trailed off. *You were in the force*, she wanted to say, *you know the score.*

'For these Crucifixion Killings?'

What else? 'Yes.'

'Oh, I don't think so, my dear.'

For a minute she thought he was refusing to help. He sipped his tea, looking out of the window as though she didn't exist. All his annoying habits were coming back to her now. She ploughed on. 'Why do you say that?'

He shook his head. 'It doesn't fit.'

'I've seen the pictures of Steele's body. McTiernan mashed it to a pulp.'

'Steele was an animal.'

'Did you ever find a history between McTiernan and Steele? Any connection?'

'My dear, McTiernan confessed. We didn't look for a reason why.'

'But you didn't accept it, did you?' She stated it as fact.

Nicholson's mouth moved on the side of his cup, his thick feminine lips incongruous with his thin face. 'No, we didn't accept it. But you can't find what ain't there. Malkie liked little boys. He was a predator, a paedophile. Sean was a good-looking wee boy; maybe there was no more to it than that.'

'But you didn't accept it?' Costello persevered.

'He confessed the minute he walked in the door,' Nicholson said, with some irritation. 'Look, I'll tell you what happened that night, as far as I remember it. McTiernan is a shrewd young man, very shrewd indeed.' Costello felt as though she was back at school. 'He served four years –'

'Three years and six months,' corrected Costello to show she was on top of things.

'Instead of life. For an assault like that, he could have gone down for life, recommended twenty. But he engineered it. It looked like culp. hom. if he was unlucky. If he was lucky, he'd get off on a plea of self-defence. And he can't be tried again. Small price to pay to get rid of somebody.'

'So there must have been some history between them? A reason to get rid of him?' Costello's mind was leaping forward now.

'Nothing that we could find. No connection to anybody, not anybody who was – anybody. There was a lot of stuff that didn't make sense. Not then. Not now.'

'For instance?' Costello persisted.

'First thing is that Steele was a hitman for Arthur Laing, a really nasty piece of work. You won't remember, too young, but in those days Glasgow hadn't yet moved out the hands of gangs and into the drug war. The crime wasn't nice, but at least it was logical, no drug-crazed nutters winding the police up.'

Costello held her tongue. She'd never given any credence to the view that the streets were safer when the Krays were alive, but she knew that was exactly where the conversation was going. 'So what did they do, Laing's lot? The usual? Protection? Prostitution? Robbery with menaces?'

'And a touch of high-level reset, stolen stuff from abroad mostly. And it was lucrative; the European Union was making international crime easier. Ask any of the Customs and Excise boys. The situation was starting to get out of control, so they set up a special squad with the Inland Revenue to try to get him. Losing Steele hit Laing hard, really hard. And it caused a vacuum that we could take advantage of. *Did* take advantage of. But McTiernan? Entrapment, hen. That's what I thought.'

'Yes?' said Costello encouragingly.

'Malkie was purporting to be a football scout. Sean, from all accounts, was not happy about meeting him, not happy at all.' His eyes drifted to the Test Match. 'He put a chisel through his hand the day he and Steele were supposed to meet, so he could engineer a rearrangement of time and place. Steele was not going to be suspicious of a wee guy like Sean. He walked up that lane like a lamb to the slaughter, and good riddance. And Sean had prepared for it all. He'd been down at his local skip that morning dumping a whole lot of rubbish, with his hand full of stitches, I may add. He emptied his flat, and when the flat was broken into, he didn't report it. He was in the process of buying a house and then pulled out the minute he'd killed Steele. I don't believe for a minute he ever swallowed the football-scout story.' Nicholson swung in his seat. 'McTiernan was not stupid. He planned Steele's killing, I'm sure of it. We all thought he planned to do a runner. He'd even bought hair dye to disguise himself,' Nicholson snorted. 'Then he changed his mind.'

'Where was this flat?' She knew from the files but decided to check his memory.

'In Ayr, Petrie Street in Ayr.' Nicholson was right about that. 'He'd lived there for about a year.'

'On his own?'

'So he said.' His attention was back on the Test Match again.

'And the house? The house he was thinking about buying?' Costello was scribbling. They were beyond the contents of the file now.

'A big house, right on the coast, below Culzean Castle.'

'That's the middle of nowhere.'

'Yeah, too big for one person, and no place for a young man on his own, miles from the nearest pub.' Nicholson shook his head. 'Bought a puppy one day and apparently dumped it three days later. Nice. Expensive it was, one of those husky things.' The lips were working their way round the rim of the cup.

'Where did the money come from? To buy the house?'

'I told you, he never bought the house. He thought about it and pulled out. Listen, hen, Malkie Steele was an evil bastard, better dead. Young McTiernan did us all a favour. You think we were going to waste police time looking any further than we had to?'

Costello decided on a different tack. 'Did you ever meet a girl called Trude?'

'She never visited him when he was being held, or in court, or in prison. He was an attractive boy, he had plenty of women coming and going. But none of them was this Trude.' Costello smiled her granny-sweet smile, willing him to talk. 'I saw him in jail, two months after he'd been sent down, and he was already changing, for the worse. I do remember him asking how my wife was, though.' Costello followed the line of Nicholson's gaze to a photograph of him and his wife, golfing. 'But she'd died the previous month. The week I finally got my retirement, can you believe it? They'd kept me hanging on all that time and what for? Another three quid on my pension.' He was bitter.

'Did Sean know your wife, then?'

'He knew she was ill and asked after her,' he remembered. 'Which is more than some of my colleagues did.' He scratched his head. 'He said to me – and I remember his exact words – *If you could have done something, anything, to save her, would you?* I answered that I would, of course I would. He just shrugged and walked out.'

'And what was that supposed to mean?' asked Costello, jotting it down in her own shorthand.

'I suggest you ask him when you meet him, hen.'

Back at the station, Costello reached for the *Clyde Coast Yellow Pages* and turned to 'Dog Breeders'. She embarked on a long series of calls, each one starting the same way: 'I'd just like to ask – do you by any chance breed huskies?'

McAlpine woke from his nightmare, sweating, his face damp with tears. He had been crying in his sleep. In sleep he'd been back among the lightning, the rain, the shattered glass and . . . then that image, of somebody – *her* – pulling him free . . .

Since his conversation in the pub with Anderson he had known that Anna's ghost was waking and stretching, reaching out to him. Every time he went into that murder room, he felt he was being sucked into a tunnel and that at the end of it was Anna, waiting.

He opened his eyes, looking at the ceiling, then closed them again, seeing two little boys running through a field, the younger one stumbling as he tried to keep up, the bigger boy stopping, holding out his hand, helping.

McAlpine opened his eyes. The pain of the loss of his brother suddenly stabbed as sharply as it had twenty-two years ago. He stroked the swelling over his jaw, more to comfort himself than to ease any pain. He turned to try and sleep, letting his mind drift, back to Anna . . . Anna, who could give him comfort . . .

But sleep wouldn't come. He got up from the sofa and went upstairs to the en suite, where it was warm. He washed his face in hot soapy water and took a good slug at the Glenfiddich he kept hidden under some old towels at the bottom of the linen cupboard. That dream had really disturbed him. Standing there, looking in the mirror, eyes focused on his bruises, he could not get the image of the monkey creature squatting on the bonnet of the car out of his mind. It wasn't the crash or the flames or the glass, the little taste of death, that was getting to him. The cloak . . . he could remember as far as the black cloak . . . but, no matter how hard he pushed, his memory went no further. He could not see the face beyond Anna's, the curve of her cheek as the lightning fell on it, the lightness of her eyes.

He picked up a towel and held it to his face; it was soft and warm. He closed his eyes, and he could see her, always her, with her blonde halo, on the beach, a shy smile playing on those beautiful lips, her hair more curled than it had been. It suited her.

'There's clean stuff in the wardrobe.' Helena walked in, rubbing sleep from her eyes. 'Sorry, I did mean to wake you.'

He tried to shake the confusion from his head. 'I've been asleep for two hours. And on a Tuesday afternoon too. Oh, God, my head hurts.'

'You haven't seen the papers today?'

'No, somebody else been murdered while I was asleep?'

Helena smiled wryly. 'Only my reputation.'

'A lost cause, then?'

'I hope it doesn't cause you any hassle. Terry put his foot in it more than once in an article yesterday. I would sue except his sister is my best friend and an advocate,' she giggled. 'Some people.'

'Goes with the territory. I'll survive.'

Her voice was suddenly full of comfort. 'You know that stuff you left behind? I put it all on the piano. Those photographs and your brother's award?'

'Yes.' The response was sharp.

'You left them in your pocket, and they nearly got put in the wash. If they're that important to you, you should be more careful.' He looked at her, his eyes hard, so she tried a different tack. 'If you want, I'll get the commendation framed, then you can hang it in the hall.'

McAlpine shook his head.

'Anyway, I'm going to have a shower now. Then I'll get back to the gallery, see what they've managed to get done without me. You going back to work?' She stood up, opened the linen cupboard and pulled out three fresh fluffy white towels. 'Look at you, Alan. You're a mess,' she added quietly.

'I'm snowed under with this case, you know that.'

'Yes, I do know. Try to get something to eat before you go back to work. There's some soup in the fridge.'

He lifted his hand, caressing her cheek with the back of his fingers. Seeing blonde hair rather than auburn, a younger, more beautiful face.

'You will come to the exhibition, won't you?' Helena went on. 'You can walk around insulting everybody's work and saying, very loudly, that a five-year-old could do better.' The phone echoed its way up the stairs. 'I bet you that's the station.'

He leaned forward to kiss her. The phone was insistent. He left.

'Fuck! Fuck! Fuck! Fuck!'

Costello shook her head infinitesimally at Anderson before gently closing the door. Neither had ever seen McAlpine so angry.

On his desk was a copy of that day's *Evening Gazette*, folded open, showing the gossip snippet that somehow merited two column-filling photographs; one showed McAlpine, face battered and bruised, looking very drunk, which was ironic, because he had been sober when it was taken. The other showed Helena in profile, her hair up, wearing what looked like diamond earrings, with a man, also in profile, hovering by her left shoulder. Costello had already read the original piece in the quality broadsheet, Terry

Gilfillan's preview of Glasgow's art scene for October, the main topic being Helena's exhibition. It was the picture they had used that had caught Costello's attention. Helena laughing, her head inclined towards Gilfillan . . . suggesting an intimacy that wasn't there. And from that seed this snide little item had grown. She knew there was no truth in it. But she did wonder what Gilfillan was thinking, to allow them to use *that* photograph. Under the headline 'Hanging Out' half a dozen lines invited readers to judge for themselves whether the long hours DCI McAlpine was putting in on the Crucifixion Killer case had driven him to hit the bottle, and his gorgeous wife – 'owner of the swanky Gallery Cynae' – into the arms of her 'good friend and business associate, Glasgow art dealer Terence Gilfillan'.

'Fucking journalists! I'd like to take every single copy of this paper and stick it up –'

'Alternatively, you could phone Helena right away,' Anderson ventured. 'The press will be –'

'Get out.'

Anderson took a deep breath. 'I think you should let her know that –'

'Out!'

'It's half four, and you've a press conference to go to . . . *sir.*'

'*Out!*'

Anderson squeezed a breath through clenched teeth and left McAlpine's office, shutting the door with precision, showing just how much he would like to slam it.

Costello watched him go, his concern for the Boss's wife duly noted.

McAlpine slammed himself into the seat so hard the wheels bounced with the recoil. He seemed to be muttering every single swear word he knew, and a few Costello didn't.

She stood her ground, leaning back on the low filing cabinet, waiting for his rage to pass.

Through the glass screen she could see Anderson, gesturing that the press were queuing up outside and they needed a decision fast. It was up to her to bring the Boss round.

'Fuckin' media! Fuckin' sharks!'

'Yes, but the bite these sharks want is a soundbite. Something that'll sound good on the telly.'

'Fucking vultures!' he muttered.

Anderson was gesturing wildly now. The gentlemen of the press were not happy.

'Boss, you were just lucky they didn't do this before.'

McAlpine turned on her, counting points on his fingertips. 'One, I've got three unsolved murders and not a single lead on the biggest fucking psycho since Bible John. Two, my team have worked for a solid week with mostly unpaid overtime.'

'I have noticed that one,' said Costello with feeling.

McAlpine was already on to point three. 'And I've dislocated my fucking shoulder.'

Costello stayed calm. 'Boss, they strapped your shoulder up just fine. And I've paracetamol in my bag if you –'

'Fuck your bloody paracetamol! We have the ACC as well as his entire office – most of Pitt Street, in fact – the First Minister, and a room full of irate, *sober* journalists, if that's not an oxymoron –'

'No doubt. So why not just make a written statement, dish out the usual platitudes . . . and maybe send Mulholland with the media liaison officer to the press conference? He looks the part, nice smile, big ego, big suit. Your face would frighten children at the moment, sir,' she said, smiling encouragingly.

McAlpine jumped to his feet, suddenly back to his old

self. Costello retracted herself as far into the wall as she could. 'I have a bloody murder inquiry to run, so I am not – fucking – *going!*'

'So, that's a no, then.'

'That's a no.' He sat back down again. Costello caught Anderson's eye through the glass, jerking her head in Mulholland's direction, mouthing the words 'conference room'. Anderson cottoned on and walked away, shaking his head, practising a few swear words of his own.

McAlpine had switched off one argument and turned on to another. 'How did you get on with finding out about McTiernan?' He tipped the dregs of yesterday's coffee out of his mug. 'Put some coffee in that, will you?'

Costello flicked the switch on the kettle behind her. The kettle started to bubble; he must have had it boiled before all this started.

'McTiernan did his apprenticeship with White's.'

'The joiners?'

'Hugh White offered to put up bail when he was arrested, and they've given him his job back.'

'Really?' He was rubbing the bruises on his face again.

'White's do the maintenance at the Phoenix,' Costello continued. 'And Sean was sent to fix a leaking skylight at Elizabeth Jane Fulton's address. So we have him potentially connected to two of the three victims. And if he works at the Phoenix . . .'

'We might find a connection with Lynzi. But so far only one of those connections is certain. The waitress Littlewood spoke to at the Ashton Café was pretty sure he left with Arlene. Eyewitnesses place both of them later at the disco, the beat coppers saw him running down the street, and . . .'

She suddenly thought about the other girl, the girl he was

up the lane with, petite and pretty. She bit her lip. Take away the black hair . . .

'And what?'

Costello backtracked. 'Arlene might have pissed off McTiernan in the disco. But, sir, I'm wondering if it's all just one coincidence too many.'

There was a knock at the door. DC Irvine stood there, too nervous to come in. 'Somebody to see you, sir.' She read the name from a piece of paper. 'A Reverend Leask.'

'Good!' He stood up, picking up the file from his desk. 'I'm going to see Leask for a civilized chat, get his version of the goings-on at the Phoenix, find out whether somebody's telling porkies about Tom and Elizabeth Jane. Next time you're there, see what you can get out of Leeza about O'Keefe and Co. and we'll compare notes. You can tell the bosses at HQ to go to hell, or refer them to . . . whoever. After that you can reinterview Arlene's friend from Clatty Pat's. I notice nobody's got around to that yet.'

'Tracey? We have it arranged for tomorrow. The thing is, sir, we're run off our feet, and it's a second interview. It went on the back burner,' she added lamely.

'Well, arrange it for today, then. Just get some decent answers out of her. And focus on Sean. He's ticking all Batten's boxes.'

All except the box marked 'Religion', Costello thought.

They had put Leask in Interview Room 4B. He sat quietly, dressed in an old anorak, head bowed, clasping and unclasping his hands between his knees, deep in thought. He looked exhausted. There was a greenish tinge around his blue eyes, a yellowness to his lips; the tone of his skin did not take tiredness well.

'How are you doing, George?' McAlpine put out his hand and was greeted by a febrile handshake.

'Not so good. Sorry to disturb you at work, though I didn't honestly think you would be here. It's nearly six, after all.'

McAlpine smiled and put the file down on the table. 'My work is done when it's done.'

'Don't you ever go home?'

'My wife is very busy these days; she hardly notices whether I'm there or not. Gives me a chance to catch up with the paper-chasing. So what can I do for you?'

'There's something I think I should tell you, in case it's relevant. I got a phone call from Ian Livingstone's mother this morning. He's in hospital, an overdose of sleeping pills.'

It was McAlpine's turn to look at the floor, the lino burned through with old cigarette dowts. There had been no harassment. Just three interviews, and exhaustive checking of Lynzi's boyfriend's alibi. 'How is he?'

'He'll make it. Naturally, he was very upset over Lynzi. He had his stomach pumped. Though to be honest, it was so mild they think it might have been accidental. He'd been put on some medication to help him sleep, he was in such a state. And he maybe lost track of how much he was taking.' Leask placed his hands outstretched on the table; he seemed to be concentrating on how far he could span his fingers before relaxing. 'I'm obviously very sensitive to such things, losing Alasdair the way I did.'

McAlpine nodded in understanding. 'Would you like a coffee?'

'No, I'm not taking up any more of your valuable time. The hospital's keeping Ian for a day or two, just in case. I'm going to phone his mother tonight, so it would be nice if I could put his mind at rest. It would be . . . appropriate.

234

He seems to think that he is still a suspect, when I know, as I'm sure you do, that there is no way he could have done such a thing. Not to Lynzi, not to anybody. The man who's doing this is an animal –'

'Our profiler tells us to focus on the fact that he's a human being,' McAlpine interrupted, his hands flat on the Christopher Robin file. 'Not an animal, not a demon.'

Leask's eyes followed the DCI's hands. 'A human being *haunted* by demons, certainly,' he said carefully. He put his hand on the file that lay between them, his fingertip tracing the doodled writing. 'Christopher Robin? What a picture of innocence.'

McAlpine smiled. 'Depends on which Christopher Robin. But you can tell Livingstone his alibi's been checked, again and again. Of course he couldn't be in two places at once. He's not an active line of inquiry. But, as I said to you on Sunday, we'll need to interview him again as a witness.'

'And, as I told *you*, he has been through this again and again.'

'But he may unwittingly know something that could be of help to us. If he wants to stay where he is, we can send somebody down.'

'Thanks. I'll pass that on to him.'

'George, did Elizabeth Jane give you the impression she knew Tom well?'

Leask looked stunned. 'Oh.'

'Oh?'

'I've since learned that Elizabeth Jane had a habit of –'

'Exaggerating?'

'Exactly . . . the extent of her friendships with men. I thought at the time she was a bit forward in the way she spoke about him, him being a priest. The way her parents said she spoke about him with them sounded to me more involved than it should be. But now I know it was just her way. I've never actually seen them together. If that clarifies the matter for you.' Then Leask straightened in his chair, the change in his manner subtly altering the balance between them. 'There was something else I wanted to say. Something personal.'

'Go ahead.' Half defensive, McAlpine knew he was being seduced by that voice, the delicate almost-soporific Highland accent filling the room with a slow-paced musical cadence as the man spoke.

Leask looked a little uncomfortable. He spoke carefully. 'I see many things in my line of work, many men driven so far that they don't see what they risk losing.'

'Losing?'

Leask held his hand up. 'Just look at the hours you work: it's starting to take you over. It's commendable, such devotion to duty, but there are many victims in this. Marriage is a sacred thing, a union before God. This man, this killer, has claimed three victims. Don't let your marriage be another. You have a choice, Mr McAlpine, as a detective that you do not have as a husband. The ego that drives you to catch this man must be quelled. I'm not stupid; I know the hours you work. My advice? Go home, see your wife. It'll make things better in the long run. You can't have two mistresses.'

'You have the Church.'

'And only the Church. I could not give a hundred per cent to both Church and wife. Wives need looking after; they need attention. When I had to make the choice, I chose the Church, as did Thomas O'Keefe. Your place is with your wife, not here.' He stood up and walked round the table, placing his hand on McAlpine's shoulder.

*

236

Mulholland had parked in Byres Road at about half past seven; he and Costello were sitting in his BMW watching the door of the Whistler's Mother pub and the small huddle of smokers gathered at the mouth of Whistler's Lane. It was busy for a Tuesday night; a karaoke competition had just started at Babinski's Balloon and the drunken strains of 'You've Lost That Lovin' Feelin'' were echoing down the street. Mulholland, as usual, had the heater on, and the windows were steaming up; Costello wiped them from the inside and tried not to keep count as Mulholland sighed for the tenth time.

'She's not going to turn up, is she?'

'She'd better, otherwise the Boss will put out a warrant. And I'll personally frogmarch her in. I'd a list of things to do today and I haven't done any of them.'

'But tomorrow is another day.'

'Some sleep would be nice too.' Costello suddenly sat upright. 'Look, that's her, if I'm not mistaken.' She rubbed the side window with her gloves. 'There, in the white skirt. And remember to try not to act like the polis.'

The girl stopped walking and leaned against the wall of the Whistler's Mother, her foot up on the bricks behind her, her face petulant. She was bored already. Tracey was a pretty girl, much younger than Costello had imagined, with long straight black hair that was clean and shiny. She wore a black leather jacket and a white peasant skirt, the bottom of it already heavy with rain. Costello noticed her feet were cased in black dancing pumps, entirely unsuitable for the weather. She looked very naive for a prostitute.

Her face brightened as Mulholland got out of the car. She ignored Costello but smiled sweetly at him. Mulholland had the audacity to smile back. Costello stepped in front of him. 'DS Costello. DC Mulholland. Tracey Witherspoon?'

'Yeah.' She managed to answer Costello while keeping her eyes on Mulholland. Costello had to admit she was impressed. She could feel Mulholland's ego being flattered.

'Want to go inside? Better than getting soaked out here.'

'If you're buying,' said Tracey, peeling herself away from the wall.

The Whistler's Mother was half empty. The usual crowd were at the bar like beasts round a watering hole, but most of the tables were free. As Costello headed towards a table, she noticed the manager gesticulating that Tracey should either put her cigarette out or get out herself.

'Get three Cokes, Vik, and show him your warrant card. Ask him how many times he's put her out of here for soliciting. We'll be over by the window.'

'You want to talk to me about Arlene?' Tracey arranged herself on the seat, automatically pouting.

'Yes.'

'She was an idiot.'

'That's not a crime.'

'But in this game it can be dangerous.'

Mulholland arrived with the drinks. She thanked him with some sincerity. 'No chance of getting a vodka in that?' She was well spoken, a well-educated girl.

'No,' said Costello.

'It might loosen my tongue a bit,' she suggested, running her tongue over her lips to prove the point. Mulholland had the decency to look away.

'Oh, get on with it or we'll take you down the station,' Costello snapped. 'I don't have all day.'

'Look, I'm sorry for what happened to her, but it could happen to anybody.'

'Yeah, but it happened to Arlene. She was a good friend of yours,' said Mulholland, moving into the good-cop role.

Tracey shook her head, her hair moving like a curtain. 'She wasn't a friend of mine. Who told you that?'

'You were out together, celebrating.'

'We had a night off. We went out for a drink, about six of us, and three of us went up to Clatty Pat's afterwards.' She shrugged. 'That's all there was to it.'

'All?' said Costello. 'Don't think so, Tracey. Try again.'

'Well, I think she wanted to be me,' Tracey said with no trace of modesty.

'She wanted to be you?' asked Costello.

'Yeah, you deaf?'

'No, just confused.'

'Look, I'm eighteen. I'm going to stay on the game until I'm thirty, and that will be me set for life. I have a plan. This is a career for me.'

'Do you know how many times I've heard that?' said Costello wearily.

'I can imagine, but I'm clever. I don't do drugs, I smoke only ten a day, and I don't drink often. I have my regular clients. I'm saving for a deposit on a flat, then I'll be up the property ladder and within five years I'll be working in the city centre, around Princes Square. That's where the money is.'

'Claiming what as a profession? Don't tell me – exotic dancer.' Costello sighed wearily. 'Everybody knows what that means.'

Tracey sighed with impatience. 'Look, I can talk in company, I don't let people down. I can behave. I'm going for escort work. That's where the money is.' She realized she had repeated herself. 'I'm expensive, but I'm good. It's a business. I work hard at it.'

'And Arlene?'

'Was just a streetwalker. She turned tricks up a lane. She

had a kid, and it ruined her body. I told her losing weight and going blonde would bring in more money. I was being ironic, but she believed me. She took everything I said as gospel. She wasn't the brightest. She drinks – drank – too much, she used to have a drug habit. She wasn't going anywhere. I was on the way up, she was on the way down, so she latched on to me. She was a good laugh, sometimes. End of story.'

'Was she on a course of self-improvement?'

Tracey snorted, choking slightly on her Coke. 'Sorry, that went down the wrong way.' She cleared her throat. 'She was an idiot, but she had this idea that if she got a better flat she could earn more money. She didn't have her boy – Ryan, is it? – living with her because her flat was so damp and he's asthmatic, apart from everything else. To stand a chance of getting a new flat, she had to get on some sort of training programme and show a change of profession; then she could apply for the return of her son. She needed a sponsor, somebody who'd give good references to her change of character.'

'Was any of this genuine?'

'I don't think so.' She reconsidered. 'No, it wasn't. She was just jumping through hoops for what she could get. I tell you, she had those muppets at the refuge eating out her hand. And good for her.'

'Who, at the Phoenix? Who was her contact?'

Tracey shook her head. 'He was kinda cute, nice voice. He was there for the taking, she said. No names.' Tracey wriggled in her seat a little. 'Can we go out for a ciggie?' she asked Mulholland.

'He doesn't smoke,' said Costello. 'What does "there for the taking" mean?'

'Guys like that can be naive. You can say they tried

something on, blackmail them. Not for much, but most guys would give you money just to make you go away. It's a game, isn't it? No harm done.'

'I think somebody was playing another game, where harm was done.'

Tracey shrugged again. 'Look, I do know she had some photographs taken, and she took them to one of those computer-print places to get postcards made up.'

'What kind of postcards?'

'Oh, her dressed as a schoolgirl in black suspenders, that kind of thing. As if men are interested in that nowadays. She thought it would bring in a better class of punter, that's how stupid she was. Anybody can pick up that type of thing.'

Costello resisted looking at Mulholland.

'What did she intend doing with them? Phone boxes?'

'That kind of thing, yeah.'

'Very upmarket.'

Tracey laughed. 'I had some quality shots done at a studio, and she thought she was doing the same thing.'

'Either way it's a good way to get yourself killed.' Costello stood up. 'Do us a favour, Tracey. Stay off the streets just now, we're busy. I don't want to be looking at your battered face on a slab, OK? Take care,' she added cheerfully. 'Come on, Vik.'

'Yeah, go on, Vik. Bye.' Tracey rippled her fingers at him. Costello looked heavenwards and sighed.

At exactly eight o'clock on Tuesday evening, the Reverend Shand returned Anderson's phone call from a small hotel in rural Minorca. The voice on the phone was the voice of a minister who had been in Glasgow all his life and had seen and heard everything. He didn't sound surprised that they had tracked him down – he had, after all, left the phone number with his daughter. He seemed more interested in telling Anderson about that day's birdwatching. Anderson found himself scribbling it all down, wondering what it was with men of the cloth and their avian friends.

By the end of the phone call he had gleaned a few interesting facts about the feathered fauna of the Balearics and many more interesting things about Elizabeth Jane Fulton. Each little bit made some kind of sense, but he could in no way pull it all together. He reached for his notes, claimed the nearest empty keyboard and started to type up a report of the conversation, in the hope that it would all look clearer on paper.

True to form, it was exactly ten o'clock that night when Anderson banged a stapler on the desk for silence. And was ignored. He tried rattling a spoon against the side of a coffee mug, and the room hushed, but only a little.

'Can you cut it out for a minute?' He tried to raise his voice over the background noise of phone calls and computer printers, pulling his finger across his throat. The two officers still on the phone wound up their calls, taking numbers and saying they would get back in five minutes. Wyngate, having a better idea of how long this was going to take, was telling the switchboard the inquiry room would be shut for half an hour.

'Right, boys and girls, just a minute of your time, and then half of you can go home. Christ knows we don't have much time to spare. We have a couple of definite leads, so there is a lot to do. Littlewood will brief you as to the specifics of today in a minute, but first, a point.' He placed his hands on his hips, waiting for absolute silence. 'Everything goes through media liaison. The press are desperate, and they will snap at anything. Batten says the media coverage is feeding Christopher Robin's ego. It shows we're under strain, so it gives him a feeling of superiority. He will interpret it as God being on his side. I'm going for a chinwag with the good doctor and Costello. Littlewood, you're in charge, come and get me if you need me.'

'When did the good Dr Batten get so bossy?' Costello whispered.

'I would ask why, not when.'

The canteen displayed a sign that said CLOSED FOR CLEANING. However, at least two shifts had passed since the place had been cleaned. From the litter of plates and discarded trays, it looked more like somebody had given the order to evacuate.

'Great,' said Batten. 'No phones, no interruptions, no nothing.'

'No food,' muttered Costello.

Batten opened his leather bag and started to put the contents on the table. Costello looked at the clock. Time was slipping past, she had a lot of work to do, and she wanted time to allow her thoughts on Sean McTiernan and Trude to form a cohesive picture. She wanted to morph the girl in the lane into Trude. She had found an ally in Gordon Wyngate, who seemed happy to sit and trawl the computer for anything she wanted. He was now tracing the life of Trude Swann from the registration of her birth as far as he could, and he'd got on with it, no questions asked. He'd come up with only one thing they didn't already know: her given name was Geertruijde. 'However you pronounce *that*.' But he had found nothing else; some years earlier the girl had ceased to exist. Which intrigued Costello all the more.

'Wyngate tells me you've been chasing somebody called Trude,' said Batten, reading her thoughts.

'Only following up the McTiernan lead,' she replied honestly.

'Maybe you can enlighten us,' asked Anderson.

'But what about this Trude, why does she attract your attention?' insisted Batten.

'Trude Swann – two *n*'s – is an orphan, and at the age of sixteen she walked out of the Good Shepherd Orphanage and off the face of the planet. That's not an easy thing to do. Wyngate tried the Good Shepherd for the name of the solicitor that looked after Trude's affairs, but they stonewalled, citing every act and statute you can think of. Wyngate can't find a name change, an emigration application or a death certificate. A member of staff who was there at the time remembers the connection with the lawyer just led to another lawyer.'

Batten nodded as if it was of some interest, but refused to enlighten his colleagues.

Mulholland arrived, looking fresh-faced and smug, McAlpine glowering behind him.

'How did the press conference go?' asked Costello.

'I dare say he used lots of big words to tell them nothing,' said McAlpine, his rage having passed. *Which was just what you wanted, Boss.*

Batten started to shuffle some photographs, keeping them face down. 'Brainstorming session. We are going to mind-map.' He looked at McAlpine. 'All right if I go ahead?'

The Boss nodded, seemingly happy to take a back seat, quiet with his own thoughts, his eyes never straying far from the battered copy of the *Evening Gazette* on the table.

'Mind-map? Like joining hands and contacting the dead? We could just ask bloody Arlene who killed her,' said Mulholland sarcastically.

Costello reached for a can of Diet Coke from her bag,

her suspicions confirmed. This was Batten's way. So much for teamwork from the guys in the squad; he had gathered the brains. This was divide and rule. 'Anybody want a mouthful of Coke?'

Anderson nodded and handed over a glass, desperate for caffeine to keep him awake.

'Three piles, one for each victim.' Batten dealt more photographs round the table, like cards.

Irvine appeared with a brown envelope. 'The powers that be left this upstairs for you.'

Batten took the envelope. Irvine hung around, wanting to be included. 'Could you close the outer door, please?'

'No probs.'

Costello watched as Batten subtly called the shots. Mc-Alpine was muttering something over and over to himself, stroking the bruises on his face with his thumb, watching as Batten opened the envelope. The doctor pulled out six close-ups, three wounds, three faces. 'Three women,' he stated. 'On the surface, we see no connection.' His hand travelled from one to the other. 'But Christopher Robin can.' His hand rested on Lynzi's picture. 'Here we have a happily married woman, but she's fucking around behind her husband's back. Doesn't even have the guts to admit to her family why she has left them.'

He moved his hands over to Elizabeth Jane. 'Costello tells us Elizabeth Jane was to be chief bridesmaid at her cousin's wedding, and that the bride said that Elizabeth Jane was mixing it –'

Anderson raised his hand to interrupt. 'I got Shand on the phone from God knows where in Minorca, just a few hours ago. For a good Christian man of the cloth, he'd some harsh things to say. He described Elizabeth Jane as' – he flipped the pages of his notebook and read from them – '*a highly manipulative, unpleasant piece of work.* He thinks she was determined to stop the wedding. Apparently she told him her cousin's fiancé had the hots for her, hinted that he'd no right to be marrying her cousin, practically said he'd be in breach of his marriage vows before he started. Well, Shand was in an awkward position, as he knows all three families really well – Paula Fulton's family, her fiancé's, and Elizabeth Jane and her parents. Of course Elizabeth Jane's parents wouldn't have a word said against their darling daughter, but he knew her well enough to know she'd stir enough shite – not that he said it quite like that – to cause real trouble. So he had a quiet chat with the boy.'

'Paula was right, it was Elizabeth Jane doing the flirting?' asked Batten. 'She would probably be naive and maybe a little obvious in her sexual pursuit.'

'The boy had no time for her.' Anderson opened his palms and smiled at Costello. 'Exactly what the bride said. But Shand felt sorry for the girl, and thought he should try to help her. So he hinted to her to come to the Phoenix. His initial plan was to get Tom O'Keefe or George Leask to act as some kind of mediator, but events overtook them. Tom had – quote – *a hairy fit* when Shand mentioned it.'

'I've read the reports, all of them carefully, and everybody says they *sort of* know everybody. O'Keefe says he knew *of* Elizabeth Jane but didn't *know* her. Her parents *thought* she knew him but only because Elizabeth Jane said so. And Leask distanced himself from his Tom comment, didn't he?'

McAlpine nodded.

'I phoned the Fultons. They'd never set eyes on Tom but had witnessed Elizabeth Jane talking to him on the phone,' clarified Batten. 'So we don't really know who was on the phone.'

'We know Leask knew *of* Elizabeth Jane,' Costello said

quietly. 'He was in their house. But it might be the priest who's lying. It was his number that showed up on her phone records. So Leask could be telling the truth, and O'Keefe might be lying.'

'But anybody could answer that phone. O'Keefe is out and about a lot,' Anderson said. 'Just because his phone rings, doesn't mean he answers it.'

Dismissing Elizabeth Jane, Batten pointed to Arlene's wrecked face. 'She was only out pissed. No crime in that.' He frowned, as if he was trying to establish a link in his mind. 'She was trying to stay clear of drugs, and that was the reason she was at the Phoenix. She had no problem being a prostitute. In fact, she seemed to be trying to make something good of it. That honesty does not fit with the other two at all.'

Costello replied, 'Honesty? I don't think so.' They listened as she related her conversation with Tracey. 'But does pulling a fast one justify getting your guts cut out?'

'Maybe in Christopher Robin's eyes it does,' said Batten, taking a Silk Cut from his packet, remembering and putting it away again. 'It doesn't really matter what *you* think. It only matters what *he* thinks. So you have to think like him. And whatever Arlene, Elizabeth Jane or Lynzi may have done, it does in his eyes "justify getting your guts cut out", otherwise we wouldn't be here.'

'So you're saying that all of these women were being something they shouldn't be? Is that what's outraging some warped sense of morality in Christopher Robin?' Anderson was unconvinced. 'I'd be much happier if they all had the same window cleaner.'

Costello opened her mouth, hesitated, then said, 'We have checked that, I suppose?'

'Yes,' Anderson stated.

'So our line of inquiry is the Phoenix.' Batten tapped the table with his finger. 'Even if we don't know who we're looking for, I think we know where to start. What do you think, McAlpine – we investigate the Phoenix and work our way out from there?'

McAlpine was gazing into the corner.

'Sir?' prompted Costello, turning to face the DCI. 'You agree we should focus on the Phoenix?'

'Yes, of course,' he said absent-mindedly. 'Look, I have to go.' And he was away, flinging open the canteen door so hard the restraining arm hit the wall and shed plaster.

Costello and Anderson exchanged glances as Batten just raised an eyebrow and nodded.

'See you, then,' said Mulholland under his breath.

'So remember: intelligent, religious, charismatic. How many boxes are being ticked?'

'Has forensics come up with anything?' asked Anderson. 'I know O'Hare is thinking about having somebody rebuild Arlene's face, scraping enough skin together to get a shoe print, but that'll take for ever. No disrespect, Doc, but I'm a stickler for fingerprints and DNA.'

'No forensic evidence as yet, no nothing. I'm all you have,' said Batten. 'What you *don't* have is time until the next one.' He didn't sound all that happy about it.

Mulholland said, 'What about McTiernan? Nobody is mentioning him.'

Both Batten and Anderson looked at Costello. 'What do you want me to say? I think it's a long way from whacking Malkie Steele, who deserved it, in my opinion, to whacking these women . . . who didn't,' she added.

'No violence against women at all?'

'No,' she confirmed. 'And in the café Arlene spoke to a man before she spoke to and left with Sean. Littlewood showed the waitress in the Ashton Café a photograph of Arlene; she's certain about Arlene leaving with Sean. It was Saturday lunchtime, they were busy, and the staff were keeping an eye on punters who were just taking up tables and not eating much, so she noticed when Arlene shimmied over to Sean's table. And she remembered the green stiletto ankle boots.' Costello felt the three men were looking at her, so she geared herself up to play her ace. 'But before that, a man called in to speak to Arlene and left without ordering anything. Dark clothes, lighter hair, dog collar or something similar. I'm sending Littlewood back to the café with photographs of Leask and O'Keefe.'

'Leask was at the Fulton house by lunchtime?' queried Mulholland.

'He has a car he never mentions,' said Costello.

'And Sean was having a chat to some old bird earlier as well,' said Costello, a slow dawn of realization coming over her. 'We didn't follow that up, though. Did anybody?'

'Scraggy old bird with glasses and a mole on her face? That was Littlewood's description,' Mulholland snorted. 'Hardly his type.'

'You said a mole. That wasn't in the notes. Where was the mole?'

'How should I know?'

'But they were talking?' Costello persisted.

'For quite a while.'

Costello bent over her notebook, the biro digging into the paper as she scribbled agitatedly, trying, and failing, to bend the features of that beautiful little girl to match Arlene's. Then she tried the image of the girl running out of the disco, Sean following. She could make that fit.

'So do we bring McTiernan in?' asked Mulholland.

'Not enough yet. It's only circumstantial. We can't put

him and Arlene together at any time that's relevant. The locus is easily explained: there are two lanes here, 50 per cent chance it would be the same one.'

'He has returned to his previous killing ground,' commented Batten.

'And the damage to the face!' said Mulholland. 'It must be him.'

'It doesn't fit the profile. Sure, stamping on a face does. But just using a kick to disable an attacker doesn't. Christopher Robin would have turned back while Steele was on the ground and had a real go.'

'I've seen the photos. He didn't have to.'

'I'm not sure the use of Whistler's Lane is relevant either. Both Ashton Lane and Byres Road are busy 24/7. Whistler's Lane is always quiet . . . apart from the drunks and the druggies,' argued Costello. 'McTiernan knows that, he has a strong connection with the area and with White's the Joiners.' Sheepishly she went on to explain the connection, to stony silence. 'But that other witness said Christopher Robin had an Irish accent, and Sean doesn't.'

'Why didn't you say all that before?' asked Anderson.

Batten put his hand up. 'Wait a mo. I'll come back to that. This O'Keefe has an Irish accent. He's the right age, right build.'

'Leask would sound Irish if you didn't know. Not many can tell the difference between an island and an Irish accent,' said Costello. 'And I'd say he has little time for the fairer sex.' She tucked her hair behind her ears. 'However much he may act differently.'

'Christopher Robin *does* appear to like women; that's what Batten's been saying,' said Mulholland. 'O'Keefe is charming, I would say extremely so when he wants to turn it on. His entire career relies on his charm.'

'But,' Batten said quietly to Costello, 'McTiernan is the one who is charming *you*. And you haven't even met him yet.'

Costello snapped her notebook shut and waited for Batten to move away from her before she breathed out and clipped the top back on her biro.

'So – from having no religious nutters we now have two, plus a joiner on life licence. Good going,' Batten said with some enthusiasm. 'I want to do a profile on McTiernan, ASAP. Can I have five minutes of your time in the office upstairs, Costello?'

'In the DCI's office? Yes, of course,' Costello answered coolly.

'Tomorrow we are going to go through the Phoenix with a fine-tooth comb. I want Leask and O'Keefe laid out in front of me like suckling pigs. Costello can go for McTiernan, seeing as she is the expert.'

'What about DCI McAlpine?' asked Anderson, but nobody was listening. They had drifted away up the stairs. He heard Littlewood's rough accent barking at the meeting upstairs as the doors opened and closed again. There was a clatter of footsteps as somebody came down to use the toilet. Then silence. He put his head in his hands and rubbed at his eyes; he needed sleep, but he couldn't face going home to be met with Brenda's rantings. He reached over and picked up the newspaper and started reading, wanting to see for himself what everybody was getting so worked up about.

Outside Partickhill Station, McAlpine stood for a moment letting the wind blow the rain in his face. The meeting had been suffocating; he needed a shot of nicotine in his bloodstream and the cold spatter of the rain to clear his head.

He turned up the collar of his raincoat and began the short walk up Hyndland Road, choosing to have the wind behind him rather than in his face. Although he could hear the ever-present snarl of traffic on the Great Western Road, Hyndland Road itself, winding between the houses and flats, neat gardens and parked cars, was quiet. He felt his breathing relax, the tension seep away.

Out on the main road again, windborne rain pecked at his face, awaking his senses for the first time in ages. He had begun to feel as though his brain had stopped working, but he could think straight now. He had always prided himself on his ability to get a squad working, squads bigger, more disparate, than this one, and without half their abilities. And there was the truth of it: they didn't need him any more. Ten years ago he would have been two steps ahead of Anderson and Costello, even with a hangover and both hands tied behind his back. At least he knew he had taught them well.

Now the whole investigation seemed to be sliding past him, out of his grasp. At glacial speed, but sliding it was. Mick Batten, so bright and charismatic, with his wise words, seemed able to rally a team the way he himself used to. McAlpine couldn't pinpoint when it was that all that had slipped away from him, when his ability to stay in charge had left him, like a slow-setting sun. *And left me in darkness,* he thought.

'Why are you not happy with McTiernan being a suspect?' Batten asked. He was sitting on Costello's desk, chipping fragments off the rim of a polystyrene coffee cup and flicking them in the direction of the bin.

'Intuition tells me we're barking up the wrong tree.'

'Exactly the intuition Christopher Robin will give you,

Costello. You have been warned.' His words were brutal, though his voice was kind.

'You know,' said Costello, 'I'm starting to think that if I say I think some guy is OK, then he's bound to be Christopher Robin. And if I say I think someone's a creep, then it's *because* he's Christopher Robin. So I can't win.' Costello flung her empty cup against the wall, and it bounced to the floor. 'This is not a game. Women are dying, and sometimes you lot talk about it as if it's an intelligence test, a case of who gets there first.'

'But why are you not happy with McTiernan being a suspect?' Batten persisted.

'Female intuition,' she sneered.

Batten was in psychologist mode. 'But why do you feel that way?' He was like a dog with a bone. 'Female intuition is in fact a scientific thing: women pick up the nuances of body language, of weakness and strength, of guilt, of honesty. So – why is it not McTiernan?'

She looked at him blankly. 'Like I said . . .'

'You've reached a conclusion. But you've no idea how you reached it. If you explain it to me, you'll explain it to yourself.' Batten pressed his hands together, taking great care to push each fingertip precisely on to its counterpart.

'The situation with Steele doesn't ring true,' Costello said.

'I've read the report. I agree. I believe it was premeditated. A case like that has a voice. It's as if the killer were a master puppeteer . . . with Steele as the puppet. Brains over brawn. If it proves to be McTiernan, there will be a connection between him and Steele. Or between him and somebody who wanted Steele taken out. What was happening in gangland Glasgow in those days?'

'It's always been a power struggle between the same two families – the Laings and the Fernies.' She made a note in her notepad. 'The previous investigation team couldn't make a connection from Sean to either of them. There's been something bothering me about Sean. He bought a husky puppy. I tracked down the breeder, and they remember selling a dog to someone, then two days later seeing the guy on the front page of the *Daily Record*. He was going to call the dog Gelert, they remember that.' She waited to see if that meant anything.

Batten pulled his hands apart. 'Gelert. So?'

'It's a famous story. Welsh. King Owen has a dog to protect the baby prince. Owen leaves to go to war, he comes back, the baby is missing, the dog has blood round its mouth. He makes the natural assumption that the dog has killed the baby and slays the dog.'

'And then finds a dead wolf, and the baby alive and well. The dog had killed the wolf to protect the baby. I do know that story. Isn't there a place called Bedgelert, the grave of Gelert?'

'He got a village and a monument and a sword through his heart for his trouble, poor dog. What do you make of that, Mr Psychologist?'

'I see where you're coming from. It's a romantic notion. *I'm going away, so here's a great hairy beast to protect you.* But how does that help us?'

'The thing is: Sean *knew* he was going away. The breeder tried to trace the puppy after Sean's arrest. But it had gone. And Sean effectively made himself homeless before he went to meet Steele.'

'So you agree he knew he was going to kill him?'

'Of course he did,' answered Costello without hesitation. 'He's a sharp cookie. He's only done three and a half years for a premeditated murder masquerading as self-defence. The woman in the Ashton Café – not Arlene but the old one with the mole . . .' She flicked open the file and removed two photographs from the back. 'That one, the old dear in the pinny – that's who I need to trace. She is the one link with Sean's past, the only link. Everyone else goes nowhere.' Then she put down in front of Batten the other photograph that Lorna Shaw had given her, of the gaggle of little boys on the beach, and the enigmatic little fairy child off to one side. 'Just look at that face. Tell me what you think.'

Batten was impressed. 'She would be a beautiful young woman by now.' He put the photograph to one side. 'OK, while there's no evidence that he had sex with Arlene, we're pretty certain he did have sex with the girl up the lane – you're saying it was this girl?'

'Maybe. But we do know it was the place where he killed Malkie Steele. What's the psychology of that?'

'Going back to the scene of a previous crime? Common psychological trait. Can be many things. But we should be careful to distinguish between the facial injuries. If you were trained in martial arts, a kick in the head is instinct. Stamping on someone's head while they are on the ground is deliberate, and stamping on the face is very personal indeed.' He looked steadily at the black-and-white snapshot for about a minute. 'Look at this again. Look at him and her particularly. What's the first word that comes to your mind?'

'Protection, devotion,' answered Costello without hesitation.

'But who's doing the protecting?'

'He is. She's just an object of adoration. He looks as though he never takes his eyes off her.'

'And how powerful an emotion is that in a kid with a background like Sean's?' Batten raised his eyebrows, questioning.

Costello's answer choked in her throat.

Wednesday, 4 October

It was raining again, cold, constant, dark, dirty, Glaswegian rain. McAlpine stood in the queue of late-night drunks and taxi drivers at the Tardis Kiosk, soaked through, his cotton shirt glued to his shoulders. He glanced at his watch: the gold hands told him that it was ten past midnight. He was too wired to sleep tonight. He ordered a bagel and a double-shot Americana. The caffeine wouldn't make any difference.

All the seats at the taxi rank were taken, so he turned into the Botanical Gardens and sat down on the first bench he came to, choosing to ignore the homeless man in curled-up occupancy. His cardboard sign was sodden with rain, as was the tartan blanket that covered him. A few pennies lay submerged in the polystyrene McDonald's burger box at his feet. Unless he was a light sleeper, they wouldn't be there tomorrow.

McAlpine rested his elbows on his knees as he sat, head down, letting the coffee warm him from the inside. The homeless guy had chosen well; the bench was slightly sheltered from the wind and rain by the glass Kibble palace behind it.

He looked at his watch – it was long past midnight – and pulled his mobile from his pocket. No point trying to call Helena at home; he knew the clever money would be on her being at the gallery. His efforts were rewarded by a steady beep as his phone went from low battery to no battery.

He brushed the rain from his face, cursing loudly, which got him a polite reprimand from the tartan rug.

'Sorry, mate,'

'Nae probs, pal.'

'Here.' McAlpine stood up, tipping two pound coins into the polystyrene lid. As he set off for home, from the corner of his eye he caught the movement of a hand retrieving the coins to the safety of the soaked blanket.

Even with the windscreen wipers on fast, Helena still had difficulty seeing the road. She had spent all day putting the finishing touches to the exhibition, and when she'd closed the door at 12.35 a.m. and set the alarm, she'd felt pleased. Now it was going on one in the morning. She wasn't tired, she decided; absolutely bloody knackered was more like it. Wednesday, Thursday and Friday would be a series of temper tantrums involving caterers, artists and moneymen, and she desperately needed her sleep. By the time she pulled up outside Kirklee Terrace, the headache that had started as a minor percussion had become a full rhythm section, with somebody practising the timpani behind her right eye.

She tried to slip the car into reverse, then remembered it wasn't her car. The Three Series wasn't automatic, and she tried to think what the man at the garage had shown her. She had to lift the collar, shift down, left and forwards. She tried it, but all that happened was a loud crunch, and she cursed. The rising wind rocked the car gently. She couldn't find the switch for the internal light. In the end she opened the door slightly to use the courtesy light, and a buzzer sounded as the cold wet wind rushed in.

White lights shimmered towards him on Byres Road, and red tail lights fluttered as the traffic halted at the lights on its incessant slow crawl into the city. In the distance Mc-Alpine could see the low flat roof of the Beatson, where Helena would be fighting a few battles of her own soon. But she would keep the fight to herself. 'Oh yes, we mustn't let the stiff upper lip wobble,' he muttered bitterly, 'mustn't breathe a word about it. I'll cope with it when I have time to cope with it.'

He stopped walking and looked over to the tower of the Western Infirmary, sure that the room Anna had been in was lit up at that very moment – there was more life in there than in his own home. He sighed and wiped the drizzle from his face, unsure whether it was the rain or a tear, and jogged across into the mêlée of Byres Road and down to Peckham's Deli for a bottle of good malt before heading back up to Kirklee Terrace. He couldn't face the accusation of an empty house without it.

By the time Helena had parked, it was gone one o'clock. She got out of the car, the wind immediately whipping her hair against her cheek. She quickly ran round the car to the pavement, pointing the alarm remote control all the time, pressing and pressing, but there was no returning bleep, so she gave up. As she turned, she walked straight into the wheelie bin, still out on the pavement after the weekly rubbish collection; the wind had pushed it up against the railing. She grasped it and tried to wrestle it down the stairs to the basement terrace, its lack of weight making it difficult to manoeuvre in the wind. She spun it round on its wheels and bumped it awkwardly down the wrought-iron spiral steps to the basement, the howl of the wind suddenly dropping in the subterranean shelter, though it still had enough strength to chase the leaves into circles along the corner of the house. Helena wiped the rain from her cheek, trying to think what was unusual. It was that noise, a metallic *clank clank*, both insistent and inconstant. Somebody's gate was open. She stood underneath the stairs that led up to her front door, looking left and right, cursing the bin men. All the houses in the terrace shared another terrace below street level, each front door having a bridge of steps up from the pavement. In the tunnel this created, most had fixed hanging baskets, ivy and creepers, and subtle wrought-iron gates, an ornamental separation of one property from its neighbour. The bloody bin men had left the McAlpines' gate open and, judging by the noise, the two beyond it. Helena left the shelter of the stairs and walked along, past her neighbours', stopping at the second gate and securing the iron bolt. She turned back to her own basement, walking in the darkness under the arch, then turning slightly to go upstairs. She put her hand on the wrought-iron rail, stopping dead as another hand covered hers.

Colin Anderson was sitting in the old Astra, so old its seat had moulded to his body, thus achieving perfect comfort. He sipped his hot coffee and reread the newspaper that he'd spread across the steering wheel. He had received a message on his mobile from his mother-in-law to say she would stay the night if he was working. He had texted back his grateful thanks, wondering where Brenda had got to but glad he didn't have to explain why he was easier in his mind sitting in McDonald's car park, concentrating on his growing feeling of unease. The digital clock on the dashboard clicked round to zero one zero zero, but that didn't mean much; Peter was always sticking things in the reset button. Anderson sighed and flicked his mobile open. He phoned Helena's gallery and got the answer service. He phoned the McAlpines' home number; ditto. He switched on the radio, quietly . . . Don McLean singing about Vincent on a night with better weather than this one. He sipped his coffee again, slowly wiping the condensation it had left on the windscreen with his other hand. His sense of unease had erased any hope of sleep. He folded the newspaper in front of him, collapsing the image of Helena's face over on itself. It was no use: he would have to take a drive up to the terrace, just to make sure.

Helena's first reaction was to wonder why her neighbour hadn't just said 'hello'. She first felt fear when the gloved hand gripped her wrist tightly and pulled it into her own stomach, trapping her between his forearm in front and his body weight behind, pushing the breath from her. She tried to sidestep as the grasp slackened slightly, then tightened again, with more power, crushing her lower lungs.

She pulled her head back, then forward, trying to free her face, trying to inhale enough air to call out, to scream, and for a moment they were both perfectly still, caught in a deadly embrace. Her eyes went blank, little arrows danced in front of her, and she could feel a needling numbness in her lungs. She was going to pass out . . . Then the pressure eased, allowing her to take a single deep breath.

Of chloroform.

Don't breathe, don't breathe, was all Helena could think. Don't breathe it in. She pressed her tongue into the back of her teeth concentrating, her heart hammered at her chest wall. She tried to locate him precisely, where his body weight was, looking for a way to break free. She tried to relax, to surrender, wanting him to think he had won. She breathed out a long, slow breath, her mind working hard. One hand covered her mouth, his elbow was clenched into her sternum; the other arm was tight on her waist with a powerful grip that did not yield. Her head pounded as she felt herself drop, letting her body weight be pushed by his, waiting for the flitting second when her weight would force him to step forward. She slumped even more, her brain willing him to lose balance, just for a nanosecond. Then she felt the slow, painless pressure of the knife in her stomach.

Anderson sat five cars back at the traffic lights on Great Western Road, the queue of traffic sitting in the outside lane by force of habit, leaving the bus lane empty. He looked to his right, across the grass, up on to Kirklee Terrace, sitting high but parallel to the road . . . he was staring straight at the McAlpines' house, dark, lifeless. Nobody home.

Helena heard a scream echo round her head, a primordial cry that shattered her eardrums. She gathered every ounce of energy she had from her body; she was dying, she knew it now. The noise penetrated her brain; she thought about nothing but falling on to that knife. It was her own scream-ing. A light flickered somewhere above, something changed. She raised one shoulder half an inch, an inch? Something kicked her hard in her stomach, but the pressure round her chest slackened, then was gone. She could see nothing; she could still feel the knife against her skin, the blade working its way; she tried to fall sideways on to the steps. She felt the wet concrete kiss her forehead, she felt the grit on her face, then nothing.

Anderson was still looking out the side window of the Astra, his vision speared by the javelins of water, but he saw a figure, dark and indistinct, jog down the pathway, quickly. Too quickly. Something about the figure struck him . . . the clothes too bulky for a jogger. Anderson quickly reversed enough to pull out and get past the car in front, spilling the coffee from the consol as the Astra took off. He raced up the wrong side of the road and turned the hairpin into the terrace while the lights were on red. The McAlpine house was still in darkness, but both neighbouring houses were ablaze with light. He slammed his brakes on.

Helena was lying, curled against the wall of the spiral stairs, her head at an angle, where it rested on cold hard brick. Anderson could hardly see, but the dark trickle from the corner of her mouth was easily visible against the pallor of her face; a perfect tick of blood marked her forehead, catching her hair.

'Helena, Helena? Can you hear me?' There was no answer. He slipped his hand into the exposed contour of her neck: the pulse was weak but fading with every beat. A man in a tartan dressing gown appeared at the top of the stairs and stopped, shouting for somebody to call the police.

'I am the police, get an ambulance,' Anderson commanded. 'Now,' he added, fumbling for his warrant card, as the neighbour hesitated.

'We heard her screaming from upstairs. Is she OK?'

'No, she's not. She needs an ambulance. Now.'

Anderson was aware of a small congregation at the top of the stairs, murmurings of concern, then an authoritative voice saying the ambulance was already on its way.

The tartan dressing gown was now at the bottom of the stairs. 'Don't move her, son. Irene!' he shouted, his hands moving confidently to check her pulse. 'Get towels. And a blanket.'

Irene was already halfway down the staircase and simply about-turned, the revolving orange light of a squad car making her shadow dance. A torch appeared over the terrace railing.

'Get along the main road, look out for any single males, get it radioed out there – Christopher Robin,' Anderson snapped tersely.

The torch beam flicked away, and crackling radios chattered to each other. Another squad car appeared. In the little island of darkness he asked, 'Did he hurt her?'

'Yes,' answered Helena weakly, stirring to consciousness. 'It's bloody sore, God, my side hurts.'

'Don't try to talk, Helena, we need to get you to hospital,' said the neighbour, shaking his head, frowning. Slowly Anderson raised his hand, blood running slowly from his palm, and then he looked down and realized the rainwater he was kneeling in was warm.

At the bottom of Kirklee Terrace, McAlpine took a slug of malt from the bottle, then stuffed it back into his coat pocket. Illumined windows shone like fairy lights through the roadside trees, lighting up the row of white four-storey Adam-style town houses that climbed up the hill away from the city centre and the river.

Except for his own house, which sat sulking in its own darkness.

Well, there was nobody to turn the lights on, was there?

Two police cars passed him, heading into the city centre. Going home, he thought. Lucky them. He opened the little gate that would take him up the garden path to the terrace above, wondering why so many houses had their lights on at this ungodly hour of the morning.

Anderson knocked quietly on the door before entering. Helena was lying on the hospital bed, still wet from her shower, wrapped and double wrapped in a white towelling robe. Her wet hair was pulled from her face, her hands clasped across her abdomen.

He sat down on the bed beside her. 'How are you feeling?' He wanted to touch her, comfort her, but couldn't bring himself to do it.

'Better, much better. I got burned when I pulled his hands away from my face. I touched something soft and wet.' She looked at her palms, studying them. 'I think that might blister. They said I might have cracked a rib, and I needed ten stitches but none of them internal, thank God. At least I'll have a nice scar to illustrate the story. I was a bit upset there was such a lot of blood and only a small hole.'

'Does it hurt?'

'A little, but I've a bumful of morphine. I feel better now.' She opened her eyes, looking directly at him. 'It was him, wasn't it? Your Crucifixion Killer? You nearly caught him. Were you there already?' She was still looking at her hands, avoiding his eyes.

'I was driving past, that's all.' Anderson tried to make light of it. 'Saw somebody running away – copper's instinct. And whoever it was, he fairly legged it. They should sign him up for the Rangers' defence. He must have run the full length of the terrace and down on to the road in five seconds flat.'

'He was lying in wait for me.' Helena screwed her face up. 'I don't understand it.'

'Well, Christopher Robin, the Crucifixion Killer to you, kills immoral women, or women he thinks are immoral. Maybe that piece in the *Gazette* means that's how he sees you,' said Anderson.

She pulled her face into a frown, pain etched in her eyes

as she stared at the ceiling. Her hand went to her breast, feeling for her little lump. 'Me? An immoral woman? God, I wish I had the energy. Where was that bastard I'm married to when this was going on, why didn't the killer go after *him*? He's the immoral one . . .'

'That's the whole point – you're a woman. Do you feel like making a formal statement?'

Helena tried to sit up and failed. Anderson gently helped her up, feeling the boniness of her shoulders under the hospital robe. 'I don't know that I've anything useful to say. It was blowing a gale. It was pitch dark down there. I couldn't see my own hand in front of my face, never mind anybody else's. Anyway, I wasn't looking.' Tears started to well in her eyes. 'I didn't see anything.'

'Did he smell of anything? Aftershave? Dettol? Mansion Polish?'

'Wet wool. I smelled wet wool. And something – oily. Like linseed oil, almost.'

'Good. Height?'

'I had the impression he wasn't old, he was slim, he moved fast, strong but not bulky, light on his feet. Nothing else. He wasn't much taller than me.'

'You're what – five nine?'

'Yeah.'

Anderson continued, 'You don't recall anything being said? You can't recall a voice?'

'Only David next door coming down the stairs, you shouting. I was holding your hand . . .' She gazed at him, and his heart turned over. 'Did that wee girl get anything from me?'

'Alison the SOCO? We'll wait and see. You put up a good fight, so there might be some transference, that's the good news. The bad news is it will be ages before you get

265

your clothes back.' He put his hand on her shoulder. 'Alan's outside now. He's in a state. Do you want to see him?'

Helena thought for a moment. 'Yes, I'm fine. It's not his fault he's a copper.' Her humour ended as her mouth closed in a resolute line. 'He tried to kill me, just like the others, didn't he? I felt that knife in my stomach, you know.'

'Best not to think about that. Those thoughts will pop up in your head, so you just put them away.' Anderson got to his feet. 'Before Alan comes in, can I ask you a question, Helena?'

'That's your job,' she reminded him, holding on to her stomach and breathing out through pursed lips.

'When Alan lost his brother . . . and his mother . . . was there somebody else? Somebody who –' Anderson was ready to expand his theory, but Helena cut him short.

'Her?' She closed her eyes, her face defeated. 'I have no idea who she is, but she occupies his dreams, I know that.' She took a few deep breaths. 'She's buried near my mum. And she was Dutch. That's all I know. Well, that and that it's too painful for him to remember.'

'That's why I asked you. I hope you don't mind.'

'Can I ask why?'

'I'm afraid not.'

'Be careful. With Alan, I mean. And her.'

'I will. I'll send Alan in, but remember you're safe here. There's a guard at the door. Can you sign this? Just so we can take your clothes.'

Mechanically she signed it. *Helena Farrell.*

'How is she? Really, I mean? I know I was getting the brave-girl act when I went in but I could tell she was dreadfully shaken,' said McAlpine, collapsing on his own sofa.

'Hardly surprising after what happened,' said Anderson curtly, closing the door on a couple of uniforms who were sheltering in the hall.

'But then I always get the brave-girl act.' McAlpine looked around him. The house felt different somehow, for lack of Helena. 'How long will they be out there?'

'It will be taped up for a few hours yet, I think. Littlewood is on the scene, Burns is helping, so we're in good hands.' Anderson looked at his watch: it was heading on for half past four. 'So Helena was still calm when you left her?'

'She does that stony calm very well.'

'I think the shock will hit her later. She said she didn't want to go back to the house, so she wants you to take in some stuff, and Denise will take her home with her tomorrow . . . although she was going to discharge herself there and then.'

'Her dad was in the army,' said McAlpine, as though that explained everything. 'Batten got it wrong, didn't he?'

'No, he got it dead right.'

Anderson looked up as a car door slammed outside, his eyes passing over the coffee table. At McAlpine's knee was a glass that had contained whisky. He hadn't even put the top back on the bottle. 'Did you have a lie down, even for a couple of minutes?'

'Too much going on in my head.' McAlpine poured another drink. 'Have they figured out what happened yet?'

'I think he was waiting down there. We had a scout about; most of the gates were open, so he could have run either way. He must have thought his luck was in when she came down the stairs to him. But I had a word with O'Hare; he says Helena's height might have made it difficult for Christopher to get a good grip, so her weight worked for her, against him. He wants to look at her upper arms

267

tomorrow, see if there's any sign of bruising coming out. It could be a good indicator of his height.'

'Leask, McTiernan and O'Keefe are all much of a much-ness, height-wise.'

'And you,' said Anderson pulling himself up to his six feet. 'Maybe once this is over, you should take some time off. Spend some quality time with her. I'll get somebody to make you a cuppa. Christ knows, I could do with one.' McAlpine, still staring into space, didn't respond. Anderson reached forward to put the top on the whisky bottle. 'Don't even think about it, Alan. Stay there and don't touch anything.'

Costello appeared at the door in mid sentence, telling a disembodied voice to get back to the station. She looked at McAlpine but addressed Anderson. 'Scene-of-crime are finished downstairs.'

'I'd better check what's happening.' He got up to leave.

'Col?' said McAlpine.

'Yip?'

'Thanks.'

'Any time.' Anderson walked out, pausing briefly to say to Costello, 'Keep an eye on him. It hasn't hit home yet.'

'He's too drunk for that,' Costello sighed.

'We'll have to keep him out of trouble. And keep the press away from the house. You OK?'

She nodded.

'Good girl.'

McAlpine's mistrustful gaze flickered round the room and came to rest on the sideboard. And on Anderson's car keys lying there. He looked away quickly before Costello noticed.

The sky darkened, rain started to pour from the heavens. In the dim light, rain streamed down her face, water mixing with blood, her cheekbones melting away. Slowly her hand pulled the shawl over the head of the infant, and she turned her back, shielding her from the rain.

Then she turned to him once more, and the hood fell, her beautiful face smiling at him as her features dissolved, all the colours of her running and melting to black. She raised her hands, holding a stick. She lifted it high into the air, her arms spreading like wings. Rain and glass shattered on to him, on to his face, again.

And again.

He woke up, his head leaning on the leather arch of the steering wheel. He rubbed at his eyes, easing the pain.

This time it was a dream. As it had been last time. A different dream. A different car.

Here he was, back on the Heads of Ayr Road at four in the morning, cold and drunk and tired, too drunk to remember driving here. He was in a car he did not know, littered with empty Hula Hoops packets and Ribena cartons, a McDonald's coffee cup at his feet.

He recognized the dark grey silk of the sea in front of him, the beach laid out below twisting like a ribbon; he recognized the castle up on the cliff.

And he had recognized the blonde angel.

Anna.

He knew now that he was remembering something a little more substantial than a dream.

He held the bottle close to his chest, wondering why his subconscious mind had taken so long to bring him here. He smiled to himself and took a wee drink. Looking out on to the water far below, he sensed the presence of Anna arriving home to comfort him after all the others had turned their backs.

Yet Anna had always been there.

Always *here*.

He watched the sea, its constant motion, gentle waves rising and falling on the distant beach. He got out of the car and began to walk. It was dark down the path, truly pitch black, the blackness that the human eye barely adjusts to. Its density seemed to envelop him body and soul as he walked along, a slow lumbering gait, arms folded round the bottle as a drowning man holds on to a rope.

He made his way down the hill, picking up a stick from the hedge, walking towards the welcoming water, past the whitewashed cottage where his good Samaritan lived, the old dear with the ridiculous mole and friends in low places.

'*Shiprids Cottage,*' he read, rolling it round his mouth. Giggling to himself. 'Oh, fuck,' he said. 'To the sea, the sea.' He stumbled a few times, the stick steadying him, before he reached the beach, the darkness, the drink and the sea air making him dizzy. He was laughing, giggling to himself, trying to sing a John Denver song about Anna filling his senses, but he couldn't remember how it went beyond the first line.

He stopped laughing, trying to remember, telling himself the tears running down his face were from the sting of salt.

He made slow, unsteady progress along the beach. The roll of the land was severe here; God had moulded it with an angry hand, the cliffs twisting into the contour of the hills and plummeting into the water, flattening on to the beach. Geologically it did not make sense, but it had confounded better men than him. He stood and took a deep breath, the heels of his shoes sinking into the sand. Slowly and deliberately he drew an ampersand in the sand, writing LAN after it. Then he drew another, adding NNA. You fill up my senses, he thought. And shivered.

He walked on, noticing another cottage, right down

underneath the cliff. A little white gingerbread house, with a half-built veranda. He turned, looking along the beach. To the left, to the right. This wee house was a long way from anywhere.

'Hello, hello,' he said, waving to it vaguely, losing his stick and his footing in the sand and nearly dropping the bottle. He took another few mouthfuls, wiping the top clumsily with the palm of his hand. A strange white house, an ugly house, right on the beach . . . stupid place to have a house . . . sitting like a sleepy kitten, coiled in a womb of rock and dune. Through the mist a single light flickered in one of the upstairs rooms.

Or maybe it was the mist in his eyes.

A single light in the darkness. A single flicker against the wall of cliff.

A lone flame.

Alone.

He was alone too.

A painted sign, two swans with necks entwined, *Keeper's Cottage* written on a diamond of crafted driftwood. He leaned on it, breathing hard, before moving slowly closer to the water's edge.

Walking unsteadily down the sand, ever closer. The moon was the smallest sliver in the sky; the stars seemed very far away, but their reflections still twinkled in the water.

He felt small.

He shivered in the silence. He was well away from the road now, the only sound the soft rush and fall of the waves, a faint bubbling as the water filtered through seaweed and pebbles. He walked on, slow and clumsy at first in the soft sand, then quicker as the sand grew harder. The tide was running from him, receding when he got there.

Had his mother felt like this before she died, glad to let

go, glad to let herself slip away? Was the minute before death warm and comfortable, with the world slowly going black?

Anna's death, slipping as the life bled from her – had that been warm, comforting? Certainly more comfortable than whatever faced her alive. Now he understood how it felt to have no reason not to die. Anna . . . killing herself and setting her daughter free. His mother . . . killing herself because she could not bear life without her favourite son. And he, with the woman he loved separated from him by some sort of Great Divide of mortality . . . the woman he loved . . . Anna . . . Helena . . . Anna . . .

He shook himself sharply awake. Robbie's death had not been a choice, not warm and comforting at all. His final moments had been cold and lonely, fighting for a life taken before it was ready to go.

To drown in cold lonely stinking water, quiet and infinitely dark . . .

He could not die the long and painful death his mother had. That Helena might die. He could not injure himself, pick up a knife and cut into his own flesh, like Anna. But he could allow himself to drown.

The only thing really to be scared of was fear.

He bent down, cupping his hands, washing his face, the water cold and gritty, leaving a film of salt on his skin. But it was better than tears. He didn't want to do it with tears on his face. He stuck the bottle of whisky under his arm, not noticing the contents running into the water that nibbled at the sand beneath his feet, and pulled the photographs from his pocket. Robbie. Robbie . . . and Alan and the snowman . . . He ripped them into a dozen little pieces, flinging them into the air, where they fluttered round his head, whispering at him like evil little demons. He stepped backwards, then forwards, dancing with the waves, following their ebb and flow, his arms holding the Glenlivet out to one side. He twirled, waltzing across the little white horses.

Then he stopped.

He took another slow, determined step into the water. As the longest journey begins with a small step, so does the final one, the big one. He started to laugh. The first few minutes of life were the most dangerous, so he supposed that the last few were pretty tricky as well.

He sank to his knees, then, through the darkness, his eye caught a movement along the beach – a bird maybe, a rush of white on a wave – something moving in the darkness, the colour of the night, moving silently, deadly, too low to be human. Floating, not touching the sand, but moving with purpose. Staring hard into the darkness, a subtle wind ruffling his hair, an unseen breath on his face, he dropped his arms. He was chilled to the bone. The hairs on the back of his neck stood on end. He felt his body collapse, a cold rush of fear, then the water washing over his face, not as cold as he'd thought it would be. Warm, comforting almost, he felt wave after wave come up and kiss his face.

Then something warmer, firmer, taking hold of him. Warm fingers stroked his hair, the scent of seawater filled his senses, he saw tendrils of blonde hair dance in front of his eyes as he imagined soft lips being pressed against his. Loving words spoken in quiet ghostly whispers, carried with the lapping of the water.

With this kiss, I shall wake you.

'What the fuck are you doing here?'

Anderson got up from the chair at the kitchen table. 'I've been here for hours,' he said. 'Your wife was attacked just a few hours ago, if you remember.' Not 'Helena'. *Your wife.*

'I didn't think the house should be left. Quite apart from some drunken bastard nicking my car.'

'Is she –'

'She's fine. The hospital say she's fine. She's asleep. I'd suggest you leave her to rest, at least until you've cleaned yourself up. She's talking about going back to the gallery this afternoon. There's no telling her.' Anderson deliberately turned his back, checked there was some water in the kettle and switched it on. 'You need some coffee in you,' he said. Then he turned round, leaning against the kitchen unit as though he were in his own house, and folded his arms.

'So where have you been? You're soaking wet.'

'This is quite dry; you've a good heater in that Astra, I'll tell you that. And the driver's seat is soaked.' The kettle boiled and clicked off, and Anderson started opening and closing cupboards, looking for mugs. McAlpine slumped down at the kitchen table. 'I was thinking.'

'Thinking? Drinking's more like it. Alan, get a grip! I've seen stiffs with more life in them. What's going on? What was going on this morning?'

'I stopped at Peckham's . . . bought myself a bottle . . .'

'And you left that one at the house, empty.'

McAlpine dropped his face into his hands and started to rub his eyes, trying for recall. 'Christ! After . . . well after . . .'

'After the attack on Helena, you went to the hospital, you went back to the terrace, you necked a half-bottle of whisky and gave Costello the slip and then nicked my car. It's after that I want to know about,' Anderson demanded.

'I drove down the Ayr Road . . . I needed some sea air, I needed to think, and that's the truth. I think I took a bottle with me.'

'Think? Think about what, precisely?'

'About Robbie, my mum, Anna . . .'

'Anna who?'

'Just Anna. Who's dead. Who's lying in an untended grave in the Western Necropolis.'

'Anna who had acid thrown in her face? That Anna?'

McAlpine nodded distractedly. 'Helena . . . I'll go to the hospital to see her now. I might run her to the gallery if she's ready, then I can keep an eye on her,' he said, trying and failing to get the papers back into his wallet. The photograph of Helena fell out on to the table. He turned it deliberately to look at it. 'The thing about women like my wife is, nothing defeats them. Nothing! She just gets up, dusts herself down and keeps going.' McAlpine went on, 'They can emasculate you just by breathing. But you'd know all about that, wouldn't you?'

'I do, right enough. Which is why I envy you being married to a woman like Helena.' Anderson sat down opposite McAlpine and leaned forward on folded arms. 'Look, Alan, the man who attacked Helena . . .'

The clouded, tortured eyes hardened. 'Of course. Christopher Robin?'

'Think,' Anderson said urgently. 'He kills women he perceives as immoral. I suppose he must think that of Helena. That piece in yesterday's *Gazette* might have triggered him in some way, that's all.' Anderson got up and poured a mug of coffee for himself. 'And the one thing Batten will ask is: why you? Why her? We are assuming all other victims are connected in some way to Christopher himself. Is Helena too? We'll be going through her life with a fine-tooth comb, and if DCI Quinn is put in charge she'll start with you. Did anyone see you after you left Peckham's? Christ, do you even *remember* when you left Peckham's?'

'What are you saying?' The pain in the dark eyes had been replaced by steely fury. 'That I attempted to kill Helena? To murder my own wife? And I suppose you want me for the other three too.'

'You've no alibi for any of it,' Anderson persisted doggedly. 'No *reliable* alibi. I have to make sure. If it goes to court, I'm not leaving any loopholes for some wanker to find. Helena's your wife. If you weren't a DCI, you'd be first suspect, you know that. Do you have any witnesses at all?'

McAlpine thought of the rain-sodden tartan blanket, the thin hand groping for the change. Not exactly what you'd call a witness. 'Nope, you're out of luck. Case solved. Because nobody saw me.' *Except my guardian angel.* 'Except my guardian angel,' he said out loud.

Anderson smiled for the first time. 'You've no right to be home in one piece. Look at the state of you. Guardian angel, eh? That I can believe.'

Outside the back door of Partickhill Station DI Anderson was sipping coffee from a polystyrene cup. He had stuffed a full cooked brunch down his throat at the University Café, but his sleep-starved brain demanded yet more caffeine. Costello's car swung into the car park, and he waited until she had finished fiddling with the key and run across the yard before he caught her by the elbow.

'Freddie?'

'Yes?' She was always suspicious at the use of her first name.

'I want you to do a couple of things for me, and I don't want you to ask why.'

'Hmm.' Costello folded her arms. 'What?'

'Talk to whoever's in charge of the burial register at the Western Necropolis. Find out if anyone was buried there – I'm guessing about twenty-two years ago, but it was during the summer she died, it would be the year the McAlpines married. Check for a young female, death certificate signed at the Western. Traumatic cause of death. Might be a slightly foreign name. Dutch or Dutch origin. First name might be Anna.'

Curiouser and curiouser. 'I can find that out. Anything more on the name?'

Anderson sighed, 'That's the best I can do.'

'OK, what's the other thing?'

'Get on to central records and dig out whatever you can find about the death of Robert McAlpine.'

'*Robert* McAlpine?'

'Yeah. I've no idea when he died, but I guess also about twenty-two, maybe twenty-three years ago. And he would have been – say, twenty, twenty-five. Strathclyde, probably. I'd check that first.'

'How did he die?'

Anderson shrugged. 'No idea. Not peacefully in his sleep anyway.'

'So what are you thinking?'

'I don't know what I'm thinking. The Boss rolled home this morning with a skinful and a sore head. All the while I was with him, it wasn't Helena on his mind. He was thinking about something else . . . somebody else. The DCI's not an idiot. Somewhere in his mind, I'm pretty certain, a connection's been made between his brother's death and the attack on Helena. Something he's been aware of since all this started.'

'So why hasn't he said?' Her hand rested on her hip, and her head was cocked to one side; she was thinking she knew where this conversation was going.

'I'm not sure he knows himself. But the thing is: Helena thinks he's flipped since he came back to this station. He's

277

been looking out old photographs and stuff, brooding over them. He was here about twenty-odd years ago, when his brother died, and his mother too, come to think of it. So, if Robbie was murdered, then maybe –'

'Maybe what?' Costello started to flick little stones with her foot; one of them hit its target, twanging against the drainpipe. 'What are you saying?' she asked petulantly.

'That's what I don't know. Maybe the Boss has buried something so deep in his subconscious that he doesn't even know it's there.'

'And Batten would say that's a self-protection thing – something too painful to surface on its own.'

'And that's why we have to find out. The Boss is back at his own house, stinking and soaking wet, barely coherent. He was a gibbering mess when he arrived back in the wee small hours, talking about angels. I took a strand of his hair and O'Hare's doing a DNA test on it. Sorry, but there it is. I said I wanted a comparison on hand. I'd expect the Boss's DNA to be all over his wife's clothes, but just in case we find anybody else's . . .'

'You checking out Terry Gilfillan?'

'That's not funny, Costello, not funny at all. Get back to me, and only me.'

'Touchy!'

Anderson glared at her and walked away.

'Colin?' She trotted after him, catching him before he entered the swing doors of the station. 'I'm sorry, but it's the way you talk about her sometimes.'

'You should have seen the state of her last night – this morning, I mean – after she was attacked,' Anderson said, his voice breaking. 'And Alan could hardly bring himself to comfort her. I don't get it.'

'Other people's marriages, Colin – don't get involved,'

Costello advised. 'Come on, before Wyngate starts lip-reading through the glass.'

'I asked you this morning, where have you been? If I asked you again now, would I get a sensible reply?' asked Anderson. 'You do look better now.'

'Had a bath and a sleep. Well, I tried to. Had a word with Helena on the phone. She seems OK.' McAlpine was sitting at the dining table, a cigarette hanging out of the corner of his mouth, looking like death slightly warmed over. His eyes were red and swollen, his nose and cheek grazed and pitted with dried blood. A copy of the *Daily Record* lay open, his own picture staring back at him. They were marking off a calendar, one set of crossed bones for every day the killer remained at large.

'Bloody tabloids!' he muttered.

'Could be worse.' Anderson dumped in front of him a mug of coffee so strong the spoon almost stood up in it unaided. McAlpine ignored it, so Anderson lifted it up and slammed it back down again, accompanied by two dihydrocodeine.

'I went for a walk, tried to clear my head.'

'A walk on water, was it?'

'In it, more like.'

'And that's what I have to tell DCI Quinn?'

'I'll tell her myself. Any further forward with the attack on Helena?'

'Quinn has been talking to her. I think the new DCI knows we are all too pally to look on it objectively. And she does have Helena's safety right at the front of her mind.'

'You mean she suspects it might be one of us?'

'You were stinking of drink that night. Helena couldn't smell anything off Christopher Robin. And don't look at me like that, it's not me you have to convince; while Quinn is talking to Helena, I think we're taking our eye off the ball. Batten has been right so far. He thinks somebody already in the field went for Helena on your behalf, so to speak, but it could just as easily have been at Brenda on my behalf. You happen to have the high-profile wife.'

'Yeah.' McAlpine was contemplating the coffee steaming in front of him, tumbling the tablets between thumb and forefinger, gathering the effort to wash them down. 'I'll come in to work.'

'You can't do that.' Anderson took a deep breath. 'This attack on Helena means you have a personal interest now. You know you're off the case.' Anderson sighed and hung his head in his hands, wishing he smoked. This would seem like a good time to start.

'Is Quinn definitely taking over? The whole thing? She can't take this case, bossy wee shitbag. She'd put a match to the Phoenix as soon as look at it. You're going to need people like Leeza to help crack O'Keefe; he's a very tough cookie, that one. And I don't think Quinn's the man for that.' McAlpine swirled the tablets down with a mouthful of coffee.

'She's not a man at all.'

'More balls than you and me put together, though, eh?'

'That wouldn't be difficult.'

By the time Costello got back to her flat it was half past five, and she was so groggy she had to look at the paper put through her door to confirm it was still Wednesday. She had been on her feet for thirty-two hours: crime scene to briefing, briefing to central records, central records to station, station to headquarters, headquarters to Paisley, Paisley to Arlene's flat, then a brief phone call to Arlene's mother, which caught the woman in a brief moment of sobriety. The only thing Costello gained out of that was a tasty titbit about Arlene and a priest, and the distinct feeling that Arlene's mum was so sectarian she would not have been happy about her daughter being friendly with any clergyman who was *not* a Roman Catholic priest.

In the shower Costello tumbled the relationships of all three girls with O'Keefe and Leask around in her head. After thirty minutes she emerged, much cleaner but no further forward.

She put some bread in the toaster straight out of the freezer. But the cheese, two weeks past its sell-by date and mouldy, ended up in the flip-top. She forgot all about her toasted cheese and put the kettle on instead.

The answering machine winked at her, over and over. She knew it was the records office, and she didn't want to hear what it was going to tell her, not on an empty stomach anyway.

She settled down in her favourite chair, feet up on the footstool, a cup of tea, two slices of warm bread and a packet of broken HobNobs to hand. She flicked the remote control for her Bang and Olufsen stereo, and let Julie London take the edge off the silence as she called some lady a tramp. Peace, perfect peace.

After a few minutes the constant winking of the answering machine started to play on her conscience. She pressed 'Play' for the first message, noted the number and called back. The call took all of two minutes. A Robert McAlpine from Skelmorlie had been killed while in the service of HM Customs and Excise. The cutter HMS *Alba* had engaged a yacht called *Fluisteraar. Fluisteraar* had been holed, her crew had gone overboard, and James Weir and Robert McAlpine had jumped in to their rescue. Nobody knew exactly what happened in the darkness, noise and confusion. Weir had been pulled from the water immediately, and a Dutchman's body had been retrieved by the *Alba* within the hour. They had to wait three days for Robert McAlpine to be washed up at Bowling on the Clyde estuary. The PM showed his skull had been smashed between the two hulls. Death might have been instantaneous, but there had been water in his lungs. No matter how, he had died in the course of duty. Both he and Weir had received the Queen's Commendation for Bravery. Reports that *Fluisteraar* was smuggling had turned out to be groundless.

Costello's head began to thump. She read her notes again: Dutch. Another coincidence?

In direct answer to her next question, she learned that Robert McAlpine had been the twenty-year-old son of Annabel McAlpine, née Wallace, and Alan McAlpine. One sibling – Costello knew already – another boy, Alan, called after his dad.

She hung up, just as Julie London was interrupted by a sudden rush of wind at the French windows, and felt the spaghetti of confusion in her head start to unravel. She had no answers. But she was starting to make sense of the questions. The blow of losing a much admired brother like that – no wonder McAlpine drove himself so hard. But for Anderson's purposes she could dismiss the contents of the call – Robert McAlpine was a dead-end in the truest sense of the word. Anderson had been right to check it out, but an accident was an accident.

She listened to the second message, glad that the girl on the switchboard at McKillop's, the estate agents in Mauchline, was not the brightest. What she learned half confirmed what Davy Nicholson had told her and taught her a great deal more. Sean McTiernan had indeed come very close to buying a house called Keeper's Cottage, at Culzean. To Costello, Culzean was a castle, not a place, but that was something she could check out at her leisure. But at the last moment Sean had backed out of the sale with no explanation. 'Mr Laidlaw', whoever he might be, remembered the purchase, because both properties at the location had been on the market for so long, and Shiprids and Keeper's had been snapped up at the same time. And by a woman Mr Laidlaw considered far too old to be living in such a remote place. Costello's eyes narrowed. *Far too old?* The old dear with the mole? So McTiernan was still as snug as a bug in the bedsit his social worker had got for him. Mrs Mole might be on the coast. But who was in the other house? And where was Trude? Costello made a mental note to speak to Mr Laidlaw.

Her instinct was right. She knew she was on to something – she had no idea what – knew she had the start and finish of something, but no clue as to the bit in the middle. She closed her eyes, nibbling the HobNobs from the edge and working her way round, a habit she had had since childhood, when such treasures had to last her a long time. She wondered what had happened to the dog. The wind slammed into the glass again; another burst like that and the window would be in.

She sat motionless for about an hour, then dragged herself to her feet. One day – one day, please God – she was going to be able to come home and just fall into bed. She looked at her watch. Half eight, but as soon as she thought about catching some shut-eye, her brain woke up. She reached for the phone.

In answer to her question, Wyngate said, 'Batten's in the Boss's office having a private chat with DI Anderson. He's almost asleep on his feet. The whole squad's coming in.

283

Having the Boss's wife attacked like that – well, it makes it very personal indeed.'

'Has DCI Quinn put in an appearance?' Costello wanted to know.

'Not that I know of.'

She rang off and ran the receiver across her lips a few times, deep in thought. Sleep? Who was she kidding?

It was five minutes to nine at night when Costello entered the main incident room, which was fetid and stuffy after a day's hard labour. The hum of the fluorescent lights seemed louder than ever as she walked up to Anderson and whispered in his ear, quickly summarizing the conversation with the records office and adding a few words about the estate agent. Anderson did not look up. 'So we've no evidence that Sean had money to buy a house. And nobody was responsible for Robbie's death,' he said half to himself. 'Pure accident; it's happened twice since that I know of, something to do with suction of water between two boats –'

'There was another fatality that same night.' She realized even as she said it. 'A Dutchman.'

Anderson frowned and leaned across to say something, but was interrupted.

'You two finished?' asked Batten. He was sitting in McAlpine's office, feet up on the desk, a pile of pictures on his knee. Today's T-shirt said 'I started at the bottom and worked my way down'. A small set of stairs disappeared into the top of his jeans.

'Yes, thank you,' said Costello cheerily. 'Would you pinch the Boss's grave so quick?'

'Sorry, Costello,' said Batten, smiling but staying in McAlpine's seat. 'I was getting a better view of that lot.' He indicated the rest of the squad, meandering round the room

284

outside. 'Look,' he said urgently to them both, 'if DCI Quinn takes over, she gets the credit for all McAlpine's work, and we all know what this case has cost him – his sobriety, his reputation, and, if we're not careful, his marriage and his career.'

'Nice of you to be so concerned,' said Costello sarcastically. It hadn't gone unnoticed by any of them how easily Batten was taking over.

'So if the original team cracks it, it's best all round. You get my drift?'

'Indeed,' Costello said non-committally. 'But we'd have to wind it up fast.'

'So, how would you say it was going, DS Costello?' Anderson asked, in an uncharacteristically formal manner.

'Like swimming the Channel through treacle. With one hand behind your back and cramp in the other.'

Mulholland came in. 'Is this a private party or am I allowed to join you?' He pulled a chair away from the wall and sat down.

'DS Costello was about to give us a run-down on her own investigations,' Anderson said, slightly turning his own chair towards her, so that Batten was almost imperceptibly distanced from the three of them.

'Can't we get on with looking for Christopher Robin?' asked Mulholland.

'We are,' answered Batten coldly. 'Can you call in Irvine, get her to take notes and get it typed up for the rest of them? And don't turn your back like that. I'm a psychologist, I feel threatened when you do that.'

Costello ignored him and deliberately perched herself on the corner of his desk. 'What I'd like to do is tell you all a story, and see what you think. Once upon a time, in the Good Shepherd Orphanage, there were two little orphans called Sean and Trude. They were inseparable, so much so that they contrived to be sent back from foster homes again and again so as not to be parted, and once they grew up the inevitable happened. But they couldn't stay in the orphanage for ever. Sean left and trained as a joiner. Trude left when she was sixteen – that was six years ago – and has never been seen since, except for, we think, one trip to a lawyer when she came of age. Also, when she was eighteen, Sean turned himself in for killing Malkie Steele down Whistler's Lane, claiming self-defence, and served a bit over three years. Shortly before the killing, he backed out of the purchase of a house out at Culzean. He also bought a dog – an expensive pedigree husky – which was never seen again. Since he's been out, he's worked at White's the Joiners, which is where he worked before he went down; they were pleased to take him back. They sent him to Fortrose Street to work on a skylight, and he's been to the Phoenix. And he's been living in a wee bedsit at Gardner Street. On the night of Sunday, the 1st of October, into Monday, the 2nd, he was again seen up Whistler's Lane, having apparently had sex there with a black-haired Goth in a long dark cloak. An odd place to choose, you might think. And Arlene – witnesses place Sean and Arlene together twice, don't forget – was found dead there not long after. Malkie Steele had been kicked so hard one of his eyes was dislodged and his liver fatally damaged, mashed to a pulp – we know that from the PM. And Arlene Haggerty's face was damaged, but not in the same way, admittedly. But damage to the face is . . . well . . . extremely personal, no matter how it's done.'

Costello realized she was subconsciously painting the sequence of events to look as bad as it could for Sean, in the half-hope that one or both men would demolish the pattern. 'His mother abandoned him when he was young, and there's no family that we can find. But he's in touch with the woman who was the cleaner at the Good Shepherd. There's evidence that he was looking for a house for her to buy, but I've not got to the bottom of that yet.'

'He's not having an affair with the old dear with the mole, is he?' Mulholland asked facetiously.

'No,' Batten said seriously. 'But she's a substitute mother figure. And don't read too much into the damage of the face. Go on, Costello.'

'He's good with his hands –'

'And sharp objects,' Anderson muttered.

'According to DI Nicholson, he's strong-minded enough to injure himself with a chisel if need be,' said Costello. 'That's how he changed the time of his meeting with Malkie Steele. Steele was supposed to watch him playing footie, but Sean injured himself and re-engineered the meeting . . . to a private place on the doorstep of his childhood haunts.'

Nobody said anything for a minute or two. Batten rubbed his chin, fingertips rasping on day-old stubble. 'Any sign that McTiernan was paid for the hit on Malkie? That would be the only trace of a contract killing.'

'None that we can find,' said Costello. 'But the timing of his house hunting is suspicious.'

'But no payment was ever made.'

'We haven't found any,' Costello repeated.

'Or if he's hidden it,' Batten went on, 'he's hidden it well, waiting until he's off parole, then he's home and dry.' He sat back again in the chair. 'The black-haired Goth – we think she's Trude, do we?'

'Except that Trude has white-blonde hair. But it's possible. Trouble is, no one's seen her either,' said Anderson.

'Because she does not want to be seen. Nothing changes a woman's appearance more than changing her hair colour.'

'True, true,' Batten said, 'but in the meantime, back to basics. We trendy psychologists would say *follow Arlene*. She's the different one. The other two were comparatively gentle murders – yes, I know, I know – I mean that there was a formality about them, a carefulness, he still exerts a degree of self-control. But Arlene – Christopher Robin was angry with *her*, her personally. Look at the damage to her face. Why?'

Mulholland said, 'McAlpine saw an echo of McTiernan and Malkie when he saw that damage. We don't know what McTiernan evolved into, but we do know what he evolved from. You've seen the social worker's report . . . what his childhood was like. We know for a fact that Arlene met him, for God's sake.'

'Of them all, he fits the profile,' Batten put in quietly.

'Apart from the fact he's too young,' countered Costello. 'And has no faith to speak of. And if we're going the religious-nutter route, Arlene's mother used the word 'friendly' when talking about the *priest* and her daughter. I think if Arlene had meant O'Keefe she would have used his name. But she might have been referring to Leask, and not wanting to tell her mother he was a Protestant. If I wanted to wrap a naive clergyman round my finger, he'd be the easiest.'

'If she wanted to keep a tasty priest to herself, O'Keefe would be the easiest. Good Catholic or not, women are attracted by men like that.'

'Sean might not have a motive, but he is the bastard son of a Catholic mother,' Mulholland persisted.

'It's only a profile, not a road map, but you've made your point.'

'There might be a connection through White's the Joiners to the two other girls,' Costello said. 'One phone call from

Sean to them, being charming and asking to come round to look at the job, would be all it would take.'

'I just feel he's too young . . .' Anderson said.

'But very mature,' Costello insisted.

'Indeed. All roads go in circles, eh?' said Batten. 'So we go back to Arlene – anything else about her that might have caused a spark, any change?'

'Nothing that we haven't already looked at,' Mulholland started. 'She had some hare-brained scheme to get a new flat, but no real plans to better herself. She was just trying it on to make more money. On the game, I mean.'

Costello opened Arlene's file, idly looking through the girl's life and death. 'She was cautioned often, arrested twice. There're photos here from her vice file. Look at these. See, here she's a geisha girl. Black hair. A schoolgirl. Brown hair and pigtails. What would you call that?'

'Personally, I would call that repulsive. Was this what she was putting in phone boxes?'

'Yes.'

'Christ! No wonder she had no money.' Mulholland screwed his face up in distaste.

'Look, this is the most recent, with red hair. She had still to take Tracey's advice on the hair.'

'I don't see your point, Costello,' said Batten.

'She was blonde when she died, but there are no photos of her blonde.'

'Tracey said she told Arlene it would bring in more money if she went blonde,' Mulholland enlightened the rest.

'You're not fucking telling me Christopher Robin goes bonkers because some daft bint bleaches her hair!' snorted Anderson.

'You said she was *the obvious one*, killed because of who she was?' Costello turned on Batten.

'Yes,' he answered mechanically.

'You wanted a recent event, a change? That's a recent change.'

Batten had his foot on the desk, swinging McAlpine's chair back and forth. The squeak was getting on Costello's nerves. 'I suppose there was no positive ID on the clergyman who spoke to Arlene in the café?'

'No,' said Costello. 'When people see a dog collar, they don't look at the face, seemingly. Sean's a good-looking boy, the waitresses were all looking at him. So no joy there. Wyngate looked at the CCTV footage, but for some reason that camera looks out at the road.'

Anderson cursed inwardly, jumping as somebody banged on the window. 'We're sending out for pizza before the shop shuts. Anybody want anything? Last chance to eat before daybreak.'

Thursday, 5 October

At the Phoenix Refuge, a harassed-looking Leeza was doing her best to tidy up the kitchen after the Thursday breakfast sitting; the police presence had done little to reduce the numbers at breakfast, but it had totally annihilated the volunteer support, and today she was on her own. The smell of fried bacon hung stale in the air, and mugs of all shapes and sizes covered the work surface, gathering round the sink like wildebeest at a watering hole. Costello noticed that Leeza did not touch anything without the protection of industrial-strength rubber gloves. She looked tired; the piercing above her eyebrow was red and angry, and she kept backhanding her fringe from her face.

There was very little noise in the place; even the radio in the corner of the kitchen was silent. There were no shuffles or whispers of anybody else in the building, just a resonance of emptiness. Costello looked up into the high ceilings and the dark wooden beams. It was a church and always would be. Outside she could hear the noise of workmen, somebody sawing wood.

Costello knocked gently on the open door. Leeza turned and looked through her with jumpy eyes. 'Oh, hello. Come in, if you have to.'

Despite the unwelcoming words, Costello sensed relief. 'I'm DS Costello. I see you're busy.' She wasn't shaking hands with those gloves. 'You look shattered.' Costello said, aware she had to build a bridge here. 'Why don't I make you a cuppa?'

'That's a first. Thanks.' Leeza turned away and began to attack the plughole of the larger stainless-steel sink with more venom than it warranted. 'I'm sorry, but I'd best get on with this while I'm protected.' She picked up a bottle of bleach and stood well back, aiming the bottle and squirting hard.

Costello picked up two cups, taking a good look at the knife cabinet. No empty spaces.

Leeza smiled at Costello, ignoring Mulholland, who was hanging round the door, and spread the cloth across the taps to dry. She indicated that Costello should refill the kettle, and then began the slow and noisy process of pulling the gloves from her fingers, prising them from her hands without bare skin touching rubber.

Mulholland moved so that he could lean back against the worktop. Out of the corner of her eyes, Costello saw him pick up a clean mug and peer into the bottom of it, rolling it round, scrutinizing it for dirt.

Costello waited for the kettle to boil. 'It's not you we want to talk to, actually, Leeza. Is Father O'Keefe about?'

'No, he left a message on the answering machine. Won't be in till later. He had a hard night.'

'What about Mr Leask – is he here?'

Leeza walked back over to the cupboard and lifted out a jar of Nescafé marked 'For Staff Use Only' and a bag of Tetley's. She said, 'No. He's up in Ballachulish; he goes up sometimes on a Thursday, birdwatching or something. He's very into birds and photography.'

'Was he up there last Friday?'

'No, he was back here. He often goes up just for the one day. You'd think he'd go for the whole weekend. But he had business to attend to, I think. I hope he gets a decent break this time. All this has been getting to him.'

'When did Mr Leask go north this time?' Costello asked casually, appearing to concentrate on making the tea.

'Early hours of this morning.'

Mulholland scrawled a quick note to check the timing – those roads, in this weather, how long would it take?

'He's already phoned in.'

'Really?'

'He mentioned he'd seen that piece in the papers, about DCI McAlpine. He sounded concerned. How is she? His wife?'

'As well as you'd expect.'

'Bet you that was a bit of a shocker. You never expect it to hit so close to home.'

'Suppose so,' Costello said. 'And Mr Leask was concerned, was he?'

'Of course he was. He thinks a lot of your DCI, and George Leask is not an easy man to impress.' Leeza was aware of the disbelieving looks from the two detectives. 'I'm not making it up, you know.' She rubbed a persistent drop of water from her nose.

Costello gestured that Mulholland should leave them alone for a couple of minutes. 'Have a seat and enjoy your coffee, Leeza; you're knackered.'

Leeza sat down a little uncertainly, cradling the mug in both hands as if she was cold.

'Take the weight off your feet and relax, the place is deserted.'

Leeza sighed deeply and dropped her head into her hands, tears not far away. 'You know, sometimes I think George is the only one who ever notices me around here. Tom is so busy and full of good intentions . . . to everybody else. But just because I'm a volunteer I'm supposed to take –'

'All the shit of the day?' offered Costello. Leeza nodded and took a mouthful of hot coffee. 'You're not alone in that. So, does George talk to you a fair bit? I just wonder how he reconciles his faith with a place like this? How does Tom, for that matter?' Costello swirled her coffee but didn't sip from the cup.

'Tom takes the Good Samaritan view, but he likes the publicity, he likes the kudos it gives him.'

'And George?'

'Different kettle of fish altogether. A lovely man, kind of quiet. He was a bit lost when he came down here. Just sold the family farm – his brother had died – and he needed to confront his issues head on. It's very easy to have his faith in a wee place like Back. Bit different when confronted with the big city. George said DCI McAlpine has his burdens as well – his very words – and that he'd a great weight on his shoulders.' Leeza waved her hands indecisively. 'With – you know – this case. He thought your boss was under enough stress without that as well. What with his recent loss –'

Costello took a deep breath and frowned. Leeza picked up a mug and stood up to shout out of the window. 'Do you want a cuppa?'

The noise of sawing stopped, and a voice answered indistinctly.

'Who's that?' Costello inquired.

'The joiner. He's fixing a window; we got a brick through it last night.' Leeza squeezed the used tea bag with a spoon and dropped it carefully into the clean mug. 'Could you take this out to him? It'll stink of bleach if I touch it.'

Costello took the mug but didn't move. 'Who has DCI McAlpine lost recently?' she asked innocently. 'You said *his recent loss.*'

Leeza looked confused. 'Did his brother not die recently?'

'Only recently in terms of Ice Ages; it was twenty years ago. More.'

'Maybe I misunderstood. I know Alasdair – that's George's brother – died recently, but from the way George was talking I just presumed . . .' Leeza looked very sheepish. She scratched at the piercing in her eyebrow and sat down.

'Easy to get the wrong end of the stick.' The Phoenix was suddenly very quiet. Costello watched the dust motes dance lazily in the still air. 'Talking of getting the wrong end of the stick, could you help us out with George's brother? What's his name again – Alistair?'

'Alasdair . . . with a *d*.' Leeza twiddled the ring in her eyebrow. 'There's not much to tell; it's a straightforward enough story, from what George says. He moved down here, met a girl, was totally besotted with her. Between you and me I think she was leading him up the garden path. He was naive, and the Leasks are not poor.'

'I get your drift.'

'Then she leaves him, he was heart-broken.' Leeza pulled at the ring, raising the skin underneath to a point. 'No more to it than that. I think Alasdair must have been a bit doolally beforehand, but you can't say that to George, can you? Most men would get drunk for a week, but Alasdair killed himself. Poor man.'

'How did he –?'

'I think he hanged himself, but I'm not sure.'

'What about her? What did she do for a living?' asked Costello.

'No idea, nothing much, I think. She just up and offed, left him shattered.' Leeza bit her bottom lip and sighed. 'It's strange, but when you think about it, that's how a lot of men get here.'

'At the Phoenix?'

'Yeah, wife leaves, they lose their anchor and start to drift. No reason to go to work, no reason to get up in the morning.'

'So much worse if the wife takes the kids; seen that often enough.'

'Yeah, it's the kids that tear blokes apart.' Leeza nodded at the cooling mug. 'But time moves on. And this tea's getting cold. Can you take that out to Sean?'

Costello's heart was in her mouth as she rounded the corner, following the noise of tuneful whistling and the gentle click of metal against wood. She found Sean McTiernan sitting on a wall and stopped dead in her tracks, hearing the door slam shut behind her.

His appearance surprised her. He looked much younger than twenty-five, younger even than the photograph in his file. Fresh air suited him. Lean, fair-haired, dressed in jeans and a long-sleeved T-shirt washed to a faded blue, he was sitting on a low wall that banked up the narrow garden running the length of the church. He wouldn't have looked out of place on Bondi Beach. Beside him, stacked against the sandstone, were metal grilles taken from the high windows. He was whittling at a long thin piece of wood, shaping it to fit, his eyes slightly screwed in concentration, and whistling the 'Skye Boat Song' so well that even Costello recognized it. She stood for a moment watching the strong brown hands cut and carve the wood, powerful, talented fingers that stopped every now and then, the thumb feeling the depth of every cut made by the sharp single blade. *Confident and skilful use of a knife.*

Anderson felt he was getting somewhere, if slowly. Sarah at the Parks and Recreation Department had got quite excited.

She'd never spoken to the police before, but it made a nice change from Americans phoning up asking, 'Do you have any McKenzies buried there?' *There* meaning Scotland.

Anderson told her, 'I can be more specific than that.' He heard Sarah tap away at a keyboard, and in a few minutes she came up with three names, though she had great trouble pronouncing the third. 'Just spell it for me, love,' Anderson said. 'And can you give me the number of your office in North Ayrshire?'

DS Costello pulled her ID from her pocket, flicking it open at shoulder level with arm outstretched, frightened to admit to herself that she was scared to get too close. McTiernan caught the movement in the corner of his eye, glanced up and smiled, both charming and disarming.

'You looking for me?' He stood up and wiped the sawdust from his open palm, strong long fingers against the denim that covered his thighs.

'Sean McTiernan?' asked Costello, aware her voice was shriller than it should have been.

'Aye.'

'DS Costello.'

'Hello, DS Costello.' He sounded faintly amused. Costello could not help but smile back; McTiernan's easy charm invited confidence. 'I hope you've said something to put Leeza's mind at rest, she's so jumpy about all this I nearly gave her a heart attack this morning.'

'Me too.' She smiled. 'It's understandable – her being nervous – this place almost deserted.' Her voice hardened. 'Can you tell me where you were Saturday, the 16th of September, in the evening?'

'Are you going to caution me?'

'I'm not supposed to be talking to you.'

McTiernan smiled, very charmingly. 'Don't bother. I remember it, it was the third week of my phased release. I went for a swim, then I had a pint in Jinty McGinty's. Got some fish and chips and went back to the bedsit in Gardner Street.'

'You remembered that well,' said Costello sarcastically. 'And last Friday? The 29th?'

'Last Friday? I think I was working late. You can check it out with my boss.'

'We will. Where were you working?'

'I was on 24-hour call all week, broken windows and that. We had one in the' – he clicked his fingers together trying to remember – 'that deli down in Byres Road, can't remember its name, and then there was another one, up round Prince's Gardens.'

'Another what exactly?'

'Broken window. I boarded it up,' he said, looking at the pane of glass leaning against the wall. His blue eyes narrowed for a moment. 'I have signed in, you know. I've seen my social worker, I haven't broken the terms of my parole or anything.'

Costello looked at him, thinking. His face seemed open and honest. Yes, she would let him help if her car broke down in the middle of the night. She would let him in the house if he wanted to use the phone. 'What time were you finished at?'

'Late, early morning. Half one, I would be guessing. Like I say, it was stand-by.'

'All week? That's a lot of stand-by.'

'In my circumstances, I'm glad I have a job. It helps me get out. Meet people.'

'Do you know a girl called Arlene Haggerty?'

McTiernan seemed to think for a minute, then smiled

sadly. He kicked at a piece of wood. 'Yes. The Ashton Café, Saturday lunchtime? Blonde hair, short skirt? I think a lot of men knew Arlene Haggerty.'

'So you noticed her skirt in particular?' asked Costello, her voice hard.

'The lack of it.'

'And you met her later?'

'I took her back to my bedsit.'

'Why?'

'Why do you think?' Sean smiled at her wryly. 'I've been in prison for a long time. It's a man thing,' he said.

'Did you pay for it?'

McTiernan looked past her as if he had not heard right, his lips forming a wider smile at something so absurd. 'Do you think I need to?'

She didn't think so. 'Talking of paying for things – do you own a cottage out by Culzean, paid for in cash?'

That question did take him by surprise. He nearly managed to hide it but not quite. 'Well, that's a new one.' A slight lift of the eyebrow.

'Immoral earnings,' Costello hinted, smiling at him. 'I don't really want to do anything about it. I just want to know. You can't serve time twice for the same crime.'

'Immoral earnings? Yes. But my mother's, not mine. She left me three things in this world: a tough heart, a good smile and a small wad of cash. I'm working hard, keeping my nose clean. I have my job back, and I'll get a flat when I can afford it. But to get back to your original question – yes, my mother was a prostitute. But I, myself, do not have to pay for sex.' He winked at her.

Ain't that the truth. Costello tried to keep her mind on the job. 'Where would you be looking for the flat? The Ayrshire coast seems to be a favourite of yours.'

McTiernan swallowed hard before answering. 'I lived in Ayr for a couple of years, you know that. You lot seem to know everything. So you'll also know the Boss has a company down there. Property was cheap to rent, and the job was on my doorstep, nothing strange there.'

'Did you live there alone?'

'Yes.' It held the glibness of a lie.

'You weren't there with Trude?'

His answer was instant. 'I haven't seen Trude for years.'

'We have you on CCTV tape, running out of Cleopatra's Disco on the weekend of the 1st and 2nd of October.'

'I know. I was there. What of it?'

'You were seen *running*. Were you in a hurry?'

'Yes, I was.' He smiled to himself, as if thinking about something recent and finding the memory pleasant.

'Why?'

McTiernan looked at her for a moment. She felt a shiver run through her and shifted her weight from one foot to the other, knowing the next thing out of McTiernan's mouth would be a lie. He had spent too long thinking about it. And there was something else, a subtle change in the expression: those friendly blue eyes were not so friendly now. 'Could you tell me why you left in such a hurry?'

'I met somebody. Shagged her as well. Is that a crime?'

A different reaction. Eat your heart out, Viktor Mulholland. Female intuition says McTiernan has feelings for the second one. He's lying. *Protection and devotion* . . .

'Is it?' he persisted.

Costello raised one eyebrow, inviting him to continue.

'I don't chase women, but I take it when it's offered. I was chasing some bad memories. It was in the same lane that . . . well, you know.'

'I think I do know, Mr McTiernan.' For a minute their

eyes locked. He looked away first. 'I would like her name, even if she's married. I can be discreet.'

'I'm sorry,' he said. 'I don't know her name.'

That she didn't believe.

The Three Judges was crowded even on a Thursday night, which suited them fine. It was warm and cosy in the booth, and a draught rushed at their ankles every time the door opened. It had been raining steadily for the last three hours, driving even the most committed smokers indoors. On the television Davina McCall was screeching with excitement about something nobody was interested in watching.

The squad were sitting at the back of the pub, heads down in a scrum formation. McAlpine was biting on the skin round his thumbnail, gnawing to relieve the tension. He had had a shower and a change of clothes, but the bruising on his skin had darkened, and his face looked thinner. Anderson was sure healthier-looking people had walked out of Belsen. It was the end of a long day, at the end of a long week, and there was a faint hope resolution was not far away. It just wasn't there yet. McAlpine looked tense, sitting slightly apart, giving the impression he no longer belonged, but Anderson was glad he was there.

'We have to get this closed and get it closed soon,' said Batten as an opening gambit. 'Remember, this is an unofficial meeting, so if we come up with any touches of genius, they get minuted as tomorrow's briefing. I've met DCI Quinn, and I share your misgivings; she's already counting the biros in the office. But enough said. We have to get closure on this now; we are so close. How's Helena doing, Alan?'

'She's fine. She went in to work for a couple of hours. The show must go on, as they say.' A slight colour flamed in McAlpine's eyes and then died. 'Quinn's already in my office, you say? I didn't make it in to tidy the desk. I've been in the hospital. They wanted to X-ray me again. I've a broken clavicle.'

'Good for you,' said Anderson. 'Peter made less fuss when he broke his, and he's only five.'

'Right,' said Mulholland, ignoring them and spreading out a sheaf of photographs in front of him. He held up the original one of Elizabeth Jane, and another of her looking very different. 'This is the most recent; we got it from her mother. There were only four weeks between these two photographs, but look: the shorter hair, the highlights she had put in for the wedding –'

'Which she had dyed back again. Gail Irvine reckoned the last-minute fuss about the turquoise bridesmaid's dress would be enough to turn Paula homicidal,' Costello put in, starting to feel a bit light-headed. 'Good thing she and her fiancé were both at his mum's that evening.'

Anderson spoke up. 'You remember I spoke with Shand? And he said he'd discussed the whole Elizabeth Jane situation at the Phoenix, suggested getting her to go down there so one of the other priests could get involved? O'Keefe went berserk, absolutely apeshit. Said he hadn't spent years working to get the refuge up and running just so some bored middle-class bint could come in and use the place to stage her attention-seeking charades. His actual words were stronger.'

'He has a strong ego, O'Keefe. No doubt about that,' said Batten thoughtfully.

'And about Arlene, Shand said it was common knowledge she was not a misguided little innocent battered by social injustice. He advised O'Keefe against being alone with her or with any of the girls.'

Batten nodded. 'He's a shrewd judge of character, then.'

There was a frustrated silence round the table while the barmaid appeared with a tray of drinks, jostling her way through a couple of guys leaning against the booth, watching the TV. One, his hood still pulled up from the rain outside, had elbowed Costello twice already. Any more of it and he was going to get his brown Barbour covered in orange juice.

Anderson caught her eye. 'Don't,' he said. 'He's had it rewaxed; you can smell it from here. It'd just be a waste of drink. Talking of which, I'll join the Boss in a malt. Christ knows I deserve it.'

'So, as the good doctor here predicted, our friendly serial killer, Christopher Robin, sees all these women as part of the monstrous regiment,' said Mulholland to Costello, misquoting John Knox.

'What are we discussing? Manslaughter or woman-slaughter?' she said bitterly. 'I don't see any guys getting cut up and left to bleed to death.'

'OK, OK,' said Batten, peacemaking again. 'This is starting to have the right feel about it.' He put his hand over the photograph, dropping his eyes to look at Arlene's pixie-ish features: the upturned nose, the exaggerated epicanthic fold over the eye. 'Bitches? Manipulators? It's a good hypothesis, but we need to look behind it, to see what Christopher Robin sees.'

McAlpine was not seeing anything except a daft bint with a new hairdo. He closed his eyes. *Bitches. Manipulators.* Was that how Christopher Robin saw Helena? How Leask had seen Anna? No, Leask had said that it was Anna who'd taught him a lot. She had died to save her child. And he had been ashamed of the way he'd thought about her.

'Well, tomorrow O'Keefe will be back in the Phoenix, Leask will be down from Ballachulish, and McTiernan will be back to finish his window,' added Mulholland. He nodded

303

at Costello. 'And I'll have a root around his toolbox, if I get a chance. I'll keep it legal – only if in plain sight and all that.'

'So tomorrow we get them all on the same menu. How lucky can we be?' Anderson looked at his watch. 'Right, troops, home-time. Big day tomorrow. We can sleep easy tonight; Quinn is having all the main players watched. Unofficially,' he added.

Mulholland left quickly, clearly glad to get away. Batten wandered back to the bar. Anderson got up to leave, then took one look at the Boss and sat down beside him. He looked hard at Costello.

'I'm too wound up. I'll stay on for a bit,' she said, understanding quickly. 'Too wound up. I'm not sure I'm getting this. I'm not sure I'm getting any of it. I need to hear how Wyngate got on trawling the books of White's the Joiners. I want something concrete.'

'Don't we all? Wyngate wasn't hopeful when I spoke to him.'

'He's playing us along, this Christopher Robin,' said McAlpine, grinding the edge of a beer mat into the table. Anderson resisted the urge to take it off him. 'Is McTiernan in the frame?'

'Yes, but the White's set-up looks well run and secure. It would have to be, if they're sending a guy with McTiernan's record out to jobs. I'd say O'Keefe looks tastier.' Anderson got up to order another drink.

'Look at that face, jumped on, pulped.' McAlpine stared at the mess that had been Arlene. 'That was McTiernan, I've no doubt. I've had the benefit of seeing his work before. All these comments about what a nice guy he is? Exactly what I heard the last time. He's a vicious little sod. His mother insisted he was brought up a Catholic, yet she had the morality of lesser pond life, so there's your religious conflict. I'd run down that joinery job; get forensics to go over it.'

'But he admits he did the work, so that gets us nowhere,' Costello pointed out quietly.

Suddenly McAlpine's face was in hers. 'I told you he was clever! I've seen what his feet do to a face, and I've seen it with these eyes. So don't give me any crap. He's guilty. He shagged one of them, for God's sake, and he knew where the other two lived. And anybody with half a brain cell could work out where I live after that bit in the press. Helena was left wide open by that!' Costello recoiled in her seat, her head jammed up against the Barbour jacket behind her, feeling queasy in a reek of lanolin and linseed. 'Do your job, Costello. You're looking for a trigger? Well, how about: McTiernan gets out of prison and all this starts. You're looking for a motive: his mother thinks so little of him that she abandons him as a baby, and the only thing she gives him is the guilt that goes with being brought up Catholic.'

Anderson held his breath until he caught sight of the time. 'Christ, I'd better be going. Costello, can you take these back to the station?' He held up the photographs. 'And make sure the Boss gets . . . somewhere.'

'Don't tempt me,' Costello glowered. 'Just put a broom up my arse, I'll sweep the floor as I go.' She fumbled as she put the photographs back in the envelope. She stopped at Arlene's picture. The high sweep of her cheekbone, her hair well cut and off her face, made her look almost classy, a million miles away from the common tart she had appeared to be on the slab. 'It's funny how that picture changes her. Maybe she was getting somewhere after all,' she said to nobody in particular. She noticed Anderson had left a full half-inch of Talisker. 'But at the end of the day her wee boy is still going to grow up without a mother. Is he another Sean

McTiernan in the making? Another Christopher Robin?'

'We all have choices, Costello,' whispered McAlpine.

'Yes. Having a father I didn't know and an alcoholic mother, I should be a serial killer . . . well, on the days I'm sober. But all I'm admitting to is a HobNob addiction.' She swigged the Talisker to dramatic effect. 'Like you say, it's all a matter of choice.'

'But you do have your ghosts.'

'Yes, I do.' She caught McAlpine's eye and longed to stroke that bruised face. 'Indeed I do.'

'And that gives you the fire in your belly to do the job right. Not all ghosts are bad.' McAlpine began upending the photograph between finger and thumb. His voice was dead, his mind elsewhere. 'We should be looking backwards, not forwards. It's our past that makes us what we are. And sometimes it comes back to haunt us. Or worse.'

'What are you talking about?'

'Someone I once knew. I think. I mean, I think I knew her. I think I still do. I don't know. I'm too tired to think straight. Now you know why I drink. Keeps the demons and memories away.'

Costello smiled and took another slug of Anderson's Talisker.

Friday, 6 October

The minister was sitting behind the desk, a mug of tea and a plate covered with toast crumbs to one side, opening that morning's mail and placing the bills in a neat pile, while enjoying his late breakfast. Even though he was casually dressed, his shirt and collar were tucked precisely underneath his jumper. He could have been any minister in any church attending to his office duties.

The whisky the night before had warmed Costello to the best night's sleep since the case had started. Now she could feel the anger come back; now she was ready to take on the world in general and George Leask in particular.

She knocked at the already open door. 'Mr Leask?'

The minister rose from his seat and nodded to her very politely.

'Hello. Police, I know, please come in,' he said. 'Oh, it's you, Mr . . .'

'Mulholland.'

Leask sat back down. His hair ruffled, his fine features slightly reddened as if he had been caught in foul weather, he had a wholesome attractiveness about him when he smiled with sincerity, like Dr Kildare. Costello summed him up as a man that women would trust. She smiled back at him. There was a flickering response in the ice-blue eyes. Costello wondered if he was shy. Or gay.

'Where were you last night, exactly?' she asked, her voice tough but friendly.

'I drove up to Ballachulish. Just a quick up and down. I'm sorry for going off like that, but after the events of the last few days, I felt I really had to get away. To tell you the truth, I needed all my strength to come back. I did leave a number,' he added defensively, directing his words over Costello's shoulder to Mulholland. 'I'd spoken to DCI McAlpine.'

'Well, you're talking to me now,' Costello persisted. 'We believe there might be a link between the murders and this place . . . or with one of the staff,' she added deliberately, keeping her voice hard. This man believed in the wrath of God. He wouldn't scare easily. 'How well did you know Arlene Haggerty?'

He pressed his palms together. 'Oh, I knew her. We tried to offer some help.'

Suddenly Costello smiled her sweetest smile, the one that charmed confused old ladies. 'I asked *how* well. I mean, you belong to a faith that objects to an air ambulance landing on a Sunday because it's the Lord's Day, yet you happily help a girl who is out drinking, and, worse, on a Sunday night. I don't get that.'

Leask steepled his fingers and chose his words with care. 'That's why you do your job and I do mine.'

'Sorry if I offended you, but it is difficult to understand.'

'I know she sold her body for money. That should have outraged me, I suppose, but *saddened* would be the word I would have chosen. She was also, for the record, slightly antagonistic to those who didn't belong to the Church of Rome.' For the first time Costello saw Leask smile with genuine humour.

'I was born in Glasgow. You get used to it. You sound as though you quite liked her.'

'She had an inquiring mind.'

'An inquiring mind?'

'Yes, we talked about faith and belief. People are not always as they seem, DS Costello.'

'You can say that again.' He looked at her with those blue eyes. She didn't look away. 'But she talked with Thomas more than she did with me.'

'Father O'Keefe?'

'Yes.'

Costello made a conscious effort not to glance at Mulholland. 'Did she get on well with him?'

'Maybe. Being a Roman Catholic, she felt he was more approachable than myself. She'd reached a turning point in her life. She was doing her best ... But she is in God's hands now, and we can comfort ourselves with that.'

Costello felt like pointing out that far from being in God's hands, Arlene was on a slab in the mortuary, cold as stone, sewn up the midline. She said, 'But the minute she got on the right road she was murdered. She was found lying next to a rubbish skip, half naked on the coldest night of the year, ripped open, left to bleed to death. How could you not let that test your faith?'

'My faith is uncompromised. Miss Costello, I have no crisis of faith. My own brother left his faith, and he died in very tragic circumstances.' He put his hands in front of him, palm to palm. He was a man of great control. 'If faith could get me through that, then believe me, I can face Armageddon and not have my faith shaken.'

'Very difficult to lose a close family member, something we both come across all too frequently in our jobs – unfortunately. DCI McAlpine went through a similar experience to your own.' Costello paused, but there was no reaction from Leask. 'Tragic, wouldn't you say?' she continued. Then paused again, inviting a response.

'Very tragic,' said Leask, nodding slowly, his eyes narrowed slightly in suspicion, but he did not elucidate.

Costello leaned forward, softening her voice a little. 'Mr Leask, could you help us out here? I don't like listening to rumours, so could you clarify for us the circumstances of your brother's death? I know you touched on it with DCI McAlpine, I know it's unfortunate, but we do have to cover all the angles.'

Leask stroked the side of his face slowly before answering. 'There's no great mystery, DS Costello. He took his own life while the balance of his mind was disturbed, that's the correct phrase, I believe.' The stroking stopped. 'Tragic, as you said, but that's all.'

'Thanks,' Costello said, as she smiled her sweet smile. 'None of that will go any further than it has to.'

Leask nodded gratefully.

'And, while we're here, could you tell us if you recognize this phone number?' She held out the number they had found on Arlene's phone.

'That's the one in this office,' the minister said carefully. 'This phone.'

'And that one?' She held out the number taken from Elizabeth Jane's phone bill.

'Where did you get that?' His voice flickered a little. It was the first sign of weakness Costello had picked up.

'Never mind. We know it's registered to a phone in here. Which one?'

'That's Tom's private line.' Then adding, realizing the implication of what he had said, 'Well, not *private* exactly. It's the one we phone him on – the staff, I mean.'

'Do you think Elizabeth Jane might have been attracted to Father O'Keefe in some way?'

The question unnerved Leask. 'I can't really say.'

'Between us,' said Costello, leaning forward, 'she was a single girl. Thomas O'Keefe is a young and attractive priest. Do you think something could have been going on there? Some kind of crush, maybe?'

'No.'

'Not even on her part only? You seem very sure.'

'I am.'

'Nothing's more attractive in a man than being unobtainable. You never got the impression that Father O'Keefe felt some resentment towards her? After all, she wasn't exactly using the place for the greater good, was she? All that fuss about the wedding, for instance.'

'I can't really say,' repeated Leask.

'And can you say, Mr Leask, whether Arlene spent more time with you or with Father O'Keefe?'

'Him. As I said, she was of the same faith.'

'And would you say, Mr Leask, that Elizabeth Jane spent more time with you or with Father O'Keefe?'

Leask looked around, as if he wanted the floor to open up. 'Him probably, but only because she hardly spoke to me. Please don't be under the impression I knew the family well. I only went round to see her parents because I was representing Andrew Shand, representing the Church. The family are Church of Scotland; you know that.'

'But not the same Church as yours?'

'What's that expression you use in Glasgow? We kicked with the same foot.' He smiled again. 'Why are you asking me all this?'

'Because Elizabeth Jane's parents never set eyes on Tom O'Keefe. We have no corroborative evidence as to who "Tom" actually is. And nobody can tell us who Arlene's priest was.'

'Oh – meaning they could be the same person? I'm going

to paraphrase myself.' He said, with genuine distaste, 'I'm glad I do my job. And I'll leave you to yours. I will pray for you.'

'Thanks,' she said lightly. 'I need all the help I can get.'

'Just one more thing,' said Mulholland. 'Do you know where we can find Sean McTiernan? Is he around?'

Leask visibly relaxed at the question. Costello wondered how much strain he had been under while he was talking; lying was stressful. 'No, I thought he would have been in today. He hasn't been seen since yesterday, not that he is obliged, of course. His social worker has been on the phone to Leeza.' The phone went again, and Costello raised her hand to say goodbye and half dragged Mulholland into the hall.

'Right, you hang about here. O'Keefe will be arriving in a minute.'

'Where are you going?'

'Outside to phone the station, I'll be back in a mo. Keep an eye on Leask and don't let him out of your sight. I've a couple of phone calls to make about Messrs McTiernan and Leask.'

'Leask? Why him?'

'You don't think I believed all that twaddle about his brother, do you?'

After five minutes of pacing up and down the hall, the dust irritating his sinuses, Mulholland felt his mobile vibrate.

'It's me. My battery's low. McTiernan's done a runner, cleaned out his bedsit, the lot. I think I know where he is. Stay put, Anderson's on his way. Tell him to expect a call from –' The phone cut off.

'No bloody option but to stay put, have I? Silly cow.'

It was just gone two o'clock when Costello pulled the car into the lay-by at the Electric Brae and took a sip of her bottled water, enjoying the silence. The weather was clear, bright and sunny, but the wind bit with a grip that foretold winter round the corner. Ailsa Craig sat like a tea cosy in a sea of watercolour blue. Ireland lay low behind, sleepy and indistinct.

She remembered this road as a child, and its strange phenomenon: a parked car runs uphill if the handbrake is slipped. People who knew about such things said it was all to do with the lie of the land, an optical illusion. Costello preferred the theory of the Electric Brae, a strange force that pulled cars against the force of gravity. She turned off the engine and gently slipped the handbrake off, and the Toyota, imperceptibly at first, began to roll up the hill. As it gained speed, Costello pressed her foot on the brake. She smiled to herself: physical proof that the world was just that little bit crazy.

She put on the handbrake and got out the OS map. The estate agent at Mauchline had been very helpful. Mr Laidlaw had made her a cup of Earl Grey and explained that he could say nothing about who *had* bought the two houses. But he could say plenty about who *had not*. He had pointed out the location of the two cheap rundown cottages and had let slip that he'd had to drive to Ayr to get the purchaser to sign, because *she* wouldn't leave her flat.

Costello looked down at the bay. This was where the cottages, and the answers, should be. If she wanted to hide from the world, she couldn't think of a more beautiful place than this.

She pulled the car out on to the road and went along to the next lay-by, which had a lane running off it down to the shore. She looked at the map again. This was the closest the headland road got to the shore, though it was still a good half-mile from the beach. She drove on, slowing to look at a stall selling watercolour pictures of the castle and the sea beyond. She was searching for another lane closer to the beach, looking for a house close to the water, out of sight of the road.

To her left, Culzean Castle shone burnished gold in the strange light, the hills behind purple, fading to lavender. It was so beautiful, she wanted to fill her eyes with the rich colours. Scotland was a country coloured with an autumn palette. She noticed the castle drifting on the skyline; the road was swinging inland. She had gone too far.

She did a U-turn on a long straight stretch and headed back the way she had come. She looked again at the stall she had passed on the way out. Profitable in the summer, she thought: this scenery was so picturesque, so near the castle. Yet it was October now and freezing cold. How profitable could it be?

No tax. No VAT. And, she supposed, a wee backhander to the tourist coaches that ploughed up and down this road. It would be on the itinerary for every McKay's Tour doing the West Coast.

She indicated and pulled in. They would know how many houses were on the beach: from the look of it, they had painted the place often enough. A woman was sitting behind the table on a folding chair, reading the *People's Friend*, a knitted bunnet pulled over her head and a tartan rug wrapped round her legs. Behind the range of watercolours on the table was a red tartan flask. She would need it.

'Hello, dear,' said the woman, looking up from her story, her eyes framed by steel-rimmed glasses, the bristles on her mole twitching.

Costello felt a tingle of adrenalin. 'These are lovely.'

The woman nodded, totally off guard.

DS Costello held up her warrant card. 'I'm looking for Sean McTiernan.'

'Aye.' The woman was good. The beady little eyes looked unfriendly behind the glasses, a keen intellect calculating how much to tell, and the only sign of unease a slight shuffle of the fingers over the tartan blanket. 'I've had a few women looking for him in my time. Usually younger than you, though.'

Costello made a note to get her done for unlawful trading. 'Do you know where he is?'

'No.'

'He missed his meeting with his social worker, and he hasn't been seen at his bedsit,' said Costello casually.

'I knew where he was staying in Glasgow, but if he's not there, he's not there.'

Costello could not argue with that logic. 'You saw him in the Ashton Café, last week?' The narrow face looked blank. 'A coffee shop in Glasgow, Saturday midday?'

'Oh, aye, weak tea, uncomfy seats.'

'And you have no idea where he is?'

'Why should I?'

'Do you know where Trude is?'

There was a hesitation. More than that, a look of slight panic. Pain? 'I've no idea where she is. I've not seen her for years.'

'Are you sure?'

'Of course I'm sure. Goodbye now.' The old woman opened up her magazine again. It was as effective as slamming a door in Costello's face. She walked back to her car. A silver BMW, one of those with the quartered wheel-trim, had driven past but was now reversing, as if curious to have a look. Maybe McAlpine should buy Helena one of those, to make up for ruining hers. She got into her Corolla and drove off, unaware of the look the two men in business suits gave her as she accelerated away.

Mulholland was getting pissed off with waiting. He had been told to wait, and that Anderson was on his way. His instructions were not to speak to O'Keefe alone.

The Irishman had come in, carrying some carrot cake and a takeaway cappuccino. He'd waved the paper cup at Mulholland.

'Oh, if I'd known we were to be having company I would've brought another.' The familiar keys had jangled as O'Keefe balanced the cake on top of the cup and opened the door.

Mulholland had been tempted to follow him in, have a crack at him on his own, but his career meant more to him than that. He murmured to O'Keefe that he would look around if that was OK, and disappeared down the hall. O'Keefe didn't answer, already drawn into the room by a ringing phone. Mulholland turned back and listened at the door long enough to know it was a call about a client; he recognized the name of a local GP, spoken informally, as though O'Keefe knew him well. He wandered off towards the laundry, a small room panelled in chipboard and dwarfed by a huge yellow industrial washing machine, and stinking of damp wool and disinfectant. There was a rack of clothes, unsellable stuff from the charity shop, dead men's clothes. He wondered if Lynzi had brought any of them in. Probably. The smell in here was affecting his sinuses even more. He opened a small door into the yard, his shoes crunching on broken glass, and looked up at the newly fitted glass of the window, still imprinted with puttied fingers. The trestle and the saw were still lying there: the repair had been recent. A can of Coke, ring-pull up, stood on top of the sandstone wall. He looked into the plastic toolbox. The tools were not new, but they were kept the way Mulholland's dad had kept his tools, the saw blades wrapped in hessian to protect the teeth. He stepped over the toolbox, the top still propped open, and noticed *SMcT* etched on the lid and then scribbled over repeatedly with ink. He bent down, raking around with the tip of his pen. His eyes rested on the knife, long and strong, beautifully polished. And he blessed his Russian mother, who never used to let him out of the front door without a pristine white handkerchief in his top pocket.

Anderson found the front door of the Phoenix lying on the snib. He opened it cautiously, entering into the darkness and the familiar smell of dust and polish. He paused, then gestured to Wyngate to stay with the car. O'Keefe's door was open, and Anderson observed him for a moment: the priest looked calm and relaxed. He seemed totally untroubled, happy even, biting into his carrot cake with gusto, his hand cupped underneath to catch the crumbs.

Anderson rattled a knuckle on the side of the door. 'Sorry to disturb you.'

'Not at all.' The priest was expansive. 'Have a seat.'

'I just wanted a word about Arlene,' Anderson said. 'How well did you know her?'

'Not well at all.' The priest shrugged, licking crumbs from his fingertips. 'A pathetic girl, really. I went to see her mother after she died.' He pulled a face. 'An alcoholic, poor woman. A terrible life.'

'We all have our crosses to bear.'

'And Christ knows, Arlene had hers.'

Anderson was looking past O'Keefe at the photographs – happy times, people having fun – on the wall behind him.

'We think that the answer to all this may lie within these walls,' said Anderson quietly.

'I gathered as much. I find the thought unsettling.' O'Keefe ran his hands through his hair. 'Please, you know you have the run of the place.'

'We appreciate that, and nobody doubts the sincerity of anybody who works here, but you cannot guarantee who'll walk in that door. If the devil himself came in, you wouldn't know.'

O'Keefe looked at Mulholland as he walked in, the younger detective tipping the wink to Anderson. If O'Keefe noticed the signal, he didn't respond, and continued to talk to Anderson.

'You know, you always think that you know right from wrong. I always thought that my faith would bring me through anything. But this is awful. For the first time, I feel I want to pack it all in and just walk away.'

It seemed to Mulholland a much more human reaction than Leask's – or maybe Thomas O'Keefe was just a better actor. 'And how do you feel about that?'

'How would you feel? Look at this place. Empty. Years of hard work down the drain. People should be here waiting to be fed, but there's nobody. We won't recover from this.' He bit on his bent forefinger, looking out of the window for a minute. 'The word is out. Six years I've been painstakingly building up goodwill. And it's gone. I was officiating at a funeral yesterday, and there was more talk about the murders than about the deceased.'

'How did you know Elizabeth Jane?' asked Anderson gently.

'I'm not sure I did. I didn't recognize any of the pictures you showed me. But who knows, maybe my memory is worse than I thought. A poor excuse for the living slipping through your fingers. I'm told I spoke to Lynzi, but if so I never knew her name. A few women would come in and sort out old clothes; I used to just say hello and leave them to it. I did know Arlene, but no better than I'd know a hundred other people that walk in here.'

'You never spoke to Elizabeth Jane on the phone?'

'Not that she identified herself, no. But that phone rings all the time, so I might have. And if I'd known it was her, I would have had a few things to say to her.'

Mulholland noticed how O'Keefe strove to distance himself from the victims, never making a definite statement that could be disproved.

'You never met her parents?'

'No. Why would I?'

'Do you know this girl?' Mulholland asked gently, handing over two pictures of Arlene.

'That's Arlene Haggerty? I spoke to her mum, like I said.'

'Do you remember seeing her looking like that – with that hair colour, to be specific?'

O'Keefe glanced at the dark-haired version. 'No,' he said with no hesitation. 'She was always blonde when I knew her.'

'Do you know Helena Farrell?'

'Runs that posh art gallery? Wife of the Detective Chief Inspector, the dark-haired guy? I know who you mean, and Leask told me what happened to her. How is she?'

'Comfortable,' Anderson answered with easy vagueness.

'I don't think she was ever down here, was she? I don't think I ever met her.' O'Keefe's phone rang again, and he picked it up. 'Sure, fine, yes, I'll have a word. Can I have a few minutes?' he said to them, covering the mouthpiece with the palm of his hand. Then back to the phone, 'I'm really sorry to hear that. How is she coping?'

319

Anderson whispered as he got up, 'Just one quick question – have you seen Sean McTiernan?'

O'Keefe shook his head and pointed to his own hand. At Anderson's shrug he asked the caller to hold on 'while I close the door'.

'I haven't seen Sean today,' said O'Keefe, his hand clasped over the phone. 'He had to go to get his hand stitched yesterday. He left in some hurry.'

'He left his tool kit here,' said Mulholland, patting the knife in his jacket pocket. 'It's out the back.'

'Leeza said the wound was bad, and Mr White, the boss, came to get the van to take him to the Western. I have to get on,' O'Keefe said pointedly.

Anderson felt his mobile vibrate against his leg and cursed inwardly. 'Bye for now.' He left the room and stood in the corridor, his face pale and carefully expressionless.

Mulholland followed Anderson from O'Keefe's office and stood in the draught of fresh air coming through the front door. He silently acknowledged Anderson's turned back, a need for discretion while the Boss was on the phone. Mulholland made a point of not listening and watched Wyngate look aimlessly at the cars parked on the circus. He stood leaning against the wall, his arms folded, thinking: in the file, in Costello's handwriting, was a note about Sean putting a chisel through his hand. And they said at the meeting that he'd used that trick before, so it was another convenient accident to rearrange the timing of events to suit himself. Mulholland listened for a moment, but Anderson was still on the phone. He felt the knife in his pocket as his own little treasure, not wanting even to mention it while there was a chance of being overheard. He thought about the photograph of O'Keefe, benign, charming and affable. In the midst of all this murder, the priest's only genuine concern seemed to be for the future of the Phoenix. An ego out of control?

Anderson snapped his phone shut. 'Yes, yes, yes, *yes*!' His fist punched the air. 'That was O'Hare. The blade had a broken tip, and it twisted when it contacted bone. We have a fair idea of length, so now we have a distinctive blade we can identify. He's sent some pictures to the station, and I've asked Burns to bring them over here.'

'Why? Why don't we go back there?'

'I'm not leaving. If that knife's anywhere, it's here. Where's Costello?' he added as an afterthought.

'McTiernan's done a runner, and Costello's gone after him. Don't get on to me about it, she was out the door before I could stop her.'

'Oh, shit!'

'And if you're looking for something like this, it was in McTiernan's toolbox.' Mulholland looked behind him to ensure they were alone and took the knife from his pocket, still wrapped in the handkerchief. He held it up to the light. 'It's covered with something dry and flaky. It used to be liquid. Look, it ran down the handle.' He held it against the skin on the back of his hand. 'It looks like blood, recent blood.'

'Evidence bag, Mulholland. Fuck! Where did you say Costello was?'

'She's gone after McTiernan,' said Mulholland.

'But where? And who with? You're here, I'm here, Burns is on his way over here and Wyngate's outside. So who's with her?'

'Nobody.'

'You let her go on her own?'

'I don't see how I could've stopped her. You know how she is; once she gets an idea, she's off and –'

O'Keefe opened his door apologetically. 'Look, I have to leave, I'm needed at the Western – last rites, you know.'

'Yes, of course. Do you mind if we send somebody with you? He'll be discreet; but it's for your own protection, really.'

O'Keefe muttered under his breath, and Mulholland thought he heard a few swear words he never thought would leave a priest's lips. They followed O'Keefe back into his room as he grabbed a black zipped bag from under his desk and hoisted it on to his shoulder. 'I'll be in the red 2CV out the front,' he said tersely.

Anderson followed him back through the door and got hold of the nearest uniform, instructing him in a voice so low neither O'Keefe nor Mulholland could hear.

'Right, where were we?' Anderson sat on O'Keefe's desk, picked up his mobile, thought a moment, then put it back down again. 'I'll get back to the knife in a minute. Where did Costello say she was going?' he demanded again.

'I don't know.'

'What d'you mean, you don't know?'

'She said she had an idea.'

'Fuck. The stupid cow.' He stuffed his mobile in his pocket. 'I'm going to get a team in here. This has been going on too long.'

'Don't we need a warrant?'

'You heard O'Keefe – we have his full cooperation.'

'I'm not sure he meant it.'

'Neither am I, but who gives a toss?'

Costello drove back down the Heads of Ayr Road and parked in the lay-by near the first lane she had seen. She had been right; she had found the old dear with the mole.

Sean was near by; this was the place. She was looking for a small cottage with a big dog. She thought about going back to Ayr and requesting assistance, but the cottage was still half a mile away. She could get down there and not even be seen. She saw a gap in the hedge and tyre marks in the field beyond, and wondered if this was where the Boss had crashed the Beamer. It was certainly along this stretch of road somewhere; the same geography that made the bay so attractive was exactly why it made such an accident black spot . . . and indeed why the new inland road had been built. If this was the aftermath of his accident, he had been lucky.

She got out of the car, checking she had her binoculars and pulling the phone from its charger. It was bitterly cold, even in the sunshine. Pulling her fleece up round her neck and flattening the hood of her duffel, she walked down the lane towards the sea, which sparkled from a dull grey through a myriad of colours to dazzling white, where the wind kissed it into white horses. She shivered.

There was a small white cottage halfway down the lane, *Shiprids Cottage* written in black italics on the whitewashed wall. Was that an old Scots word for sheep? Shepherds? Something like that. Everything in sight had been whitewashed.

She rang the doorbell.

Nobody answered.

She tried again.

Nothing.

Shit. There was no evidence of another house down here. She was debating with herself whether to go down to the beach or to walk back up to the car, when her phone rang. She knew before she answered it that the decision had been made for her.

'Costello, you stupid cow! Where are you?'

'I can hardly hear you – the signal's bad.' She looked up at the hills behind her, the sea in front: no chance. 'What?'

She heard 'stupid cow' but she was too happy to be upset. 'Just wait, sir. I've traced Sean's old friend, from the Good Shepherd. I've made the connection . . .'

'. . . found . . . McTiernan?'

'McTiernan . . . Well, not really, but . . .'

'. . . arse back . . . here . . . *crackle crackle crackle*. Now!'

'Yes, but . . .'

'Costello . . . *now*!' McAlpine would talk to her like that, but Anderson? That meant trouble. She put her finger in her other ear, turning her body this way and that; a few words came over crystal clear – 'I mean it, keep away from him' – before the buzzing started again. She felt a cold handclasp over her heart, a deep shiver that went through to bone. It was a lot colder than she had thought.

'You have no idea where McTiernan is?' Anderson asked. The air in O'Keefe's office was getting very stale, and he waved his hand in front of his face.

'No, I really don't. I know his address is a bedsit near here, but that's it,' Mulholland replied.

'How long's Costello been away? An hour or so? Where was the house? It was in that report. Christ, she told me right after she spoke to the estate agent.' Anderson pinched his fingers over the bridge of his nose. 'There's only one road that follows the coastline, isn't there?'

Mulholland nodded. 'Yeah, the Heads of Ayr Road.'

'Get a car down from Ayr,' Anderson snapped. 'If he follows type, as Batten would say, he'll head to his "mother". Tell them they're looking for a white Corolla parked near a remote house. Get to it.'

While Mulholland dialled, Anderson tried to get hold of Costello. But every time, the mobile was dead. 'Wherever she is, she's out of range . . . down beside the water. Tell them that.' He put his phone down and started to fiddle with the binoculars on the windowsill.

'Sorted!' Mulholland snapped his phone shut. 'You a birdwatcher too?'

'Feathered or two-legged?' said Anderson.

'Either.'

'Neither. I'm an expert on Postman Pat and Edie McCreadie from *Balamory*.' He looked out of the window again, his finger tapping the telephone on O'Keefe's desk. 'If this line is busy, does it stop anybody else ringing through?'

'No.'

Anderson was holding his mobile in his palm, willing it to ring. It stayed silent, its green light ridiculing him.

'Where's the Boss?' Mulholland inquired.

'McAlpine? He was going to visit Helena and then have a good sleep, I hope.'

'Leask goes birdwatching up at Ballachulish,' said Mulholland, flicking through a pile of magazines with *Leask* written on the front cover.

'He has family there as well. Bloody sight closer than Stornoway.'

'Was that true, about Stornoway Airport not allowing landings on a Sunday?'

Anderson nodded. 'Yeah, they're a funny lot. Where's that team? Where's Burns? He should be here by now.'

'Do you want me to run this over to forensics?' Mulholland held up the evidence bag, desperate to get out of the dusty, smelly office.

'No, no, I've phoned it in, and somebody's coming to get

it. I want a search team and I need you here. We need to wait.' The office seemed darker, more oppressive. A delivery had come in, and a pallet of dried soup was stacked on the floor, along with litre bottles of detergent and floor cleaner. Boxes upon boxes of what looked like man-sized tissues were stacked to desk height. Mulholland's curiosity got the better of him.

'Gloves,' he reported to Anderson. 'Latex gloves.'

'Eh?'

'Latex gloves? No fingerprints?'

'No fingerprints because he doesn't touch anything that would retain them, Mulholland; don't get carried away.' Anderson bit his teeth into his lips. '*Phone*, you fuckers!'

Her day ruined, Costello walked back up the lane slowly, past the patch of burned grass where the car had crashed and gone up in flames. There were bits of glass everywhere – small cubes of windscreen sparkled on the ground like diamonds of dew – and fragments of blue metal. It was the same colour as the Beamer's paintwork. She could see a pattern of something here . . . She was starting to sound like Batten.

She climbed the fence to look down at the bay, a last look before the lane climbed to the height of the main road and she lost sight of the beach altogether. It was a strange place, mystical even. It was blowing a gale down on the shore, yet there was no wind here. A dull grey cloak of cloud had fallen over Ailsa Craig, and it looked as though another storm was on the way.

Costello climbed up on the second-highest spar of the fence, hitching her leg round it to steady herself, and pulled out her binoculars. She could see a fair way along the waterline from here, not much of the beach, but she could see as far as the cliffs and then up to the castle. She scanned the binoculars back and forth; she could not see any other buildings anywhere.

To her, it was the obvious answer. This place had a hold on Sean McTiernan. So if the old biddy had one cottage, who had the other? Was that what the estate agent had *not* said? *Keeper's* . . . What secrets was it keeping?

That shiver ran through her again, as though someone had walked over her grave.

She dropped her binoculars. Looking again without them, she saw a movement at the water's edge. Blond, the colour of driftwood, it seemed to roll and undulate in the water, a piece of wood caught in a riptide. Then it moved quickly. Costello put the glasses up again: a dog, wolf-like, was playing with the breaking waves, wet legs comically scrawny compared to the huge fluffy body. Costello always said the only thing she knew about dogs was that the end with the teeth was dangerous, but she knew a husky when she saw one. Gelert. Who had never been dumped.

She reached upward on her wooden perch but could see no further.

She clicked her tongue in irritation. She couldn't walk down there and risk coming face to face with Sean. She checked the map again. It clearly showed the other cottage, almost on the beach, further along, but she couldn't see it. She tried to get her bearings, turning the map so it matched the orientation of the land. She faced inland, with Ailsa Craig behind her, the castle on her right. The other cottage was closer to the sea, almost underneath the castle. She sighed. She had found the old biddy, and she had found Gelert. She would get back and tell Anderson, force him to listen.

She took one last look, scanning the beach through her

binoculars, envious of whoever had the peace and beauty of this place to enjoy.

'What do you think? It's starting to get dark,' said Mulholland.

'Don't know, I'm still thinking. Wait to see what forensics say about that knife. They'll make it a priority. Burns should be here any minute with the stuff from O'Hare about the knife that was used on Arlene. Somewhere we should get a match. How long has it been since I phoned Costello?'

'About ten minutes. She'll be all right, she's not daft. Is it just the pictures Burns is bringing over?'

'A blueprint for the blade and some dimensions.' He pursed his lips. 'As for Costello not being daft, I'll reserve judgement on that.'

Anderson opened the shutters at the window, but the dank mustiness of the place persisted. Darkness was falling fast. It was the end of the seventh day. He wished somebody would open a window in this place every now and again. He put his fingertip against the window, drawing in the grime.

Leeza came in. 'Are you going to go, or hang around, or what?' She dangled a key in her hand. 'I'll need to lock the door.'

'Don't worry, we'll wait. We'll make sure nothing goes missing.'

Not the answer she wanted.

Mulholland found he could not stop looking at her face. After clearing up from tea, she had applied some lipstick, but must have been interrupted because the colour had missed her mouth at one corner, giving the appearance of a permanent leer. The ring that dangled from her eyebrow had infected the skin underneath it. With that, and her damp dungarees, she looked like a perverted rag doll. However, she was trying to be nice. Somehow Mulholland found that even more unnerving.

'Do you want another coffee, tea, anything?'

'No, thanks, we're fine. We would prefer it if you hung around, though, just in case.'

She looked troubled. 'In case of what?'

'Just in case.'

'Not much choice, have I?'

'Not really. We'll try not to be long.'

She considered for a minute. 'I'll take some of those magazines through to the kitchen. There's loads of them there, if you're bored,' she said sarcastically to Mulholland. 'No *Playboy*, I'm afraid.'

Costello walked back up the lane, thoughts rattling through her head. She turned on to the road at the top of the lane, her eyes down as she put her binoculars into their little plastic case. She put the case back into her jacket pocket. Her fingers were numb; she hadn't realized how cold she was. Eventually she felt the key fob in the deep recesses of her pocket.

She was walking quickly to the car now, anxious to get back to the Phoenix to find out what the boys, particularly Anderson, knew about McTiernan. So near and yet so far.

She walked into the lay-by, pulling her chin deep behind the cowl of her fleece, breathing through the warmth of the material. It was much windier up here. She didn't look up till she saw the feet, the white trainers. Standing there, leaning casually against the door of the white Toyota, hands in pockets, face raised towards the cool autumn sun, was Sean McTiernan.

*

Anderson looked at his watch. 'How's the search going?' he asked Mulholland anxiously.

'Carefully. We've no idea what drugs may be stashed in this place. The team's called for full HIV protection, and you know how slow that makes things. Wyngate's in charge. He's taken the kitchen knives for testing. And he said, to give them their due, that Leask, O'Keefe and Leeza have given us carte blanche.'

'Which means we could have nothing to find.'

'Or, if we do, they don't know about it.'

Anderson walked over to the wall, looking at the photographs, listening to the footsteps of the search team outside. 'It's McTiernan; I can taste it. Costello could get sucked in, just like Elizabeth and Lynzi.'

'It wasn't you who sent her. It was McAlpine,' pointed out Mulholland. 'And she's not some stupid bint, she's a serving police officer.'

'I could have stopped her, though. And I didn't.' The door opened tentatively.

'Do you mind if I just pick up some stuff? We seem to be under siege.' Leeza came in, followed by a female officer who retreated to wait outside when she saw Anderson there. Mulholland thought Leeza's hair looked less spiky than it had previously. In fact, Leeza herself seemed less spiky, and he saw vulnerability in the way her eyes flickered from side to side. She was uneasy at the police invading a space she clearly thought of as hers. Or maybe she was glad of their presence with the shadows of Leask and O'Keefe hanging in the air. He smiled at her offering reassurance and got a tight-lipped smile back.

She settled down at her desk and began to rifle through the same papers that Leask had, muttering nervously, 'We paid this; we've definitely paid *this*, so why are they sending us a reminder?' She looked at the calendar, which was stuck at September, and walked across the room to change it. 'Are you any closer to finding anything?' she asked, her voice catching a little.

'Not yet. These things move slowly.' Anderson sat casually on the two-drawer filing cabinet, emphasizing that he was in control. 'How well do you know Sean McTiernan?'

'McTiernan? I know he's done time. And I know what for,' Leeza replied, carefully folding over the next page of the calendar, a Canadian seal popping its head through an ice hole.

'Has he ever mentioned any family? Anybody he was close to?'

'You mean, he's disappeared and do I know where he is?'

'Top of the class.'

'No, I don't know. And I don't know him well.' She added, with some bitterness, 'You could talk to him all day and not know him any better. He only tells you what he wants to. And I suppose, in his circumstances, I would be the same.'

'Do you like him?'

'What kind of question is that? If you're asking do I ever feel threatened by him, the answer is no.' She tilted her head, biting her lower lip, and for a brief moment she almost looked attractive. 'He's self-assured, easy in the company of women. Like a happily married man.' She stood up. 'Believe me, I know a happily married man when I see one.'

'Really?'

'Yeah, they're a rare species.' She made a point of looking at Anderson's wedding ring on her way out. 'McTiernan wouldn't hurt a fly.'

'Sounds like our man, then,' Mulholland muttered to himself.

*

331

'Well, hello, DS Costello.'

'Hello, Mr McTiernan.' She kept her voice calm.

'What brings you down here? It's a bit off your patch.'

'They're going to start looking for you.' She looked him straight in the eyes, eyes she remembered as being blue, kind and friendly, and felt a tightness in her stomach when she realized they were now neither so kind nor so friendly. Her fingers crawling round the phone in her pocket, she cursed herself for not calling for back-up.

Sean folded his arms over his chest, letting the good arm take the weight of the sore one. The white bandage was already filthy. Costello wondered if the accident had been a pretext to hide teethmarks or scratches, or some other injury. It wouldn't be the first time he had damaged himself with a tool for a good reason. McTiernan didn't move from the car. He was looking at his feet, as if thinking deeply about something.

Costello's fingers closed round the key fob, her thumb finding the button. She could unlock the car from here, but then what? She tried to read his body language, his facial expression, any threat in his eyes. There was something there, but she couldn't identify what.

'Anything you wanted to know, you could have asked me yesterday. Saved yourself a long drive. How did you find me?' His words were curt.

'Power of deduction.' She shrugged her shoulders, attempting a smile. 'And an estate agent who was a sucker for a warrant card and a nice smile.'

He turned slightly to face her, leaning on the driver's door. There was no way she could get past him to get in. She felt her stomach sink. He wasn't stupid; he knew what he was doing.

Costello moved from foot to foot as though her feet

were cold, even as she felt the sweat pouring down her back. Key fob in right hand, mobile phone in left hand, neither of any use. She had gone past shock; she knew that. It was him or her.

She tried to take deep breaths so as not to let him see her tension, but she could feel her heart thumping against her rib cage. She had been trained for this sort of situation, but her mind had gone blank.

'You left your bedsit. What about the conditions of your parole? You have to go back, you know that,' she said, her voice steadier than she'd thought it would be. 'I was the one who knew where you were. As you notice, I'm here on my own.' She glanced at her watch. 'I've got to radio in soon, though.'

'So you say.'

'Sean. Look, you served your time, don't mess it up now.' She took a step nearer to him, trying to draw him away from the car door, some courage coming from adrenalin. She stared at his feet, innocent-looking in white trainers, and saw images of Malkie Steele, kicked to death, lying in a puddle of his own blood, pale shards of fractured cheekbone serrating the skin. She lifted her hand to her face, feeling the soft flesh of her own cheek.

McTiernan's body tensed as though he was going to move away from the car, but he took a packet of Silk Cut from the back pocket of his jeans with his good hand and drew out a cigarette. She watched his long, strong fingers caress its length and place it delicately between his lips. His eyes never left her face. He lit it, waving the match in the air until the flame was extinguished. He settled back against the car door, his eyes steely cold.

Suddenly he moved, firing his cigarette to the ground and moving away from the car. Costello instinctively moved

333

back, her finger through the loop of her key fob, keys in the palm of her hand. She could jab at his eye and then . . .

He paused, giving her a strange look, as though he thought her not quite sane. 'I'll be in touch with my parole officer, and I'll be back up in Glasgow to get my stitches out.' He waved the bandaged hand at her. 'OK? Nice of you to be so concerned.'

He was some yards away from the car now. Or was he letting her think she was free to go?

She stepped closer to the car, McTiernan watching her all the while. She pressed the button on the key fob. Nothing happened. She tried again, nothing happened. The lock had jammed again. She cursed the AA man under her breath, feeling sick with tension, expecting a blow on the head or the cold grip of chloroform at her throat at any moment.

Keeping her voice light, she asked, 'That dog down there – is it called Gelert?' McTiernan smiled but did not answer.

She clicked the key fob and heard the central locking spring open.

Then lock again.

The sound made him turn. She pulled her left hand into a flattened claw, fingers drawn back to her palm, knuckles ready for the windpipe, while angling the sharp end of her ignition key in her right hand, ready to go for the centre of his eye.

If she could bring him down, get to the car and slam the central locking shut, she might have a chance.

Lynzi, Elizabeth Jane and Arlene had probably thought they had a chance as well. Or had the chloroform blocked everything out before they even had a moment to realize they were doomed?

*

Anderson checked the clock on the wall, comparing it with his own watch. Apart from the fact that it said Thursday rather than Friday, the time was right – five fifteen.

'Would you sit in a bathful of cold porridge for charity?' asked Mulholland.

'Would I bollocks.'

Mulholland stopped picking imaginary fluff from his jacket sleeve and picked up another birdwatching magazine. He was not a man who could hide his boredom; he could hear the search team ripping the Phoenix apart, and for a brief moment he wished he was back in uniform. Exciting things were going on in the building, and here he was babysitting his boss in case two phones rang at the same time. 'There's a picture here of O'Keefe doing exactly that.'

'He's Irish – what do you expect?' Anderson turned to the wall, studying the photographs with faint interest. The one of O'Keefe looking slightly foolish in the bath of porridge was labelled *Priest Gets His Oats*. There was a group of six men, none of whom he recognized, in trainers and running tops, false breasts dangling precariously, miniskirts rucked up over their shorts, hanging round each other's necks in exhaustion.

'Do you know how common blue tits are in this part of the world?' said Mulholland, agitated, flicking through the magazine.

'If that's a preamble to something smutty, forget it. Leeza will have your balls.'

They both jumped when Anderson's phone went.

There was a brief exchange of words, most of the talking coming from the other end of the phone. Anderson shot a look at Mulholland. 'Oh, great,' he said into his mobile with weary sarcasm. 'Look, just get them to send a squad car from Ayr, down to Culzean . . . and take the Heads of Ayr Road.' He swallowed hard as he flicked the phone shut.

'Costello?'

'She could be in trouble. That was Wyngate, tracking down McTiernan's money.' He turned on Mulholland. 'McTiernan came into a little money when he was eighteen but nowhere near enough to buy a Wendy house, never mind a house on the coast. So what's Costello playing at?'

'I'm sure DS Costello can look after herself,' Mulholland ventured. He sounded more confident than he felt.

Anderson looked at his watch again and started pacing as far as the little office would allow, muttering under his breath and looking at the photographs on the wall without seeing them. 'There's nothing else I can do, is there?'

'Not really, sir.'

When McAlpine woke up, the house at Kirklee felt like a mausoleum: no sign of life, no sense of family, no sense of home. It was chilled, the way only an empty house can be. He had staggered into bed sometime in the last twenty hours but had no idea when. He had woken up in the spare bedroom, feeling as if he had not slept at all. Horrific nightmares had tortured him in his sleep: Robbie rising from the water, Anna and Robbie kissing, laughing and cheering in the waves. Anna her face grey and dead, dark gaping holes where her eyes used to be. He heard himself call to Anna, calling to her that he was drowning. She had turned away. Nobody heard his screams. He woke up as the water closed over his head.

He looked at his watch, the Cartier that had been his lucky charm for twenty-two years. Now its stern square face was telling him that it was half five, and that if he got a move on, he could make it to the gallery for the exhibition.

He could show Helena some support; he could stand at the back and be proud of his talented and clever wife.

He undressed and stepped into the shower, turning up the power so hard it was painful to stand under it, before noticing something odd about the shelf under the window.

Spaces.

And, casually, near her bottle of bluebell perfume, sat her wedding ring. On top of it rested her engagement ring, its blue diamond reflected in the glass. So Helena had taken some of her toiletries, because they were important to her. And left the rings behind. He picked up the diamond, stroking the single stone against his lips. She had asked him to do that single thing, to take some of her belongings to the hospital, and he had forgotten. The ring suddenly felt cold in his hand. Maybe she'd taken them off only because her fingers were blistered . . . But *she* had gone.

Had gone to stay with Denise Gilfillan.

Gone to protection of sisterhood.

He spent an age shaving, taking care round the cuts. He dressed carefully, choosing his good suit and a tie that went with the shirt. He even walked over to the mirror, holding both up to his chest, to check the colours. He went downstairs and poured out a Glenlivet, then went into the kitchen and poured it down the sink. He switched on the kettle instead.

Anderson was still looking around abstractedly, his eyes skimming the collage of photographs on the wall. 'That's some amount of money this place gets gifted,' he said, looking at a formal photograph of a giant-size cheque, made out to the Phoenix Trust, being handed over. There was a series of photographs of Scouts and Boys' Brigade activities. The last two pictures showed one perfect triangle of logs, and another not so perfect. Anderson looked a bit closer, tracing the outline of the fence round the grass with his finger. The lower flats of the building behind were clearly visible.

'Vik? Get Leeza in here.'

Mulholland opened the door and shouted down the hall.

'It stinks out there; they have the floorboards up.' Mulholland wiped imaginary grime from his face, remembering why he was glad after all to be out of uniform. He resumed his reading of the magazine. 'Some interesting stuff in here,' he said flicking through. 'Nobody's drawn bras on these tits.'

'Oh, piss off, Vik.' Anderson's finger was pointing to one of the photographs. 'Do you think that's Victoria Gardens?'

'Looks like Victoria Gardens. But have a swatch at that.' Mulholland put the magazine right in front of Anderson's nose and watched the face of his senior officer as he scanned the line drawings. How to bait a trap, the trapped mink and a third captioned *Anaesthetized Mink.*

'What do you think that means?'

'Well, sir, what do you know that can knock something out in a confined space? Look at the picture: they put the whole trap in a bin bag, pour something in and hold the neck of the bag until –'

'It stops struggling. And you gain a controllable victim. Costello said that's why he uses the chloroform.' Mulholland flicked the magazine over to show Leask's name written in the top corner.

'The name means nothing; it's been kicking around here for weeks. But if that's the source of the chloroform? Find out what that anaesthetic is – oh, just get a move on.' Anderson pulled out his mobile phone. 'Go out to my car, plug that in, phone the RSPB, the guy who wrote that

article, anybody you can think of. Find out what they use
... *exactly*. If it's chloroform, use your initiative and back-track. Find out if it's registered, regulated, whatever.'

'And who has it where?'

'Yeah, in particular the Ayrshire coast. McTiernan keeps nipping down there for something.'

Mulholland went out of the door so fast he nearly knocked over Leeza coming in.

'Yes?' she snapped.

'Where is that?' Anderson asked, indicating the photo-graphs of the log piles.

'Victoria Gardens. A tree came down in the storm, and we had a sponsored log-clearing, the Scouts versus the Boys' Brigade. It raised a few bob. Who's interested? Do you know your lot are ripping the toilets out?'

'Yeah, we're looking for illegal substances.' He sniffed; her hair smelled faintly of good dope. 'Was there a key to Victoria Gardens kept here?'

'How should I know?'

'*Was there?*' He let his anger show in his voice.

'Probably!' she shouted back. 'The gardens are locked, aren't they?'

'Who would have them, the keys? Think, it's important.'

Leeza's hand went to her throat, trying for total recall. 'I really don't know. Either George or Tom, one of the young ones – they organized it.'

Anderson swore loudly. 'So an extra set could have been cut, the originals handed back.' If they had picked that up after Lynzi's body had been found there, the investigation would have been over. 'Are these pictures in any particular order?'

Leeza's voice quavered a little. 'No. That's the Jewish Women's Circle with Rabbi Shaffer. That's –'

There was a knock at the door, and Burns's huge frame appeared. He was carrying an envelope; there was a note pinned to it with his thumb. 'Thank God. Do you mind, Leeza? This could be confidential,' said Anderson. Leeza closed the door behind her. 'No sign of Costello out there?'

'No.'

'Shit.' Anderson emptied the envelope on to the desk.

'O'Hare said you were to look at that, and Quinn said you've to phone this number ASAP.' He handed over the note. Anderson glanced at it and frowned slightly, not recognizing the code.

'Where is that, now?'

'Stornoway, same code as my Auntie Dolina. It's the number of the manse. Costello's already phoned the minister, but Quinn says it's important you speak to him.'

Anderson relegated the number to his breast pocket and concentrated on the contents of the envelope, now splayed on the desk. 'Right,' he said, glancing at the pictures; if he had not known better he would have said they showed pieces of badly damaged concrete. It was Arlene's spine.

Somebody had drawn a circle round the crescent-shaped notch on the front of the bone. The next showed the same picture blown up, the image grainier. Again the indent had been circled, with an arrow going clockwise.

'So what does that mean?' Burns asked.

'It means the knife was twisted when it went in,' said Anderson.

'Was that what O'Hare said on the phone?' asked Burns, his broad finger outlining the waisted vertebrae.

'I'm sure that's what he said.'

Burns shifted from one foot to the other.

'If you have something to add, please do,' said Anderson. Burns was not the brightest, but he was eminently sensible.

'It could be, sir, that the knife was twisted on the way out rather than the way in.'

'Does that make a difference?' asked Anderson.

Burns gestured cutting open his own stomach, causing Anderson a shudder of recognition. 'The sort of knife you'd use for that, there's a gutter that runs up the middle of the blade, to act as a channel to let the blood out; otherwise the knife can get stuck. Suction . . . you need to twist the knife to break the grip of suction.'

Anderson was feeling sick. He handed Burns a piece of paper from Leask's desk. 'Draw it. Draw it life-size. O'Hare says we're looking for something one inch plus wide, seven inches long, with a two-millimetre slice off the top, a saw-tooth blade.' He watched as Burns's big hands moved quickly over the paper.

'Bowie knives, bayonets, they're all made the same way, with a blood channel,' Burns said. 'What were those measurements again? And you want it sawtoothed . . .' He smiled.

Anderson immediately pointed to Sean's knife, lying in state on Mulholland's white handkerchief. 'This is longer than seven inches,' he said. 'And thinner.' He shook his head. 'We'll still send it up. I don't trust these measurements. What do you think?' he asked Burns. 'I remember you saying, about the sharpness of a knife that could almost cut through a leather belt . . .'

Burns ran his eyes over the knife. 'It's sharp, right enough.' He felt the tip with his thumb, careful to touch it only through the handkerchief. 'And it's a wee bit damaged, look, here at the end, as though it's been used as a lever, maybe to open paint tins. But I don't see this being the weapon, sir. It's not strong enough. Too long, not enough weight.'

'And I don't see Christopher Robin leaving a bloodstained weapon lying around.'

Mulholland came back in, rattling the door against the jamb. 'Surely the fact that it's bloodstained is the point,' he said breathlessly, pointing at the evidence bag containing the tiny dark red flakes.

'I was saying Christopher Robin would be too clever to leave it lying around. So the blood is McTiernan's, probably. He did cut himself. Burns, will you take that straight up to forensics? A uniform was supposed to come, but we can't wait any longer. The sooner we find out the better. Somebody's either perfectly innocent or being very clever. But before you go – were you brought up on a farm?'

'Aye, sir,' answered Burns.

Anderson was pacing again. 'So disembowelling, gutting animals – is that the kind of thing only a farmer would know: a farmer, a gamekeeper, a soldier?'

'Somebody like that, sir. Don't suppose it's common knowledge.' Burns sketched quickly, annotating the drawing.

'So answer me one question, yes or no. A Glasgow-born-and-bred joiner, interested in football and running – would he instinctively know how to do it? Yes or no.'

'Instinctively? No.'

'That's all I wanted.' Anderson was thinking about a connection with what Burns had said. Somewhere, in the recesses of his mind, he remembered seeing a bookcase, full of books, reference books, well worn and tattered, but he couldn't quite focus on where it had been. There was a pattern here, a pattern of country life, someone used to handling a knife, used to being at one with nature, but set on righting the wrongs of mankind in the worst way possible. What had McAlpine said – *the smell of morality* . . .

'Sir, I managed to –' Mulholland started, but he was

interrupted by the outer door opening and closing, the sounds of chatter.

The door of the office burst open and Costello came in. 'Present for duty, sir!'

Even though she was red-cheeked and trying to be cheery, Anderson could tell she had had a fright. His relief turned to anger. 'You, Costello, are on a charge.'

'Of what?' she asked.

'Being a stupid bitch. Where have you been?' He slumped in the seat.

'I know where Sean is,' Costello beamed.

'Don't ever, *ever* go off like that again.'

'Sorry.'

'We found his knife, Costello. It's being checked,' Anderson whispered. 'Bloodstained,' he added for effect, trying to ram her fright home. It was a lesson she had to learn; she might not survive a second time. Giving her no time to answer, he went on, 'They had the keys here for Victoria Gardens all along.'

Costello's eyes widened.

Anderson walked over to look at the photographs on the wall, feeling sure the answers were there. He recognized a few old players from Rangers and Celtic in the line-up, a few from Partick Thistle, a couple of local radio DJs and a Glaswegian who once came second in the Song for Europe competition. Both the football teams were listed, name by name, with date and venue, their moment of glory captured for ever.

'What you've got there is a diagrammatic reconstruction of the knife we might be looking for,' he told Costello. 'Burns here recognized it.'

'Do you two mind if I get a word in edgeways?'

'Sorry, Vik, did you get through?'

'More than got through.' A slight smile played around his lips. 'The mink of Ayr are few and far between. Mink create a big problem with the ground-nesting birds in Ballachulish, though.'

Costello froze, looking from one detective to the other. A slight smile passed from Mulholland to Anderson and the DI said sweetly, 'We'll ask Quinn to apply for a warrant to search Leask's place. I'm just in the mood to see those beautiful floorboards pulled apart.' Anderson looked at his watch and plucked the phone number from his breast pocket. 'And on we go – getting closer and closer to Christopher Robin.'

It was getting on for eight o'clock when McAlpine parked his car in Bath Street, as close to the gallery as he could get. It boded well for the success of the show, the opening night being this busy. In the light of current events, Helena had rearranged things; she had been standing in the middle of the gallery, pointing, while Denise and Terry and the staff ran round her. Business first – Alan knew that aspect of her personality well. Maybe they weren't so unalike after all. Her gamble had paid off, and the place was crowded, just the atmosphere was different. As he walked past, instead of the gentle swirl of jazz punctuated by bubbles of conversation and laughter, he heard the lament of a lone piper above the subdued buzz of chatter, the chinking of glasses, but no frivolity. The exhibition had certainly got plenty of publicity – nothing like a good murder attempt for getting the parasites of the press involved.

The girl on the door handed him a catalogue and said hello. He resolved again to behave himself, to be all sweetness and light, no matter what. Glasgow's finest had turned up in force; from the steps he could see some honoured guests from Holyrood and the Provost of Glasgow having a serious chat over some champagne. Girls, all dressed formally in black suits, all with their hair gelled back, steered their way through the throng with trays of glasses filled with champagne, orange juice and mineral water. He picked up some champagne, put it back and then, feeling naked without a glass in his hand, picked up a mineral water.

He saw Helena up on the mezzanine, looking beautiful and curvaceous in a black silk suit, her red hair tumbling down, amorphously melting into a flame-red scarf. She looked her normal self, but her make-up was a little too heavy, her smile a little too wide, as though she was rearranging her features for a photograph. She kept the palm of her hand protectively over her stomach, appearing to smooth down her suit. But she was coping. She was talking to an art critic in front of a painting that, to McAlpine's untrained eye, looked like an aerial photograph of one of the more boring Scottish islands. Helena was gesturing at something, but, as the critic turned to see where she was pointing, her smile disappeared, her face reverted to the slightly drawn politeness of someone in pain.

McAlpine made his way up the stairs to talk to his wife.

'Hello. I didn't expect to see you,' she whispered to him. 'But I'm glad you're here.'

'I thought I would come along, offer some moral support.' He looked around him. 'It looks as though it's going well. Lots of people in kilts.'

'That's as it should be. Do I look nervous?'

'You look just fine.'

'I've been doing this for years, but I keep thinking people are going to jump out and stab me.' She took a deep breath.

'I was thinking it was really busy, all these people I don't know. Then I realized it's all members of the Strathclyde police force in plain clothes.'

'They could do with some culture.'

Helena gave a delightful smile to somebody walking past. 'How's your arm?'

'Sore. How are your ribs?'

'Sore. But I win, I've got stitches.'

He lifted up the mineral water. 'Well, I've given up the drink because of the painkillers. One bad habit at a time. How are you, really?' he asked.

'Fine, until somebody asks me how I am *really*. I'm going to change the subject now. See the man over there, long hair?'

'With the tartan blanket over his shoulder?'

'That's Peter Kolster.'

'Don't tell me that's the McKolster tartan.'

Her smile began as a mischievous flicker on her lips. They looked at each other as if they had only just met.

'You left these in the house.' He handed her the wedding band and blue diamond engagement ring.

She took them slowly. 'I did. I'm sorry; my fingers are sore.' She spanned her fingers revealing the red ugly blisters on the palms. 'I don't want to wear them on the wrong finger in case I lose them. Tell you what, you look after them for me.' She put the rings back in the palm of his hand and squeezed her own fingers round them. He pulled her towards him and kissed her gently. He put the rings back in his pocket. 'Your tie is squint.' She straightened it, recognizing the silk one she had bought him last Christmas, her hand lingering on the front of his shirt. 'How's the case going?'

'I'm off it. They've put Quinn in charge,' he said bluntly. 'Once he attacked you, it became personal.'

'Oh,' said Helena, as her husband's mobile rang.

He spoke into the phone, listening, saying 'yip' twice before ending the call. 'Something's up.' He snapped the phone closed. 'But the one thing I do not want to do now is rush out of here, on your big day.'

'But that's exactly what you are going to do, isn't it?' she asked.

'I was trying to be a good husband.'

She sighed. 'Al, just be the husband you've always been, kind of hopeless. I'm used to that.'

'I'm trying to do the right thing.' He sipped his mineral water, wishing it was whisky. He had only been teetotal for half an hour, and it was hurting.

She swirled the champagne around in her glass. He looked at her, his eyes melting to a smile, and for a minute she saw the handsome man he used to be. She smiled back.

'So, are you all nice and cosy at the Gilfillans'?' he asked.

The smile died. 'Quinn sent somebody round to interview them. She seems to think I'm crucial to the case somehow.'

McAlpine seemed to consider this for a minute. 'I'd better be going.' He turned to leave, then turned again to plant a warm kiss on her cheek. She reached out to touch his arm, but he had gone.

Late on Friday night, the Three Judges was at last quiet, just the local crowd at the bar refusing to go home until the rain eased off.

McAlpine put a Diet Coke down in front of Costello, who was gripping the bridge of her nose between thumb and forefinger, trying to relax. 'Get that down you. I'd buy you something stronger, but I know you want to get back across the road and get amongst it.'

'Don't you?'

'Not really. I want to pop in at the post-exhibition party. See how it went.'

'Good on you, Boss. First time you've been there for, well, years.'

'First time I've been there full stop.'

'And I don't think it's a good idea for you to go over there. Quinn is ripping Helena's life apart as well, trying to find the connection between all the victims. Her picture is up on the wall, and yours. It's not nice to see when it's somebody you know.'

'The connection is me and this case, surely?' argued McAlpine.

'That would seem the obvious answer, and we've pointed it out to DCI Quinn more than once. But, you know DCIs, sir. They sit at God's right hand. She's up and running with Helena and Leask, they're her two main lines of inquiry.'

'Do you think we've been wrong about this all along?'

'I don't think we're wrong,' said Costello defiantly. 'Leask.'

'Leask just doesn't strike me as a fucking nutter. No forensics as yet, no eyewitnesses, no ID parade. Just because he's a birdwatcher and –'

'And had access to chloroform,' pointed out Costello.

'You have yet to prove *he* had access. Don't get carried away. It's not enough to bring him in, not enough for a search warrant. And, in spite of Batten's guidance and all the wee boxes, they could get nothing out of him at the interview. There's nothing, absolutely nothing, we can prove. I thought I'd taught you lot better than that,' said McAlpine.

'Do you want something to eat while I tell you the latest? I'm starving.'

'You are a sweet person, Costello.' He downed his orange juice in one. 'So you think it's Leask?'

'Yeah,' said Costello, her voice flat. No elation, no victory.

348

'The chloroform put the tin lid on it for me. All that driving up and down to see some ancient uncle. Where's my purse?' She emptied her bag, notebook, photographs and all, out on the table.

McAlpine looked at the photographs.

Costello was still talking. 'It was here two minutes ago . . . And that reminds me – I've got to write up that report on our big development – about Alasdair Donald Wheeler's girlfriend and that comment by Leeza . . . Leeza . . . Leeza?'

'McFadyean,' McAlpine said vaguely, unscrewing the top of a bottle of mineral water.

'She said Alasdair hanged himself. So half an hour on the phone to our colleagues in Stornoway, where Anderson had a nice chat with the minister, a few emails to Ballachulish, and we found out some things that made Batten's ears prick up. DCI Quinn's a bit iffy about it all, but the rumour is she smiled, so something about all this must be pleasing her.'

'Alasdair Donald Wheeler? Should I know that name?' McAlpine studied his empty glass.

'Leask's half-brother – and how he died.'

McAlpine paused, the water bottle halfway to his mouth. 'That's still very raw with him. I don't think I'd bring that into the inquiry unless you have to.'

Costello was about to comment that it was he who'd taught her to leave no stone unturned, but one look at her boss's face told her to think again.

McAlpine's eyes closed briefly. Then he opened them and stared at her. 'What exactly did you find out, Costello?'

'Well, Wheeler was down here, working. Left uni, got a good job as a trainee accountant, sent money home regularly to help out; a perfect son, until he met a woman, Christina Morton. She was a fair bit younger, introduced him to drink

349

and fornicating and all sorts of things his elder brother would extremely disapprove of. Instead of going home when he was fully qualified, they moved in together; he paid the mortgage and all the bills, while she seemed to spend her entire salary on clothes and beauty treatments.' Costello opened her purse and pulled out a lone tenner. 'Why can I not get a man like that?

'It was Leeza who put me on to it. Christina dumped him with no rhyme or reason and left him bereft. Personally I think she spent his money and then legged it. And I've a little theory – that I'll feel very clever about if it pans out – about the downward spiral of depression for Alasdair. It's not an unusual story, but I'm wondering how Leask coped with that.'

'He probably just let it go, just let the memories float away.' McAlpine passed the mineral water back and forth under his nose, wishing it had the perfume of malt. 'The past is the past. Behind us. And that's where it should stay.'

'You're very philosophical.'

'I know. I'm sober. Look to the future, always look to the future. After all, that's where you'll spend the rest of your life.'

'Are you sure that's only mineral water?'

'How did Wheeler kill himself? Did you find out?'

'A bottle of whisky, a plastic bag over his head, and then hanged himself from the Connel Bridge. The place of all his childhood holidays.'

'At least it was picturesque, must have had a good view as he dropped.' McAlpine thought of Anna, lying with her arms ripped open, her beautiful feet speckled with blood. What had her last memory been? The feel of the lino floor cold against her face? No, he knew that her final thought had been of him, and him alone. *He* had been her dying memory. As she would be his.

'You turning into a psychologist?' Batten cut in, flinging three packets of cheese-and-onion crisps on the table and sitting down. He patted Costello on the head.

'She's got a head start – female intuition, remember?' said McAlpine.

'And what a great thing it is.'

'She was pregnant, wasn't she?' Costello asked.

Batten nodded. 'She aborted the baby. Alasdair was devastated . . . more than that . . . it laid waste to all his reason for living.'

'I knew it. I knew it had to be more than just their splitting up.' Costello ripped open a packet of crisps. 'I think Leeza had guessed something like that – female intuition again.'

'Bloody women,' said McAlpine, and was totally ignored by the other two.

'I've been going over the dates, like Quinn asked me,' Batten said. 'Nothing fits exactly. No anniversaries, nothing like that. I think it was simply that when Christopher Robin realized what a fake Arlene was, he went into some kind of religious meltdown. And each time Lynzi lied, each time Arlene pretended to read the Bible, each time Elizabeth Jane tried to manipulate him, that piece about Helena in the paper – it was another turn of the screw. Each one, by behaving deceptively and dishonestly, was like a hammer slamming it further into his head.' Batten attacked his packet of crisps, as unmoved as if he had been talking about the racing results. 'Every single one of those women knew the power of their femininity in some way . . . a duplicitous way. Speaking from the viewpoint of Christopher Robin of course,' he added for McAlpine's benefit.

McAlpine wasn't listening. 'Whores, you mean?' he asked. 'Masquerading as angels.'

'Wouldn't exactly say angels, but . . .'

McAlpine wasn't listening; his eyes fell into the middle distance. 'Playing at being an angel,' he muttered. *And all the while . . .*

Costello asked, 'Sir, what do you mean – an angel? Hardly angelic, any of them.'

'Nothing.' McAlpine's eyes suddenly focused on the present. 'I was thinking about somebody else. But an image can stay with you for life, like an everlasting scab you just pick, pick, pick at.' He signalled to the barmaid, who brought over a Talisker without being told. McAlpine asked her for an orange juice instead. She turned and bumped into a man in a brown waxed jacket, the same waxed jacket Costello had seen before. Its owner edged into the booth beyond theirs, the one with the good view of the television, and sat down.

'Do you think anything good is going to come out of this case at all?' Batten asked. 'It's always good to think on the positive side.'

'The only good things I can see are that the over-sexed mink of Ballachulish will live a wee while longer. And Sean McTiernan will live a long and happy life out at Culzean with whoever bought the house, the one who has the dog – the girl in the lane, I suspect. His own little blonde seraph.' She frowned. 'You know the house, Boss . . . right where you smacked the car, huge hole in the hedge . . . you can't miss it.' She lifted another two photographs from the file, the backs of them yellowed with age. 'I can't help thinking I'm missing something. Right at the start, you said: *with Sean, he shows you one thing to stop you looking at another.*'

'He's not daft, that's for sure.'

She smoothed out the first photograph on the table, flattening its creases with her thumbnail. 'So what was he hiding? I would like to know why he killed Malkie Steele. I really would like to know that.' She noticed McAlpine had finished his drink. 'And one day I'm going to ask him. I'm going to ask him how he went from being this innocent little boy' – she handed McAlpine Lorna's photograph of the children on the beach – 'to someone who could do that.' She handed over the picture of Malkie Steele's crushed face.

'Somebody offered him money,' said McAlpine, looking at the menu, feeling a bit peckish.

'You don't go up to a twenty-year-old with no record for anything and offer him forty grand to kill somebody. Davy Nicholson was right; there's more to it than that. I'll get you another before I go up the road. You want a toastie, Mick?'

'Aye, cheese and ham. I'm just away to the gents.'

'What about you, sir?'

McAlpine didn't answer. Costello got up and went to the bar as McAlpine picked up the photograph and turned it to get a better look. Four children on a beach. Three boys standing at the back. A sand-boat with its flag flying. A wee girl with long blonde hair flying in the wind, a beautiful face with perfect features, fine arched brows and large grey eyes, wide and innocent. And one of the little boys was gazing at her, his own eyes full of devotion . . .

'Do you want salad with it?' said Costello, turning back to him, but McAlpine had gone.

Batten bolted his toastie and drink, and disappeared off, while Costello finished hers at leisure. She was just reaching under the seat for her bag to find her notebook and pen when Anderson eased into the booth opposite her.

'I thought you were on your way home,' she said.

'I am. But this came through just after you left. I've only been waiting two days, although it was urgent.' He handed her a fax headed Parks and Recreation Department. In two seconds Costello's forefinger had run down the list of names and dates and come to a halt. She looked sharply up at Anderson. 'How did you know?'

'I didn't. Just something the Boss mentioned, about a case he was involved in once. A young woman who died following an acid attack.'

'Leaving a baby daughter, named after her mother. Well, the pronounceable version of her mother. Geertruijde – Trude. Who would now be – twenty-two, say?'

Anderson nodded. 'We don't really *need* to dig out the records on that case.'

'But we're going to. Well, I'm going to. First thing to-morrow.'

McAlpine parked the car in a lay-by and turned off the engine, taking a few moments to calm down. It had taken thirty-eight minutes to drive the forty-seven miles from Glasgow to Culzean, bypassing Ayr and then taking the high coast road, thrilling but not legal. He had stopped on the way and bought a half-bottle of Jack Daniel's. This was too good not to celebrate. He got out of the car, and twisted the cap off the bottle. The alcohol hit his bloodstream and was welcomed like a long-lost friend. He was about to meet another.

He was in heaven, a dark and windless heaven; the air hung expectant, waiting. The darkness was intense. He could sense her; she had been speaking to him all along, whispering in the darkness. He just hadn't been listening.

He stood there, his eyes closed, seeing her face in his mind's eye, tasting her on his lips.

He saw movement on the beach, a young man moving through the moonlight, silhouetted against the darkness of the waves as he ran along the waterline. A man out for a run on a beach with a dog, a white glove or bandage on his hand, punching the air as he ran.

At midnight.

McAlpine watched him run into the distance, into the darkness.

He came to the white cottage, Shiprids, sidestepped two planters filled with something woody and spiky that had been cut back for the winter, and walked on, passing a little red car parked covertly under the hedge. The cottage was dark and deserted, no sign of life. The little old lady protected the lane like a sentinel. But *she, his angel*, had pulled him from the car. She was here, he knew that now.

He walked down the lane to the sea, listening to the gentle hush and rush of water he could no longer see now the moon had passed behind a cloud. She had been here; here, then gone.

He walked along towards the castle, to the little white cottage, much further than he remembered from that night. He saw the sign with the two swans, their necks entwined, the words *Keeper's Cottage* wrapped in a diamond of lighter wood. The swans were for her, de Zwaan. The swan. And a diamond. It was only yesterday that he had sat at the side of her bed and held her hand, that fragile hand, watching that little tendril of blonde hair fall over the pillow. He smiled, twisting the imperfect blue diamond in his pocket. At last he was going to give it back to her.

Sea birds squawked from their rest on the high point of the cliff, disturbed by some noise. There would be caves along here, cavern haunts of smugglers and cannibals. Things secret and things hidden. Yes, he would have kept her down here, tucked away like a treasure, away from the Christopher Robins of the world.

She was drifting and whispering through his mind, beautiful, so beautiful, with her grey eyes and lovely hair, as she lifted his head from the water and leaned forward to kiss him, reclaiming what was hers. She was telling him to come back, to come back to her, that she did not want to live only in his dreams, in his nightmares, but with him.

He turned up a makeshift path towards the little gingerbread house, towards its still flickering candle-flame. His feet stumbled clumsily over driftwood on the path as he looked for signs of life. But he could see and hear nothing apart from the constant noise of the waves and the occasional sea bird.

He pushed the door gently with one finger. The wrought-iron doorknob rattled. He turned it slowly, and the mechanism released immediately, the door swinging open, revealing the kitchen, a huge oak table in the middle.

He recognized the smell immediately. Turps and oil paint. Paintbrushes were suspended in cleaner over at the sink, hanging from a wire contraption used by professional artists.

Stained rags had been left behind the taps; two canvases, sized and primed, were drying on the wall, far enough away from the Aga so that they did not dry too quickly and warp. Watercolour paper was stretched on boards, ready to be used. It could have been Helena's studio. There was even the same type of scalpel she used, a pile of them lying next to a cloth marked with pigment. He picked one up, waving it from side to side, as if conducting an invisible orchestra.

Two cups stood upturned on the draining board, among an incongruous mix of palettes and dippers. Underneath the smell of the paint and the smell of fuel in the Aga, he could smell dog. A square of carpet topped by a woollen rug covered in dog hair lay in front of the stove. Two bowls lay on the floor, one full of water that looked fresh, the other speckled with brown flecks. He tasted a memory of the dog in his dreams, a huge wolf-like creature with yellow eyes and wicked teeth.

He walked slowly into the hall, past the door to the half-built veranda. The hall at least had a rug covering the bare boards. The stairs, five feet wide, only two inches on each rise, were more suited to a hotel than to a cottage this size.

He paused for a minute, waiting and watching, tapping the scalpel on the wood of the banister. There was no noise, apart from the deep *tock* of the granddaughter clock in the corner of the room, the incessant whisper of the sea, the wind walking around in the rafters above his head. And in the noise there was stillness, as if nothing would move from here, as if time and space were standing still.

He crossed the hall into the other room. This was a room that was never lived in. It was tidy, with dusty, unread magazines stacked neatly in the corner, and paintings – good paintings – hanging on the wall. There was an open fireplace stacked with sun-bleached driftwood, but the window had never been opened to let the freshness of the sea-salt breeze inside.

In the darkness beyond the glass he saw her again, the image of her, on the bonnet of the car, that dark stormy night, the wind blowing the hood of her cloak from a face suddenly highlighted to white by the lightning, just as he opened his eyes and focused through the pain and the rain. His eyes clearing as she brought the stick down on the windscreen, again and again, closing as the glass shattered. He could feel the relief of being dragged upwards and out through the window, his feet kicking against the seat. She had lashed out at the glass with her heel, so she could pull him clear without cutting him. He could remember it now, could remember it all.

He went up the stairs, the treads creaking underfoot, measuring each tread with a tap of the scalpel on the handrail.

At the top of the stairs there was a bathroom, or at least a small room with a sink, a bath and a toilet. There were no blinds or curtains at the window, and the floorboards were bare. He could make out a white towel, a pile of clothes left on the floor in a heap, but no make-up, no trappings of femininity. Nothing.

He went up the rest of the stairs, feeling his way in the darkness, feeling that somebody was here in the house with him, breathing, keeping it alive. The old plaster walls were warm, flaking in his hand as he climbed the stairs. In the darkness, he saw a picture on the wall, a photograph, the only photograph. He was beside it, level with it, before he could make it out. He had seen it before, one fleeting glance across Graham's desk, the day he had learned the truth about how Robbie died. The photograph was grainy – it had been blown up from a smaller picture – and the colours had faded; the blue sea had drifted off to a metallic green, and chemical deterioration over the years had edged the figures with brown.

Two men and a woman, squinting their eyes against a strong Continental sun, were hugging each other in front of a yacht moored in some Mediterranean port – Monaco? St Tropez? The land rose in chocolate-box hills, white stucco houses freckled a hill scarred by a fine line that might have been a funicular railway. A road ran off the picture to the right, a promenade of open-topped cars and beautiful women. The taller man, the one who looked like Steve McQueen, had the even sun-tanned look of somebody who spends every daylight hour out of doors in a sunnier place than the west coast of Scotland. *Your brother didn't hesitate – just went straight in to get him.* A dark man in a T-shirt – John? Jan? – was laughing, living for the moment. *He'd been tortured before being shot.* And, between them, there she was, a sunhat on the back of her head, her hand in the pocket of her denim shorts. Her brown feet bare on the wooden deck, in a balletic pose. All three were smiling, laughing, happy. A portrait of tragedy.

Warm fingers of love caressed his heart. She had been here, waiting for him, all along.

'Hello again,' he said, tenderly. On the glass his fingertip traced the lines of the yacht, the metal stanchions, the white rope looping from one to the other, the dark blue hull, the name of the boat hidden as *she* leaned like a swan twisting its neck towards its mate.

It was an insignificant noise, a slump of something soft hitting a wall, the ghostly flit of somebody moving across floorboards. McAlpine turned to the bedroom and looked in through the door. She was standing there in the mild darkness, her hands over her mouth, her back against the wall. The moonlight danced on the halo of blonde hair crowning her pale face, her eyes closed slightly, and a small sigh forced its way from her mouth as she slowly but steadily collapsed to her knees, a slow stain of red seeping through her white gown, spreading across the dusty floorboards. Her eyes flickered, closed. Then opened, trying to focus on him. Her hands grasped her dress, then as she crumpled full length on the floor, she reached out, pointing at him, her hand quivering.

Then she lay still, a question poised on the most perfect lips he had never kissed.

He stood motionless, watching as the persistent stain of red began to seep across the floorboards.

He tried talking to her, words of comfort, anything he could think of. 'Come back to me, come back, come on, honey.' He pulled off his jacket, wadded it up and pressed it to the centre of the wound. She convulsed, moaning slightly, a slow involuntary sound from deep within. All the time he talked to her, hiding his own panic and confusion. Her head tilted back slightly; a faint trickle of blood was born at the side of her mouth and began a meandering path across her cheek. Thin arms fell outstretched, like a marionette with broken strings.

'No, no, no, not again,' whispered McAlpine, doing the first-aid stuff, straightening her head, clearing her airway, the familiar procedure clearing his mind. He folded her arms across her wound, holding the jacket firm. 'You hold that there now.'

He pulled his mobile phone from his pocket, his other hand a comforting pressure on top of hers. 'You hold on. Keep calm. And keep breathing.'

She moaned again.

He glanced at his mobile, knowing they were low on the beach, a huge cliff behind them. The signal would be weak. Was there a phone here? What about the figure on the beach? 'Connect, connect,' he said to his mobile. The display flashed at him, casting faint blue light – emergency calls only.

'Thank God,' he said.

'Indeed.' A floorboard creaked behind him. 'I knew you would come, Alan.'

McAlpine didn't turn round but stayed crouched, allowing the mobile to be lifted from his grasp, snapped shut and thrown across the room. He continued to press his hands to the wound, his fingers going deep into the crimson darkness of her dress. Blood was spreading out from under her as well now. 'Oh, God.' He closed his eyes and prayed for her to keep breathing. 'George?' McAlpine's mind was slow, emotion clouding his thoughts, but he kept his voice calm, authoritative. 'I would like you to call an ambulance. She is badly hurt.'

'Nemesis, Alan; that's all it is.'

McAlpine held his hand to her forehead, smearing blood on her beautiful face. The dim light made her look as though life had passed already. Then he saw a single, weak pulse flutter under the skin of her neck. 'You shouldn't have done this,' he said through a pall of sorrow. 'This one is innocent.'

'How can she be? How can this be innocence? Alan? Alan? Look at me. Even now, after all these years, see how you are captivated by her. Let her go, Alan; let all of it go.' Leask's voice was kind. He placed his hands on McAlpine's shoulders, as if comforting him. 'It's her fate, as it was the fate of her mother. Look around you, look at all this. She has all this because your brother died. *Your* brother.'

'No.' McAlpine lifted his blood-soaked jacket and tried to press the edges of the wound together. Trude whimpered slightly. She was so very, very thin. 'We need to get help,' he insisted.

'She has your brother's blood on her hands.' Leask was almost singing now, the island lilt seductive, as though McAlpine were his whole congregation. 'They don't change, do you see that, they don't change. Her mother looked just the same, too good to speak to me, too beautiful, too important. Laughing at me just because I didn't know about good coffee, laughing at me because I carried my Bible everywhere. Too important to give a thought to anybody

361

else. And all those policemen going on about how beautiful she was, and what a victim she was. What victim!' Leask scratched his eyebrow gently with his forefinger, talking all the time. 'You see, Alan, it was all over the news that week, how a Dutch yacht was holed by a government boat and a Mr McAlpine lost his life. Well, I had a little Dutch girl upstairs. Then she was attacked and a PC McAlpine came to investigate. Then she died.' Leask stopped scratching and shivered, as if somebody had walked over his grave. 'And then PC McAlpine was taken off the case, because his brother was involved as well. That's when I realized. I have a talent for being invisible, I think. People talk in front of me as if I'm not there. Also I have a talent for never forgetting a face. Well, not any more, not after this.'

McAlpine turned to look at him, remembering the ugly little transient that had passed him on the stairs, clutching his Bible for comfort. How he would have welcomed helping the police, boiling the kettle to make cups of tea for the search team, being the hub of the investigation.

'They told me it all at the time, Alan; they told me about the boat, about your brother. Everybody talks to a minister, Alan, everybody. Your brother lost his life, so a spoiled little rich girl could continue to be just that. Look around you. Look at all this . . . she's a parasite, she is living off your grief.'

McAlpine turned back to look at Trude as she moaned, the slight gurgle of breath escaping through the blood that pulsed slowly from her mouth. Her eyes flickered open, those huge grey eyes came to life, moist and so full of pain McAlpine could hardly bear to look at her. But she was the image of her mother. Every memory he had ever known, every touch, every smile, rushed over him like a kiss.

'You'll be fine, baby, you'll be fine,' he whispered. He

pulled the ring from his pocket, the ring that he had kept, the ring that Helena had worn for twenty-two years. He picked up her limp hand and fitted the diamond on to a finger slippery with blood. 'It's yours. It's always been yours. You should have it back,' he said.

'She lies like Ophelia, don't you think? In a river of red, with her blonde halo of flowers.'

'How did you find her? I've waited more than twenty years to find her.' McAlpine pulled the hair from her face; her breathing was laboured now, quickening, then fading.

'Women, Alan. Your little blonde detective should learn to keep her voice down in the pub.' Leask scratched the side of his face with the broad blade of his *skean dhu*, leaving a smear of Trude's blood on his cheek. He wiped it off with the cuff of his Barbour, disgusted. 'You said she was good at her job. Well, you'd think she would be more observant . . . of being followed. But she's another one who finds me invisible,' he added chillingly. He went on, 'I saw her in the street once. *Her!*' He flicked the point of the knife at the gasping figure on the floor. 'It couldn't be anyone else. That same face, after more than twenty years . . . I've never forgotten.'

Trude breathed out. A slow stream of breath bubbled through the blood at her mouth and a crescent of foam curled at the corner of her mouth. It was a long time before she breathed in again.

McAlpine stood up. 'She needs help.'

'No,' Leask said matter-of-factly, the madness in his voice as well as his eyes. 'No. God will have his way.'

'I'm not letting her die.'

'She's not worth it. You know that.'

McAlpine turned to look at Leask, pointing to the knife. 'Hand it over.'

'No.' The minister was calmly certain. 'Alan?' he said gently. 'This one is for you.'

'For me? But I loved her.'

'She beguiled you. Your brother died for all this. All of this. You never knew her. But *I* knew her. She was a bitch.'

'She was an angel,' McAlpine said. 'You were wrong. But you have the chance to do the right thing now.' He held his hand out for the knife. 'Please, George.'

'No. Not this knife, this knife is mine.' Leask looked at Trude, like an artist contemplating his work, wondering whether it is finished. The minister looked pleased and turned away.

McAlpine backhanded the sweat from his upper lip, knowing he had to play for time Trude didn't have. 'That knife's yours? What about the knife you used on the others?'

'Couldn't get near it, could I? Not with your lot all over the Phoenix, but I thought it fitting that this one should be used on her.'

McAlpine shook his head; his hand remained steady. 'Give me the knife, George. This is not absolution, this is not justice; this is revenge; and you – of all people, George – you are above that.'

Leask did not respond, he merely tested the point of the *skean dhu* against the tip of his thumb. Trude coughed slightly, and her lungs wheezed quietly. Then nothing. 'And that's how you see it, Alan?'

'That's how I see it, George. Now you are going to do the right thing. I'm going to phone for help. We are going to save her life. And then we'll sit down and have a long chat.'

Leask nodded. 'If that's the way it has to be,' he said.

And smiled slowly.

*

364

Sean was running, running at night, running effortlessly, his feet hardly touching the sand, the wind in his hair, fresh sea air in his lungs. Behind him, Gelert lolloped along the waterline, his paws splashing in the shallow waves. Sean put a little speed on – the sand was harder here – his legs pumping, his arms driving, oblivious to all noise but his own breathing, regular and slow, never puffing, never panting. In. Out. In. Out. Steady.

Then he noticed the dog was no longer with him. He jogged to a halt and turned.

Gelert had stopped in his tracks and was looking back along the beach, ears pricked, a faint growl coming from the back of his throat. Sean ran back and slapped the dog on the neck.

'Come on, come on, another three miles yet.' But the dog trotted forward, then broke into a run and galloped back towards the cottage.

The phone went, its noise drilling through the first night's sleep Anderson had had for ages. It was Burns down at the Phoenix. 'Good news, sir. We've found a knife.'

'Does it fit?' Anderson asked, immediately awake.

'In every way. It's an old black blade, right enough, a proper working knife with a bog-oak handle and a wee bit of sawtoothing up the back of the blade. The tip's slightly damaged. It's got the initials ADW on it.'

'ADW? ADW?' He tried to pull something from the back of his sleepy head. 'Alasdair Donald Wheeler,' Anderson said suddenly. 'Where did you find it?'

'In a toolbox, tucked away under the stage, wrapped in the cloth the Brownies use as a prayer mat or something. But it looks clean. The sheath might prove more fruitful.'

'Has anybody touched it?'

'No. Wyngate found it. Don't worry, he was thinking at the time. That's the good news. The bad news is that we don't know where Leask is. He went up to his flat, the lights went on, but there's no answer to the phone or at the door.'

'And the minder was left in the car?'

'Leask waved to him on the way up, so he presumed he was going to bed. Didn't know there was a back door from the close.'

Anderson sighed, feeling his career slip away from under him. 'Send a couple of uniforms round. Kick the door in if there's no answer, say we're doing it in case he goes the same way as his brother. But first get the knife to forensics ASAP. I'm on my way.' It was out of his hands now. He felt desperately tired. His system, so long wired with caffeine, had taken no time at all to deflate. A headache began to roll over his forehead; he rubbed gritty eyes and sighed. He could not remember the last time he had had a good sleep, a decent meal and a quiet moment to himself with his children.

He could not remember a time before Christopher Robin. And now, just as they thought they could see light at the end of the tunnel, it was probably that of an oncoming train.

Red.

Nothing but red.

It was all he could see, on the floor. The life pouring out of her.

Nothing.

Then breathing.

Rhythmic breathing.

Nothing more than the tranquil ebb and flow of life.

Her eyes were open. There was no response. Nothing. In there, in the bloodied mess of her white dress, Sean could sense the rise and fall of her breath. He put his finger between his teeth to stop himself crying and stood up, stepping over the man stretched out on the floor. He ignored the standing knife, its tip embedded in the floorboard, and reached for the abandoned mobile sitting in its little pool of blue light.

Saturday, 7 October

She was lying in a white tomb, staring at the ceiling with unseeing eyes, bathed in an eerie light, so small and thin on the bed she seemed hardly there at all. A halo of blonde hair curled round her perfect face, the beautiful profile spoiled only by the tube that ran from her nose to the drip stand. Across her stomach a set of wires coiled from her heart to the monitor that caged one weak, thin line, peaking every now and again. Her heart was still beating.

Sean was standing, wearing a white paper gown, leaning his forehead against the window, his eyes closed.

'You left this. You might need it,' said Anderson, his voice cracking. He handed the young man his jacket.

'Is there any news?'

'Nothing yet, but don't worry, we'll get him.' His voice more assured now.

'You had better get him before I do.'

'Don't worry, every hour that passes builds the case against him. His fingerprint was on the picture at the house, a thumbprint on the phone, his knife is covered in blood. We just have to find him now.' Anderson watched the thin line race across the screen, such a thin line, a fine balance. He swallowed hard. 'How is she?'

Sean shook his head, not trusting his voice to speak. For a moment they shared a silence, while a nurse fussed around the room for a minute.

'She's in the best place.' Anderson waited until the nurse had walked away. 'This might not seem the time or the place, but we are alone and you can deny everything after-wards.' Sean gave no response. 'I've been wondering about something,' Anderson said. 'And I'd like my curiosity satisfied.'

Sean imperceptibly moved away, but Anderson kept talk-ing. 'Suppose your girlfriend inherited some diamonds. Suppose somebody else thought they had a right to them. I imagine you'd have to keep it a secret, wouldn't you?' Anderson stopped, as if thinking the problem through. 'Bit awkward, as you couldn't sell them – the money would attract all kinds of attention. So what would you do? What would *you* do, Sean?'

Sean didn't move. Only the weary sag of his slender body stiffened slightly.

Not looking at the boy, Anderson said, 'Help me out here.'

There was a long silence before Sean spoke. 'You know how there's no such thing as magic? By the time the trick's seen to be done, it's already been done? I'm a great believer that if you show something, you'll get away with not showing much.'

Anderson frowned.

'She's a good artist, Truli. She makes a lot of money. We can sell those paintings all over the world to tourists. A painting is really only worth the price of a canvas and the frame, but sometimes they have deeper . . . value. A small diamond is untraceable. And very small,' he added unnecessarily.

Anderson felt a slow penny drop, and nodded. 'A trickle of money.'

'Self-employed artist, tax paid, earned income. Nothing illegal in that, if anybody asked.'

'I get your point.' Anderson leaned his back against the

glass, neither man looking at the other. 'How the hell did you set that up? Who do you sell to? Who knows? Without exposing it, I mean?'

Sean bit the corner of his lip, stopping the smile before it got any further. 'You can make useful contacts in jail. Diamonds are, in a strange way, respectable. Gentle crime.'

'Until folk like Malkie Steele get involved.'

'Indeed.' It was hardly more than a whisper.

'And you were happy to do the time for killing him.'

'I was. I've spent all my bloody life in institutions, and this time I had something to come out to.'

'But you had to keep Trude safe. She and Nan together.'

'That's how that woman – Costello? – found us, wasn't it?' Sean smiled, biting his own tongue.

'Sean, how did you get hold of the diamonds in the first place? The entire might of Interpol only got as far as her mother coming from Amsterdam to here . . . but then nothing. She died, and the trail ended. How did Trude end up with the stuff?'

Sean sighed. 'The two years we were together in Ayr were perfect, just me and her. Then a letter arrived, a few days after her eighteenth birthday – just a few lines on a white page. From a lawyer. That lawyer sent us to another, somebody up in Edinburgh. He had a photograph, and it was obvious Trude was exactly who she said she was. She and her mum are like peas in a pod. That done, he just hands over an envelope. Trude opened it, and cried and cried.' Sean smiled, pinching the tears from his eyes. 'She ripped it up. Then we were sent to a bank, and they treated us like royalty, ushered us into a small room, and they walked out and left us alone . . . with a little metal box on the table and a key. They wouldn't let us open it until they had all gone. It was only a collection of stones, just a handful of little stones. It was only then Trude told me what was in the letter.'

'I've heard enough,' said Anderson. 'You don't need to tell me any more.'

'No, I want you to understand. She wouldn't touch them. She never has.'

'If I'm thinking right, she's happy to live off the spoils of the crime, though.'

'She's lost enough, don't you think? You should have seen the way she held on to that photograph, as if she would never let it go. She knew what was important to her. I think she thought the diamonds – *knew* the diamonds – were a curse right from the start.' McTiernan smiled. 'Even more so when I blagged my way into the Mitchell Library, and they had all these newspapers on these small rolls of film.'

'Microfiche?'

Sean nodded. 'And there it was, all the details about the theft. Just the theft, nothing about the killings that followed. That's when I realized what we had. And Trude was right. From that moment he was on to her.'

'Malkie Steele?' Anderson prompted.

Sean nodded. 'He was the one who came after her. I thought he would be the first of many, and if we could just get away, live in a remote place, drop out and disappear, we would be safe. But Malkie was the only one who ever came. The real threat – *this* – came from . . . well, another source altogether.'

'How did Malkie know? A long time had passed.'

'I can only think he was involved in the original . . . incident. He would only have to pay attention to Trude at – what? Eighteen? Twenty-one? Even if he lost sight of her, people are not hard to find, if you know where to look.' The boy shrugged and turned to face Anderson. He looked pinched and deathly tired under the midnight fluorescent lighting. 'But when no one else came after us, I reckoned he'd decided not to tell them he'd found her, to keep everything for himself. But I really don't know.'

'And when you decided to do away with Malkie Steele, she disappeared from sight; you made a good job of that.'

'That was the worst day of my life. Closing up the flat in Ayr. She left, dressed as a boy. I didn't think I would ever see her again.' Sean pressed his hands to his face. For a moment Anderson thought he was going to cry.

'And she went to live in your cottage by the sea until you came back.'

Sean nodded. 'Nan had to pay the deposit, money laundering and all that. She had to keep them going until I got out of jail, but they sorted things out themselves pretty good. They started trading without me.' Suddenly, Sean cried out with agonized desperation, 'I would have done anything – anything – to keep her safe!'

Anderson moved to put an arm round the slender shoulders. 'I know,' he said. 'I know. I hope I'd have the courage to do the same. But I don't think I would.'

'Oh, you would. If a guy like Steele came round your daughter, you'd kill him. You would.'

Anderson gave him a squeeze on the arm, turning to lean against the wall, keeping an eye on the green line. 'I should warn you, there's no statute of limitation on stolen goods over a certain value. On the other hand, it's nothing to do with me; it wasn't my case. And I don't imagine anyone's going to be interested in digging it all up again now.'

'We just want to be left alone. She's suffered enough.'

'Look, anything we could do to you now would be a walk in the park after everything you've been through.'

Sean nodded again. 'All those years I worried about Trude,

looked out for her. Yet the bigger threat came out of the blue.' Sean turned to watch the green line chase itself from left to right, left to right. 'They said Leask knew her mother?'

'It seems so. She lived upstairs from him when she came to Glasgow. He might have liked her face, her quiet manner, the fact that she was foreign and alone. But he was a theological student, and she was unmarried and pregnant, so it would have torn him in different directions. I think he probably mistook her secretiveness for rejection and that just burned him for years. Our psychologist thinks he loved her, in a weird sort of way. If Trude looks like her mother, I can see why. She's very beautiful, beguiling.'

They both looked at the figure in white, the green line still moving, and shared another silence.

'Mr Anderson?' said Sean.

'Colin.'

'I'm truly sorry.'

Anderson nodded slightly and walked away, leaving the swing doors to close quietly behind him.

Anderson tried not to think, but his brain was moving at the speed of a runaway train.

He had been sitting in the incident room for half an hour, maybe an hour. After an initial burst of frantic activity, time had compressed itself into deep thought and strong coffee. He put the cold coffee down on the desk and sat, cradling his head in his hands, the palms against his eyes, pressing so hard that he could see stars dance on his eyelids.

There was a discreet knock at the door. He shook his head, trying to get his thoughts together.

'Hello, Colin, how are you?' It was Costello. 'Sorry to interrupt.'

'I wasn't really doing anything.'

Costello sat down on the desk opposite him. She looked wrung out. 'I'm just here to pick up my stuff. I'm off on the sick for a week. With all this I don't think I can cope with –'

'Quite right,' Anderson interrupted, not wanting her to push that conversation to its natural conclusion.

'Well, I just need some sleep. I seem to have lost the ability to put my head on a pillow and fall asleep. So the Doc said take a week off. I've cleared my desk. I think Quinn is reorganizing everything anyway.'

'Good for her.'

'Helena McAlpine and her friend are downstairs talking to somebody about clearing out Alan's stuff. Bit awkward, as I think Quinn's filed most of it in the bin. I thought you might like to deal with that one. How was she when you –'

'Don't talk about that. It was awful,' Anderson said slowly, biting his lip.

'I thought I should start putting the report together. We've put Leask in the cottage at Culzean, we've got the Leask knife with' – she paused – 'two sets of blood. The ADW knife has blood-type matches to the victims, but we've sent it away for DNA. Quinn insisted.'

'Fair enough.'

'Burns traced the maker of the knives, hand-made in Back, one for each boy, presents from their mother on their twenty-first birthday, and the maker can ID his own work easily. So we have him. We just need to find him.'

'And I got these from the fax machine.' She handed him three typed pages, still curled. 'Quinn requested a brief background report on Leask. The local police sent some official stuff through, but they sent another copy. They'd a bit to add on a more personal level, seemingly. The signature looks like the Gaelic spelling of Macdonald. And the report we requested on the brother has come through.'

'Mr A.D.W.?'

'I think you should look at this; it makes some kind of sense of it all.' Costello slithered from the desk and pulled out a chair. 'Leask's story is not pretty. Will I condense it for you or do you want to read it?'

'Just tell me please.'

'Brought up on a remote croft they had, miles out of Back, a long walk to school, a long walk home, usually just him and his mum. His dad was dour, depressive, used to beat his wife senseless. Wee George used to try getting between them and would go to school covered in bruises. Once his dad let him rear a lamb, which followed him all over the place. Then he slaughtered it, in front of him. He was six years old, poor wee sod.'

'God's sake, I phoned every bloody pet shop on the south side when Peter's goldfish died, to find a match so he wouldn't notice.' Anderson shook his head. 'Some folk.'

'He'd be sent to bed on a Sunday for laughing, often going hungry for misbehaving. OK, things were like that in those days, but Leask senior took it all a wee bit too far.'

'Is that all in the official report?'

'No, in the margins of this one. I don't think the local police were too surprised when they heard what had happened. Batten was quite interested when he read in there that when Leask was ten, he saw his dad gored by a cow, right in the stomach. He was in such shock he didn't go for help. He basically stood there and let his dad bleed to death.'

Anderson nodded with some understanding.

'Leask had gone on to the Nicholson Institute in Stornoway by then, but was still totally devoted to his mother.'

'And then the mum remarried and had Alasdair, a sibling rival?'

'The new husband was charming but the marriage didn't

375

last. He was good-looking but not much use in the way of family duties. George took on himself the role of the good father, the man of the house. The new husband legged it pretty quickly. Couldn't cope with George's closeness to his mum. George helped bring up the younger one; little Alasdair apparently adored his big brother. Then, when the mother died back in the spring, some batty old cousin at the funeral kept saying how alike the brothers were, with their "lovely blue eyes". Turned out the whole of Back had realized George Leask wasn't his father's son, but no one had said. That was when George first knew that he and Alasdair were full brothers. Nice, eh? What a fall from grace for womankind. That coincided with Alasdair having trouble with his sanity; later he was flipped over the edge by Christina.'

'I don't believe all that is in here.' Anderson was trying to decipher the cramped, scarcely legible writing.

'A lot of it is. Also, DC Burns's family is from Stornoway, don't forget. And don't dismiss his Auntie Dolina as a source of local knowledge. She was the one who said, and I paraphase, he could accept it when Alasdair was a half-brother but not when he was a full-brother.'

'Meaning?'

'Alasdair's fall from grace was now definitely down to the influence of a bad woman.'

'And bearing in mind he now knew his mother had been having an affair all along . . .'

'And wee George had been getting the shit kicked out of him for a mother who didn't deserve such devotion. It all starts to add up. He put his career, his whole life, on hold to keep the croft going –'

'He looked after his mum and did all kinds of stuff around the farm, which was how he came to be so handy with a knife?'

376

'A present from his mother.'

'Only to be repaid with dishonesty, and the knowledge that all the good he'd tried to do had been useless, a lie.'

'Batten was right – you can see where it all comes from, can't you?'

'So he came down here, and Leeza believes he came down to live among these women to try to help them, but it just all went wrong in his head. It wasn't just the girlfriend's fault or Arlene's fault. It all went back much further. If it weren't for the fact that he'd left three women dead, he'd be more to be pitied than scorned, as my granny used to say.' Anderson flicked through the papers. 'Do we give this to Quinn as it is?'

'We can give her this copy.' Costello handed over another set of papers, the official version, devoid of the gossip in the margins.

'Nowhere near as enlightening as that.' He nodded towards the annotated report.

'She can have this. It's the medical report on Alasdair Donald Wheeler. It shows quite clearly the downward spiral of a healthy young man into depression, neurosis, suicidal tendency, hospitalization for chronic depression ... all stemming from his girlfriend taking him for every penny and then aborting their baby. He died less than a year later.'

'What of this do we take credit for?'

'I'll wait and see what we have to carry the can for. You're the senior officer. I leave it to you.'

'Ta, matey.'

She stood up. 'I'll see you, then.'

'Try to get a good rest, Costello. We've all been through a lot.'

'You should take your own advice.' Costello caught a

movement in the room outside. 'I'm out of here. Quinn's on her way.'

'Just what I need.'

Costello left quietly, leaving Anderson feeling worse than he would have thought possible. So much they hadn't known, couldn't have known. They were all going to be tormented by *if only* for a while to come.

He could block out the images, but music was playing in his head, worming in his brain. A tune he could not quite identify, annoying him, distracting him. He knew it was a tune he liked, but he would for ever associate it with this moment.

Ella Fitzgerald, 'Every Time We Say Goodbye'.

He saw DCI Quinn walk past the glass panel in the door. She gave him a compassionate smile, a slight raise of the hand before opening the door.

'DI Anderson? I am so, so sorry.'

Anderson did not reply.

'I know this isn't the time –'

'You're right, it isn't.'

'I'll be brief. Lab says there were three blood types in the sheath on the ADW knife.'

'Yes, I know.'

'But I've requested the DNA. Better chance of identification, with the passage of time and everything. Only Leask's prints on the handle. So I think we'll be safe and sound once we get the reports in.'

'Good for you.' Anderson's voice was flat. 'All you have to do now is find him.'

Quinn ignored him. She tugged at the sleeves of her beige suit with some irritation. 'There's somebody here to see you. I'll bring her in here. I think it's a private visit.'

He sniffed loudly and, for the first time since he was a

boy, he wiped his nose with the back of his hand. The figure at the door was tall, wearing a dark coat, standing too close to the door for him to see through the window. Quinn let her pass.

Helena McAlpine walked slowly, clutching a small holdall, the charcoal drawing of her husband sitting on the top, its little bit of Blu-Tak still visible. Helena looked half the woman she had been, as though somebody had switched off the light in her life.

'I don't know what to do.' She looked perfectly calm, pale and composed.

Anderson found that harder to deal with than tears. 'Neither do I,' he said honestly.

She pursed her lips a little. 'How's the girl? Any progress?'

'Touch and go. But Leask would have killed her, if Alan hadn't intervened; it's worse than they first thought. He saved her life.'

'It's no consolation. I just don't understand.' Helena sniffled. 'No. I do know, and I think I understand perfectly.'

'Just the daughter of a woman he once knew.'

'The daughter of a woman he once loved,' she corrected.

Anderson didn't know what to say.

'*Once* loved?' Helena went on. 'He never stopped loving her. She's buried in a grave with white tulips.'

'Then you know she died very young, very tragically. She left her mark on a vulnerable young man. That's all, Helena.'

'He didn't trust me with that secret. Did you know about her?'

Anderson opened his mouth.

'Too slow to answer, DI Anderson. You knew.'

'Only a few days ago and not all of it. I had to figure out the connection between Anna and Robbie myself. If he had told me, I could have done something official about this,

379

and Leask would not have found her. The outcome might have been different, but he had his reasons for playing it his way; it was a part of his life that we weren't entitled to, Helena. Alan was a good man. He had his reasons.'

Helena nodded. 'I'm sorry.'

'Nothing to be sorry about.'

'Colin, even my engagement ring was hers.' She sat down wearily. 'I've just seen him in the morgue. I looked at his face and hardly recognized him. He looked so content. I think he spent his whole life feeling guilty about her, and now he has repaid his debt. Well, that's what Costello says.'

'Costello is a born romantic. Alan was killed protecting somebody defenceless.'

'His demons have gone now.' She sighed. 'She will pull through – the girl?'

'She's getting the best attention.'

'Once a policeman, always a policeman. When I get him back, could you come with me to do the –'

'Of course I will.' He opened his arms, laid her head on his shoulder and began to cry.

The Connel Bridge spans Loch Etive like a wrought-iron big cat leaping from shore to shore. In the late-autumn mist, kissed by the lightest of frosts, there is a fragility in its strength, as if the slightest breath of wind from Ben Cruachan would break sinew of steel and bone of iron.

It is a skeleton of a bridge, its superstructure lightly sparkling in the weak sun. Through the mist, the surface of the bridge is illumined, as if with a peppering of fairy dust.

There are a few dull footprints on the road. They stop at the edge of the bridge. An empty bottle of Glenmorangie, a tribute to the Glen of Tranquillity, lies where it rolled to rest against a neatly folded brown waxed jacket. In the neck of the bottle is a rolled piece of paper containing a few lines written in a precise italic hand and a signature framed with inverted commas: *'Christopher Robin'*. The handrail of the bridge shows the imprint of a human hand, where the warm caress of a palm has melted the frost beside a frayed knot of rope, tightly tied. The rope disappears towards the water.

At the end of the rope swings a body, a gentle sway, just moving and no more with the touch of the breeze. The feet are swinging north by north-west. The face is masked by a polythene bag, the features obscured by condensation. The rope is tight around the neck, cutting an inch into purple flesh already tinged with a black fringe of necrosis. Just below is a crescent moon of brilliant white, a sliver of pristine dog collar.

He looks as if he is smiling.

Epilogue

The spokes of the wheels cast shadows over the floor, the white-grey-black-white-grey-black of old cine film. Sean's hands moved on the circular rail, faster and faster, muscles pumping, fingers grasping, then opening, slipping the rail through, then tightening and driving onward, leaving skid marks on the wooden floor, an accompanying scream of exhilaration echoing round the cottage.

Gelert trotted along behind, panting, totally unimpressed.

The wheelchair rolled out on to the balcony and came to an abrupt halt. Gelert stopped too, sniffing the air. Man and dog turned to look at Trude, lying snuggled like a child in the hammock, dead to the world.

Sean looked at his watch. Medication time. He picked up the four brown bottles on his lap and stood up, kicking down the brake on the chair. The sun was strong on the veranda, the sea sparkled dark blue and diamond, a slight breeze tinged the air with salt. Ailsa Craig was in soufflé mode, rising from the sea fully baked. He had nailed a blanket over the balcony rail to keep the strong glare of the sun from Trude, but now he twisted it back on itself, letting some of the light and the warmth flood in. Prison had made him a great believer in the vitality of sea air, sunshine, sea breeze.

Although still asleep, she instinctively turned her face away from the wind as it caressed her face, lifting the fair hair in gentle wisps . . . that face, that beautiful face that still haunted him in his sleep. Her lips and eyelids were tinged with blue, the twisting path of the veins of her temple clearly visible through the transparent skin.

He stood all the bottles in a line on the wooden rail of the balcony, arranging them in order of size. Gelert with his big mouth open, tongue hanging out, put his ears back and watched with meticulous intent.

Sean hated this bit, waking her up. She slept deeply these days, the sleep of the dead. The doctors said it was good: her mind was at rest and not remembering, her body taking time out to heal. But he was always afraid that she would not come round when he tried to wake her, afraid of finding that life had slipped away unnoticed and that she was lying, still and cold.

Now, if he looked at her for one minute more, she would be alive for a little longer. He would never come so close to losing her again.

His hand was shaking as he leaned forward and kissed her on the forehead, then again, deeper and stronger. She did not stir.

He rubbed her forearm delicately, the way the hospital had shown him – *don't nudge, a steady pressure, wake her up gradually* – reeling her back in from no man's land.

'Truli,' he said quietly. Her eyes flickered open, closed, then opened again, squinting into focus. Confusion, pain and then realization crossed her face, her eyes smiling slowly and waiting for the rest of her face to join them.

'How are you feeling, Truli?'

Her eyes looked past his, out to the sea and the sky above, helpless and searching, probing the dark recesses of her mind with questions she was not ready to answer.

'Tablet time.'

She smiled at him, a little secret smile, and the dimple on her cheek creased and deepened. She pulled her arms from under the blanket and stretched, pulling the sleeves with slender fingers, retracting her head into the neck of the jumper. It was Sean's jumper; her head went the whole way in. She began to giggle.

'Tablets, Truli!'

He turned round, ready with the medication, and her head popped out of the jumper again. The wind caught her hair, blowing it into a halo round her head.

With the last tablet swallowed, he cradled her face in his hands, making sure she was all right. She smiled at him, lazily regarding him through drugged eyes. She looked slightly drunk, suggestive, inviting.

'OK, Truli, time to get up; four hours' sitting sleep and four hours' lying sleep, that's what the doctor ordered,' he said, repeating the hospital mantra. *Keep her circulation going*, they had said. He placed her bony arms round his neck, and they held firm now in helplessness as they once had in passion. He lifted her bodily, her feet swinging clear of the floor. Last week her head had swung like a rag doll's; this time it still lolled a little but she was managing better. Her arms were strong enough to grip him. Another little step along the long road to recovery. She was looking at him straight in the face, a faint curve on those lovely lips, as he lowered her, her feet taking the strain for a fleeting moment before her knees gave way and the rag doll was back.

She hadn't spoken a word since the stabbing. He preferred it that way. Now he could do all the talking, all the thinking. To get to her, they had to get past him. But nothing would get past him, and they would be safe. And now he had Anderson as back-up, an honourable man.

He sat down and pulled the wood towards him, four bits fashioned to make a frame, and clipped them together. He had already cut the hole in the wood: in that would nestle a small grey stone, a priceless small grey stone. Together with one of Trude's watercolours of Culzean Castle, the frame and its tiny cargo would pass through Customs as a pleasing memento of a holiday to Scotland.

Nan would be along soon; she would take it and the rest of the paintings up to the roadside, and sit there till they came. She would have the odd coach stop, and the American tourists would keep her amused, but it was the silver BMW with the quartered wheel-trim and a packet of Swan Vesta matches tucked on the dashboard at the passenger side that got the painting with the expensive frame.

The money was already in a safety-deposit box.

He looked out over the water, the water where the *Fluisteraar* had been caught and Robert McAlpine had died. He knew about all that now, but it didn't change a thing. It was calm today.

He selected a watercolour of Culzean on a wintry grey day. The castle looked dark and foreboding. They were lucky to live under its protection. They would be happy here, happy away from everyone, here on the beach in their own personal paradise.

Gelert ran on to the sand, a happy dog, plumy tail up, chasing seagulls with the energy of unbounded joy and freedom. Sean dropped the frame and jumped up to join him, running down the beach, arms out, running in circles, their footprints in the sand intertwining, leaving a tideline of ampersands for the waves to wash away.

Acknowledgements

Writing a novel can be both lonely and uncertain. The whole, often painful process has been made bearable and enjoyable by my supporting network of kith and kin.

Heartfelt thanks to my agent Jane Gregory – she's the best – and all 'Gregory Girls' for showing faith in my talent at the best and worst of times. And to Mary of course – such a font of knowledge and wisdom on so many subjects; she's a veritable encyclopedia.

Much gratitude goes to all at Penguin, especially Beverley Cousins, an editor of supreme 'tact', and all the creative team for making the publishing process a pleasure for a total novice like me.

Not forgetting my own crew: Karen, Catherine, Annette, Vadim, Elizabeth, Liz, Jessie, Irene, Antoinette, Noreen, Linda, Selena, Gillian, Biriani, Lorna, Lorraine, Safaa, Francis . . . told you I was a creative genius! And Heather 'the blether' Graham, the 'Tweenies' expert. And her granny for the tablet.

Many thanks to all those whose brains I have tapped: Robert J. P. Kerr and all my friends in Strathclyde Police for their expertise given so freely and with infinite patience – all the inaccuracies are mine. Special mention to Archie McKenzie and Cameron McKichan, two true gentlemen. Without forgetting all the others who chipped in with their tuppence' worth, Anna McC. and Janet S. Specially to Helen W. and Margaret P. for keeping me supplied with Irn-Bru and latte respectively.

Acknowledgement also to Gavin Bell, a true wordsmith. His passion for the written word is catching, but I hope one day, on some distant tropical shore with the waves lapping at his toes, he will discover the wonder of crime fiction. But what do you expect from a Motherwell fan . . . the only club that could double the stadium seating capacity by buying a sofa. Regards as always to Patchers Patch.

Which turns me to my dearest and nearest – the four-legged companions that provide sanity in a world of madness – or should that be vice versa – Kimberly Kim, Chloe Big Dog, Katie Wee Dog, Rusty Thin Dog and Emily Pit Bull. Not forgetting Pi Pi for 'helping' work the keyboard – if only cats could spell. Properly.

Some gratitude, I suppose, to all at Johnstone Writers Group – right bunch of nutters that you are. I suppose I should mention John Coughlan in particular, nasty piece of work that he is! And to Ian Hunter for keeping the group together no matter what.

And Christopher 'Skippy' Koster – Tooting's own Crocodile Dundee for all your support in moments of true madness and despair – usually when the computer crashed . . . again. Which brings me to Tracy the Moth, computer genius. I appreciate everything you do for me and my random memory, but I still have no idea what you are going on about. And with credit to Colin the Bruce, fellow creative genius and inhabitant of Abba Land.

This book was produced with aid from a Scottish Arts Council Grant and with help and support from Ajay Close, an underestimated genius. Ajay looked at me once on a Thursday night group and said, 'Try sending that thing you wrote to Jane Gregory.' I did and look what happened!

And indeed, to Glasgow itself, my green city. I apologize for messing with your geography but needs must. And yes,

I did go to Hollywood once, but there were no potato scones, so I came back.

Last, but by no means least, to Mater and Pater for all their help, support, dog-walking, vacuuming and helping me with the juggling act that is my life . . .

Thanks to you all,

Caro

Read on for an early taster of

TAMBOURINE GIRL

By Caro Ramsay

To be published in hardback in Summer 2008

Tuesday, 19 December 2006

He was supposed to have been at school, but his ma couldn't be bothered to walk that far. She couldn't be bothered most days now.

She'd been in such a hurry to get out the flat he'd not had a chance to put his jacket on. Once he'd gone back to get it and she'd locked him in and left him all night. So all he had was a wee fleece from the Oxfam shop, and that was soaked through and sticking to his back. Shite, he was cold. He was always cold.

Christmas shopping at Woollies, she'd said, but she never made it further than the offie. So there'd be nothing left to buy presents.

It was getting very dark now; soon they'd be turning on the big light at the end of the playground. He sat on the swing, shivering in the slow-falling sleet, not daring to touch the freezing iron chains with his bare hands. If you work a swing up high enough, his dad said, you can kick the clouds up the arse. But that was two Christmases ago, a long, long time; he was only five then. If his dad was here now he'd give him a push, but he didn't know where his dad had gone to, and he was too cold to swing himself.

So he sat watching the lights come on one by one in the tenements, a growing patchwork of comforting brightness, and played a game with himself, betting which window would light up next. The playground was empty. Everyone else was somewhere warm and bright and happy.

He watched his ma wiping the rain from the bench seat, using her sleeve like a big paw. She'd a huge coat on, made from a dead sheep; she'd got that at the Oxfam shop too. Now she was taking a bottle out the bag at her feet, unscrewing the cap. She always came to the same bench, her favourite place for a wee drink.

His feet were so cold he couldn't feel them. To warm up a bit, he scuffed his Oxfam Nikes. Scuffed and scuffed, working the seat round and round, the chains twisting above him, until he couldn't hold it any longer, and the whole thing spun back. The icy chains shrieked and clanked, but his ma didn't look up. She was taking another swig from the wee, flat bottle with the stag on it.

He wound the seat round and round the other way and let it go, sticking his feet out and leaning back to watch his scrawny white ankles spin round, and the yellow flashes on his Nikes light up in the dark.

But after a few goes he was bored. He wanted to see if he could give the clouds a kicking even though it was too dark to see them. So he shouted to his ma to give him a shove. But she wasn't listening.

There was that old woman again, the one with the wee white dog. He waited to see if she had a go at his ma. It wouldn't be the first time. They hung about for a bit, the wee dog crapped on the path, then they buggered off up the road.

He wanted to go home too. Maybe there'd be something to eat. So he slid off the swing and went over to his ma. He tugged on the sleeve of the dead-sheep coat, and she slumped sideways, her eyes hazy, unable to focus. Pissed again. She looked older than everybody else's ma, and he didn't like the way she pulled her hair back in an elastic band. It made her look like the dead cat he'd seen floating in the canal last summer. He could smell her whisky breath through the rain.

The bottle was balanced between her knees. If she stands up it'll get smashed, he thought.

He took a few steps into the darkness.

He wasn't allowed on the roundabout in the rain ever since he'd fallen and broken his arm and they'd tried to take him into care — again. But she wasn't watching, so he'd not get a skelping. He pushed and pushed, went round once, twice, and got the wheel going really fast, all by himself.

Suddenly, the floodlight came on. In the brightness he could see a syringe abandoned, close to the roundabout. Next time round, he'd *kick it right on to the grass . . . But he stretched too far, his numb fingers slipped, and suddenly he was on the ground.*

He lay there for a little while, whimpering, frozen hands stinging with pain. Then he rolled over and sat up wearily. In the floodlight he could see his knee skinned raw and tiny red bubbles of blood welling up. He'd ripped the knees out of his trousers. His ma would kill him.

Out beyond the light it was really, really dark. And his knees and hands were hurting. And he was so cold.

Then a tall shadow fell between him and the floodlight, a grown-up wearing a long black coat, and an enticing smell of hot soup enveloped him.

'You've hurt yourself,' a kind voice said. 'I've just got some pies and chips to take home. Why don't you come and have some?'

He sniffled and wiped his nose on his sodden sleeve. All he wanted at that moment was for somebody to pick him up, cuddle him and take him somewhere warm.

And feed him a nice hot pie. With chips.

Wednesday, 20 December 2006

DI Colin Anderson held a handkerchief to his nose, trying not to breathe, his eyes watering in the acrid smoke, and looked at the remains of the ground floor flat, 34 Lower Holborn Street. The fire had been out for half an hour but the flat was humming with the intense humidity of a tropical rain forest. Two firemen, boots squelching, emerged from the smoke-filled kitchen and stood for a moment in the sanctuary of the hall, sweat tracing veins of white skin in the soot on their faces. The younger of the two stared at the sagging ceiling, looked troubled and sighed. A close call, but too late.

The older one gesticulated with a tired wave of a heavily gloved hand – Anderson could have a look if he wanted.

DI Colin Anderson tiptoed forward and squatted beside the black plastic sheet as Woodford, the senior fire investigator, lifted the corner. What lay beneath was only vaguely human. The crouching pugilistic pose, limbs contorted into flexion, clenched hands pulled up to the face – the muscle contraction was typical of a body caught in intense heat. Anderson leaned forward for a closer look, coughing into the back of his hand, and Woodford pulled the plastic away further. They knew it was the body of an old man, they surmised he was seventy-six-year-old John Campbell, but the mass of burnt flesh could have been anyone, anything. The body was black and yellow, darkened with dried blood, devoid of hair and eyebrows, clothing either melted on or burned away. Small patches of coloured fibre with frazzled

394

strands were dotted around the shoulders. Had he been wearing something woollen? A cardigan, maybe dark blue? Anderson looked closer and saw a melted button. He remembered his own granddad wearing those cardigans, Fair Isle with metal buttons like little medals. He picked one up on the end of his pen, and slipped it into an evidence bag.

'What time was it called in?' he rasped.

'A few minutes past ten, so an hour and a half ago,' Woodford replied. 'We were here in minutes, but too late is too late. There's no debris underneath, so he was already on the floor when the fire took hold.' Woodford gesticulated with the back of his hand.

'Is that suspicious?' Anderson started to cough again.

'Probably not. He was old, the smoke would have knocked him out quickly, or he could have had a coronary, collapsed and that's why the pan went up in the first place.' Woodford pointed to where an open can, a cracked plate, and the remains of a knife lay on the floor. Close by was a twisted plastic strip of pills, and a seven-day dispenser melted into the shape of a flower. 'Signs he was on medication, wouldn't you say?'

'No indication that he tried to put the fire out?'

'No extinguisher, no fire blanket and the smoke alarm was bugger all use. The place went up like . . .'

'The proverbial house on fire?' Anderson smiled and nodded, signalling for the body to be covered up; his eyes were streaming so much he couldn't see any more anyway, and the noise of a generator starting up was deafening. He retreated, looking at all the boots in the kitchen, tramping everywhere, contaminating the scene. *Site*, he corrected himself. Nothing so far to indicate that it was a crime scene.

He gingerly dipped his head under the door lintel, now supported by an inner metal frame, and felt the vicious heat eating through the soles of his boots. Even Anderson's inexpert eye could tell the ceiling was starting to sag like an empty hammock.

One of the fire-fighters tapped along the wall none too gently with a hammer. 'Do you think this is weight bearing?' he shouted, keeping his eyes on the crack in the plaster that ran the length of the room.

'Tap it any harder and we might find out,' answered some smartarse through the smoke.

Anderson knew they were on the ground floor of a four-storey tenement and felt his stomach sink.

Somebody handed him a hard hat.

Great.

He shuddered, casting his eyes round the room, as Woodford shouted and the generator was cut. The hammering died abruptly and all was quiet apart from the walls cracking and sighing as they relaxed after the intense heat. Anderson stayed still, thinking they were listening for further signs of life, but they had stopped only because somebody senior was taking a phone call.

In the relative silence, Anderson looked back at the kitchen. Everything, in the aftermath of the rage that had passed this way, was consumed and blackened, warped and twisted. In the heat the lino on the floor had shrivelled into leaves that now floated on little pools of water. He could hear something still sizzling. Yet, amid all this destruction, this was still recognizably a kitchen. Two hours ago somebody had been cooking a leisurely Wednesday morning breakfast. Part of a worktop remained, sticking out like a jetty. An oval-shaped biscuit tin with a picture of a green Bugatti on the lid sat waiting, incongruous, as if it had been kissed by the flames and rejected. Anderson noticed that the fridge, the same model as his own, had buckled under the pressure of sheer heat. The focus of the rage, the cooker, was a dark tangle of metal, with the odd bit of chrome stubbornly shining through.

A fire officer appeared with a video camera, nodding to DI Anderson for tacit approval to keep filming. Anderson nodded, pulling the hard hat further down over his eyes, trying to ignore the savage heat that still gnawed at any exposed flesh. He knew a fire investigation officer could read a fire in a way a run of the mill SOCO never could; best leave it to the experts. The camera whirred into life, the operator complaining about the lack of light. Anderson felt the smoke irritating his throat again, and coughed deeply. No amount of money in the world could persuade him to do their job.

'You OK?' asked Woodford, holding his hand out. 'You were a bit late for the barbie.'

Anderson smiled wryly and reversed out of the flat, keeping his fists clenched and his arms folded; it was easy to forget and put a hand down and get a palm full of burns. The soles of his feet were complaining loudly, he was going outside to stand in a puddle. He started to cough in earnest, a dry hacking at the back of his throat. Then he retched.

'Yip,' DCI Quinn snapped down the phone. Its high-pitched ring tone made the fillings in her teeth hurt. Twice she had asked for a new one but she might as well ask to be made the next queen of England. '*Yes?*' she said again, but whoever was at the other end totally ignored her and said, 'Left a bit, left a bit,' to some unidentified other. 'Wyngate!' she shouted. The incoming code said reception and there were only two people at reception – Costello and Wyngate. The latter, she knew, was unkindly known as Wingnut. And it was DS Costello who had the brain cell.

'Yes, ma'am. Wyngate at reception, ma'am.'

'I know that. What is it?'

'Well, Costello's not feeling too good, ma'am. And some of the rest of the squad have called in sick . . .' He began reeling off a list of names. 'It's the flu, ma'am; it's everywhere,' he added helpfully.

'Might be quicker to send me a list of who's actually in,' Quinn said, and put the phone down. Apart from DS Costello, she had no idea who any of the names were. Over 60 per cent of the squad was down with flu now, and it was Christmas next week. Just as well things were relatively quiet.

She glanced at the clock. The briefing was in ten minutes; she could hear the remnants of the squad gathering on the other side of the blind. As usual, she was well dressed in the navy blue classic suit that she considered her uniform, her red hair precisely pinned back, but her lips were pale. She opened her make-up bag, and applied her lipstick carefully, pursing her lips, watching the coloured lower lip blot the stain on to the upper in the mirror in the lid of the bag. It was one of her little rituals; like Beryl Reid saying that if she got the shoes right she got the character right, so was DCI Quinn with her lipstick. Without it she was a human being; with it she was a cop. And a good one.

She checked there was no lipstick on her teeth, no loose hairs on her collar, and turned back to her desk. The pile of files added up to nothing much – seven-year-old Luca Scott had disappeared forty-eight hours ago. The boy had more or less lived on the streets and it wouldn't be the first time he had done a runner. The family, such as it was, belonged to that inner city underclass which was of no fixed abode but always seemed able to afford the latest mobile phone and a bad-tempered pit bull. Quinn sighed.

The next file was forty pages thick, a document circulated

to all Strathclyde stations. Rock legend Rogan O'Neill was flying back into Glasgow airport, and a brief itinerary of his castle-hunting plans was attached, plus details of the Hogmanay concert which had been rumoured, but was now definite in the light of the earthquake appeal. Nothing like a good disaster to jumpstart a flagging career. There was page after page about the security involved, with special notes for Partickhill Station. No extra manpower, Quinn noted, just more work. This had landed on her desk because the aging rock star was staying at the Hilton round the corner, with – rumour said – his blonde model girlfriend, or at least the latest in a long line of blonde model girlfriends.

She opened a few more bits and bobs, determined to make her way to the bottom of her in-tray before the briefing – she wouldn't put it past this lot to leave something really important right at the bottom, then ask her about it. The usual pile of memos, her expenses form (last month's) . . . She pulled out a piece of stiff white card: *Alan McAlpine, 1960–2006.* His picture on the front of the funeral Order of Service looked back at her, a relaxed and handsome man with melting eyes and a smile that was more intriguing than friendly. She looked at it for a minute, a pleasant memory stirring, and stuck it at the bottom of the pile.

She jumped as the shrill ring of the phone reprimanded her.

'DS Costello here.' Female, clipped, abrupt, only just this side of insolence.

'Yes, DS Costello.' Quinn spoke with pointed politeness.

'Any news on Luca Scott, ma'am?'

'Am I not supposed to be asking you that?'

'Well, I'm still trying to get some sense out of his mother, but she's more concerned about where her drug dealer is than where her son's got to. There's something else – a Mrs Cotter of Horeselethill Terrace . . . that's near where . . .'

'Yes, I know . . .'

'Well, she's reported that her neighbour came home last night without her son. Too drunk to remember where she'd left him. I checked on the database and it's not the first time *this* boy, Troy McEwan, has been reported missing either, so in light of Luca Scott . . .' Quinn heard Costello flick over a page of her notepad . . . 'Both seven years old, blond-haired, both within half a mile of each . . .'

'Send me up anything you have.' Quinn pulled Luca Scott's file from the small stack on her desk. 'And get DI Anderson back here, as soon as.' She hung up.

She shut her eyes for a moment, willing the two little boys not to be connected. Not *two* missing children, not in her first week; just before Christmas, not for her first case with this team – McAlpine's team.

They were good – Anderson, Costello and Mulholland – McAlpine's handpicked little squad, a tough team to crack. But the King was dead, long live the Queen. *Long live Quinn* – she allowed herself a little smile. DI Colin Anderson was the one she had to break. He was a quiet, intelligent man, who thought before he spoke; each action was considered. She had expected some resentment from him, but there was nothing. Well, not exactly nothing – more of an indefinable something – as if he was merely going through the motions, like a clever pupil with a slightly dense teacher. Quinn had been hoping he would blow and say what he had to say and get it over with, but so far, nothing. Anderson was obedient, end of story. But the squad respected him. Get him on board, the rest would follow.

Annoyed, she saw the picture of DCI McAlpine looking up at her; he had worked his way back up to the top of the pile, just as he had in life. *Bastard*, she muttered to herself, picking it up and wondering where to put it. The bin seemed disrespectful, and in any case someone might find it there.

She knew she was not the only one who had succumbed to McAlpine's charms more than once in the last twenty years, not by a long chalk. She spun her leather seat round, away from prying eyes, and kissed McAlpine's picture gently, before feeding him slowly into the shredder.

She sat for a moment, watching him go. Then she stood up.

In-tray empty, desk tidy, lipstick in place – she was ready.